Masquerade
(Heven and Hell #1)

*To Heidi
Thanks for everything!*

Cambria Hebert

MASQUERADE Copyright © 2011 CAMBRIA HEBERT

All rights reserved, including the right to reproduce this book, or portions thereof, in any form without written permission except for the use of brief quotations embodied in critical articles and reviews.

Otherworld Publications, LLC
125 ½ Main Street
La Grange, KY 40031
www.otherworldpublications.com

Interior design and typesetting by Lynn Calvert
Cover design by MAE I DESIGN
Edited by Amy Eye, The Eyes for Editing

This is a work of fiction. Names, characters, places, and incidents either are the product of the author's imagination or are used fictitiously, and any resemblance to actual persons, living or dead, business establishments, events, or locales, is entirely coincidental.

Paperback ISBN: 978-1-936593-25-5
Hard Cover ISBN: 978-1-936593-28-6

Masquerade

Dedication

I dedicate this book (at the risk of sounding corny) to anyone who has ever had a dream. To anyone who has had a fire in their belly and a determination in their bones. Don't ever give up, even when it seems like the world works against you. If my dream can come true then so can yours.

And also,

I dedicate this book to myself. What? I worked really hard.

And always,

For Shawn.

Acknowledgements

Being a writer is a solitary journey but becoming an author takes a team of people. My journey from writer to author could not have been possible without the help and support of a lot of people.

First, I want to thank my husband, Shawn, who patiently endured my far away moods when I was lost in my own head. For not saying a word when the house fell into disarray because I was pounding at the computer, chasing a dream that might not ever be realized and for always believing that it would. Without you I might never have put my butt in that chair (and stayed there) long enough to see this through. I want to acknowledge my children who patiently waited while I wrote "just one more line" before getting up to play.

I am lucky enough to have a great group of friends who never told me I was crazy (even if they thought it) when I announced I was writing a book. To Andrea, who always read everything first and would call me at all hours of the night so we could dish about it all. Our talks kept me motivated when my motivation dipped. To Jenn Pringle, who has been there to support and champion me. Your support got me through some stressful times. To Christy, who listened to me go on and on (and on) about cover design, characters and networking. Thanks for never acting bored. And for reading everything and always giving me the truth when I asked your opinion. Oh yeah, and for naming your daughter Heven, so that I might come along and borrow it. For Melanie, one of my oldest childhood friends, the sister of my heart, your unflappable personality and phone calls sometimes got me through the day. And to my Mom and Mommom, who never asked me why I didn't get a 'real' job because you understood that this was the only job that would ever matter.

To my editor and good friend, Amy (theeyesforediting.com), your eyes saw things that mine never did and you made me think about my characters in ways I never had. Without your insight this book would not be as good as it is today. I never dreaded the red on the pages because I knew that with the red would come laughter. You are my accomplice in all things literary and my partner in crime. Thank you for all your support and willingness to do whatever you could to see this book in print. To Regina Wamba (Mae I Design), your cover designs blow me away every single time and so does your willingness to work until it's just perfect.

To Lynn and the entire staff at Otherworld Publications for taking a chance on me and this book. You saw potential where others did not and you gave me the path to my dream.

Finally, to all the others in my life who have supported me and cheered at the top of their lungs when I told you the news. I am beyond blessed because your names alone could fill pages of this book. Never doubt how much every single bit of support or praise I received meant to me. You all honor me by being my life and nothing could ever replace you.

Chapter One

Heven

The street was dark and deserted. I wished, not for the first time, that I had a car. But I didn't, and I'd spent too long in the library, so now I had to walk home in the dark. It was a clear night, and there were a million stars nestled in the sky, twinkling brightly alongside the moon. I was nearly home, my street just yards away. The night was quiet, exaggerating the sound my heels were making on the pavement. Usually, I liked the clicking sound; it made me feel womanly, and it announced my arrival. However, at this moment, it seemed I shouldn't announce my presence. I slowed slightly, gentling my steps and glanced to my right at a wooded, overgrown lot. I imagined something hiding in the brush, watching. I laughed a little at my silliness, but quickened my pace. This time, allowing my heels to slap loudly on the pavement, hoping the sound would ward off any animals that might be around. Behind me I sensed movement and whirled around to confront it.

There was nothing there.

I began walking again. I'd walked this street many times, I knew it was safe.

Wasn't it?

Just as I passed an empty lot, I heard some rustling and turned back. Something was definitely there, a dark shape unfurling from the weeds.

My heart beat fast, and my stomach cramped with nerves as I began to run. I wasn't fast enough, and whatever was stalking me caught up. I fell forward, something heavy and warm pressing me down onto the cold pavement. I tried to scream, but the sound lodged in my throat. A hideous sound built low and filled my ears…

I bolted upright, heart pounding. It was just a dream. A stupid nightmare. Except it wasn't stupid, and it wasn't just a dream. I tossed the covers off and headed to the bathroom, feeling sticky and clammy with sweat. The water was cool and felt like silk running through my fingers. I scooped the water in my hands and splashed it on my cheeks. I froze, fingering the raised, puckered scars that distorted the left side of my face. No, it hadn't been a stupid dream. It was an unnecessary reminder of reality.

The dreams had been haunting me so long I knew that it would be impossible to find sleep again tonight, so I didn't bother to go back to bed. The soft sheets and fluffy pillows didn't offer the same comfort they had *Before*. Bed was now the place I was haunted by unanswered questions. I shut off my alarm and turned, glancing at the window. A strange feeling of being watched crept over me, and I padded over to peek out from behind the curtain. I don't know what I was looking for, only that I had a feeling that something was there. Chills raced along my skin and the hair on the back of my neck stood on end as I looked out into the dark. I resisted the urge to turn and look over my shoulder, but then something caught my eye – a movement within the shadows. I squinted and pressed closer to the cold glass of the window hoping for a glimpse of whatever was there. After long, tense minutes, I gave up. Of course, there wasn't anything there. I was beyond exhausted from lying in bed at night worrying, paranoid about being watched, knowing that I wasn't. Why couldn't I shake this feeling that I wasn't safe?

With one last look at the empty yard and a deep sigh, I went back into the bathroom, careful to avoid the mirror. I went through my usual routine of brushing my teeth and washing my face. I grasped my brush and looked up into the mirror above the sink. I began brushing the very long, very blond thickness of my hair, taking care to part it low on the right and smooth it over to conceal as much of my face as possible. I tried distracting myself with the features that weren't so bad like my sky blue eyes and pimple free skin. There was a light smattering of freckles over my nose and cheeks and my lips were full and a natural peach color. *How close I came to having the left side of my lips ruined.* I shivered, and the action sent my hair momentarily away from my face, revealing what I hadn't wanted to see.

A large, raised scar began at the corner of my eyebrow and ran jaggedly down, dangerously close to the corner of my eye and didn't stop until well past my cheekbone. It was puckered and dark pink. If that wasn't hideous enough, it wasn't alone. A pair of wide scars, one on each side of the larger scar ravaged my skin, making me look like a freak. Adding to my freakish appearance, I had nerve damage, and the left side of my face was slack…the skin not as taut as it once was. When my hair concealed as much as it could, I left the bathroom to get dressed. It didn't take me as long to get dressed as *Before*. I didn't see the point of dressing nice when my face was ruined; whatever effort I made with my clothes wouldn't matter. I selected a pair of jeans and slid them on, adding an oversized hooded sweatshirt. Getting ready so early, I had to wait for what seemed like forever before I went downstairs to make a show of grabbing a granola bar and carton of orange juice from the fridge.

"You look nice this morning."

"Thanks, Mom," I said, mustering a smile even though I didn't feel like smiling. I know she was trying to be supportive, trying to make me feel good. I appreciated her efforts even if they never worked.

"Gotta go, I'm late."

"Have a good day," she called behind me.

I paused just before walking out the front door. *Get it over with.* Taking a deep breath I stepped back and prepared myself to look up. You'd think after months of this routine it would get a little easier. It didn't.

I gazed into the mirror at my reflection, making certain my hair covered as much of my face as possible, knowing it was what everyone would be whispering about when I walked through the halls at school. They still whispered, even after all this time. You would think they would forget, I wanted to – like I ever really could. It was *my* face after all, and it was disfigured.

Kimber pulled into the driveway just as I shut the front door behind me. The bright red VW Bug was a happy announcement that she was here, an exclamation point that was her life. I used to love that car and all the attention that it drew. I'd hoped for something like it. But that car didn't fit into my world anymore; I'm no longer the girl who would drive something so flashy. But I rode in it anyway, grateful not to ride the bus.

"Hey, girl," Kimber chirped as I slid in the passenger seat.

"Hey." I smiled and shoved the uneaten granola bar and juice into my bag. It would join the rest of this week's uneaten breakfasts in the bottom of my locker. I was aware of Kimber watching, but she didn't say anything. Her eyes were hidden behind a pair of sleek, dark purple sunglasses.

As she backed out of the drive, I checked out her outfit. She was wearing a pair of dark skinny jeans and a pair of tan Uggs that came to her knee. Her top was white but far from plain. It was a long sleeved, button-up with a bunch of ruffles along the chest. The first three buttons were unbuttoned, and a sparkly silver tank peeked from beneath it. To top it off she had on at least four necklaces. One had huge aqua colored beads on it while another had small yellow pebbles. The other two were silver and sparkled when the sun hit them. It should have been way too much, but on her it was perfect. It was exactly like something I would have worn. *Before.*

Her Blackberry began singing a Taylor Swift song, and she sighed. "Who is it?"

I picked the phone up from the cup holder and glanced at the screen. "Cole."

"Ugh." She took the phone, hit the 'ignore' button, and dropped the phone back into the cup holder.

"Are you fighting with him again?" Kimber and Cole have a definite love-hate relationship. They'd started dating freshman year and had broken up and gotten back together so many times in the past two years that I'd stopped counting. It used to amuse me. Now I wondered why they bothered.

"I broke up with him." She sniffed.

"I'm sure by lunch everything will be fine."

"Not this time," her voice cracked.

"Kimber, you know this is the usual pattern with you two."

"I caught him kissing Jenna last night after the game."

"He wouldn't!"

"Oh, yes he did! I know we usually fight and make up, but this is different. He *cheated* on me!"

"With a skank!" Jenna Hoffman was a snotty brat. She flirted with everyone's boyfriend and talked about everyone behind their backs. Unfortunately, the teachers all thought she was great. She got straight A's and sucked up to all the right people. It didn't hurt that she was next in line to be head cheerleader, and that her parents had serious money.

A giggle escaped Kimber.

"What?" I asked. Dealing with Jenna was no laughing matter.

"You said 'skank'."

"So?" I shrugged. "You act like I've never called anyone that before."

"It's been a long time. I almost forgot how…" She pressed her lips together and fiddled with the radio.

"How fun I used to be."

"I wasn't going to say that."

I snorted.

"It's just nice to see you excited about something."

I didn't think calling Jenna a skank for acting like one was me being excited. "So what are you going to do?" I asked, wanting to avoid this conversation.

"About the skank?" Kimber grinned. "Nothing."

"About Cole."

Her grin faded, and she stared at the road. "He keeps calling me."

"Have you talked to him?"

"I told him to leave me alone."

Her phone went off again, and I picked it up. "It's him."

"Just turn it off."

This was serious. She never ignored his calls. She always answered to yell at him and then hung up. It was part of how they worked things out. Suddenly the idea of Kimber and Cole breaking up – for good – seemed like too much. I always thought they would be together, fighting forever. It was something I counted on – a constant. In a world full of change and uncertainty, I always thought I could count on them to be there…well, fighting.

"You okay?" Kimber asked, slowing the car.

"Yeah, I'm fine." *Breathe.*

"You having a panic thingy?"

"I am NOT having a panic attack." *Please, not now.* I took a deep breath. Then another. The tightness in my chest eased. Kimber was watching me.

"Need me to pull over?"

"No. I'm fine. Sorry."

She nodded, and we rode in silence for a few minutes.

"I'm sorry," I said as we pulled into the student parking lot at school. "That was really crappy of Cole."

"Yeah."

"You going to be okay?" I asked, reaching out, laying a hand on her arm.

She looked momentarily startled that I touched her, but she recovered fast. She smiled and said, "Shopping? After school?"

Shopping was the last thing on earth that I wanted to do. All those people. All those bright lights and mirrors. "Sure," I agreed. She stood by me through a lot this past year and without her I probably would have gone insane. I would never be able to repay her, but this was one small way I could make a dent in the debt I owed her for all she'd given me.

She let out a loud groan as she pulled into her usual parking spot. I looked out my window at the car parked next to us. Cole was leaning against his dark blue pickup waiting with his cell clutched in his hand.

"I can't do this right now," she confided.

"Go," I said, "I'll talk to him."

"Thank you." She grabbed her book bag and scurried from the car. I heard Cole shout her name.

Kimber kept running, yelling over her shoulder, "Do not follow me!"

I was slower to get out of the car, reluctant to begin the day, but still I moved faster than normal. Surprisingly, Cole listened to Kimber and stayed behind. He stood at the back of her car, his hands shoved in his pockets, watching her run into the building.

I slammed the car door and dropped my book bag at my feet; reaching up to pull the hood of my sweatshirt up, I made sure my hair was smooth around my face. Cole turned to look at me. He looked miserable.

"Jenna, Cole? Really?" I sniffed.

"It wasn't what it looked like." He walked over and stood in front of me.

"So you weren't kissing her?"

"No – I mean yes!" he yelled, frustrated.

I flinched.

"Sorry." he sighed, bending to pick up my bag to hand it to me.

"It's all right."

"No, it isn't."

"Really, I'm fine." I was busy pulling at my hood.

Cole noticed me pulling the hood even further forward and said, "Quit hiding all the time."

"You gonna to tell me about Jenna?" I avoided his words because I always felt like hiding.

He sighed and ran a hand through his rumpled, dark hair. It stood out all over his head, and his normally bright blue eyes were bloodshot. Even looking as wrung out as he did, he was still good looking. He stood almost six feet tall with the broad shoulders of the football player he was. He was a popular guy, one of the most popular in the class, but he was still a nice guy. Even though he did a lot of things to make Kimber mad, he never did anything like cheat. We began walking toward the school entrance.

"I could explain if she would just talk to me."

"How do you explain what she saw?"

"It didn't mean anything. It was a dumb bet. She shouldn't even have seen it."

"That's your story? It was a bet, and you did it because you thought you wouldn't get caught?"

He made a frustrated sound in the back of his throat. "I'm not into Jenna."

That I actually believed. He was too good for her. "You went too far this time, Cole."

"Funny thing is – I did it for her."

I stopped in my tracks. "You kissed another girl for Kimber?"

"It was a bet. I made a lot of money. Kimber's birthday is next week."

"You have a job." I pointed out. He worked at the local grocery store bagging groceries.

"I don't make enough to get her what I wanted to get her."

"Looks like you won't have to get her anything now."

We went up the front steps; he walked ahead and held open the door for me. I paused before going in. *Just another day, just like yesterday.* I went in, and Cole followed.

"She's not going to forgive me, is she?" He sounded miserable.

"I don't know." I shuffled from foot to foot. Did that mean I couldn't forgive him either? He was like a brother to me. He was one of the very few who still treated me like I was normal, even though I wasn't. I sighed. "I'll see if I can get her to talk to you."

"You're the best, Hev."

"Give her a few days okay?"

"You got it." He grinned. "I'll call you later."

I nodded, and he went down the hall calling out greetings as he went. I tried to remain invisible as I walked to my locker. There were only a few stares this morning, which was good. One of the girls I used to cheer with called out a timid greeting. I gave her a little wave and a small smile before returning my gaze back to the floor. Just because people weren't staring didn't mean they weren't looking. They tried not to stare, but they couldn't keep their eyes away. I was a freak now. I made people uncomfortable – and not necessarily because of my scars – but because what my scars represented. Danger, fear, and the unknown. Something bad had happened to me, something not even I could remember. They all probably thought that I was crazy, that I somehow did this to myself. I couldn't blame them. How could I? They might be right.

Chapter Two

Heven

"What did he say?" Kimber asked before I'd even sat down. I pulled out a chair, facing her and the wall away from everyone else. Kimber's fashionable lunch bag was open before her, along with a bottle of Smart water.

"Where's your lunch?" she asked, frowning.

"I'll get something from the cafeteria."

She grimaced. She didn't eat food from the cafeteria. She said that if she couldn't tell what it was, she wasn't going to put it in her body. I used to feel the same way. She reached into her bag and pulled out a turkey sandwich on wheat with avocado slices. "Here."

"I'm not going to eat your lunch, Kimber."

She pulled an identical sandwich from her bag and raised her eyebrow. "Eat."

She stared at me until I was chewing. Only then did she start eating. "So you talked to him this morning?"

I nodded. "Maybe you should talk to him."

She shook her head adamantly.

"He said it wasn't what it looked like."

"Do you believe that?"

"Maybe." I put the sandwich down. It was hard to swallow.

"You're on his side?" She looked absolutely wounded.

"No!" I cried. "I'm on your side. I just hate to see you so upset."

"Cole cheated on me, Heven."

"With a skank," I added, hoping to make her smile again.

"The skank is headed this way," she whispered under her breath.

I resisted the urge to turn and look. A scent of freesia wafted toward us announcing her arrival. Before I looked up I pulled my hair to the side and over my left shoulder.

"What do you want, Jenna?" Kimber asked, her voice full of annoyance.

"Just wanted to remind you that we're having an extra practice Saturday morning. The competition is next month, and you need all practice you can get so you don't embarrass the squad."

In my lap my hand balled into a fist.

"Well, if I need extra practice it's because you taught the team the cheer we're doing. It's hard to get the moves down when your form is so sloppy."

I giggled.

The breath hissed between Jenna's teeth. "Speaking of sloppy," she purred. "I'm going to have to teach Cole how to kiss…clearly he's learned nothing from you."

"Bitch," Kimber growled, standing.

Jenna laughed and flicked a glance at me. "Freak," she taunted under her breath then walked away.

"She's evil," Kimber said, sitting back down.

"She's just jealous you're a better cheerleader than she is."

"We still on for some shopping after school?"

"Sure. I'll meet you at the car after the final bell."

Kimber packed up her uneaten lunch, looking more shaken than normal. On the way from the lunchroom she put her hand on my arm. "Hey."

"Yeah?"

"You know you're not a freak, right?"

"I know," I assured her with more bravado than I felt.

"Good. Because if anyone is a freak around here, it's her."

"You missed Bible study."

Mom's voice startled me, and I jumped. I looked around guiltily, relieved when I saw she was talking from the kitchen. How had I not heard her come in? I grimaced at the book and notebook in front of me, my attention certainly hadn't been on homework. Ever since the sky began darkening, it became harder and harder to not stare at the window worrying about what might be out there. At one point I drifted to sleep, bored to tears by my chemistry homework, and woke to a light scraping sound over the glass of the nearby window. My heart hammered in my chest when I saw a single sharp claw slowly slide down the glass then pull away only to slam back into the pane, causing it to vibrate. I jumped up, sending my chair clattering to the floor, ready to run, when I realized it was only the branch of a tree. I was an idiot. But knowing that didn't make me any less afraid.

I heard the fridge door close, and something hit the counter. I stifled a groan; please not chicken again tonight. Somehow my mother had gotten the idea that she should cook chicken in every way she could think of. So far, none of her creations tasted good.

"Sorry," I said, walking into the kitchen. "I have a ton of homework, and I'm not feeling well." It wasn't exactly a lie. Shopping with Kimber was overwhelming and left me with a headache, and the smoothie she'd insisted I drink was sitting in my stomach like a rock. When Kimber finally dropped me off, I let myself into the house and was so grateful to be alone I could have wept. I tried to distract myself with homework, but it was impossible to focus.

"You look pale," Mom clucked, placing a hand to my forehead. "No fever. Did you eat today?"

"Yes."

"Well good. Hope you saved room because I have a new chicken recipe!"

When she turned around I glared at the chicken on the counter. "Actually I have homework." I stepped backward toward the door.

"I'll call you when dinner is ready."

I went to get my book bag, wondering how to get out of eating the newest chicken delight. My cell phone rang, and I reached into my pocket silencing the generic ring. "Hello?"

"He sent flowers."

"What kind?"

"Roses. Pink. They're too pretty to throw away."

I smiled. "He really is sorry."

"Sorry isn't good enough," Kimber's voice wavered.

I sighed, throwing my book bag onto my bed. "I guess it isn't." But why couldn't it be?

"What are you doing?"

"Homework and trying to get out of another chicken dinner."

"Want to go grab a Panini and an iced coffee?"

"I'm not sure," I said. I was still a little on edge from our trip to the mall earlier.

"Come on, Hev. If I don't get out of here I'll go crazy looking at these flowers all night."

"I don't know. Mom might not let me because I missed Bible study." For once I might be grateful of Mom's strict rules.

"Leave that to me."

Before I could question her plans, she hung up the phone.

The doorbell rang ten minutes later, and I heard Kimber's voice downstairs. I rolled my eyes and went to see what she was up to.

"It's just awful, Mrs. Montgomery! He broke up with me!" Kimber sobbed at my mother.

"Maybe it's better this way, dear. You're too young for a boyfriend." Mom reached out and patted Kimber's shoulder.

I bit my tongue trying not to laugh.

"Maybe you're right," Kimber agreed seriously. "Can Heven come have dinner with me? It would make me feel better."

"Why don't you come in and have dinner with us? We're having chicken."

Kimber stepped into the house glancing at me. "Chicken sounds wonderful, but I was hoping we could go to the library too." She hung her head. "I kind of need help with my chemistry."

Mom nodded. "All right then." Before turning away she patted Kimber again. "With no boyfriend you'll have more time to study."

Kimber nodded gravely and wiped at her eyes. When Mom turned away, she grinned. I stifled a laugh.

"That was quite the performance," I told Kimber once we were in the car.

She grinned. "I knew it would work."

At the café on Main Street we settled into a corner booth with our drinks: a mocha latte for Kimber and a hot green tea for me. My nerves were already shot from my dream and our trip to the mall, so I figured the less caffeine I drank, the better.

"I've decided what to do about Cole."

"You have?"

"I'm going to give him a taste of his own medicine."

"What do you mean?" Although I was afraid I already knew.

"I'm going to make him jealous." She nodded, taking a sip of her coffee.

"Do you really think that's a good idea?"

"It's perfect."

"He's really sorry, Kimber. He's already miserable."

"He's the one who cheated," she snapped.

Our Panini's arrived, and we were silent for a minute. Kimber picked at her chips, pushing them around on her plate. "I'm sorry."

"Me too. I didn't mean to make it sound like he's innocent."

"It really hurts, Hev," she whispered, leaning across the table. "He really hurt me."

"I know." I'd never seen her so down.

"Why would he do that?"

"He told me that it was a bet."

"What?" she exclaimed.

"He said he did it for the money. He wanted to get you something really nice for your birthday."

Kimber laughed without humor. "He cheated on me…for me?"

I shrugged. I thought it ridiculous too. I watched her green eyes narrow, and she smiled.

"Kimber, what are you thinking?"

She picked up a chip and popped it into her mouth. "Payback's a bitch."

"You're serious? You're going to kiss another guy to make him jealous?"

"No." She sipped her latte.

"Then…?"

"I'm going to *date* someone to make him jealous."

"What? I don't think that's a good idea."

"When I'm done, Cole will never cheat on me again."

"So you're going to forgive him?"

She sighed, and her green eyes melted. "Yeah, I love him." Then her voice rose, and her eyes hardened. "But he needs to be taught a lesson. One he won't ever forget."

I took a sip of my tea, trying to figure what I should say. I didn't think this was a good idea, but saying so would make her angry. She'd already accused me of choosing his side over hers. She was

13

my best friend, my only friend since the accident – well, except for Cole.

"Who do you plan to make him jealous with?"

She pursed her lips, thinking. "He has to be hot, popular, and have a car."

"It can't be one of his friends," I cautioned.

"He has a lot of friends," Kimber complained. "Why does he have to be so popular?"

"Yeah, why couldn't you be dating an ugly, clumsy nerd?" I wondered sarcastically.

Kimber laughed. "It would make it easier."

We lapsed into silence. I surprised myself by eating a few bites of my Panini. It was pretty good. Kimber was staring off behind me, her attention caught by something or someone. I didn't turn around; I didn't want to draw attention to myself.

"Too bad he doesn't go to our school."

"Who?"

"That guy over there. He definitely has what it takes to make Cole insane with jealousy."

I resisted the urge to turn and see for myself.

"He's totally hot. Look," she urged. "I haven't seen him around before."

Slowly, I peeked around the back of the booth. He was standing near the counter, waiting for his coffee with his back turned. He was tall, well-built without being bulky, and the back of his head held shaggy, dark blond hair. When I kept looking Kimber whispered, "Told you."

Despite my usual need to keep hidden, I wished for a fleeting moment that he would turn around so I could see his face. Then he did. He looked right at me. The booth vibrated with the force of my retreat from sight. Butterflies fluttered around in my stomach, and my hands shook slightly. I pressed my back into the wood of the booth and willed myself to calm down. I looked up at Kimber, embarrassed over my reaction, but she wasn't paying any attention to me. She was waving at him and smiling.

"Stop it," I hissed.

She looked at me, and her smile was replaced with a frown. "What?"

"Don't draw any attention to us."

"Too late," she whispered. "He's heading our way."

My head swam. He was coming! I didn't want him to see me. "I have to go to the bathroom," I said rushing out of the booth. It would have been the perfect escape if I hadn't run right into him. I bounced off his chest, and his arms came out to steady me, but I cringed back into my seat, letting my hair fall around my face. "Sorry," I mumbled, looking down.

"No problem." His voice was raspy and low. My stomach fluttered again. He was more gorgeous than anyone I had ever seen. I wanted to look up so badly, but I wanted him to look at me less.

"Haven't seen you around before," Kimber said boldly.

"I'm new in town."

"I figured. I would have remembered if I had seen you around."

She was completely wicked. A part of me was jealous of that wickedness.

"What's your name?" he asked. His voice was unlike anything I'd ever heard – yet confusingly familiar; it filled me with something that I could only long for these past months: a sense of safety. It was beyond understanding because, right now, I shouldn't feel safe. I never felt safe around anyone new, but his presence was like a blanket to my shivering insides, whatever he projected reached out and wrapped around me, keeping my fear at bay.

"Kimber."

"Cool." he turned to walk away. I felt the urge to reach out and grab his hand. *Stay.*

"What's your name?" Kimber asked.

I inched closer desperate for the answer.

"Sam."

"Well, Sam, I'm sure I'll be seeing you around."

After he walked away it occurred to me that my attempt to be invisible worked really well. He never asked my name, and even though I hadn't wanted him to notice me (had I?), I couldn't help but be slightly disappointed.

I woke again that night to another frightening, unfinished reminder of the night my life changed forever. It was too early to get up for the day, and once again, I was too edgy to lay there, so I paced around my room. It was no surprise that I found myself at the window, looking down at the dark yard, my eyes always drawn to the trees and bushes, searching for someone I felt was there though always just hidden from sight.

"I know you're there," I whispered, even though, once again, I saw no one.

Something darted from the edge of the yard and disappeared around the side of the house. My stomach clenched. I watched awhile longer, waiting for whatever it was to come back. It didn't, and nothing else moved, but I knew my chance for sleep tonight was gone.

A shiver built low and raced its way up my back, making my body shake. I was just about to turn back to bed when my attention was caught by something up in the sky – the stars. It was a clear night, and many were visible. It made me remember the many nights when I was little that my dad would take me out into the yard on his shoulders and point out the many constellations. We always stayed outside until we saw at least one shooting star to wish on. I always felt safe with him; I missed him so much.

Just before I closed the curtain, I glanced back at the sky. There was a star twinkling so brightly that I wondered how I couldn't have noticed it before. It was the brightest and biggest in the sky, and it radiated warmth. As I watched it began to move, shooting through the sky and leaving a glittering path behind it. I didn't bother to make a wish because it already made me feel so much better.

Maybe sleep wouldn't be so out of reach after all.

Chapter Three

Heven

"Jenna is such a witch," Kimber growled. I abandoned my lunch to watch her drop into the chair across from me.

"What did she do now?"

"She scheduled extra practices all week for the competition coming up."

"So? We always have extra practices when a competition is close." I grabbed my water and took a long sip, just now remembering the fact that I didn't cheer anymore.

"I know." Kimber sighed. "I just hate her. I wish you were still cheering."

I placed the cap back on my water. "Have you talked to Cole at all?"

"He's called," she hedged.

"Kimber…"

"No."

"Maybe you should answer next time he calls." I was convinced that if they just talked, they could work it out.

"I can't."

"Why not?" I leaned across the table.

"Because I'll forgive him," she whispered.

Relief washed through me. She still loved him. Kimber and Cole would be back together, and everything would go back to normal. I ignored that tiny bit of relief that her plan to make Cole jealous would be no more. And the boy she thought would be perfect for that plan would be no more. "It's okay to forgive him."

She shook her head. "I can't just forgive him. I want him to know what it feels like."

Oh, no. "What do you mean?"

Before she could answer, Amber, one of the girls I used to hang with when I cheered, ran up to our table. She gave me the smallest of smiles before turning to excitedly beam at Kimber. "Did you hear?"

"Hear what?" Kimber asked.

"There's a new guy."

My stomach dropped.

"He's so hot," she drawled.

"Who is it?" Kimber asked.

"I don't know his name." Amber looked up, toward the cafeteria door. "But he just walked in."

With a lump in my throat I turned to see. It couldn't be.

It was.

"His name is Sam," Kimber told her with a slightly haughty tone.

"You know him?" Amber asked, awed.

"We've met," Kimber answered mysteriously.

The girl responded, but I didn't hear. There was a ringing in my ears. I couldn't drag my eyes away from him. He was so…

His eyes found mine; I felt my own widen.

I looked away, smoothing my hair around my scars.

"Did you hear me?" Kimber asked, leaning across the table.

"Sorry, what?" I looked up. Amber was gone.

"I *said* it looks like I've found my man to make Cole insanely jealous."

That's what I was afraid of.

It was spring, but the air was still cool, and I was grateful. Warm weather was not my friend; I couldn't wear hoodies and layers of clothes to hide behind. I huddled a little deeper into my jacket and hustled toward my destination. Just the sight of the weathered red barn was enough to soothe some of the day's worries away. I'd always liked this place, but ever since I woke up in the hospital with huge ugly scars on my face and no memory of how I got them, my grandmother's home was the only place I felt truly at ease. She was the only person in my family that didn't coddle or smother me with unwanted pity and worry.

I heard the soft rustle of hay, and I smiled. He knew I was coming. Once I reached the barn I walked directly to the first stall and looked into waiting, coal-black eyes.

"Jasper." I crooned, reaching out to stroke him. "Hi, boy. I've missed you."

The chestnut colored horse made a soft sound and pushed his nose toward me. Gran had three horses, each of them unique and special in their own way. But Jasper was my favorite. He was a balm to my wounded spirit.

"I brought you something." I reached into the bag I was carrying and pulled out a crisp red apple. The horse stomped his foot impatiently. I laughed. "Here you go." As he chomped, the other two horses neighed for their treats. I passed out the fruit and returned to Jasper with a small caddy of brushes.

As I curried him my thoughts wandered a place it shouldn't…to Sam. I didn't want him to be a new student at my school. I didn't want the halls to be buzzing about how cool and good looking he was. I did not want him to be in my seventh period home economics class. I absolutely did not want Kimber using him as some sort of pawn. I did not want to feel anything for him. But I did. I wasn't even sure what it was. Maybe it was just nerves. A new kid would be curious, interested in knowing how I got to be so ugly. People would talk to him about it – talk to him about me. I could just hear what they would say…

No one knows what happened…not even her.
She's a freak.
She used to be so popular…now she's nobody.

Jasper nuzzled my arm, bringing me back to the moment. I shook my head, clearing it. I went about my routine of brushing and saddling the horse. I did a good job of keeping my thoughts at bay until I rode Jasper out to my favorite wooded trail where my thoughts went right back to Sam. Right after the final bell at school, I rushed to my locker wanting to get out of there. I was hoping to avoid Kimber, but I wasn't fast enough. She wanted to talk about Sam and her plan for revenge. Thankfully, Grandma was waiting outside for me, and I managed to escape, but not before promising to call her when I got home.

I wanted to tell her that this plan to use Sam was stupid. I wanted to tell her to forgive Cole already and move on. But I wouldn't. I was chicken. I didn't used to be this way. *Before*. Whatever happened changed the way I viewed, not just my appearance, but my worth. Sometimes I wondered which was worse. Maybe if I still had the confidence I used to have, I wouldn't care that half of my face was disfigured. But my confidence was gone – just like cheerleading, the drama club, my fabulous fashion sense, and my friends. All I had left from my old life was Kimber. So, if concocting some stupid scheme to get back at Cole for cheating was what she wanted, then I would go along, because if I didn't, I wouldn't have anything left at all.

Jasper danced beneath me, and I patted his neck to settle him. I took a moment to gaze off into the newly budding trees ahead. Soon the forest would be a canopy of green, and I looked forward to it. I always felt at peace and protected among the trees here. Somewhere off to my left I heard a branch snap. Startled, I looked to where I'd heard the noise; there was nothing there. I nudged a reluctant Jasper along, feeling silly, yet I couldn't convince my heart to slow down. A few feet farther there was another snap, this one a little closer than the last. Jasper's ears pricked up, and he turned toward the sound. Suddenly his nostrils flared, and he took off running. I grasped at the reins but didn't bother to try to slow him down; if he sensed danger then I wanted him to run. I tucked my head down and urged him faster. I thought I heard another scuffle behind us, but I didn't turn to look. Broken memories and feelings began building in my chest. I felt like I might burst with anxiety. A sob escaped.

"Not again." I trembled, urging Jasper faster. The roof of the barn came into view, and I held on to the sight. I was almost there. I tried to listen for anyone following but heard nothing except the pounding of my own heart. When we reached the barn, I took a deep breath and turned to look behind me. There was no one there.

I felt silly.

Though, silly as I felt, I didn't slow Jasper down until we were safely inside the barn. Once there, I dismounted and swung the barn doors closed, bolting them. I ignored the trembling in my knees and hands as I lead Jasper to his stall. I tried to take comfort in the fact the horse showed no signs of distress.

I couldn't.

With Jasper in his stall, I walked to a corner of the barn filled with hay, sank down and cried my eyes out.

The Hate

Her crying amused me. She came prancing into the forest on that silly horse not even realizing I was watching. The horse noticed, but as always she was too involved in herself to notice that it was trying to warn her. She trotted right past me, so close that I could have reached out and touched her. Ahh, to see the terror in her eyes when she realized that all that looking over her shoulder wasn't for nothing. That there really is a monster in the shadows…waiting. But the time isn't right yet, and it was all too easy to scare her. All I had to do was make a single sound to send her fleeing the woods with fear on her face. Her cowardice annoyed me.

Months I have been stalking her, and I still can't figure out what it is that he loves so much. I guess some might call her beautiful – well they would have. I took care of that. With those huge, disgusting scars on her face, no one can stand the sight of her. Still, he watches her. He obsesses over her. He doesn't see the real her, he sees what he wants to see. He's blind to her. What he needs is a lesson…an education on all things about 'little Miss Priss.' Maybe then he would finally see what world he belongs in. He's fooled himself into thinking that there might be some good left inside him. But no more. I wonder who he will turn into when he sees her dead and lifeless body lying before him. Yes, when she is dead he will finally accept what he is and who he isn't.

The Hope

Her crying was unsettling. I wanted to reach out to her and take away her pain, but without pain there would be no joy. I took a moment to close my eyes to feel the warmth of love and peace course through me, and I sent it out to her for comfort.

It disturbed me that she was being watched by those with sinful agendas. Her path was so tentative it could turn either way. I prayed that she would choose the path that would lead her towards happiness. She could be the answer — but she would need help. I looked upon her once again; she lay crying in a darkened corner, looking alone and lost.

You are not lost. You are brave.
Love is the answer to it all.
Your turn for love is near.

I prayed that he was deserving of her love. I prayed that he could cast aside what he probably should be. It takes a brave and strong soul to deny part of yourself, not many can accomplish it. I watched her for another long moment. It was still too early to know which way this would go.

The road ahead holds many tests challenging everything she ever believed. I whispered a prayer for her inner strength to guide her on her path. She was going to need it.

Heven

A long while later I let myself into Grandma's kitchen. I wasn't crying anymore; I was seething with anger.

"How was your ride?" Grandma asked, her back turned, as she stirred something in a pot on the stove.

"Fine."

She turned and glanced at me as I poured a glass of water. "I saw you and Jasper run into the barn from the forest."

"Thought I heard something."

"Probably just a squirrel, they've begun coming out now that the weather is warming."

I said nothing because that was why I was angry. It probably was just a squirrel, and I acted like I was being hunted by a…well by who knows what? I was a stupid scaredy-cat! My own shadow scared me, and it was embarrassing. At the moment it also made me extremely angry. I didn't want to be a baby.

"I made spaghetti," Grandma said, pretending not to notice my foul mood.

"It's Thursday. I have Bible study at church, remember?"

"Not tonight. I called your mother and told her I needed you to help me with some chores around the barn."

"Everything looked done to me."

"It'll be our little secret," Grandma said, turning to wink at me.

I smiled. "I'm surprised she agreed. I didn't go earlier this week either." This meant that I would probably get a lecture later on skipping church and being unavailable to God. I sighed.

"I'm sure you could use the break," she said, placing a plate of spaghetti in front of me. Could she know how tied up I felt inside?

"Thanks."

She joined me at the table with a plate of her own and a basket full of garlic bread, which she placed directly in front of me. I took a piece, not wanting to seem unappreciative of the meal.

"How is school?"

I took a small bite of spaghetti; it was warm and slightly sweet. "Fine."

"Nothing new going on?"

"Kimber and Cole broke up."

She smiled. "I'm sure it's temporary."

I nodded, not wanting to go into details. I took another bite, and I surprised myself by saying, "We got a new kid."

"How exciting."

I shrugged. "He's in my home economics class."

Grandma leaned across the table to whisper, "Is he handsome?"

I giggled. "Yes."

"Have you talked to him?"

My smile faded. "No." *He doesn't even know I'm alive.*

"Maybe you should say hello."

"Why would he want to talk to me?" I felt embarrassed to say it out loud.

"Why wouldn't he?"

I shrugged, sorry to have brought up Sam.

Grandma sighed. "You are far more than those scars, Heven."

My eyes flew to her face. Not many people brought up my face. It was dangerous territory. Instead of getting angry I felt my eyes fill. "I'm hideous."

"You could never be hideous."

"Forget it." I wanted this conversation over.

"I can't forget it," Gran said, not giving up so easily. "I don't like to hear you talk about yourself that way. Your scars do not define you, young lady. Your actions do."

"It's hard to act confident when I feel anything but," I mumbled.

"I know that." Gran reached across the table and covered my hand with hers. "But hiding from who you are isn't going to make you feel any better."

I let my fork fall to my plate. I didn't want to hide who I was – I just wasn't sure who that was anymore.

"Pass me the bread," Gran asked.

It was right next to her, so I figured that was her way of telling me that she was finally going to let it go. Grateful, I passed the bread.

We finished the meal in silence.

The next morning Kimber laid on the horn earlier than usual. I ran down the stairs calling a goodbye to Mom, not even bothering to pretend to have breakfast. As usual I stopped at the big mirror by the front door and forced myself to look up. My blond hair hung over my shoulders and face, concealing as much as it could. It wasn't as shiny or healthy looking as *Before,* and my blue eyes were a little dull. I told myself it was because I hadn't slept well the night before. I never bothered with makeup anymore, but at least my skin was clear. I was dressed in my usual baggy shirt and jeans. Kimber laid on the horn again, and I ran out the door.

"You in a hurry?" I grumped, sliding into the passenger seat.

"You didn't call me last night," she accused.

"Sorry."

"I called you like a hundred times!"

"I was tired. Is something wrong?" I looked over at her. She was dressed just as fierce as always. Her thick red hair tumbled over her shoulders and she was wearing a long knit dress with a bold, colorful print. Her denim jacket was scuffed up and worn in all the right places. She didn't look like anything was wrong.

"We have been invited to a party this weekend!"

"Great."

"Ask me who."

"Whose party is it?"

"Josh Turner's!"

"The varsity quarterback?" I asked curiously.

"Yes!" She clapped her hands, about to burst.

"Wow."

"I know, right? It is going to be awesome! His parties are legendary."

"Yeah." His parties were always the topic of conversation for weeks afterward. Even though Kimber and I had never been to one, we always heard every last detail in the hallways at school.

"Aren't you excited?" she asked, exasperated.

"Thrilled." I tried to inject some enthusiasm in my voice.

She pinned me with a look that made my stomach hurt. "You are not getting out of this one. You're going."

I wet my lips with my tongue.

"It's tonight."

"Tonight!" I gasped.

"Yes. Come over after school, you can borrow something to wear."

"I can't."

"Please..." she sang.

"I can't."

"Please, please, please…"

Her begging was pathetic.

"We have been waiting for an invite to one of these since freshman year!"

That was true. "You go…without me."

"If you don't go, I don't."

"That isn't fair," I groaned.

"I'll hold it over your head forever!"

"Fine," I agreed, weary.

She squealed as she pulled into the parking lot at school. I was actually glad to be here just to get out of the car. "Have you talked to Cole?" I asked just because I was mad that she'd guilted me into going to the party.

She made a face. "Yesterday. Something else you would have known if you'd have called me back."

I straightened the hood on my head and stifled an eye roll.

"He wants to get back together."

"Did you forgive him?" Hope bloomed in my chest.

"Are you kidding? I told him I wasn't sure what I wanted."

"Why would you say that?"

She shrugged. "Let him wonder for a while."

I opened the door to get out.

"He's coming tonight," she said over the hood of her car.

Great. More drama. Maybe I'll have a panic attack, and it will *really* be fun.

"My plan begins tonight."

My heart froze. "You're plan?"

"Sam is bound to be there tonight. He's, like, the biggest attraction at school right now."

"What are you going to do, Kimber?"

She smiled. "You'll see."

Chapter Four

Heven

I looked down at the clothes draped across my bed and frowned. How did I get myself into this situation? Just minutes before, Kimber had dropped me off with a promise to return to get me later. I stood there wondering if she'd believe me if I suddenly got sick. Not likely.

The outfit she picked out was gorgeous, of course. Too gorgeous. I didn't wear stuff like this anymore. What was the point of trying to look pretty? The dark denim jeans were designer, and so was the top. It didn't have a hood. It was a V-neck. Ugh.

There was a knock on the door before it swung open. "Have a good day?" Mom asked.

"Great," I lied. "You?"

"Yes, thank you." She eyed the clothes on my bed. "Do you have plans tonight?"

I nodded. "If it's okay Kimber was invited to a party, and she asked me to come too." I threw the 'party' word out there in hopes she would tell me I wasn't allowed to go.

Her eyes narrowed. "Who's party?"

I told her. She stared at me for long moments. I waited for a lecture – I was overdue. She hadn't said a word about me missing Bible study again last night. She asked about Grandma, and I told her about school, and that was all. I came home late today, and now I was asking to go to a party. She wouldn't let me get away with it.

"His mother is in my Bible study group. She's very nice."

I nodded.

"Be home by eleven."

That was it? Just like that? "Really?"

"Yes. We'll have breakfast in the morning, and you can tell me about it."

"Okay." She shut the door and left me standing there, empty. Now how was I going to get out of this?

I didn't get out of it. At precisely the designated time, Kimber pulled into the driveway. I went slowly down the stairs toward the front door. Mom looked up from her book, her eyes running over me. Did she look slightly relieved?

I wasn't wearing what Kimber wanted me to wear. I couldn't bring myself to wear that top. So in concession I was wearing the jeans, but they didn't look the way Kimber thought they would. They were too big; everything of mine was. Instead of hugging my curves, the jeans hung off of them, which was fine by me. I elected to wear a hoodie, but a nice one. It was made of a fine knit and it was a nice shade of blue. It wasn't as baggy as all my other ones. In an attempt to dress it up further, I wore a silver cross pendant.

"You look nice. I haven't seen that necklace in a while," Mom said.

"Thanks. I'll see you later." I hoped that she would call me back and say she changed her mind.

I opened the front door and looked back.

She'd already returned to her book.

In the car Kimber demanded, "What happened to the outfit I picked out for you?"

"I'm wearing the jeans," I answered defensively.

"Those are my jeans?" She sounded shocked. "How much weight have you lost anyway?"

I shrugged. I was thin *Before*, but she had always been thinner. I guess not anymore.

She muttered under her breath and backed out of the drive. I looked out my window and wondered how bad this night was going to be.

The party was bumping, and there were far more people than I expected. It seemed like half the student body of Windham High was there. "Kimber, I..." my voice cracked and fell away as I looked at the front door.

"Chill, Heven. Everything is going to be great!"

Before I could throw myself into the bushes, the front door opened and loud music vibrated out around us. "Ladies!" Some drunk dude from the senior class boomed. Kimber grabbed my hand and pulled me inside as I smiled thinking of what my mother would say now about her friend from Bible study.

We chatted (rather Kimber chatted) with everyone we knew, and she dragged me into the kitchen for a drink. She tried handing me a cup of red punch, and I lifted an eyebrow at her. "Seriously?" I yelled over the music.

Kimber rolled her eyes and reached into a cooler to pull out a Coke and handed it to me. I watched in horror as she took a long sip of the red 'punch.' "It's definitely loaded," she called to me, taking another sip. I held out my palm, and she rolled her eyes, but surrendered her keys without argument. "Let's find Cole." She grabbed my hand and towed me through yet another huge crowd out into the back yard.

The back yard was huge, and it had a kidney-shaped pool, a hot tub, and a gazebo. People were dancing and yelling to each other over the loud music, but at least it was fairly dark. The only illumination came from the few lights on the deck and the back of the house. Kimber pulled me off to the side of the deck and pointed. "There he is."

Cole was on the other side of the pool, lounging against a large brick planter. He was surrounded by half the football team, and while he was smiling, his eyes scanned the crowd every few seconds. "He's looking for you."

"Yeah, and I'm going to give him something to look at." With her declaration she released me and strutted away, her hips moving seductively and attracting the gaze of every guy she passed by. Except she wasn't walking toward Cole. I felt the blood drain from my face when I looked past Kimber to whom she was strutting toward.

Sam was standing in a crowd of people who were all openly staring at him, yet he wasn't really part of the group. He seemed separate somehow. He was wearing a black leather jacket, a snug navy shirt, and a pair of beat-up jeans. His dark blond hair was messy, falling over his ears and right eye, and when he saw Kimber heading toward him, he pushed it up onto his forehead. He didn't smile as he watched her slinking toward him but watched her like a predator might watch his prey. It made gooseflesh rise along my arms. As he watched her his eyes flashed up over her shoulder – searching for something or someone – and not knowing why, I stepped back into the shadows so he wouldn't see me. Kimber walked around the open fire pit that separated her from her target and reached out her manicured hand and placed it on his arm, drawing his eyes back to her. Her mouth moved, and the side of his mouth kicked up in a small smile. His lips barely moved, but I knew he'd spoken, and I wished I was closer to hear the deep, raspy tone of his voice. Kimber laughed and her hand went a little more firmly around his arm. It made my stomach hurt, and I looked over at Cole to see if he was watching the show.

He was seeing it all right. He was standing erect, watching with his fists balled at his sides and an angry expression on his face. Kimber laughed again, and I looked back in time to see Sam turn fully toward her and look down to smile. God, he was so beautiful. For a split second I imagined that he was looking down at me smiling that way, and my heart nearly stopped. From behind, someone bumped into me, and I stumbled forward.

"Sorry," the guy mumbled, but I ignored him because as soon as I moved, Sam's eyes flashed up to where I was standing, like he knew I was there. But I knew my imagination was working on overdrive because I was in the shadows, and I knew he couldn't see me. As if to prove my point, his eyes went back to Kimber who brazenly leaned up and whispered something in his ear.

I glanced at Cole who was clearly having a hard time staying rooted to his spot. He was so angry that the guys with him were turning to see what he was staring at. In fact, it seemed Kimber and Sam were attracting quite an audience. Unfortunately for Kimber, one of her audience members stepped forward, making a beeline for the pair.

Jenna looked like a woman with a mission and by the evil glint in her eye, whatever that mission was would not be good for Kimber.

Somehow Jenna managed to wedge herself between Sam and a perturbed Kimber. She flicked her dark locks over her shoulder and placed a single finger on his chest and leaned into him. She really was a skank, and I wanted to gag at the thought of her touching Sam. He stared down at her with an unreadable expression on his face. She said something that made Kimber go red in the face and glare daggers at her back. With a sigh I headed over toward the unfolding drama. Cole was stepping through the crowd also, and I caught his eye and waved him back. He would only make things worse.

I stopped beside Kimber who gave me a 'can you believe this?' look before putting her hand on Jenna's arm and yanking her around. "Why don't you go torture someone else with your presence?" she snapped.

Jenna hissed and slapped her hand away. "Don't touch me."

"Chick fight!" someone behind us yelled, and a crowd began forming.

Kimber pressed in close to Jenna, and I put an arm between them. "This is so third grade," I said, trying to sound bored.

Jenna turned her icy stare to me. "Careful freak, might find yourself with some more unsightly scars."

Some 'oohing' and 'ahhing' went through the crowd, but I barely registered it. Her words made my face flame with embarrassment. I knew that everyone was now staring at the girl with the disfigured face.

"You dirty bitch!" Kimber yelled, pulling back her fist. Unfortunately, my arm was still in the way, and Jenna used it as her shield, pulling my arm up so it would take the impact of the hit. It was solid and spun me backward toward the roaring fire pit. Jenna shrieked, trying to pull away from me, but like anyone who loses their balance, I groped for something to grab and right myself; it happened to be her. She didn't pull me back up, rather, I pulled her down with me. I felt the back of my knees buckle at the impact of the edge of the stone border and felt the heat from the flames through my clothes and panic stole through me. As I fell, I wondered where my scars would be this time.

One minute I was falling toward a flaming death, and the next I was lying on the ground, away from the flames, unburned and unhurt. I heard Kimber asking me if I was all right, and I blinked, trying to clear my head, trying to decide if I was or wasn't. But I couldn't think because my heart was thundering in my chest, and Jenna was screeching at the top of her lungs.

I sat up and looked at Jenna who was lying on the ground clutching her arm. "It's broken! She broke my arm!" As she screeched she rolled to the side and glared at me.

I drew back. I did not do that to her. Did I? What the heck happened? I thought for sure I was going into the flames.

Kimber stood, placing herself in front of me. "Heven isn't responsible for your arm," she spat. Then, dramatically, she flung herself to the side at someone. "Thank goodness you were here!"

Sam caught her easily and patted her shoulder as she wrapped her arms around his waist. Pain lanced through my chest, and I winced. Maybe I was hurt after all…

I looked up and my eyes fastened on Sam, who was watching me. Emotion flashed through his eyes, but it was gone so quickly I was unable to name it.

"Heven? Hey, you okay?" Cole leaned over me. He looked so sad I couldn't be angry at him for blocking my view of Sam.

"I'm sorry," I whispered.

"This isn't your fault, Hev."

"Help me up?"

He lifted me up and onto my feet with ease. When he pulled back I swayed a little, and he came back, anchoring his arm around me. "Are you sure you're okay?"

My eyes went back to Kimber and Sam. I watched as he gently tried to detangle himself from her and then push her aside. The pain in my chest eased considerably when they were no longer touching. Sam seemed more interested in my conversation with Cole and was staring between us with that unreadable expression he did so well. I looked up at Cole. "I'm fine."

"Need a ride home?" he whispered.

I nodded. "I want to go." I was extremely sorry I came at all.

Kimber was beside me instantly. "You know I didn't mean to push you."

"I know."

"I would have died if you'd gotten hurt! Thankfully, Sam has some bad ass reflexes and pulled you out of the way."

Sam saved me from the fire? It happened so fast that I wasn't sure what had happened.

I pulled Kimber's keys out of my pocket and stepped out from beneath Cole's arm. I held them out to her. "You'll be okay to drive?"

She stared at me for a few seconds like she couldn't believe I wanted to leave. I wasn't sure what I would have done if she'd said no. But I knew I couldn't stay here, but I would worry if I left and knew she wouldn't be safe...

"I'll make sure she gets home safe." Sam's husky voice made me shiver and then he touched me. It was a simple, insignificant brush of his hand as he took the keys from my palm, but I would remember that one second contact with him like it was my first kiss.

Every single nerve in my arm tingled, and my skin burned. Every coherent thought I might have had completely faded away. I stared at him, entranced by his hazel stare, caught by the golden highlights that sparked through his eyes. "Uh..."

His mouth opened and broke the spell. "You okay?"

I just knew that my face was glowing from embarrassment. Geez, he said two words, and I practically fell at his feet drooling. He must think I am pathetic. I let my head fall so my hair would curtain my face. "Thanks," I mumbled, as my eyes focused on something...I gasped and grabbed Sam's arm. "Are *you* all right?"

"It's nothing," he said, gently trying to pull his arm away.

I wouldn't let him. I stared at his leather jacket, which was burned all the way through. I brushed my finger over the hole; the fabric was still hot. My fingers grazed the skin of his arm. I sucked in my breath and dared a glance up at him. He was watching me intently, and I forgot what I was going to say. "Y-y-your shirt is...the fire burned through your jacket and shirt."

He grasped my fingers and removed them from his arm. "Forget it."

Did he reach into the fire to get me? Would I be burned right now if he hadn't put his arm in the way of the flames? "Are you all right? Are you burned?"

He cleared his throat and shot a nervous glance to the people gathered around. "I'm fine. No burns." He held up his arm, pushing back his ruined sleeve. His skin was completely unmarked.

"Oh," I mumbled, feeling embarrassed yet again. How many more times would I humiliate myself before I left? "Well, thank you–" I took a step back toward Cole. "–for pulling me out of the way."

It seemed like he might say something, but Kimber spoke first. "It's a shame Jenna wasn't as lucky."

I turned and watched Jenna being led away by her henchmen and dismissed her. She would be fine. Girls like her always were.

"Heven?" Cole asked, touching my shoulder. "Ready?"

He and Kimber completely ignored each other. "Yeah, just a second." I turned back to where Sam was standing, hoping to hear whatever he might have said.

He was gone.

The interior of the truck was dark and cool. I didn't mind either. It gave me an excuse to huddle into my jacket and not worry that my facial expressions would give away my sour mood. It bothered me that Sam and Kimber were together right now. I wondered what they were doing…

"Sometimes I wonder why I bother." Cole said quietly.

I glanced over his way. The dashboard lights cast a glow over his strong features. His jaw was set, and his brow was creased but even so he was attractive. His dark hair was mussed, but not the kind of mussed that guys do now on purpose. His was like that because he didn't care what it looked like. His brilliant blue eyes were staring out at the road, slightly squinting when he looked at a sign. I found that little detail endeared him to me. It kind of reminded me that we were all human and we all had flaws. The skin of his face was pulled taunt over strong cheekbones and a square jaw. His lips were pressed into a flat line.

"Bother with what?" I asked just as quietly as he had.

"With Kimber."

"I'm sorry about the way she's treating you, Cole." I probably shouldn't say that or anything else against my best friend, but then I got a vivid flash of Kimber pressing herself into Sam and him lowering his face towards her…I squeezed my eyes shut and blurted, "She really is acting like a bitch."

As soon as the words left my mouth I regretted them. Talking trash behind Kimber's back made me as bad as her. "I didn't mean that." I rushed out.

Cole glanced at me and laughed. He had a dimple in his cheek. "I won't tell." He winked at me before returning his eyes back to the road. "Besides right now I would have to agree."

"You really hurt her." I said, trying to make amends with my own guilty conscience for what I said.

"Do you think I like seeing her with that other guy?"

"I guess not," I mumbled. He turned onto my street and I felt a wave of relief.

"Sometimes I think it might be easier just to date someone who isn't so…" his words trailed off.

"You'll never find anyone like Kimber." I said loyal to my friend even while I asked myself why I should since she was with Sam. Clearly her loyalty to me wasn't as strong as I thought.

He pulled up to the curb at my house and shifted in his seat to look at me. "I'm not so sure about that."

Something about the way he said it and the look on his face made me swallow hard. "I should get inside."

He stared at me for another long moment before smiling and giving a nod. "Yeah."

Before getting out I turned back. "You should try and make up with her. You two make a great couple."

"I'll see you on Monday." Cole said softly.

"Thanks for the ride." I said before hurrying away and into my house. I leaned against the front door as I listened to him drive away. On my way upstairs to my bedroom I wondered who it was that Cole thought would be so easy to date. I shied away from the obvious answer because that wasn't something I was prepared to think about.

When Kimber put her mind to something, it got accomplished. It was an admirable trait to have – except in this instance. This time she set her sights on Sam, and things were definitely swinging in her favor. Since the night of the party, Sam and Kimber had been spotted together several times: in the halls at school, outside once classes were dismissed, at the local ice cream shop, and once Sam went to a game that Kimber was cheering at. I knew every detail about every encounter because I had to sit through the play-by-play at lunch. Every. Single. Day.

Ugh.

It made me ache from the inside out. I felt like a tire with a slow leak, except the leak was in my heart. Every single time she mentioned his name and every single time I saw his vibrant white teeth flash at her in a smile, a little bit of my heart deflated. I was hoping that soon there wouldn't be anything left so it wouldn't hurt anymore.

As I walked from my locker to the cafeteria, my stomach knotted in anticipation for today's report. It was Monday, the crappiest day of the week, and it just got crappier because now I had to sit through an entire lunch of her details of the weekend. Her weekend with Sam. I tried to console myself with the fact that she said all their 'dates' were strategic, meaning that they only went places where she would be seen with him, and she was certain it would get back to Cole. She told me that they hadn't ever been completely alone on a date, and I was curious what Sam thought of that. I wondered how much he liked her and how much he would hurt when she dumped him and went back to Cole. Then I wondered if Cole would even want her back. As if he knew I was thinking about him he appeared at my side.

"Hey, Hev." He said, giving me a smile.

"Hey."

"I thought about calling you after the other night…I wanted to see how you were doing."

"See how I was doing? You're the one who had to watch Kimber drape herself all over Sam." I muttered darkly.

Hurt flashed in his eyes, and I felt bad for my comment. Just because I was suffering didn't mean he had too as well. "Do you know him well?"

I glanced at Cole swiftly. "Who?"

"The new kid – Sam. The way you said his name…" he looked at me with questions in his eyes.

"Uh-no. I've heard her talk about him a lot." As soon as the response left my lips I felt guilty again.

"I'll catch you later," Cole said, stopping just outside the cafeteria doors.

"Aren't you coming to lunch?"

"I forgot my lunch money in my locker."

Before I could respond or try to apologize for my foul mood and grouchy comments, he stalked off.

Exhaling, I walked into the cafeteria to our usual table where Kimber was already sitting, lunch bag open in front of her. I slid into my chair, bracing myself.

"How was your weekend?" she cheerfully asked.

"Fine – and yours?"

"So great. I had a date." She smiled and her eyes sparkled. I was beginning to wonder if she was even doing this to get back at Cole anymore. I wondered if she enjoyed playing with people's hearts like this. Then she said, "He came over to my place."

The bottom dropped out of my stomach, and my vision blurred. I blinked several times. "Sam came to your place?"

"Uh-huh."

That's all she had to say? Usually it was, 'Sam this' and 'Sam that' and blah, blah, blah. She never shut up! But the one time I wanted just a single detail, she was being closed-lipped. It could only mean one thing. She liked him – *really* liked him.

I couldn't do this. My chest tightened, and a cold sweat prickled my skin. *Do not freak out right now. Calm down.* I took several deep breaths until I felt more in control and then looked up at Kimber who was chomping on her sandwich, oblivious. Then a bright smile broke over her face. "I invited someone to join us today."

Oh no.

Sam pulled out a chair next to Kimber and sat down. I think my heart stopped beating. So far I'd only had to listen to the gory details and see them, briefly, from across the hall. But never once did I have to witness Sam and Kimber up close and personal. I couldn't bear it.

"Sam, you remember Heven?"

"Hey, Heven." I swear his voice turned huskier than usual when he said my name.

"Hey," I returned, blushing furiously.

"Where's your lunch?" Kimber asked him.

"I need to go through the line."

"I'll save your seat." She giggled, leaning toward him.

He smiled, and I wanted to gag. I scooted my chair back so I could get out of there when Kimber turned toward me. "Here." She reached into her bag and handed me a sandwich.

I took the sandwich, laying it in front of me. "You brought me a sandwich?"

Kimber rolled her eyes. "I've been bringing you a sandwich every Monday for months."

She had? Sure, she shared sometimes, but every Monday?

At my blank look she rolled her eyes again. "Mondays are the hardest day of the week for you. You never remember food. Can't have you wasting away."

Her thoughtfulness touched me and made me regret the things I'd been thinking earlier. Then Sam cleared his throat. My eyes shot to his face; he wasn't looking at me, but at Kimber. "I'll be right back."

When he was gone I tried to escape, using the same excuse Cole had used only moments before. "I forgot something in my locker."

"Not so fast."

"What?"

She sighed. "I know you're uncomfortable around new people, and I get it, but Sam, he's important to me."

"More important than Cole?" I shot out.

She seemed taken aback. "I..."

"Don't you think he's learned his lesson? How much longer are you going to hurt him?"

"He hurt me too."

"Not like this." He wouldn't do that to her.

Kimber frowned and looked to where Sam was in line.

"You really like him?" I whispered. When she opened her mouth to answer I cut her off. "Don't answer that. It isn't my business anyway."

"Of course it is. You're my best friend."

But I couldn't stand to hear her answer, which was ridiculous, because I didn't even know him, and he had no clue I was alive. He arrived back at the table and sat down. Kimber looked at me with pleading eyes, and with a sigh, I scooted my chair back to the table.

"I need to talk to you about something," Kimber said, taking a bite of her turkey sandwich.

"Okay." I was only half-listening, distracted by Sam's presence.

"You know Jenna broke her arm?"

"Uh-huh," I answered. Sam's hands were huge; he had long fingers and short square fingernails. The fork he was eating with looked like a child's toy.

"Earth to Heven" Kimber was waving her hand in front of my face.

"Sorry," I mumbled, and Sam looked up to catch me staring at his hands. Quickly I ducked my head, but not before I saw his lips tilt up. My heart beat faster.

"Anyway, I thought you could think about it," Kimber finished whatever she was saying.

I stared at her.

"You didn't hear a word I said, did you?" she frowned.

"Uh, yeah, Jenna and her broken arm."

Kimber brightened a bit and nodded. "I want you to take her place at the cheer competition next weekend."

"Me?" I choked on the water I was drinking. The cap from my bottle flew out of my hands and landed right in front of Sam. He scooped it up before I could reach for it and held it out. It looked small lying in the center of his palm. I flicked my eyes up to his face, but then looked back down when I saw him watching me. "You lost something," he rasped and held his hand out to me.

"Thanks." I tried to touch as little of him as possible, but someone jostled his chair from behind just as I was reaching into his palm. Instead of the 'no contact' I'd planned, his arm shot out, and I automatically grasped his hand to try and steady him.

His skin was warm.

And slightly rough.

I sighed.

I swear he heard the small breath, and his eyes locked on mine. I didn't pull away as I wanted to because I was surprised by the shot of gold that was like lightning through his whiskey-colored stare. I blinked then looked back at him, but the gold was gone. Had I imagined that?

"Heven, are you okay?" Kimber worried from somewhere far away.

To my intense surprise Sam squeezed my fingers before gently sliding his hand from beneath mine. He grabbed my water bottle, and I watched as he twisted the cap back into place. When he was finished he returned the bottle beside my elbow.

"Thanks."

"Anytime."

"Heven, the cheer competition?" Kimber reminded me.

"I don't cheer anymore."

"It hasn't been that long, and I can teach you the routine." I shook my head, ready to shoot her down, but she interrupted. "Please! The team won't be able to compete because we'll be short."

I looked doubtful, and Kimber hurried to add, "Two girls are out because of injury already, and now with Jenna…"

"Find someone else."

"There isn't anyone, and you're the best!" Kimber smiled over at Sam. "Heven was going to be head cheerleader."

I kicked her under the table. Sam looked at me. "Yeah?"

I nodded, blushing.

"Cool. How come you stopped cheering?"

Wasn't it obvious? Kimber made a sound, but I held up my hand. "I cheered *Before*."

He seemed confused, so I motioned to my face and looked right at him so he could see.

"You stopped cheering because you have scars on your face?" He put his fork down like he was sickened by his food. It made my stomach hurt to see his reaction to my ugliness, and I quickly ducked my face, reaching for my hair and pulling my hoodie as close around my face as I possibly could. Desperate for a new subject, I turned pleading eyes on Kimber, but she was staring in the opposite direction, so I followed her gaze. Just entering the lunchroom, Cole was standing in the center of the room, staring at our table. He looked angry and hurt at the same time. Abruptly he turned and banged out the doors, and Kimber jumped up from her chair.

"I'll be right back," she threw out and then ran after him.

I resisted the urge to go after them both and find out what was happening. Did Kimber finally understand that she was breaking his heart? Could Cole possibly forgive her? I prayed that he would, because things just didn't seem right when they weren't together. And because selfishly I didn't want her to be with Sam. I reached across the table and gathered Kimber's forgotten lunch – I knew she wouldn't be coming back this period. I couldn't wait 'til the final bell rang so I could find out what happened between them. As I zipped up her fashionable pouch I felt a whisper against my ear. "You didn't answer my question."

A shiver started at the base of my spine and went all the way up to my shoulders. Ever so slowly I turned to peek at him from around my hood.

"Remember me?" He smiled.

Something familiar ghosted through me, but I couldn't think about that now. I would never forget Sam. I nodded. His chuckle slid over me like honey, and of their own accord, my eyes briefly closed.

"So?" he prompted.

I sifted through the fog in my mind for whatever it was he'd asked. Oh, yeah, the scars. "Yes. I gave up cheering after my accident."

"I don't think you should let a few little scars keep you from what you love."

He was closer than ever. Somehow his chair was right next to mine, and he was the only thing in the universe. "I-It isn't little."

"Your beauty overshadows it." He said the words easily, as if they cost him nothing. Yet they were words that were more valuable to me than anything, and I was very afraid that they cost me my heart. The very heart I had been trying to protect. I watched in slow motion as his hand came up and drew closer, his hazel eyes hypnotizing me. Right before he made contact I realized what he was doing, and I jerked away. No one had ever touched my scars, except for my doctor. Not even my mother. As a result of my quick reflexes, his hand brushed the side of my hood and landed on my shoulder. I kept my eyes down, trying not to struggle for air. I felt his fingers move over me, almost like a caress, and then his touch was gone. "I didn't mean to frighten you."

"You didn't." My shaky voice betrayed me.

He sat back in his chair and watched me for several moments until I looked up. He seemed angry with his jaw set and hand clenched in his lap. "I'm sorry," I told him.

"Me too." The simple words were spoken like he truly meant them, and I couldn't figure out what he might be so sorry for. Was it was the fact that he tried to touch me, or the fact I was too chicken to let him.

"I have to go, I...I don't want to be late for class."

His white teeth flashed, and he laughed.

"What?" I scowled.

He motioned to the room, and I managed to break my eyes away from his beauty.

I gasped. "How long?"

"About five minutes." He was amused.

I, of course, was mortified. I'd sat there with Sam for five minutes without noticing that the room was completely empty.

Chapter Five

Heven

The skies were dark and cloudy, matching my mood. Why did I always allow her to talk me into things that I absolutely did not want to do? From the window seat of the bus I stared out, watching the trees bow and sway in the increasing wind.

A storm was coming.

In the glass of the window I saw Kimber slide into the seat beside me. With a sigh I turned to face her.

"Want me to do your hair?"

"No," I replied quickly. "I'll do it before we go on."

She didn't press, which was a good thing. "Thanks for doing this," she said, lowering her voice.

I looked down at my lap, noting the bright colors of my cheerleading uniform – something I thought I would never wear again. I thought back to the day at lunch, the day I secretly think of as "the day Sam stole my heart", and remembered the broken look on Kimber's face after school. Her strategic 'dating' of Sam worked too well so things with Cole were not going well. In my head I told myself that it was her fault, and in my heart, I felt a teeny bit of satisfaction that she was getting a little payback for making me watch her with Sam. But she was my best friend – my only friend, and I hated to see that broken look on her face. So, when I denied her request once more to cheer for the competition, she informed me that I was their last hope. If I did not agree to learn the cheer, then the entire squad would have to forfeit. How could I do that to my old squad? It made me feel downright guilty.

So here I sat, on a bus headed toward Portland, for a very public cheering competition. The girls surprised me with smiles and welcomes. I even got a few thank yous for bailing them out of a forfeit, and it felt good to be back with the squad. The practices were fun, and the routine was super easy to learn; I even managed to change a few moves to make it better. If only I could skip the competition. Every mile that we drew closer to Portland the more nervous I got.

"You're nervous, huh?"

I nodded.

"No one is even going to notice."

She was trying to be nice, but I knew better. My puckered, raised scars were too noticeable, and to top it off we had to wear our hair up. Ugh. At least I managed to talk the coach into letting me be in the back. She wanted me in the front, but I made it clear it was the back row or nothing.

"Let's talk about something else," I said. "How are things with Cole?"

She screwed her face up. "I really messed things up good."

"He's still mad?"

"Hurt, angry and betrayed is more like it. But he's driving up here today to watch."

"That's great!"

"Yeah. I don't know if I can fix things with him. I was stupid."

I was afraid to ask about Sam and what was going on between them. She hadn't mentioned him in a while, but I saw them in the hall the other day. "His coming up here is a good sign."

"Yeah. Although I think that he might be coming just to see what I'm doing, or rather what I'm not doing."

"Oh."

"I feel bad for Sam, though."

"Why?" My heart picked up at his mention.

"Cole is pissed, and it's mostly directed at him."

"Kimber! You can't let him be mad at Sam for something that isn't even his fault!" My breath stuttered, and I felt my control slipping. The thought of Sam getting hurt was more than I could bear.

"I know," she answered miserably. "But with Cole so mad at Sam, he isn't as mad at me."

"Kimber," I gasped.

"Fine. I'll tell him."

"Want me to talk to Cole?"

"Couldn't hurt. Cole has a soft spot for you." She nudged me with her elbow. I couldn't help but smile.

"You'll be great today," Kimber whispered, sinking down to rest her head on my shoulder.

I stared out the bus window at the gathering clouds, hoping just to make it through the day.

The roar of the crowd and the loud beat of the music made me want to throw up. I stood behind the curtain waiting for the signal that it was our turn to perform. I couldn't stand still, shifting from one foot to the other and fidgeting with my ponytail.

"Your hair is fine," Kimber said from beside me.

"Well, yours looks gorgeous."

Kimber smiled. Then the announcer was calling for our squad, and the crowd was cheering. The next thing I knew, I was being pulled and pushed by the girls out onto the platform beneath bright lights. I found my spot, my feet feeling like concrete blocks, and stood still while everyone moved around me, getting ready. Panic rushed through me as the hundreds of faces in the crowd blurred to one. I couldn't do this. I. Could. Not. Do. This.

Just as our music began playing there was movement in the crowd that drew my eye. It was Sam. My eyes locked on his, and he nodded. That profound, familiar feeling of safety that he always brought flowed through me. I *could* do this. His presence meant everything to me. Air filled my lungs as the squad started moving. I plastered a huge smile on my face and performed the routine with perfection, all the while keeping my eyes on Sam.

Before I knew it the audience was clapping and cheering and the music went off. The girls bustled around me, high fiving each other and squealing with excitement. But I just stood there, a solitary being in the center of chaos. I couldn't look away from Sam. I didn't want to. He was here for me. I felt it in my core; I could practically taste it in the air. He never once looked away during the entire performance. It was as if he knew that he was the one thing that tethered me to the floor. He never once glanced in the direction of Kimber; it was almost as if no one else existed for him but me. I

MASQUERADE

marveled in the fact that I could have the most personal moment of my life in a room filled with people.

Someone tugged at my arm. "Come on, Heven. We have to go."

"Yeah, okay," I told them without taking my eyes away from Sam.

He nodded once and his lips curved up in a secret smile. A smile directed at only me. My heart fluttered beneath my ribs. Before I could smile back I was pulled away behind the curtains, and I was jarred back to life by the noise and people around me. It was such a stark contrast to what I felt only moments before I actually wondered if I had imagined everything that just happened.

I stood in front of a large mirror, wiping the stage makeup from my face. We nailed the competition and won. Everyone was thrilled. I was just relieved it was over and maybe a little proud of myself for doing it. My nerves were still raw from the stress of all the people, and sometimes it was still hard to draw a breath.

I tossed the cotton pad in the trash and reached for another, dousing it with makeup remover. The makeup was thick, and I wanted it gone. Somehow I felt that it drew more attention to my scars than away from them like it was meant to do.

"Hey, girl." Kimber smiled, coming up behind me.

"Where is everyone?"

"Loading the bus. Time to go."

"I'll be right there."

"I'll be outside talking to Cole."

When all the makeup was gone, I brushed my hands through my hair, already released from the dreaded pony and pulled it over my shoulders. When I reached down to flip the brush into my bag I caught a glimpse of half my reflection. My good side. I straightened up keeping the edge of the mirror splitting my face in half. When I looked at myself this way, I could almost believe my accident had been a horrible nightmare, and what I saw on this half of my face was exactly the same on the other.

Behind me the door creaked open, and I bent to grab my bag. "I'll be right there."

I stood to find Sam's reflection watching me in the mirror. My good side was still the only side of me showing, and for a brief moment I stared at us both and pretended that I was beautiful enough to fit with him. He took a step forward and then another until he stood just behind me. I watched as he slowly reached out and pulled my hair behind my shoulder. His knuckles skimmed along my jaw and then his hand settled around my neck, his fingers splaying lightly over my skin.

Sometimes he seems so familiar. It was a feeling, fleeting at best, and it was too complicated to explain. Mostly it was an instinct that I was safe. I shook my head, unwilling to admit such a thing.

"What do you see?" He hitched his chin at our reflection.

"What will never be."

He took my shoulders and turned me to face him. When I ducked my head he placed a finger beneath my chin and lifted my face. "I think you're beautiful."

"Half of me."

His hand rested over my heart. "All of you."

"You don't know me."

"I *sense* you." The words said in his husky tone dripped with intimacy.

"Why are you here?"

Kimber picked that moment to burst through the door. She stopped cold at the sight before her. I stepped away quickly, but Sam stayed where he was, not even turning to look at her.

"Kimber, I…"

She was shocked and probably hurt by seeing me like this with Sam, but she didn't say a word. "I'll tell the bus driver you're having a *lady issue* and need a few minutes."

"No, I…"

"Take your time. I'll see you on the bus." And then she was gone.

"Crap," I said.

Sam smiled.

"You think this is funny?"

"I think you're cute when you're flustered."

I held in a groan. "Why are you here?"

"For you."

"Me?"

"I thought you might like a friendly face in the stands."

I felt a warm blush bloom in my cheeks and hoped it wasn't noticeable. "What about Kimber?"

"Her heart belongs to another."

So he knew that she really wanted Cole. Was I some kind of consolation prize? Was he taking pity on the disfigured girl to make himself feel better? "I have to go." I tried to rush past him but he caught my hand.

"What did I say?"

"Nothing." Exactly nothing.

"I was never interested in Kimber. I'm interested in you."

I laughed. "Yeah, right."

"You don't believe me?" Why did this surprise him?

I shook my head.

He stepped closer.

My knees turned to Jell-O. But I was spared embarrassment from falling because he put those strong hands at my waist and bent his head. I swallowed thickly as he put his lips to my ear. "*Sense* it."

He was good. Really good.

"Can you?" he whispered, and then his lips brushed my cheek.

"W-what?"

His lips brushed my cheek again, and my eyes closed. But then he stiffened and rose to his full height, keeping his hands at my waist. Behind us the door burst open and something hit Sam hard. He didn't lose his balance, but the force of the hit vibrated through him into me. His eyes were sad and apologetic while he removed his hands from me.

"Turn around you bastard."

I gasped and looked around Sam at Cole. He was standing with an aggressive stance and a scowl on his face. His eyes flicked to me then back to Sam. "Go, get on the bus."

"Cole," I protested.

"I don't like you," Cole spat at Sam. "You took advantage of Kimber, and now you're doing it to Heven."

"He isn't!" I put myself in front of Sam, afraid of what Cole might do.

Cole grabbed my arm and yanked me forward. Behind me I heard a growl, and then Cole was on the ground with Sam in front of me. "Watch it," he snarled down at Cole.

Cole jumped up and charged, hooking Sam around the waist and pushing him back. Both guys went down in a tangle of fists.

"Stop!" I cried, hearing a fist connect with bone. The sound was sickening.

Kimber burst in and started screeching for them to get off each other. Of course they didn't listen. "What happened?" she asked me.

"They just started fighting."

Another sickening thud and I looked down in time to see Cole land a solid punch on Sam's face. My stomach heaved. "Don't hurt him!" I said, without the force I intended. The blood drained from my head, and my vision swam.

Kimber stepped over them and grabbed at Cole just as Sam flipped them both over. Kimber went flying backward into the wall, landing on her butt.

"Kimmie?" Cole was up and pulling Kimber to her feet before I could move. "Did I hurt you?"

"No more fighting," she cried, "this is my fault."

She looked past Cole at Sam. "I'm sorry, but I am in love with Cole, and I used you to make him jealous."

"I know," Sam said simply. "I used you to get to Heven."

Both Kimber and Cole stared at him, astonished. It was insulting. If I wasn't fighting a panic attack, I would have told them so.

With that announcement he dismissed them and turned toward me. "Breathe. In. Out. In. Out."

When I could breathe I said, "I don't like fighting. I have to go."

I saw the same sadness from earlier pass over his eyes, but he nodded. I grabbed my bag from the floor and walked to the door.

"I'm sorry, Hev," Cole called.

I kept going.

It was not my day. The sky had finally opened up and rain fell in heavy sheets, soaking my clothes and making me cold. With no sign of the rain letting up, it was equally depressing when the bus broke down not even halfway home. Most of the students got lucky because their parents were following behind the bus, and they were allowed to ride with them. I wasn't so lucky.

"Come on Heven, Cole's out there. Coach said we could ride with him."

I allowed Kimber to lead me off the bus and through the rain toward Cole's truck. I dreaded the ride with the pair. As Kimber climbed into the cab next to Cole, I looked around. Sam was parked, engine running, behind Cole. He was standing in the rain on the passenger side of his truck. He opened the door, looked at me, and waited to see what I would do.

"Heven?" Kimber called from inside Cole's truck.

Without a word I left her and walked through the pounding rain toward Sam.

The Hate

She's falling for his act. I can smell it. I can see it in her eyes. Without realizing it, she is destroying what little is left in her life. I took a moment to stare at the astonished faces of her friends as she chose him over them. How alone she will be when he abandons her.

They have no idea that I am watching them. Stalking them. I watched as he shut her in his truck and turned, and I caught a glimpse of his face. He angers me. He didn't look triumphant or even smug. He didn't look like a hunter triumphant in capturing his prey. He looked…nervous and hopeful. I should have known he couldn't do the job. He's too obsessed with her to care about what she knows. Apparently she's the one doing a number on him.

The way he watches her…would he turn his back on us and choose her? I thought that once he got to know her, he would see how pathetic she really was. How can he look at her destroyed face and feel anything but pity?

He's losing sight of the reason he's here.

He needs a reminder.

The Hope

Her love for him is palpable. She sees the good that fills him but turns a blind eye to what is beneath his surface, yet she knows that something else is there. She hesitates to trust him, and she is right to do so. He must prove himself.

It is clear that he loves her.

Chapter Six

Heven

Inside the truck it was warm, and I sank into the seat with a shiver. Sam climbed into the driver's side and reached behind him to pull out a gray sweatshirt, which he draped over my shoulders. It was soft and worn, and I couldn't resist pushing my arms through it and wrapping it around my body. It smelled just like him: deep and strong with a hint of spice.

"Thanks," I told him, pulling my soaked hair out from the sweatshirt and letting it drip down my back.

He watched me for a moment then redirected the heat vents so they all pointed at me. "Are you warm enough?"

I nodded. "What about you? You're just as wet as I am."

He shrugged. "I like water."

"Are you a good swimmer?"

"The best."

"I don't like water," I admitted. It was just another reminder that I wasn't good enough to be here. I reached for the handle. "Maybe I should go."

"Are you hungry?"

I turned back. His wet hair was hanging down on his forehead, and it flipped out over his right ear. His face wasn't wet, but looked damp, giving his smooth, olive-toned skin a dewy quality and his eyes, which looked more gold than hazel, were framed by a fringe of dark lashes that were watching me with a resigned look.

"I could use some coffee."

He flashed me a smile that made my toes curl then put the truck into drive. As he pulled around Kimber and Cole, I was aware of the pair staring, shocked, out the window at us as we drove away. I reached down and turned off my cell, knowing that I was going to have a dozen messages from Kimber later.

He drove skillfully, maneuvering through the downtown traffic with ease. For the first time all day, I found myself relaxing against the seat and settling deeper into his warm sweatshirt. Too soon, he guided the truck into a hard-to-come-by parking spot and turned off the engine.

"Where are we?" I'd been to Portland several times, but I didn't recognize this place.

He smiled. "Well, it isn't Starbucks, but it's pretty good. Different."

He was around the truck and opening my door before I could say anything. My stomach fluttered when he lifted me out, and I was slightly disappointed when he stepped back, putting distance between us. I followed him onto the sidewalk and trailed after him, smiling to myself at how huge his sweatshirt was on me. Yet I loved it. Suddenly he stopped, and I ran into the back of him. "Sorry," I stammered as he turned.

He gave me a crooked smile and leaned forward to ask, "Do you trust me?"

"Yes." I didn't even have to think about it.

He blinked at my fast response and then grasped for my hand, frowning when he couldn't find it in the huge shirt. I fumbled with the material to free my hand, suddenly cursing the very shirt I loved for keeping me from his touch. When my hand was free his large hand closed around mine, and he towed me through an open door.

"Bubble Maineia?" I asked.

"What's your favorite flavor?"

"For what?"

"For anything."

"Umm, strawberry."

He seemed pleased by this and sat me in a comfy chair before going to the counter to order. The people around me all had drinks with huge straws sticking out of them. The place was really cool and kind of funky. I looked around eagerly at all the color and decoration until I caught someone staring. Quickly I ducked my head, letting my damp hair hide my face. How could I have forgotten?

A pair of scuffed boots appeared in front of me, and Sam scooted a chair over and sat down directly in front of me, blocking me from view. "I got you something."

I looked up to see him holding out a dark pink drink. It too had a big straw that measured at least half an inch. At the bottom of the clear cup were a bunch of marble sized balls. I reached out and took the drink, fiddling with the straw. "What is this?"

"It's called Bubble Tea." I watched him take a long pull from his own drink, which was a shade of brown. "Try it."

He eagerly watched me, and I couldn't help but get swept up in his fun. With a smile I tried the drink. It was sweet and creamy, tasting of strawberry. Then, one of the balls from the bottom made its way through the straw and into my mouth. It was like a big gummy bear. It made me feel like a kid.

"This is really good," I declared, taking another drink. Then I paused. "What's in it?"

He laughed. A deep, husky laugh that drew stares from some of the women in the shop. He didn't seem to notice. "It's tea mixed with cream and sugar. Yours is strawberry flavored. The balls at the bottom are called tapioca pearls."

"What flavor is yours?"

To my surprise he held it out for me to try. The thought of my lips touching the same straw as his made me shiver. He noticed and frowned. "Are you cold? Maybe I should have gotten you coffee."

"No. This is perfect." Before he could pull the drink away, I took a sip. When I pulled back he had that unreadable expression on his face. "Chocolate."

"You like?"

"Mine's better." I held it out for him. His eyes widened, but he leaned forward and took a sip. A little thrill went through me.

"I think you're right," he agreed.

"I didn't know this place was here."

"I found it last summer. Been coming here ever since."

"Thanks for bringing me."

Just then a loud group of guys walked through the door, and I automatically tensed, ducking my head. "Let's get out of here," Sam said, standing to return his chair.

Outside the rain had slowed to a soft drizzle. Sam pulled me close to the buildings and pulled the large hood on the sweatshirt up over my head. "Are you ready to go home?"

I shook my head.

His smile was one of relief, and it made me a little sad. There was something about him that seemed lonely, and it made me want to take it away from him. He reached out and brushed my hand with his, but then pulled back to walk beside me. I concentrated on my drink and ignored the disappointment I felt.

"Can I show you my other favorite place around here?"

"Sure."

We walked a few blocks, not really speaking, but it wasn't an awkward silence. Then Sam cleared his throat. "That park over there–" He pointed, then placed his hand at the small of my back. "–that's Lincoln Park."

In the center of the park was a fountain. It was a cute find in the middle of an urban space.

"It was created after the great fire of 1866 which burned down almost all the buildings here in Portland. The park is named after Abraham Lincoln."

"How do you know this?"

"I read a lot, explore a lot."

I raised an eyebrow. "About parks?"

A very faint pink spread beneath the sun kissed glow of his skin. He was embarrassed, and it was so cute. I giggled. He smiled a quick flash of straight, white teeth then he shrugged.

"I'm kind of drawn to this place. Maybe it's the fact that it's been here for so long. Maybe it's because it was created after something really bad happened, and it was like a fresh start for the town…" his voice trailed off, and he cleared his throat.

"I really like it too," I said softly, bumping my shoulder into his side.

That seemed to please him, which gave me monster-sized butterflies yet again in my belly.

A few minutes later we came to another door. "This is your favorite place?" I smiled.

"It's not my favorite place, but I really like it."

"A comic book store?"

He grinned and opened the door for me. Inside was bright with racks and shelves full of comic books. There was even someone dressed in a *Star Wars* costume walking around the store. I prayed he stayed away from me and hurried to get closer to Sam. I could tell how much he liked this place by the way he walked around taking everything in and briefly touching a few of the books.

"So why comic books?" I asked him in a hushed tone.

Without turning around he answered, "A lot of the characters are exceptional. They're different than everyone else. They have…abilities, and they have challenges to face. But yet they're still like everyone else too."

"I guess I never thought much about it."

"Do you ever wonder what it would be like to be different?"

"No." I already knew.

He turned abruptly, and I almost ran into him again. "Heven…"

"So which one is your favorite?" I asked, ignoring his tone and gaze.

He sighed and reached for my hand to lead me to another rack. "I like all of them. But a few of my favorites are *Secret Avengers*, *X-Men* and *Iron Man*. Then there are the classics."

"The classics?" He lifted a comic off the shelf and held it out. "*Spider Man*." I smiled. "I'm familiar with him." He thumbed through the comic pointing out things I never noticed about comic books.

"Thanks for bringing me here," I said on our way out of the store. "I had fun." For the first time in a long time.

"Me too."

There was a loud clap of thunder above us and then lightning lit up the sky. I jumped, unable to stop my reaction. Geez, I was such a baby. But Sam didn't laugh at my reaction or even roll his eyes. He put his arm around my shoulders and pulled me against him saying, "Let's get you to the truck."

Once again that familiar feeling of safety enveloped me, and I smiled into his shoulder. A few fat drops of rain began falling as we approached the truck, and I spotted a trash can a few yards away to toss our empty Bubble Tea cups. I jogged the distance to the can while Sam unlocked the doors. Just in front of the trash can I was suddenly flanked by two men. They walked so close to me that their shoulders jostled me as I walked. "Excuse me," I said low and quickened my pace to get away. They moved right along with me. I threw the cups the remaining distance into the trash and turned to run back to Sam. One of the men grabbed me around the waist and turned me back saying, "Let's take a walk, sweet thing."

My heart hammered in my chest as the other one laughed low. I opened my mouth to refuse, but I didn't get the chance because Sam ran up behind me and inserted an arm between me and each guy, shoving them out and away. He had enough arm strength to do it. Unfortunately, the men were not fazed, and they came quickly at Sam, pinning him up against the side of a building.

"Go get in the truck, Heven."

"But..." I couldn't leave him there.

"Oh, we just want to talk to her." One of the creeps laughed.

Sam looked at me, appearing completely calm. "Go."

I ran, climbing quickly into the truck and locking the doors. I reached for my cell and keyed in 911 resting my finger on the SEND button, keeping my gaze glued on Sam.

Sam straightened, shoving both the men off of him, and I realized they weren't much older than us. They were both tall, dark headed and...grinning? Except their grins weren't reassuring, they were frightening. In that moment the few, fat drops turned into a heavy avalanche of rain, pounding down from the sky.

Sam said something, and one of them laughed. Sam retaliated by shoving him full on, and the guy stumbled backward. He advanced on Sam, and I tensed, waiting for the worst, but the other stepped between them and said something causing the angry one to back down, but not before he yelled something at him. Sam got up in his face, his lips barely moving as anger seethed from every pore. The muscles in the recipient's back rippled beneath his shirt, and once again I worried for Sam, but the guy backed down. The other guy said something and Sam shot a look in my direction, his eyes narrowing into slits. His jaw was set and hard when he turned back. It scared me, and I realized I didn't really know anything about him. But then he turned back to point a finger in the man's face and shout. Suddenly all three of them looked up the street, and I followed their gaze, but all I saw were shoppers running into stores, most of them covered with hooded raincoats.

Sam turned his back on them and walked, almost prowled, toward me, but it wasn't over. I beat on the window in warning, but it was unnecessary because just as one caught up to him, Sam turned, throwing a fist that connected solidly with his pursuer's jaw, and he hit the wet pavement. Sam challenged the other guy, but he shook his head and helped his buddy up.

Then Sam was at the door. I unlocked it, and he slid in beside me, starting up the truck.

He said nothing as he pulled into traffic and disappeared down the street.

"Who were they?" I gasped.

His jaw tightened as he pushed the wet hair off his forehead. "My roommates."

"Your roommates?" Didn't he live with his parents?

He nodded. He was soaked from the rain. I hurried to turn some of the heating vents toward him and pulled off the sweatshirt he gave me. "Put that back on. You're going to freeze."

"You're soaking wet!" I slid over and used the shirt to dry his arms and face, running it over his head to dry his hair.

"Smells like you now," he murmured.

"Are you hurt? Your hand?" I worried.

He flexed his hand and shook his head. "I'm fine."

"What was that all about?"

"Nothing. They thought they were being funny."

"They looked angry."

"They aren't very nice."

"Why not?" I demanded.

"They've had some rough times."

"That's no excuse for bad behavior!"

He smiled.

"I'm serious!"

"I know. Don't worry about it okay? They won't act like that again." Something in his voice told me he'd make sure of it.

"Are you going to get into a fight when you get home?"

"No."

I twisted my hands in my lap. What if he did? There was two of them and only one of him.

He reached out and wrapped his hand around mine. "Everything's fine."

"Why would you live with them?"

He sighed. "It's complicated." Then I saw a wall go up. He was done talking about them.

I didn't bother pressing the issue. Instead I turned my head and looked out the passenger window, but I stayed right next to Sam. After a few short moments he placed an arm around me and pulled me into his side. "I won't let anyone hurt you."

"I know."

We drove the rest of the way home in silence.

Chapter Seven

Heven

Kimber's red bug was in the driveway when Sam dropped me off. When I climbed out of his truck, Kimber climbed out of the bug and ran to the front door.

"You didn't answer your cell," she hissed.

"I turned it off," I hissed back, letting us into the house.

"Heven? I was beginning to worry!" Mom came out of the kitchen, wiping her hands on a towel. "Oh, hello, Kimber."

"Hi, Mrs. Montgomery."

"Sorry I'm late, Mom. The bus broke down, and I got a ride from a friend."

"Oh. Well I am glad you're home. How was the competition?"

"We won."

"Well that's wonderful. I guess now that it is over that means that you're no longer needed on the squad."

She didn't come right out and say it, but I got the impression that Mom would rather I didn't cheer. When I told her I would be filling in for an injured Jenna, she didn't tell me no, but she didn't seem happy either. She wished me luck and told me I wasn't allowed to miss Bible study to cheer. "Actually, the coach asked me to come back to the squad."

I could feel Kimber's excitement and Mom's disappointment. My head began to pound. "I told her I would think about it."

"Yes, you should take some time to think about your choice." Why did it feel like she was trying to say something else, and why didn't she just say it?

"Is it okay if I hang out with Heven for a while, Mrs. Montgomery?"

"Sure, honey. I'm making chicken. You are welcome to stay."

I pleaded with her with my eyes. She sighed. "Sounds great. I love chicken."

Mom returned to the kitchen to finish the dreaded chicken, and we escaped to my room, closing the door behind us.

"You have major explaining to do," Kimber fiercely whispered.

"Oh?" I went to my dresser and began pulling out something dry and comfy to wear. I caught a glimpse of my limp hair in the mirror and winced. Geez, it's like I tried to look hideous.

"Don't play dumb with me. You like Sam!"

"Shhh!"

She looked at the door guiltily. "Sorry."

I tossed her a pair of sweatpants and a sweatshirt, motioning to her cheer uniform. She looked at the clothes and grimaced. I rolled my eyes and rummaged around coming out with bright pink velvet lounge pants and a matching zip-up hoodie. She brightened and reached for the clothes. "You are such a snob." I laughed.

"I just like to look nice." She sniffed. "And you'd better start caring about your appearance if you want Sam."

My appearance was not up for discussion. Still, a little part of me worried that she was right.

"Why didn't you tell me that you liked him?"

I thought about my answer while I changed into the very clothes she'd snubbed. "It doesn't matter."

"Are you crazy!? Of course it matters! I never would have used him, *dated him,* if I'd known."

"I thought you liked him."

She sank down on the bed. "I do like him, he's a nice guy. Just not like that."

"Really?"

"I'm in love with Cole. I always have been."

"How are things with that anyway?" I hoped to turn the topic to her and get some distance from my own feelings.

She smiled. "Good. It seemed his fight with Sam, my confession of loving him and me only using Sam fixed things."

"You're back together?"

"We haven't said the words yet, but yeah." She smiled brightly.

"Thank God. You two belong together."

"Now, back to you." Kimber said, going to my dresser and pulling down her thick red hair. "Uh, look at all this frizz!"

I rummaged through a forgotten drawer of products and came up with some anti-frizz spray. "Here."

"Don't you think it's time you start putting your wardrobe and products back to use?"

"Kimber..." I sighed.

"I get it, Hev. I do. But it's been ten months. Enough moping."

"I am not moping."

"Then admit you like Sam."

I stared at her, mutinous.

"Did you kiss him?" she asked, eyes twinkling.

I grinned. Then I thought of something, and my grin disappeared. "Did you?"

Her eyes turned serious. "Never. I swear."

Something inside me relaxed. "Fine, I like him."

She squealed. "So?"

"No, I didn't kiss him."

"Why not?"

"I hardly know him." Yet, I felt like I did. I *sensed* him. Just like he'd said.

"Who cares? He's hot!"

I laughed. It felt good.

Kimber turned sober and came to stand in front of me. "This year has been really hard on you. I know. But please, don't hide from him, he likes you. I saw the way he was looking at you today. I can't believe I never noticed it before. He's totally into you."

That's what bothered me most. He did like me, and I couldn't understand why. He was hot, mysterious and was actually nice, too. He could have any girl he wanted, so why would he aim low?

"Hev?"

"Yeah?"

"I'm so sorry if I hurt your feelings by 'dating' him. I would never hurt you intentionally."

"I know."

Mom knocked on the door then stuck her head in the room. "Chicken's ready!"

"Smells great!" Kimber said enthusiastically.

"Coming," I told Mom.

When she was gone we both burst out laughing. "Thanks for staying," I said, wiping my eyes.

"After everything I've done, I think eating your mom's chicken is a fitting punishment."

"I think it's a bit harsh, but I am glad you're staying."

"Maybe it will be edible," she whispered as we left my room.

"Don't count on it, but it won't stop her from making it again!"

After Kimber left, Mom and I were in the kitchen cleaning up, and I was lost in thought, thinking about the time I spent with Sam earlier.

"I forgot to mention that I signed you up to help serve at the pancake brunch after the early morning service tomorrow at church."

I stifled a groan as I dried a glass and put it away in the cupboard. "Can I work in the kitchen instead?"

"I think interacting with the church members will be good for you."

I dried another glass and put it away. I hated being in a large crowd, and she knew it. All I could think of was what everyone was saying about me behind my back.

"So how are things lately?" she asked, assuming that everything was settled for tomorrow. I guess it was.

"Great."

"Still having those nightmares?"

"Not as often." Actually I had them just as much as always, but I felt it was somehow important to make light of them.

"Any more memories from that night?"

"No." Why would she bring this up? She knew it upset me not being able to remember how I got this way.

"I was talking to Father Mike and he was saying that he thought maybe you might be repressing the memories because…"

I cut her off, angry. "Because I am too traumatized to remember. I know, Mom."

"Actually, I was going to say because deep down you fear that you did something to cause what happened to you."

A plate slipped out of my hand and hit the floor breaking in half. "Crap!" I bent to pick up the pieces. "Sorry."

She ignored the plate, watching me.

"I don't think I caused the accident."

"No?"

"How could I?"

"You were on your way home from the library that night?"

"Yes!" Why did she seem to doubt this?

"It was late."

"Ms. Agnes stayed open late for me, Mom. I had that paper due."

"That was very kind of her."

"Don't you believe me?"

"Of course I do," she smiled. "I just want to make sure you don't blame yourself."

"I don't."

"Well, good. So about the cheering…"

"I don't think I want to do it." I rushed to say.

"Well, that's probably a good idea. They need some volunteers down at church with the preschool class, and I thought you could help out. Too much on your plate and your grades could suffer."

I made a sound of agreement. Why did everything have to center around church these days? I finished drying the dishes and put them away. "I'm going to bed."

Mom came over and hugged me. "I'm proud of you. You've made a good choice. Love you."

"Love you too, Mom."

As I went to my room I wondered what she would have said if I'd chosen to return to cheering, and what she would say about Sam.

The pancake dinner was a madhouse, and the crowd exhausted me. When Mom announced that she was going to stay and help the treasurer with the receipts and log book, I figured I was doomed for another few hours. But I was saved when Mom handed me the keys to the car and told me that she would get a ride home when she was finished.

Once home I went straight upstairs and did something rare. I pulled my hair into a high ponytail on top of my head. It was driving me crazy, and I was alone with no one to stare at my face. Then I changed into a pair of knit yoga pants and a tee. I just wanted to be comfortable and not care about what I looked like. I settled on the couch with a blanket and the remote. A few minutes into channel surfing the doorbell rang. I figured that Mom forgot her key and ran to answer the door.

Sam stood on the porch. "Hi."

"Hi." I stared at him, taking in his golden hair and the clean lines of his face.

"Is this a bad time?"

"No! Sorry, come in." I opened the door wider, and he brushed by me sending electric jolts through my body.

"My mom is at church," I stuttered.

"You're alone?" he asked like he already knew.

I nodded sending my ponytail into a bounce. I froze, remembering my appearance. I reached up to yank down my hair.

"Leave it," he said softly.

I went to pull it down anyway, Kimber's voice floating through my brain *you should start putting your products to use.*

Sam appeared in front of me, his hand reaching up to pull my hand away, fingers entwining with mine. "I like seeing your face."

"It's ugly."

"It's beautiful."

I shook my head and ducked my face. He used our entwined hands to lift my chin. "I like looking at you."

"What's wrong with you?"

A wary look crossed behind his eyes. "What do you mean?"

"You're too good for me."

He frowned. "That isn't true."

I went to the couch and sat down, tucking the blanket over my lap to hide my outfit. Sam followed, sitting next to me, so I turned, resting my cheek against the back of the sofa and bringing my knee up between us.

He reached out and tucked a stray hair behind my ear leaving his fingertips to linger near my face. Very slowly, his fingers moved up my jaw and my stomach clenched, knowing what he intended. I sat there debating whether or not to allow it. His touch was feather light, and his eyes held no disgust, so I watched him as his fingers moved upward just grazing the bottom of my biggest scar. Holding my eyes, gently he traced the jagged outline and explored the raised puckered parts. He never once seemed grossed out. He actually looked sad and regretful. I closed my eyes to his emotions because my own were more than enough to cope with. No one had ever touched me like this. I didn't want them too. Until now. It was sweet and made me feel not so ugly.

His fingers didn't linger on the scars but I felt the pad of his thumb brush against the underside of my bottom lip. My eyes opened. "Why are you here?" I whispered.

"I forgot something yesterday."

"You did?"

He nodded, leaned forward and I froze, the bottom falling out of my stomach. He was going to kiss me.

His lips brushed over mine once, and he pulled back a fraction before returning to settle them over mine again. He kept his body exactly where it was, but I was completely enveloped by him. His hand moved to the side of my neck and stopped, but his lips moved over mine softly, again and again. Every part of me hummed and vibrated, and something inside urged me to get closer that this wasn't enough. Yet, I was so entranced by him I couldn't move. I don't know how long we stayed like that, every part of us unmoving except for our lips, but the whole time I prayed that it would never end. Of course, it had to.

He pulled back enough to rest the side of his face against the couch, mirroring my position. The lightning storm of gold in his eyes was beautiful, but deep down a voice wondered if it was natural. I pushed the thought away because I wouldn't let anything spoil this moment. "Heven," he rasped, his fingers caressing me once more. "What happened to you?"

"I don't remember."

"Nothing?"

"I was attacked walking home one night from the library, and I woke up in the hospital like this."

"I'm sorry."

"It's not your fault."

He pulled away. "I should go."

I grabbed his arm. "Wait. Why did you really come here?" What had I done to make him want to leave?

"I wanted to see you."

I glanced at the clock. "I have awhile yet before my mom gets home. Can you stay?"

That lonely look flashed through his eyes, but then his lips tilted up. "Yeah."

He sat back and spread his arms along the back of the couch. I sat up and scooted closer, resting my head against his chest, wondering if the butterflies in my stomach would ever settle. I kind of hoped they wouldn't.

Chapter Eight

Heven

I stared at the clock as I trudged into seventh period. This crappy Monday was almost over; it seemed like the longest one yet. Sam didn't stay long enough yesterday. For once Mom finished her work at the church early, and he had to go. I spent the rest of the day doing homework and spending time with Mom. When I went to bed I was haunted with the same nightmare as always, except this time Sam's creepy roommates were the ones chasing me down the street. When they caught up and tackled me they stared down with flashing gold eyes. I woke up at five drenched in sweat with a pounding heart. I knew that if I closed my eyes again I would once again be haunted by flashing gold eyes and taunting laughter. Instead I lay in bed staring at the ceiling and replayed Sam's kiss over and over in my mind. The memory was enough to chase away the worst of my nightmare.

I looked at the clock again, wondering if I had enough time to sneak out in the hall and call Grandma to beg her to pick me up after school so I could spend some time with Jasper. But then the bell rang, and I saw Sam slip inside the door and move to his seat. It was the first I had seen of him all day. Yet another reason this day had been so endless. I stared at him, and his eyes flicked up to mine. He didn't smile or wave, but his eyes flashed gold. Scenes from my nightmare flashed before me, and I hurried to turn away in my seat. My reaction confused me. Sometimes I caught glimpses of a Sam that frightened me, sensed some kind of self-contained violence that made me wonder if I should be afraid. I wondered if I really knew him. But then he was around, that automatic feeling of safety would spread over me, and I would feel silly for ever thinking that I was in danger with him.

Mrs. Cooper hurried in carrying a bag of measuring spoons and a stack of papers. "Today we will break into our cooking groups and attempt to make this recipe." She held up the stack of papers.

Great. Just what I didn't want to do. With my luck we'd be cooking chicken.

"We'll be making mini pizzas on English muffins."

Eww.

"With a barbeque chicken topping!"

Double Eww.

"Everyone go to your cooking stations, and I'll pass out the recipe."

Everyone in my station was absent except for Emily Hall, the biggest gossip in our class. Resolved to get this over with, I began doling out paper plates and plastic silverware so we could get started. Mrs. Cooper came over with a recipe, Sam trailing behind her.

"Girls, since most of your table is absent, Sam will be joining you today."

A little thrill went through me.

"Since he's new he doesn't have a group yet." She turned to Sam and handed him the recipe. "This is your cooking group for the rest of the year."

He moved to stand by me.

"I thought you were absent today," I accused when the teacher moved away.

"Been here all day."

"Why weren't you at lunch?" Too late, I realized that I'd just practically told him I was waiting for him.

He cleared his throat and his eyes slid to our audience. Emily was staring straight at us with her mouth open. Great. Who knew what would be all over school by tomorrow.

"Aren't you dating Kimber?" she asked Sam.

"No!" we both answered quickly.

"Are you dating?" she asked us, a glint in her eyes. Sam shut his mouth and turned to me, lifting his eyebrow.

"No," I answered quietly.

"She won't have me," Sam told Emily.

Emily gasped and turned to me.

"That isn't true," I assured her.

"I've asked her out three times."

"You won't go out with *him*?" she asked me.

"Of course I would," I blurted, then blushed furiously.

"So you *are* going out?"

I grabbed the pack of English muffins and slammed them on the counter. "Let's do this."

When Emily went off in search of a missing ingredient I spun toward him. "Do you have any idea who we were just talking to?"

He feigned innocence.

"She's the biggest gossip in our entire class."

"I guess it will be all over school tomorrow that we're together." He seemed unbothered by this.

"Probably before then," I muttered, slapping some cheese on the pizza.

"Easy," he scolded, taking the bag of cheese from me. "Like this." He sprinkled the cheese on the top.

"You want everyone to think we're dating."

"Hand me the chicken will you?"

I practically threw the chicken at him.

He snatched it out of the air with ease and shook it at me. "Maybe I should handle the chicken today. Clearly you treat it the same way your mother does." His eyes sparkled with mischief, and he stifled a laugh. It was a side of him I didn't often see, and I liked it. I found myself smiling back even though I think he had just insulted me.

When he turned away I was able to remember that we had been talking. "Why?" I demanded.

"Why, what?" he asked, never turning from the chicken he seemed to be so carefully arranging.

"Why do you want everyone to think we're dating?" I said, exasperated.

"Because then you'll have to go out with me. You wouldn't ruin my reputation by turning me down and humiliating me would you?"

"Like you care," I muttered as Emily returned.

We finished our pizzas as Mrs. Cooper came around to see our handiwork, and then we put them in the toaster oven to bake. While they baked the three of us stood in the tiny kitchenette awkwardly as

I tried to avoid Sam's gaze, and Emily stared at us with open curiosity. When the little timer beeped I all but sighed in relief. I turned to grab the oven mitts off the counter and when I turned back Sam was already reaching into the oven and grabbing the hot pan.

"Watch out!" I cried as Emily and I both rushed forward.

Sam looked up with a puzzled expression on his face then his eyes rounded and he dropped the pan back on the rack. "Shit, that was stupid!" He exclaimed and shook out his hand.

"Let me see." I held out my hand for his knowing that he had to be covered in blisters. I was about to call for the teacher when his voice cut me off.

"It's no big deal, I'm fine."

"You can't be fine. The inside of that oven is almost four hundred degrees." As I spoke I leaned forward to look at his hand.

He brushed it down his pant leg then stuck it inside his pocket. "Really, I'm fine. We should get those out before they burn."

"I'll get them," Emily volunteered when I just stood there staring at him. "They actually look pretty good." She said, sitting them on the hot pad on the counter.

Sam kept his hand in his pocket and turned away to look at the pizza. Emily hurried off to get the teacher to give us a grade, and I used the opportunity to tug his hand out of his pocket. Sam didn't protest, but watched me with somber, liquid-honey eyes. I turned his hand palm up and ran my fingers across where a massive blister was sure to be.

There was nothing there. His skin was completely smooth and unmarked.

I was sure that he would be burned. I saw him touch that pan, why weren't there any marks on his skin? I thought he might say something, but then Emily and the teacher returned and the moment was lost. As soon as we received a grade Sam grabbed up his pizza and ate it in one bite.

"Did you even eat lunch?" I grumped.

"I'm hungry." He shrugged, avoiding my gaze.

I pushed my untouched pizza toward him. He ate it in one bite too. Emily sat next to him gingerly picking at hers. "What are you doing after school today?" he asked around his chewing.

"I was hoping to go to my grandma's. I have a horse there."

"Do you need a ride?" Sam asked and suddenly the pizza lost its interest for Emily, and she stared at us, trying not to make it obvious she was looking.

"Actually, that would be great." I replied giving up on trying to keep myself out of the gossip mill. What did it matter anyway?

When the final bell rang, Sam caught up with me and walked me to my locker. I couldn't help but notice the curious glances directed our way. I pulled the hoodie further down over my head and tried to ignore everyone. Kimber came running up to us just as I was entering the combination on my lock.

"You'll never guess what I heard!"

Emily worked fast. "I can only imagine," I intoned.

Kimber frowned. "Is something wrong?"

"No, nothing. So what did you hear?"

"They announced the theme for prom today!"

"They did?" I'd forgotten about prom. I'd avoided every dance this year and every other social activity I could. It had never bothered me until now. "What's the theme?"

"It's a masquerade ball!" She jumped up and down.

"Like with masks?" This idea intrigued me.

"Exactly! Isn't it cool?"

"Actually, it is."

"Does that mean you're going to come?" she asked me, sliding a look at Sam.

"I don't know." I glared at her.

Kimber grinned, and I knew she was up to something. "Well, I am sure everyone will be expecting to see you with the guy who had to practically beg you to be his date."

"Emily!" I gasped.

Kimber cackled as she walked away.

I slammed my locker shut and turned to Sam. "I'm sorry."

"For what?"

"Now everyone will think we're dating."

"I'm the one who told her that in the first place."

I sighed. "Seriously – why would you do that?"

We moved off down the hall as I hefted my book bag over my shoulder. "I figured it was the best way to get you to agree."

"To date you?"

"Uh-huh."

"Like a girlfriend?" I whispered.

"If you want." He held the door open and motioned for me to go ahead.

The sun was bright and it would have been warm if it wasn't for the breeze in the air. "Why would you want that?" I mumbled.

He took my hand and pulled me around to face him. "I do. Want that." The breeze ruffled his hair playfully, a stark contrast to his jaw, which was set like he was expecting rejection.

Something about that slightly vulnerable look in his eyes melted me. I gave in, if the hottest guy in school wanted to date me – and I know I wanted to date him – then I would stop wondering why he liked me and just go for it. "Me too."

"Really?" His eyes shone like the summer sun with a hint of surprise.

"Really."

A grin broke his face, exposing straight, white teeth and suddenly he was lifting me off my feet to plant a quick, firm kiss on my lips. When he put me down, he took my hand, and we began walking across the campus to his truck. I noticed that people were outright staring, and for once, I didn't care.

"Do you usually go to your grandma's after school?"

"As often as I can. Tuesdays and Thursdays I have to go to Bible study." He slid his eyes away from the road to look at me, then back. "My mother is very religious," I explained and noticed a tightening around his eyes and mouth. Was he against religion then? "She wasn't always that way, but then my father died."

"Your father died?"

"Yeah. A few years ago. He was on the police force here. He was shot during a robbery." That single bullet had changed everything in my entire world.

"That must have been really hard. I'm sure it still is." He reached across the seat for my hand.

"Sometimes." I liked that he didn't automatically apologize. Whenever I told someone about my dad, it was the first thing people said: 'I'm sorry.' I knew they meant it, and it was supposed to be comforting; but it really wasn't, and it wasn't necessary. It wasn't their fault that he'd died, so why apologize for something they had nothing to do with?

"Your grandma is your dad's mother?"

"Yeah. She's really special to me."

"I'm glad you have her, then."

"Who is special to you, Sam?"

"You," he rasped the word and sent goose bumps across my skin.

"Where are your parents?"

Seconds passed before he answered. "I'm emancipated. I don't see them."

"For how long?"

"About a year and a half."

No wonder he seemed so lonely, and it could even explain his rude roommates. "You're roommates…?"

"They're emancipated too."

"Oh." It was ironic because 'I'm sorry' popped onto my tongue, but I bit it back. "You're not alone anymore."

A groan built in his chest and rumbled out of him. The topic was clearly hard for him, so I changed the subject. "What do you do after school?"

"I have a job," he said it low, like he was ashamed.

"Really? Where?"

"*Planet Fitness*, at the front desk. They're coaching me to be a personal trainer."

"Wow. That's really cool." I guess his job explained the muscles I'd seen rippling beneath his clothes.

He seemed embarrassed, but added, "I just got hired for a second job too. Down at the lake renting paddle boats and stuff. It's just for spring and summer though, mostly on weekends."

"That's really responsible," I said before I could stop myself. He threw me a look, and I giggled. "Sorry." I laughed again.

He tried not to, but laughed anyway. When we sobered he said, "I can take care of myself."

That seemed really important to him, and I nodded. I guess he didn't have a choice. Undoing my seatbelt I slid closer to him. "You're doing a good job."

He cleared his throat but said nothing. When we pulled up to my grandma's house he parked, letting the engine idle. "Thanks for the ride."

"How long do you usually stay here?"

"As long as I can."

"I get off at nine. Want me to pick you up?"

Nine was later than I usually stayed, but I would wait just to see him again. "Sure. Unless you'll be tired and want to go home."

"I'd rather see you."

"See you later then." I peeked up at him from beneath my lashes.

He moved fast, taking my face between his palms and lowering his head until his lips covered mine. His lips were full and moist, and he knew how to use them. Too soon he moved back, and I gripped his wrists before he could pull completely away. His hazel eyes were an intense burning gold, and I felt my hands begin to shake. Almost as if he knew, he closed his eyes and came back to me, his lips brushing a gentle kiss over my scar. The simple act melted me.

"I'll be back," he whispered, reaching around me to open the door.

It took a moment for the fog in my head to clear. "I'll be waiting."

I stood in the yard and watched him drive away. It was only after he was gone that I realized I hadn't given him directions to get here.

Chapter Nine

Heven

I walked around in a dreamy haze for the rest of the week. Sam was my boyfriend. I had a boyfriend. Somehow I found myself smiling a lot more, and when people looked at me in the hall, I looked back. Sometimes, I waved. To my intense surprise everyone was nice. No one whispered about me when they thought I wasn't looking. Thursday night I found myself standing in front of my closet pondering my wardrobe. While I still knew my scars were ugly and the left side of my face was disfigured, I wondered if maybe people wouldn't notice it as much if the rest of me looked nice. I rummaged around and tried on a few things, but nothing fit. Everything was just too big. I reached for my cell and punched in Kimber's number.

"I need to go shopping," I said when she answered.

She laughed. "I'll be there in ten minutes."

"Wait! I can't go tonight. Bible study."

"You're wardrobe needs help ASAP."

"I'm supposed to go out with Sam this weekend. If I don't go to Bible study tonight, Mom will never let me go out with him."

"Does she know about him yet?"

"Uh, no."

"After school tomorrow?"

"Thanks, Kimber."

"Don't thank me! I cannot wait to see you in something besides a baggy sweatshirt!"

I gave up on my meager wardrobe and flopped down on my bed. My cell chirped, and I grabbed it, opening the text. It was from Sam. *Miss U.*

Miss U 2.

C U n the AM B4 class?

Can't wait.

"Heven! Time to go!" Mom called up the stairs.

Have a gd nite. I quickly wrote then stuffed the phone in my pocket and left my room.

I thrilled my mother by offering my help to Mrs. Bennet, the preschool Bible class teacher, who accepted right away. And, just my luck, they were having a special activity that night after classes, and she asked me to stay. The way my mother was smiling I figured it would go a long way to getting me out of the house with Sam this weekend.

It was well after nine by the time we had everything cleaned up from the kids, and I was exhausted. I just wanted to go home and crawl into bed. The sooner I went to bed the sooner I would see Sam. We hadn't been together long, but I couldn't imagine my days without him. Just the few hours we'd been apart I missed him.

The last thing to do before Mrs. Bennet drove me home was to take out the trash. I gathered the surprisingly full bag and hefted it out of the can. Outside, night had fallen and taken all the warmth in the air with it. I shivered as I hurried around the side of the church toward the dumpster. When I was almost there I heard a noise behind me. I looked over my shoulder but I was alone. After a few more steps I felt certain that someone or something was there.

Watching.

Waiting.

It was just like that night. A sob caught in my throat but I swallowed it. *Think!* Last time I ran and I was pursued. So this time…

I dropped the bag of trash abruptly and pivoted, walking back the way I came. Out of the corner of my eye I saw movement but nothing solid. "Who's there?" I called, sounding braver than I felt.

A low growl came out of the night.

A whimper escaped me as I scanned the area. I was going to be attacked again. If that happened I wouldn't survive. I glanced at the door to the church. I could do this. I sprang forward running as fast as I could toward the door, but something leapt in front of me blocking my way. I skidded to a stop, and it prowled closer. It was so dark I couldn't tell what it was, but I knew that it was an animal, possibly a rabid dog. It was huge; its hulking shape was terrifying in the dark. It was a dark color – most likely black – because it blended in so well with the night. It peeled back its lips and pure white flashed in the night. I stifled a whimper when I took in the size of its fangs. It made sounds that I only heard on Animal Planet and the hairs on my arms stood up. Slowly, I backed away, but it followed.

"Nice doggie." I said, trying to get the animal to realize I wasn't a threat and run away.

It lunged. I squealed and took off toward the dumpster, jumping onto the ladder built on the side. I scrambled up as the animal snapped at my heels. Without looking back I jumped into the piles of trash and froze, trying to make as little noise as possible. A loud bang sent the metal of the dumpster vibrating around me. Again and again the animal barged into the side of the container. Was it trying to leap in after me? The inhuman sounds that keened through the night were somewhere between a growl and a scream. Agonizing fear rolled through me and I slapped my hands over my ears as tears rolled down my cheeks. Why was this happening? The metal of the dumpster was humming from the force of the hits; I was sure I would feel the force in my bones tomorrow. That is, if I lived until tomorrow.

Suddenly, everything went quiet. I prayed the animal had given up and gone away.

I couldn't bring myself to climb out and see. I was paralyzed with fear and terrified of getting attacked. Slowly, I lowered my hands away from my ears and swiped at my tears. It was still there. I could hear it standing on the other side of the dumpster breathing. What was it doing? Why had it stopped? From nearby another sound cut through the dark. A long, lingering howl followed by a snarl that set me to shaking all over again. The animal just outside the dumpster made an answering sound – almost like a challenge; then it slammed itself into the side of the metal again, and I screamed. My scream set off another angry snarl, and I heard whatever else was out there race forward. The sound of bodies slamming together and gnashing teeth terrified me all over again, and I tried to sink even further into the filth that filled the container. Garbage was preferable to the beast that lingered outside. And what was even worse?

Now there seemed to be two of them.

Sam

The interior of the truck smelled like her. For me it was a scent that once tasted, I would never forget and something I would always seek out. Until I laid eyes on her I never thought feelings like this were real. *Before* her my life was a barren landscape. A world in black and white. Even as a child nothing seemed as vivid as it does now.

The first time I saw her had been an accident. I was racing through the woods, attempting to run away from what I am, from the life I lived. Before I even heard her, I caught her scent and I was lost. I stopped running and turned, seeking out what called to me. When I found her my life changed.

She was riding a horse, the animal was large and powerful looking, but it was she who commanded the attention. She was sitting in the saddle full of confidence and grace. Her light blond hair floated out around her and flirted with the breeze. It had been late summer and her skin was kissed by the sun; she was wearing a top that bared her shoulders and arms.

As I watched, the horse seemed to sense my presence and dance beneath the canopy of green the trees provided. In fluid, calm movements she leaned forward and spoke stroking her hand along the horse's neck.

"Settle, Jasper. We're safe."

Envy speared through me. I wanted to be that horse. I wanted her to stroke me the way she did it. The intensity of my reaction scared me, and I wanted to flee.

Yet I was rooted where I stood.

I felt as though an invisible tether reached out of me and went directly to her. It tugged at me as I stood there, begging me to close the distance, for just one chance to see her smile.

Of course, I denied myself the urge. She was too good for me. My parents made it clear that I wasn't good enough for anyone. Besides, what a shame it would be to taint such beauty with such a beast. Instead I settled on watching her from afar. I haunted the woods like a ghost just praying to catch a glimpse of her. Then, it wasn't enough and the fleeting glances that I caught became teasing and taunting. I wanted more.

So I followed her.

I stalked her.

I let her presence fill up every hole inside me. And that first time I saw her smile I knew that I loved her. Unfortunately, my love ruined her life.

Beneath the hood of the truck, a strange noise grinded and pulled me from my memory. I glanced down at the gauges and realized that I had been going over seventy miles an hour. Way too fast for this old truck. If I wanted it to last then I couldn't drive it the way I wanted to drive. And since I didn't have any money to buy something new, I needed it to last. With a regretful glance at the speedometer I let off the gas.

I felt edgy tonight. I counted the minutes until my shift was over at work so I could get here and reassure myself that she was okay. She had no idea of the danger that she was in. She had no idea what kind of monster was obsessed with her. But I did.

Because I was a monster too.

The only difference is that I don't want to hurt her. And because of that I am in this situation. I'm trapped. I'm caught in a web of lies so thick that I might never get out. If I told Heven the truth she would push me away, she would hate me for life. I could accept her hatred, but not her absence.

I'm the only thing standing between her and death.

As I got closer to the church my heart began to hammer in my chest. Uncomfortable, I rolled down the window and let the air rush in. Something wasn't right. I slammed my foot down on the gas, ignoring the groaning of the engine and prayed I wouldn't be too late.

I heard a cry and then a snarl and my skin started to burn. Had. To. Get. Out.

The front of the church came into view, and I swerved to the curb and leapt out of the truck. I tossed aside my shirt and pants as I went and broke into a run. I could hear her crying and I could hear loud banging and growling. At least she was still alive. I wasn't too late. I rounded the corner, resisting the pain in my joints and the fire in my veins.

The monster was toying with her, knowing that I would be here, knowing that I would see. As if on cue our eyes met. The challenge was there. Anger ripped through me and I let it out, the sounds burning my throat. My cry was met with another, and I raced forward.

We met head on, slamming into one another. The giant beast towered over me, but I held myself in check, even though it hurt and even though my limbs shook with need.

I slammed the monster into the asphalt, trying to dodge the swipe of its claws. I couldn't. Pain lanced through my side, and I realized if I wanted to win this fight, I couldn't hold back. Inhuman sounds roared out of my throat and a battle began.

You should never have come here. I told you to leave her alone.

I sent the monster hurling away, only to have it come back. Our arms locked together and I brought my legs up between us and kicked. I felt bones give way but a few broken bones wouldn't be enough to convey my message.

When I threw off the monster, I lunged, hovering over it, and sank my teeth into a fur coated neck.

I'm not playing games with you. I will kill you right now and this will be over.

Suddenly, I found myself lying against the hard ground, teeth snapped at my face and soulless eyes seemed to laugh down at me. Not ready to admit defeat, I lashed out catching my opponent by surprise.

We went at it again and again, rolling across the ground, landing punches and taking hits.

Through the snarling and the shrieking a small sound stopped me cold. A small hiccup. Heven. She could hear this fight and was probably paralyzed with fear. Who knew how long it would take her to recover from this. Because of my distraction I took a hit to the side of my head. Automatically I roared and flipped myself off the ground. In one swift movement I locked my opponent in a hold and dragged the body away from the container and into a line of nearby trees. When released, my captive sunk razor sharp teeth into my leg, but I bit back a howl and punched out, connecting with flesh and heard another crunch of bone.

The hateful eyes that watched me glazed over, but not before a streak of shock shot through them. Then it turned tail and ran away.

I thought about giving chase. I wanted to rip it apart and scatter the pieces. I was so angry I could do it. But I couldn't leave her here alone, shivering and scared to death while sitting in a trash heap waiting to die.

Heven, what have I done to you?

I raced back through the parking lot, sticking to the shadows, moving with stealth and silence. I barely noticed the cuts on my side; they had already stopped bleeding and would be healed soon. I hurried to dress, thankful that my clothes seemed to be unruffled and wouldn't look like I had been fighting. On my way back around the side of the building I heard a woman calling out for Heven.

Shit. I didn't want anyone in my way.

With a deep breath I told myself to chill, and I stepped out of the shadows.

"Excuse me, Ma'am? Is everything alright?"

The woman calling out for Heven jumped and pressed a hand to her chest. "Who are you?"

"I'm a friend of Heven's, I heard you calling for her."

The woman's obvious distress over Heven won out over her surprise at seeing me. "She came out to take out the trash…she's been gone a long time. I shouldn't have let her come out here alone." The woman wrung her hands, clearly upset. Little did she know if she had come out with Heven, she would now be dead.

"I'll help you find her," I volunteered. It took everything in me not to race to the dumpster and give away that I knew exactly where she was. Instead I poked around for a minute before going over and climbing up the ladder. Thanks to my enhanced vision I could see her in the dark.

The sight both tore my heart and sent flames of anger licking at my insides. She was so small and helpless looking. She was curled into a ball, with her hands balled into fists and hugged tightly to her chest. Tears streaked her cheeks. I could see the rapid rising and falling of her chest and the shaking of her limbs. I leapt down into the container, silently vowing to make things right.

Even if it was the last thing I did.

Heven

I was crying before, but as soon as I heard his voice I started sobbing. He was here, and I was safe. Suddenly the dumpster vibrated again, but I wasn't afraid anymore. My feeling of safety around Sam eclipsed the fear I felt of whatever else was out there. But then I realized that Sam was now in danger too. My lips worked, but no sound came out except for a small squeak.

Then he was there, pulling me up and against his chest. "Heven?" I hardly recognized his voice – which was strained and full of anxiety – but I knew the feel of him, and I dug my hands into his back, trying to get him closer. "It's all right now," he soothed.

Once again I tried to warn him, but all that came out were deep sobs. He didn't demand to know why I was crying or why I was in the trash, and he didn't try to force me out. He simply sank down into the trash with me and held on.

"I found her!" he called over my tears.

"Heven! Are you hurt?" Mrs. Bennet yelled. I completely forgot about her. Had she seen what had happened? Had she heard the horrible sounds of fighting?

I shook my head in response to her question, not realizing she couldn't see me. "She's fine," Sam called.

"Thank goodness!"

"What happened?" Sam whispered against my ear.

"There was an animal. It tried to attack me."

"An animal?"

I nodded. "I was so scared. It…it tried to get in here."

"You're safe now," he murmured, stroking my hair.

"I'm so glad you're here," I sniffled.

"I wish I'd been here sooner."

"How did you know I was here?"

"I didn't. I just got off work and drove by in case you might still be here. When I got here I heard that lady calling for you."

"I was hiding."

"I know. It was good thinking."

"You found me."

"I heard you crying."

I took a fistful of his shirt. "It was just like last time."

"You remember?" He stilled and suddenly seemed tense.

"No. But I remember feeling afraid and alone…" a shudder went through me.

"You're not alone anymore," he vowed. "Let's get you out of here."

He helped me up and climbed down the ladder first, standing at the bottom with his arms up in case I fell. Mrs. Bennet was pacing on the pavement, and when I hit the ground, she swept me into a hug. "I was so worried! What happened?"

"There was a dog out here, and it tried to attack me. I climbed in the dumpster to hide."

"Oh, dear. It probably smelled the leftover food in the trash and wanted it."

We all looked at the trash bag still lying on the ground where I'd dropped it. It was untouched.

"You probably scared it away before it could have its meal," Sam told Mrs. Bennet.

"Who are you?" Mrs. Bennet asked. Now that she knew I was safe, I could see her switching to chaperon.

"I'm Sam Kavanagh." He held out his hand. "I'm a friend of Heven's from school. She told me she would be here, and I wanted to return a book she lent me in class today."

"Hello," Mrs. Bennet responded. I could see her taking in his *Planet Fitness* T-shirt and khakis. Even though he was dirty and rumpled, the proof he had a job went a long way in gaining him some brownie points with her. "I would have been here sooner, but I just got off work." Sam explained to Mrs. Bennet.

"Very commendable for such a young man to have a job."

"Mrs. Bennet, would it be okay if Sam took me home? It would give us a chance to discuss the assignment I lent him the book for."

"Well, I don't know…" I could see her debating whether or not Sam was trustable. I held my tongue knowing if I begged she might say no. She seemed to come to a decision and nod. "Go straight home."

"Yes, Ma'am," I said, trying to calm my shaking insides.

"I'll help you to your car, Ma'am." Sam said placing a hand at the small of my back and guiding me along with him toward Mrs. Bennett's car. His hand was warm against my back, and I shivered. He watched me out of the corner of his eye as he helped the lady into her car and shut the door. He gave her wave as she drove off then he turned toward me.

"Are you hurt?" he asked, the sound of his deep voice brushed over me.

"No."

Without another word he guided me around the front of the building and toward his waiting truck. My stomach cramped with nerves – afraid that whatever had attacked me would come back. I glanced at Sam. He didn't show the least bit of anxiety, and it made me relax. If Sam thought we were safe then we were.

Once inside the truck he turned the ignition but instead of driving away he dropped his hands and turned toward me. "Come here," he commanded softly, and I couldn't comply fast enough. I fit myself against him, breathing in his scent and sighed. He pressed a kiss to the top of my head and murmured something too low for me to understand then he put the truck into drive and pulled out of the parking lot.

The next thing I knew he was nudging me awake. "You're home," he whispered.

"Want to stay with you." I yawned, snuggling closer; he was deliciously warm.

"How am I supposed to leave now?" He groaned.

"Don't."

"You know I have to."

"Yeah." I sat up, rubbing a hand over my eyes. "Thanks for coming. I would probably still be in that dumpster."

"I'm beginning to think I should drive you everywhere."

"I would like that."

"So would I."

"Will you text me when you get home?" The thought of him leaving made my stomach hurt.

"Sure." For the first time that night I looked into his eyes. They were angry and hard.

"You're angry."

"At that animal that scared you." He brushed a hand through my hair.

I didn't bother to tell him there was more than one. I didn't want to think about it anymore. I looked out at the walk. It seemed like a twenty mile hike to the front door. In the dark.

"Come on," Sam said, getting out of the truck and coming around to get me. He led me to the front door, his eyes scanning the yard as we walked. Instead of feeling reassured I felt frightened all over again. At the church he seemed confident that whatever had been there was gone, and his confidence calmed me. But here – he made it seem that he needed to protect me. That something might be watching. Like maybe whatever I imagined being out here all those nights was real and not a fragment of my imagination and bad dreams. It made me wonder if I was safe in my home.

"I'll see you first thing at school," he told me.

I nodded.

He leaned in and pressed his lips to my forehead. "Sweet dreams tonight."

"Bye."

He waited until I was in the house with the door closed and locked before he left. Once upstairs I did my nightly routine, pausing in front of a mirror before getting in bed. I stared hard at the jagged scars on the side of my face. Scars that could have been made by an animal…I searched every corner of my mind for a memory from that night, even a brief one. There was nothing. It was like the accident had never happened, except it had, and I wore the proof on my face. Did the same animal that attacked me then come back tonight to finish the job? As I climbed into bed I told myself that I was being silly and paranoid and that it was just a coincidence. But, I lay there awake and tense, willing myself to remember, until I gave up – exhausted. Yet I still couldn't relax. Only after I received Sam's text that he was safely home was I able to fall asleep.

The Hate

Come out to play little girl.

She was hiding like the coward I knew she was and whimpering like a baby. I thought about jumping into the dumpster, ripping her apart and leaving her to rot with yesterday's trash. The idea had some merit.

But that wasn't why I was here, and there wasn't enough time. As much as I wanted the little bitch to die, I had another agenda tonight. I had a point to prove. He was pushing me too far, not doing what I told him to do. I had to show him who was in control.

And just like I knew he would, he showed up. I made sure that the show was in full swing when he got there so he could see that she was mine whenever I decided to take her. She was just so easy to take advantage of. And his rage was exactly what I wanted to see. He thinks he's so much better than the rest of us. But he isn't. He tried to hold back but one gash to the side and he let go of his control.

He fought better than I anticipated. His anger gave him an advantage. But no matter. By the time I am done taunting him he will be half-crazed, and then I will make my move.

Until then I want him to worry every time he isn't with her to worry that she could be gasping for her last breath. I want him to wonder if one day he will be too late.

One day very soon he will be.

The Hope

"You should have come to me."

I understood his turmoil and I sympathized. "It wouldn't have changed anything."

"We need to do something, she is in danger."

"She is safe now." It appeared that he was special, that their love might be enough.

I turned at the sound of his bitter laugh. Bitterness had no place here. "You can't possibly believe that the sinner will protect her."

"He has been."

"He isn't suitable for her."

"Your anger is understandable, but it is misplaced."

"She wasn't supposed to be involved."

"You know as well as I that we have no control over these things."

He gave a curt nod.

I held out my hand, and he came forward and took it. "Let us pray."

Heven

After my scare the night before, I was feeling a little unsure of my decision to change my wardrobe. Staying hidden was easier, and it called less attention to myself. When I tried to get out of our shopping trip, Kimber wasn't having it.

"Clearly your inconspicuous wardrobe didn't help you last night," she pointed out.

"I should never have told you about last night," I murmured, shoving a book into my locker.

"Too late." She smiled. "Come on, Heven, it will be fun. You need this."

"Fine." I gave in. I really did want something to wear tomorrow night when I went out with Sam.

I closed my locker door and found his handsome face staring at me. With unreadable eyes he appraised me. When he was satisfied he smiled. "Hey, Beautiful."

He was the beautiful one, from the top of his messy dark blond head right down past his ripped up jeans to the black boots on his oversized feet. "Hey, yourself."

His fingers wrapped around mine, and the three of us moved down the hall toward the doors. Cole rounded the corner, his eyes fastening on Kimber. "I'll be right back," Kimber said, jogging to his side. Sam and I continued outside. When I smiled up at him, I noticed his eyes scanning the campus.

"You all right?" I tugged his hand.

"Yeah." He pulled me against him, wrapping his arms around me. It felt good, and I leaned in giving him all my weight.

"Heven, are you ready to go?" Kimber asked from behind.

"No." My voice was muffled against his chest.

I felt the subtle tightening of Sam's body. "You're not going to your grandma's?"

I tipped my chin up to see him. "Kimber and I are going shopping at the mall."

He didn't seem pleased by this, but he slowly nodded. "I'll drive you."

"She can ride with me," Kimber protested.

I stepped out of Sam's hold and turned. I was surprised to see Cole standing silently beside her. I hadn't known he was there. "Hey, Cole."

"Hey, Hev." He gave me a smile.

"I'm going to ride with Sam. I'll meet you there," I told Kimber.

She rolled her eyes but grinned. "Are you going to shop with us too, Sam?"

Judging from the way that he snorted and rolled his eyes Cole didn't like this idea. Behind me Sam chuckled, clearly amused that he annoyed Cole. "I have to work."

"Looks like the girls are shopping while the boys are working," she chimed and started off toward the parking lot.

We all followed, with Cole grabbing my arm and towing me backward. "Hey," he whispered.

"Yes?" I whispered back, smiling. I noticed that Sam stopped walking, took a step closer to me and was staring at us.

"Her birthday is next week. I need help," Cole pleaded with blue puppy-dog eyes. It would have worked better if they were gold.

Still, I giggled. "Let me think about it. I'll get back to you."

"Call me."

Sam reached over to gently pull my arm out of Cole's grasp, his hand sliding down into mine. Cole's eyes narrowed. "I'll call you this weekend," I promised, towing Sam away hoping to diffuse whatever testosterone was flowing.

In the truck Sam started the engine. "I don't like that guy."

"Cole?"

He nodded, and I let go of my seatbelt, sending it flinging backwards. "He's my friend."

"Is he?"

I gasped. "Yes! He and Kimber were the only people who treated me normal and didn't whisper behind my back when I came back to school like this!" I gestured at my face.

"Calm down." He reached across me and buckled my seatbelt.

I stuttered at the feel of his warm hands brushing across my skin. His hand pulled away, but he was still close. "I'm sorry." His breath brushed over me. It smelled like peppermint.

I nodded, dumbly. He smiled and leaned closer to kiss me, but stopped short, mere inches from my lips. I made a sound and he smiled, the corners of his lips tilting up, then he brushed his lips across mine. When he pulled away he chuckled and kissed the tip of my nose before pulling the truck out into traffic.

My skin tingled for a few moments before fading away. "You did that on purpose, trying to make me forget I was angry."

"Did it work?" His eyes twinkled.

"Maybe." I smiled. "But–" My smile disappeared. "–it upsets me that you two don't get along."

"We're never going to be friends, Heven."

"Could you try to get along?"

A muscle worked in his jaw and I thought he would say no. But then he sighed. "Okay."

"Oh, thank you!" I unclasped the seatbelt and flung myself over and hugged his neck.

He laughed. "Put your seat belt on!"

I used the lap belt in the middle to stay closer to him. The parking lot at the mall was crowded, making me nervous as to what would be inside. I was beginning to feel more comfortable at school and in more familiar places, but this was a large place with a lot of people.

My anxiety must have shown because Sam said, "Want me to take you to your grandma's instead?"

Kimber was already waiting at the entrance. "No. I'll be okay."

He seemed disappointed. "I got you something."

"You did?"

He reached into his pocket and pulled out something on a black cord. "I thought you could wear it."

"What is it?" I took his hand and flipped it up. He opened his fingers and revealed something small and shiny in his palm.

"A whistle?"

He smiled. "It's a special whistle. It makes a sound so high that only animals can hear it."

"Like a dog whistle?" I thought back to last night.

"Kind of. The sound is so piercing it will give you a chance to get away."

"Is this because of last night?"

He nodded, his eyes searching mine.

"I don't think I'll get attacked by a dog at the mall," I said lightly.

"I didn't like seeing you like that last night. I felt...helpless. The thought of you like that again...I just want to you to be safe."

I put a finger to his lips. "I'll wear it." Anything to take away the look of pain on his face.

He quickly slipped the cord over my head. The whistle was small and light and I tucked it beneath my shirt. "Thank you," he said, resting his forehead against mine.

I touched my lips to his. "Can't wait 'til tomorrow," I said, pulling back.

"Me neither," he agreed, kissing me again.

"I have to go," I said against his lips.

He made a sound in his throat but released me. "I'll call you later." He seemed worried all over again.

"Bye." I ran across the pavement toward Kimber, the cold metal of the whistle against me the entire way.

Chapter Ten

Sam

I looked out over the lake, watching the couple row clumsily away in their little boat. I hoped they figured out how to paddle sooner rather than later because I didn't much feel like fishing them out of the water. I watched as the boat rocked unsteadily, and the girl squealed. At the last moment the man righted the boat and smiled. He sunk the oar into the water and pushed off, sending the boat gliding forward. I guess he had been paying attention to me after all as I explained how to row. Maybe he had been teasing his date with the thought of falling into the water.

I wondered what it would be like to be so carefree. To be innocent to the real dangers that lurked out there. I hadn't known a moment like that in years. I turned away from the boaters and glanced over at the rental shack to make sure that no one else waited. For the moment I was alone.

I glanced down at my watch. I had two hours until I got off. Two hours until I would see her. I itched to see her, to know that she was safe. I hated having to work so much, I often worried that one day my jobs would get in the way of her safety. It was all the more reason that I get rid of the threat.

My dark thoughts got the best of me and I pulled out my prepaid cell and typed up a quick text message. *Are we still on for 2nite?*

Sharp relief and then happiness washed over me when my phone beeped just seconds later. *Yes. C u tonight.*

I tucked the phone into my pocket and looked back at the boaters. They were far out now but I could still hear their laughter. Maybe tonight I would try and capture some of that. I never thought that I would get the chance to go on a date with her. I felt a little guilty because I had to lie to get the date. I have to lie about everything. Except for my feelings. Those were true. And they were the one thing I could say out loud.

It made me wonder…

If I could make her love me. Maybe then my secrets wouldn't matter as much. Maybe then she would understand.

I shook my head. She couldn't love me. And if by some chance she did, how could I admit what I am and the part I played in her torment? It would wipe out whatever feelings she had.

But we had tonight.

All I had to do was figure out a way to make it special.

Another couple pulled up and walked to the rental shack. I rented them a boat and gave them a run-down of safety and how-tos. They were nice people, and I was in a good mood because I was looking forward to tonight, so I took the time to explain a few tips and tricks when out in the water.

I helped the man at the shoreline and held the boat as they climbed in. Once they were settled the man looked up at me. "Do you have someone special, son?"

His words sent a pang of longing through me. No one has called me son for a long time.

"Yes."

"I thought you might," he said, grinning like we shared a secret.

He could only imagine my secrets.

"I own a big lake house across the lake. We are having a big party tonight, and I am setting off fireworks. If you follow the little road there," he said, pointing to the dirt road that went past the boat rental parking lot. "You'll find a nice clearing on the water. Perfect view for watching fireworks."

"Thanks." I grinned, thrilled with the idea. It was exactly the kind of thing I was looking for. "I might take you up on that."

The man smiled, and I gave the boat a push out into the water.

Excitement coursed through my body, making my limbs shake in anticipation. My skin felt tight over my muscles, and I sighed. Sometimes living in this body was a burden. It felt as though I walked around pumped full of adrenaline at all times, and when anything happened that actually excited me – good or not – my body responded by trying to change. I guess it was its way of trying to expel some of that excess energy, but it wasn't always practical and sometimes I felt like a caged animal. Most times I could control it, but lately, I had to work harder. Knowing that Heven was in danger, knowing I was the only one to keep her safe…I could never let down my guard and because of that I was in a constant state of battle. I got tired of battling with myself.

But it wasn't all bad. I had awesome reflexes and my hearing was unparalleled to anyone else. My eyes could pick up even the smallest detail and could take in an entire room in mere seconds. Running was always a rush because I was fast and breaking a sweat always made me feel better. More in control. I think that's why I liked my job at Planet Fitness so much. Working out was an outlet for all that excess energy.

Then there was the really cool stuff. I smiled up at the sky, thinking of all the awesome stuff I could do. I was waterproof. I could never drown, and I could swim like an Olympic medalist. I was fireproof too. I could stand in the middle of a raging fire, and I would hardly break a sweat.

Yes, sometimes living in my body had its benefits. I wondered if Heven would see it that way too?

When my shift finally ended, I took the truck back down the dirt road that the man from earlier told me about. I wanted to make sure that there really was a clearing and that there were houses across the lake. I wasn't about to look like an idiot in front of Heven, taking her out into the dark and then have nothing happen.

The clearing was there, and it appeared that I wasn't the only one who had ever been there. I smiled and turned my truck in the opposite direction. On the short drive back into town I passed a few fruit stands and another stand that wasn't there earlier when I drove to work. On impulse I pulled the truck over and got out, walking over to see what the woman was selling.

It was a small table, with a white cloth covering the top. Jewelry and trinkets were lined up in rows and there were some earrings on some kind of stand. My eye caught on a locket, heart shaped, off to the side. I reached out my fingers to pick it up when a voice beside me froze my hand.

"You don't want that."

I turned and lifted an eyebrow. "No?" What kind of sales lady was this? Was she trying to talk me *out* of buying something?

"No." She shook her head. She had very dark hair and her face was shaded by a hat.

"Why not?"

She flipped the price tag up and I felt my mouth drop open. "You've got to be kidding me." I said. There was no way that little necklace was worth that much money.

"Nope." The woman said.

I turned my attention to another necklace, this one not a locket.

The woman made a noise under her breath and shook her head.

She was the worst sales person I ever met. I turned to walk away but she spoke. "I have something that isn't on the table that I think you might like."

I turned back, I felt compelled to see what it was she was going to try and sell me.

She reached into a bag beneath the table and pulled out a small bundle and unwrapped it. She held out her palm to show me. It was a charm bracelet. All the charms were keys of varying shapes and sizes. I liked it immediately. There was something about it that seemed to say it belonged to Heven.

I lifted it out of her palm, and the keys made a small noise when they hit together, almost like a chime. I jangled it again on purpose. It had a bit of music to it.

"How much?" I asked.

She rattled off a number, and I felt my eyes narrow. "Why isn't it more?" I could actually afford this – unlike everything else on the table.

"The clasp is broken; you'll need to fix it."

"Okay." I fished a few bills out of my pocket and handed them over.

The woman seemed very pleased with her sale and tucked the money into her pocket. As I was walking away her voice followed. "Be sure to fix that clasp. It would be awful if you lost it."

The back of my neck prickled, and I couldn't help but feel like there was more to her words. After a few more steps I stopped and turned to go back.

She was gone

I knocked on the front door and stepped back to wait. I couldn't stop my swift smile when I heard her soft gasp and footsteps rushing down the stairs. I liked being anticipated. I liked that someone – that Heven – couldn't wait to see me. When she came closer to the door her footsteps slowed and then paused. I pictured her looking into the mirror I remembered being by the door. A tight knot of guilt formed in my throat, and I tried to swallow it down.

I hated the part I played in what happened to her.

When she found out she was going to hate me too.

The knob turned and the door gave way. Her scent, light and pure, floated around me. Then her face filled the doorway and everything else fell away. She was certainly the most beautiful girl I had ever seen. Her hair, the color of a full moon, hung over her shoulders and around her face. It looked different tonight than usually though; it was softer and the light seemed to bounce right off it. But the biggest difference was that she was staring straight at me. Her chin wasn't tilted down, and her hair wasn't curtaining her face. There were large waves of hair framing her face, not hiding it.

"You look beautiful." The words came out as a whisper because it was all I could manage at the moment.

"Thank you." She smiled an open, warm smile and stepped out onto the porch pulling the door around behind her. She stepped close, close enough that I could see she was wearing make-up. Her cheeks were pinker than usual and her blue eyes stood out against her fair skin and dark lashes.

Without thinking I reached out and caught a strand of her hair between my fingers. It seemed to curl right around me and I tugged gently on the strand, pulling her closer. She came willingly, and I could hear the fluttering of her heart.

I kissed her then. I brushed my lips across hers and caught a hint of strawberry. Her lips were soft and welcoming, and I had to hold myself back from deepening the kiss. She pulled away first, her eyes sparkling. "Are you ready for this?"

I had been waiting for this forever it seemed. I held out my hand and said, "Let's go."

She tugged my fingers, and I marveled at how well her hand fit in mine. "You have to meet my mom first."

I didn't want to. I already knew that parents hated me, and Heven's mother made me uncomfortable. She was extremely religious and from what Heven had told me, she wanted Heven to follow her path.

I was the total opposite of religious. I didn't have to be. I knew where I stood in God's eyes: unwelcome.

"Sam?" Heven prompted, increasing the pressure on my hand. She was gazing at me openly, her freckled nose wrinkled in confusion.

"Lead the way," I prompted, motioning to the door.

I reminded myself that it was just one mother. I had faced down way worse than this. I felt my lips tilt up at the thought.

Heven's mom came out from the kitchen, her eyes scrutinizing me from head to foot. It made me glad that I took the chance to go home to shower and change. I didn't bother worrying about what she would see. I did the best with my appearance, putting on dark jeans and a plain white short-sleeved polo. It was the nicest shirt I owned. I guess I never much thought about my appearance because I learned a long time ago that a person's appearance was only a disguise for who they truly were.

"Mrs. Montgomery," I said, smiling. "It's nice to meet you."

Heven dropped my hand when her mother entered the room, and the skin on my hand tingled, wanting the contact back.

"Hello, Sam. I trust that you will respect my daughter this evening." She said, her voice cool but firm.

"Yes, Ma'am." Her hair was light, but not nearly as light as Heven's. Hers was more of a golden brown and her eyes weren't blue. They were brown and they were staring at me with mistrust. She was a little taller than Heven, thicker in form.

"I have a few questions I'd like to ask you," her mother said, pinning me with a stare.

I stopped myself from shrugging and nodded instead. She fired off questions like a drill sergeant. Wanting to know things like where I lived, how long ago I got my driver's license and what part of town I lived in. I answered them all, as truthfully as I could, and prayed that it would be over soon. Then, as abruptly as the questions began, they stopped.

"Be home by curfew." She said turning to Heven.

"Okay." I figured the meeting must be over because Heven hurried over to grab a jacket hanging by the door.

"Nice meeting you," I said, turning when Heven opened the door.

She didn't say anything, but she smiled and gave a little wave. I couldn't help but notice that the smile never reached her eyes.

Out on the porch, with the door closed firmly behind us, I reached for Heven's hand again. Every time I touched her I felt a jolt of excitement. Her skin felt like cool silk against my heated palm. If I thought God was listening, I would thank him for sending her to me.

She looked up at me, shyly and smiled. "Sorry you had to go through that."

"I'd go through anything to be here with you."

In my palm, her fingers curled closer into my hand, and I stroked my thumb over her skin.

I opened the passenger side door of the truck and watched her climb in. I couldn't help but notice the way her jeans hugged her curves. Usually she dressed in clothes that were too big and sweatshirts with hoods to hide her face. Not tonight. Tonight she wore jeans that showed off her thin figure and a light colored lavender shirt that seemed to float out around her slender waist. It was some sort of thin fabric that you could see through so beneath it she wore a white tank top. I tried not to stare at her; I didn't want to make her uncomfortable. She spent enough time like that anyway. But I couldn't seem to keep my eyes away. She looked beautiful and soft in my world of rough edges. If I hadn't been holding her hand only moments, before I might have thought she wasn't real. As if to prove that she was, I reached out to touch her again, this time, leaning over her to clasp her seat belt.

I heard her breath catch when my hands brushed against her. Could she be as affected by me as I was by her? I took my time clipping the seat belt in, and then I pulled back, keeping myself close to look into her eyes. The blue in them reminded me of a tropical ocean that I saw once on TV.

"You're wearing the whistle." I said, my voice hushed as I picked up the thin cord that lay against her chest. Her skin was unbelievably soft.

"You asked me to wear it always," she said, her eyes looking down at my hand.

"You listened." I tucked the cord back beneath her top and looked up.

She nodded, looking directly into my eyes.

I thought about kissing her, I wanted to, but I knew her mother was probably watching from the window, and I held myself back.

She raised her hand as if she might grab me as I gently closed the door and went around to the driver's side. On my way, my eyes automatically scanned the yard and street. I had to remember that I couldn't afford to be distracted. Heven couldn't afford it. When I was at my apartment earlier no one else was there. I had been glad, wanting to avoid a fight. I really needed to get my own place. But now, I kind of wished that they had been there. At least then I would know where they were. I might even have been able to scare them off for the night. Instead, I didn't know where they were. I didn't know what they were up too.

And they have definitely been up to something.

Heven

My night with Sam was finally here, and he took me to the last place I ever would have imagined. Well, not the first part of the date – that we spent playing mini golf after he patiently endured meeting my mother and answering all her questions. Turns out that my almost-being-eaten-alive-by-some-homeless-dog fiasco the other night had actually worked in my favor. Mrs. Bennett couldn't wait to tell her all about the upstanding young man who found me and came to our aide *and* had a job. Before he knocked on the door she already liked him, but his quiet respect, and I suspect his sincere hazel eyes, got me out the door.

But here, now, I began to wonder if that wasn't a mistake. After mini golf, which was pretty fun, Sam took my hand, led me to the truck and drove us here. To the lake. In the dark. With woods all around. Every step into the night we took, I became a little more afraid.

"Why did you bring me here?" I asked, hesitating to go further.

He stopped and turned back to face me. His head tilted to the side as he studied me. I squirmed beneath the scrutiny. "You're scared?"

I shook my head quickly, not wanting to admit such a thing. I mean, I trusted him, right? "It's just really dark and…"

Suddenly mere inches separated us, and I was staring at his chest. I never really noticed how very broad it actually was. I titled my head back and looked up. The golden highlights in his eyes were magnificent, making it possible that even in the dark I could see his expressions so clearly. I never imagined anyone could ever look at me that way. He cupped his hands around my cheek, the heat of him searing me to my very soul.

"I swear to you that you are safe," he whispered, "nothing or no one will ever touch you."

The only coherent thought that drifted through my head was 'I hope not,' because I sincerely wanted him to touch me more.

Then a bomb went off. Loud banging rumbled the dark and vibrated the ground.

I jumped, reaching out and grabbing handfuls of his shirt and while I buried my face in his chest. Close to my ear he whispered,

"It's your surprise." I looked up and he caught my chin in his hand, "I hope you like fireworks."

I looked up. "You brought me to see fireworks?"

"If you don't like them…" he seemed worried.

"No!" I yelled over the loud booming. "I love them."

He smiled and walked forward, carrying me with ease. The lights were beautiful. Fireworks of every color exploded against the black backdrop of the sky. Their shimmering brilliance was extended because it shimmered on the water creating twice the beauty.

I kept my eyes above until nothing more burst through the sky. I sighed, laying my head against his chest. "Beautiful," I said.

"They aren't over."

We were near the water's edge in a private little clearing that I can't imagine anyone knew about, except someone had to because of the swing. It was wooden, old-fashioned looking and hanging from a large tree by two wide ropes. Sam sat me on it, moving behind me to push.

"I think they're over." I told him, disappointed.

Just then a line of gold shot through the sky and burst into a million golden stars. I stared transfixed as they shimmered and dimmed, leaving me feeling a little empty. It was a shame for such perfect beauty to last for such a short time. But then another streaked by, and I became mesmerized by color. We watched the show for a long time, Sam coming to sit next to me on the swing.

It was perfect.

It felt like a secret.

Like we were the only two people in the world who knew about this place, and the fireworks were lighting up the night just for us. I leaned my cheek on his shoulder as he swayed the swing to and fro. When what I assumed was the grand finale began, he casually looped and arm around my waist and pulled me just a little closer, his body buffering some of the extreme booming. The very last firework to erupt into the sky was red and shaped like a gigantic heart. Just below my rib cage, butterflies danced.

"Thank you for bringing me," I told him when everything around us fell silent.

"You liked it?"

"Truly." I sat up to look him in the eyes.

His knuckles brushed over my cheek. "I wish I could give you more."

"I already have everything." I longed to reach out and touch him, but insecurities and nerves held me back.

"I got you something." He dug into the pocket of his jeans.

"But you already gave me this." I held up the cord that held the whistle.

He made a face. "In case you needed it to scare something away. It's not exactly something that shows you how I feel, or something that makes you think of me.

"I think about you all the time." Again the truth behind my words made me feel vulnerable. But I didn't care, the way he was looking at me tonight, I didn't mind being vulnerable in that moment.

His smile was quick and devastating. "Then this will just show you how I feel." He pushed back the sleeve of the cardigan I was wearing to expose my wrist and clasped something silver around it. Immediately I felt a strange feeling of rightness, as if a long lost piece of me was finally found. "Okay," he said, moving his large hands to give me a view of the gift.

"Oh my," I whispered. "It's beautiful." It was a silver chain that wove together like a rope and was so polished that it sparkled. Hanging from the chain were many charms in varying small sizes. Each charm was a key. They all looked like the old-time skeleton keys, some with rounded bottoms, while others were more ornately shaped. "I love it."

I placed my other hand around it and hugged it to my chest. "I'll never take it off." As I said the words I reached for him, forgetting all my vulnerabilities. But when I moved my hand away from my wrist the bracelet came with it, sliding toward the dark ground. I gasped, reaching to catch the precious treasure.

I missed.

Sam didn't.

"I'm so sorry! I'll be more careful."

"It's not your fault," Sam spoke quietly while reattaching the gift where it belonged. "But you do need to be careful. The clasp is broken."

I gasped. The thought of the bracelet being damaged was heartbreaking.

"Don't worry." His mouth tilted up. "I can fix it; I just didn't have time before I came to pick you up."

"Oh, good." I went back to studying the keys, trying to learn every shape and curve of each one. The largest key was slightly tarnished and seemed to be older than the rest.

He grew quiet and when I looked up he was smiling. "What?" I asked.

"You really do like it."

"Oh yes!" I rushed to say, then I frowned. "Why wouldn't I?"

He shrugged. "There was a woman near where I work renting paddle boats today selling jewelry. I wanted to buy you this necklace, a locket." He cleared his throat. "But...I didn't have enough money." My heart dropped into my belly at the thought of him spending any of the money he worked so hard for to support himself on me. I opened my mouth to protest, but he held up a hand and continued. "She told me that she was trying to sell a broken piece, and I was the perfect person to buy it. When she showed it to me..."

"What?" I was drawn in by his raspy tone and interesting tale.

"It was weird." He shook his head. "As soon as I saw it I felt like it should belong to you." He looked up, and I saw in his eyes exactly what I'd felt when he'd clasped it around my wrist. But then they cleared and he smiled. "And the fact that I thought it was totally appropriate."

"Keys?" I lifted a brow. Why on earth would he think that keys were appropriate? I never thought of keys as being romantic before. But now, the way he was looking at me, maybe I was wrong.

"You've unlocked every place inside of me and left me completely vulnerable."

Yep, I was *totally* wrong. Keys were the most romantic gift ever.

"Vulnerable?" I squeaked. No way could this calm, gorgeous, confident guy feel that way. *I* felt that way.

"I love you," he whispered.

"You love me?"

"From the first moment I saw you."

Joy shot through me, and my heart beat wildly. But the moment was ruined when my dumb brain got involved. For the last ten months my life moved in slow motion, and now everything was going at warp speed.

He was still watching me, waiting for me to say something. Probably wanting the same words in return. I looked into his hypnotic, gorgeous face wanting to say the words.

"Sam." As soon as his name slid past my tongue his eyes flashed gold. Hesitation slammed through me. Not denial, just hesitation. I struggled to put the feelings together because he was waiting, and I desperately did not want to hurt him. I reached out and splayed my palm over his chest. His hand covered mine. "I…"

His head snapped around toward the trees. Every muscle in him tensed. I swear I saw his ears wiggle and felt the muscles in his legs quiver.

"Come on." He rose from the swing gracefully, taking me with him. "It's late. You have a curfew."

"What's wrong?" I worried on my bottom lip. Was I too slow to respond?

"Nothing." He took a deep breath through his nose and quickened his pace. I practically had to run to keep up.

I dug my heels into the ground, but he pulled me right along like I was doing nothing at all. "Sam," I whined. I shouldn't have hesitated to tell him I love him back. I just – froze. The words were there, my heart practically beat just for him – so what happened with me?

He practically tossed me into the truck and rushed around to get in. As he drove his shoulders were tense, and he kept giving anxious looks in the rear view mirror. I was stupid and ruined the night and now he was angry. When we turned onto a busy street in town, he pulled to the side of the road. "I'm sorry about that."

"No – I'm sorry."

He tilted his head to the side and looked at me. "Why would you be sorry? You didn't do anything wrong."

"But, I thought – we left in such a hurry."

Sam's eyes softened. "I thought I heard something in the woods, probably an animal, but I didn't want you to be afraid. After what happened the other night at church…"

"Oh." He hadn't left because of what I hadn't said. But, he was right to have left. I was scared before the fireworks, and another wild animal sighting could have sent me over the edge, but still, we were having a moment, and now, it was lost.

On the other hand, it got me out of saying whatever it was that I was going to say.

"I wished we could have stayed longer."

He smiled, reaching over to take my hand. After another look in the rearview mirror he pulled out into traffic and drove me home in silence, holding my hand the whole way.

When we pulled up to my house I glanced at the clock. I was a whole hour early for curfew. Why did the night have to end so soon?

"I had a really great time." I said, hoping he missed the tiny catch in my voice.

"Hey, I'm sorry." He scooted across the seat to me. "I had a really great time too, and I ruined it by panicking back there."

"It's okay." I fingered the keys on my new bracelet. I knew I should give it back to him; he worked too hard and needed his money too much to spend it on me. I went to undo the clasp, but it slid open and felt into my palm. I lifted my hand out, but Sam shook his head and tucked my fingers around it.

"It belongs to you."

"It's too much."

"It was a steal. The lady practically gave it to me."

"Really?" I asked, suspicious.

"I promise." He laid a hand over his heart and bowed his head. I found the action sweet and, from him, believable.

"Okay." I smiled. "But no more presents, all right?"

He grinned and kissed me quick. "Agreed."

"Thank you again." I glanced at the clock. I wished the night was just beginning.

"If I bring you home early a few times then your mom won't mind when I take you out so often," he whispered, tracing my lower lip with his thumb.

I smiled because it would totally work.

"I love you, Heven."

I was once again saved from responding because he kissed me. It was a deep and thorough kiss that left me breathless and fuzzy headed. He chuckled, coming around to get me out of the truck and leading me to the front door. "I'll call you tomorrow."

Already I couldn't wait to hear his deep, raspy voice. "Okay." I slipped out of his warm embrace and opened the front door, looking back once before going inside. He was watching me go with an unreadable expression. I waved and went inside.

It was the last time I saw him before he disappeared.

The Hate

My taunting was becoming less of a threat. And now he blatantly ignores what I told him to do. He is more ignorant than I thought, and she is much smarter than I gave her credit for. The little witch has managed to reel him in. He is besotted with her, giving her jewelry and proclaiming his love. Our kind doesn't love. We destroy love. He knew I was watching, and like a white knight, he swept her away from danger. He knows her days are numbered. Trying to delay the inevitable is stupid. Lucky for him I like to play with my food before I eat, or she would already be dead.

He shouldn't have chosen her over me. Once I find what I am looking for, he will beg to rule with me. He will see that I am the one he belongs with. But first, she must die.

I watched him kiss her, practically attacking her mouth with his. She pretended to like it and batted her eyes at him as he walked her to her door. An incredible urge to attack her right then came over me. My body trembled with the force of how much I hated her.

I held back because he knew I was there. He was on guard and watching. When I kill her I want it to be a surprise. Even he won't be able to stop me.

She let herself in the house, and he waited while she locked the door. When he turned he looked right at me, his eyes flashing in the dark, a silent challenge. He was angry, I could smell it. He gunned the engine when he drove away. I didn't bother hiding the fact that I was following him. He issued the challenge, and I was answering. Maybe I would just kill him too.

Sam

For a single moment I thought she might say it back. The way her eyes melted when I gave her the bracelet, the way her body molded against mine as we sat in the swing. I had started to believe it might be possible.

Then we were interrupted. I smelled trouble coming; I heard its silent trip through the woods. Was one night was too much to ask for? What should have been a night to remember turned into another threat to avoid.

I couldn't sit out there in the open with her any longer, she was a sitting duck. Her safety wasn't something I was willing to chance. So instead of waiting to hear the words I desperately wanted, I ruined the moment and pulled her away.

I knew she was upset, I could see it in her eyes. She thought she had done something wrong, and for that I was pissed. How much more was she going to have to endure all because I love her?

The minute she stepped inside her house and turned the lock I turned and sought out the one who was watching. Adrenaline and anger surged through me. I have had enough. I was tired of looking over Heven's shoulder, tired of hiding in the shadows and keeping danger from her door.

It was time that I eliminated the threat. I didn't like to kill.

But that didn't mean I wouldn't.

I drove to an empty lot not far from town. I didn't want an audience for the murder I was about to commit. When I turned onto the road that lead to the clearing, I felt a weight land in the bed of my truck. I didn't bother to look; I knew exactly what it was.

I slammed on the brakes a few seconds later, letting the truck fishtail and jerk as it tried to stop so abruptly. I enjoyed hearing the banging in the back and the snarl of pain.

Once the truck was stopped I turned off the engine but left the keys in the ignition. I leaped out of the truck, my body tense, expecting the hit. It came, from over my head, a body sailing right over me. I turned and caught the attacker from above and tossed them onto the ground. Again, the sickening thud of the body hitting the ground pleased me.

I didn't wait for them to get up but leapt on top, landing a few really good punches to the side of my target's head.

Next thing I knew I was sailing through the air, and I turned to land on my feet. My enemy charged, and I ducked out of the way sending the shadowed figure stuttering forward. I shoved my enemy from behind, but my nemesis turned, sharp teeth raking down my arm. I pulled back and glanced down at the blood welling on my arm.

"I'm done with you," I spat. "I'm sick of the games you keep playing with Heven!"

I got an answering snarl, and then I was tossed through the air again. This time I landed further into the lot, in a part with trees growing closely together. I gritted my teeth when my back hit a branch, but I straightened and braced for another attack.

But something else distracted me.

The smell.

I looked down and held back a gag. Body parts littered the ground. There was a hand lying next to my foot and another laying a few yards away. A foot was sticking out from beneath a pile of leaves and there were puddles of blood in the grass.

"I told you that you belonged with us."

My gaze snapped up at the sound of the voice. I preferred them in their other forms. At least then they couldn't talk.

I took pleasure in the swollen purpling bruises that marked the monster's skin.

"I'm not anything like you."

A humorless laugh echoes around me. "Then why did you come here? *You* challenged me. *You* have death in your eyes, you came here to kill. You led me to the place that I kill too. Your instincts told you it was the perfect place to hide a body."

"When I am done with you there won't be anything left."

I saw the hit coming, and I blocked it. We went round and round, throwing punches and trying to weaken the other.

When we both pulled away I realized I had the upper hand. I smiled, knowing that the months of fear would finally be over. "I never wanted to kill you," I said. "You leave me no choice."

I pounced, wrapping my hands around a gasping throat. I heard the others coming and knew that they would be here soon. I squeezed harder, wanting to snap her neck. She was struggling so fiercely, I couldn't finish the job.

A shoulder caught me under the ribs and I was suddenly knocked aside. I smacked into a tree and landed hard. Ignoring the pain in my side, I planted my hand in the grass to stand and came away with a severed ear. I wanted to gag at the bloody appendage. *Where was the rest of the body?* I couldn't think about that now because the others had come. I hadn't been fast enough at delivering death. Why wouldn't they just let me do this? Removing the monster would make all our lives easier.

The three of them stood in a line, staring at me with eyes devoid of emotion.

I glanced at the monster who was grinning like a maniac in between gasping for breath. "I told you that you couldn't beat me. You're nothing but a little pup."

Up until this point my body quivered and shook, I held back my need to change. But now I prepared to shift. If I was going to survive a fight of one against three I had too.

The others recognized what I was about to do and they jumped into action, pinning me down and laughing.

"You need to be taught a lesson, pup. One you won't forget."

I'm not really sure how long the beating lasted. I tried to fight back, but it was useless. It was three against one, and I was pinned.

My last thought before I blacked out was of Heven.

I opened my eyes to only to blink back the sunlight. How long had I been out?

Heven.

I jerked up, ignoring the protest in my body and looked for my phone. I was in my apartment. The apartment I barely ever spent any time at. How did I get here?

"Going somewhere?" A voice beside me asked.

I turned, angry that I hadn't realized he was sitting there.

"Morning. Did you have a nice nap?"

"Like you care," I snarled. I shoved my hand in my pocket looking for my phone. It wasn't there. Then I remembered I left it in the truck. I wondered where the truck was.

"She's fine." He said, and I paused and glanced over.

"How do you know?"

"Because the person who wants her dead is busy – got a big lead on *it*."

"Why aren't you out helping to look?" I asked.

He shrugged and motioned to the unopened water bottle on the table. I reached over and palmed the water. I drank it in one gulp. It was cold and felt good going down. I was beginning to feel the effects of my beating, but I refused to show any pain.

If I hadn't known any better I would think that he stayed behind to make sure I was okay. Except why would he care? He's the one that held me down to take the beating.

I stood, ignoring the way the room spun around me, "What time is it?"

"Sit back down."

"I have shit to do."

"You look like shit, and you're about to pass out."

I moved fast, and he wasn't expecting it. I had my hand around his throat, and I was half lying across him where he sat, lounged in a beat up chair. "If you think a couple of broken ribs and some bruises are going to keep me down then you're stupid."

He shoved me away, and I landed back on the couch. I got back up with clenched fists.

"Chill." He said, rising out of his chair. "You wanna leave? Go."

"You might want to think about whose side you're on. I'm not backing down."

"Is that a threat?" His eyes narrowed dangerously.

"No." I snapped. "It's a fact." I saw my keys lying on the table, and I grabbed them.

He smirked but he made no move to challenge me. "You better do something about your face before you leave. I have a feeling that little girl of yours might not take to seeing you like this so well. How are you going to explain yourself? Huh?"

I must have showed my doubt because he laughed. "You've got a lot to learn, pup."

With that he walked out the front door.

I stood there for long moments, using my senses, making certain I was alone. When I was sure he wasn't coming back I walked into the tiny, dirty bathroom and looked into the mirror.

I had an idea of what I would see, because my face hurt like hell. He had been right. I couldn't go around Heven like this. I couldn't explain, and she would be scared to death. I looked at the dried blood covering my face and the swollen bruises distorting my face. No, I couldn't see her like this.

With a sigh I turned away from the mirror and turned on the shower. I healed fast but my injuries were pretty bad. If I was a normal person I would be in a comma. But I wasn't normal. I should be healed in a matter of days.

I bit back a hiss when the water hit my back and sides. Broken ribs hurt like a bitch. And so did open cuts and burns. I scrubbed myself good anyway, ignoring the searing pain. The soap was the cheap kind, the kind that felt like sandpaper against your skin. I washed quickly, but thoroughly then turned the water off and stepped out. I didn't have time to linger.

Just because I couldn't let Heven see me didn't mean I couldn't see her.

The next few days were going to be endless, but I could do it. I had too. Staying away from her now was necessary. I couldn't explain and didn't know how even if I wanted to. So I would go back to watching her from afar, protecting her in the shadows. She was going to be hurt if I wasn't around. I hoped she could forgive me.

But at least she'd be alive.

Chapter Eleven

Heven

"Earth to Heven. Come in Heven..." Kimber said, waving her hand in front of my eyes.

I blinked, my attention slowly coming back to reality. Back to the overcrowded coffee house that we were sitting in. I glanced at Kimber who was staring at me with an exasperated frown. "Sorry, I wasn't listening."

"Yeah, what else is new?" Kimber muttered

I sighed and looked down into my cappuccino. The foam on the top was thick and rich looking, and my stomach turned. "I'm sorry. I know I haven't been a very good friend lately."

"No, I'm sorry. That was bitchy. I would be acting the same way if Cole disappeared for three days and didn't tell me anything."

Three days. Three long, endless days of staring at my phone, the door, and the window, waiting for him to appear. I kept expecting that familiar feeling of safety that I have grown so accustomed to just wash over me, but it hasn't, and my insides feel hollow.

Where are you Sam? Where have you gone and why did you leave me?

What if he was hurt or sick and no one was there to help him? He didn't have a family, all he had were those creepy roommates, and I got the impression they would hurt him before they would help him. All he had was me. What if he was lying somewhere wondering why I hadn't come and was feeling betrayed and hurt?

I felt betrayed and hurt. How could someone just tell you that they love you and then disappear?

My cell phone beeped, a signal that a text was received. I practically dived at my phone and hit the button. 'No New Messages' was displayed on the screen. Then the phone beeped again, and I realized it wasn't my phone doing the beeping but the phone in the booth behind us. I resisted the urge to cry and shoved the phone in the pocket of my oversized hoodie.

"I don't get it," Kimber said, taking a sip of her latte. "He hasn't called at all?"

"No," I said for the millionth time. Before she could ask the next thing that she always asks, I went ahead and responded, "And, no I don't know where he lives."

"I always thought mysterious guys were hot. But now I am starting to think that they aren't good dating material."

I looked up at her and rolled my eyes. "*You're* not dating him."

"Down girl. Don't shoot the messenger."

I pushed the sleeve up and fingered my bracelet, taking care to make sure the clasp was still closed. He hadn't been around to fix it. "He said he loved me," I whispered.

"Why didn't you say it back?" Kimber asked leaning over the table towards me. She reached out and fingered my bracelet.

"I don't know – I thought I might but then he freaked over something he heard in the woods and rushed me home. I wished I would have. Maybe he never would have left." I shoved the cappuccino away. I couldn't stand its smell any longer. My stomach was in terrible knots, and I had a headache.

"This isn't your fault." Kimber said vehemently.

Maybe it was.

I scrubbed a hand over my face. The noise of the coffee bar was pressing in on me. I wanted to scream for everyone to just be quiet. My hands were shaking, and I needed to get out of there.

"I have to go," I said, rushing out of the booth.

"Wait!" Kimber caught my wrist across the table, pulling me back. I struggled, pulling away, only to stumble forward right into something solid and warm.

Arms surrounded me and for a moment I pressed myself closer, my heart beating unbelievably fast. He came back! But…something was off…his smell was wrong. It was too clean and light and I didn't fit against him the way I should. I pulled away. "Cole."

He reached out and grasped my shoulders. "You okay, Hev?"

"Yeah, sorry." *Don't cry, don't cry, don't cry.*

"Come sit down, Heven," Kimber said from the booth.

"I have to go."

"Where are you going to go? I drove you here."

I stood there trying to come up with a response. Cole put an arm around me, and I dropped my head onto his shoulder. For so many days I had been panicked and the comfort felt good.

"Come sit with me," Cole said softly, and I went with him because I didn't know what else to do.

"I'll get you a hot tea instead of this coffee." Kimber picked up my discarded cappuccino and walked off.

Cole smoothed the hair from my face, "It's all going to be ok."

I was fighting tears so I didn't say anything as he rubbed slow circles over my back.

"What's going on here?" The raspy deep voice sent my heart splintering. I pushed Cole's arm away.

"Sam!"

His hazel eyes flashed at me, but then went to Cole and narrowed. "Get your hands off my girlfriend."

I pushed Cole away and ran forward, throwing myself against him. He caught me but the breath hissed between his teeth. I tried to pull back, to see what was wrong, but his hold tightened.

"I've been so worried!" I said into his chest.

"I know, and I'm sorry," he said, leaning down, whispering into my ear. Goosebumps raced across my skin, the sound of his voice was exactly what I needed to hear.

I went to grab my bag from the booth, and Cole stepped into my path. "You can't go with him, Heven."

"What? Yes I can." I pushed Cole back with my hand and grabbed my bag.

Sam cleared his throat and came to stand at my back. "Hey, Kimber. I appreciate you looking out for Heven while I was, uh, gone."

"Where were you?" she asked.

"I was sick, I couldn't call." He glanced down at the floor when he spoke.

"You were sick? Are you alright?" I asked, turning to face him.

"Can we go somewhere to talk?" He asked.

"Of course," I said, motioning that we should go.

Cole stepped in front of Sam. His eyes were hard. "You don't deserve her. Heven deserves someone who would treat her right."

"I don't think you have much say in the matter." Sam said tightly.

Cole grabbed my arm and tried to tow me aside. "We need to talk."

"No, we don't. I'm going with Sam."

Cole shoved a hand through his dark hair. "I don't trust him."

Sam made a sound and then shoved Cole down into the booth, and Sam was pulling me along with him out of the coffee bar.

"Why did you do that?" I demanded when we were outside

"If that guy touches you one more time…" He growled, almost to himself because his back was to me. His fists were clenched at his sides and his back was tense.

"Sam?"

His shoulders dropped and he turned, his somber hazel eyes eating me alive. "I've missed you."

I groaned and went into his arms, hugging him hard. When he winced I stepped back. "What's the matter?"

"Nothing, I'm fine." He tried to pull me toward him, but I could see pain in his face.

"Are you sick? Hurt?" I began running my hands over him, feeling for any sign of injury.

He caught my hands between his. "I'm all right."

There was a faint yellowing bruise along his jaw. I brushed a finger across it. "This?"

He blew out a breath that ruffled his hair. There was a cut along his hairline. I gasped and reached for it. "This?"

"Let's go," he urged, pulling me toward the truck at the curb.

"What happened to you?" I demanded as we drove away.

"It's nothing to worry about. I'm sorry about not being around."

That's all he had to say? I wasn't about to accept that. I'd spent three days worried sick, and then he shows up clearly healing from some sort of injury and he says that it's nothing? I don't think so. He has some real explaining to do! "Where have you been?"

"At home."

I didn't even know where that was. "Where is home exactly?"

"Across town."

I made a frustrated sound in the back of my throat. "You disappeared without warning for three days. You didn't answer my calls or my texts, and I had no idea where to look for you because I have no idea where you live, and now you won't tell me what's going on."

"Don't cry," he said, hoarse.

I turned my body away from him, angry at myself for being such a wimp. I couldn't even be mad at him because I was so relieved he was all right. I wiped furiously at my eyes, ignoring that he was slowing the truck and pulling over. Broad hands caught me around the waist and hauled me backward until I encountered his solid chest. His arms wound around me and held on tight. His breath was warm and brushed over my ear, making me shiver.

"I was so scared," I admitted, fresh tears falling.

"I know, sweetheart." Somehow the tender endearment made it worse, and I cried harder.

"I…didn't know…if…I would see you again."

"I couldn't leave you."

"But you did," I accused, turning to face him.

He sighed. He looked tired, and there was an echo of pain in his eyes that I thought he might be trying to hide. "I got in a fight, okay?" He pushed a hand through his shaggy hair. I caught another glimpse of the cut on his forehead.

"A fight? With who?"

"My roommates."

So I was right to think they weren't really Sam's friends. "But why?"

"It doesn't matter," he said, his jaw hard, and his eyes flashing. Fear skittered along my spine.

"You were hurt," I began, pushing away my fear and tentatively reaching for his hair, lifting it to study the cut.

I felt him tense, but he allowed my touch and didn't respond to my words.

"Lean down," I whispered.

He lowered his head, and I trailed a finger along the cut. It was red and slightly raised and looked like it had been pretty bad. I brushed his hair further back and wondered how a cut that looked so vicious could be closed already. "Oh, Sam." I sighed, pulling away.

I opened the glove box, and a small first aid kit fell out. Exactly what I was looking for.

"I'm fine," he growled.

"That cut needs to be covered, or it's going to get infected." I found a bandage and some anti-bacterial cream in the kit and motioned for him to come closer. I knew that it was closed and wouldn't get infected, but I felt like I should do something to help him. I thought he would argue but he didn't, and I went about cleaning the cut and bandaging it. When I was done I took his face in my hands and tilted his head to study the yellowing bruise along his jaw. He had another behind his ear, but there was nothing I could do about bruises.

"Why didn't you call me?" I whispered.

"I didn't want you involved."

"I would have helped you." My voice trembled as I put away the first aid kit.

"I'm fine."

"But..." He cut off my words by pressing me into his chest and wrapping me in his arms. It felt good and safe, and I had missed being with him even more than I knew. I relaxed against him, surrendering to his warmth and love. We stayed like that a long time, but something intruded through my cloud of contentment. Sam wasn't completely relaxed; he was holding himself a little stiff. I gasped and sat back. "Where else are you hurt?" I reached for the hem of his shirt, but he caught my hand.

"I'm all right, Heven. I'm just a little stiff and sore, okay?" His eyes begged me to let it go.

After a few minutes I sighed. "You need to move."

"I'm working on it," he muttered.

I blushed, ashamed. He already worked two jobs. He was probably trying to save enough for his own place. "Sam?"

His eyes softened when I spoke his name. "Yeah?"

"Next time, call me, okay?"

"I never meant to make you worry." He held open his arms and I eased into them, not wanting to hurt him. Was he thinner than before?

"I'm glad you're back." Everything inside me calmed and settled.

"I wish I could spend the afternoon with you, but I have to work in an hour."

Disappointment washed through me, but I pushed it back. The more he worked the sooner he could move out away from his roommates. I tilted my head back and smiled. "We have just enough time to go get one of those Bubble Teas you like so much. My treat."

He smiled. "Deal." Before releasing me he inched closer, his lips covering mine. Long moments passed as our lips met again and again. When he pulled back my heart was going a mile a minute. He stared at me so intently that I began to squirm in my seat, but then he blinked, pressed a kiss to my forehead and put the truck in drive.

The Hate

I spent three days chasing down a false lead. Three days wasting my time! All because some informant thought he could give me bad information. Now he isn't giving anyone information. Except for the worms I buried his mutilated body with.

To make matters even worse, I returned, expecting to see Sam back at home. To see that he learned his lesson. Only I was informed that he left three days ago and hasn't been back. He's been out watching that little bitch girlfriend of his, protecting her from me.

Little does he know that he can't protect her from me any more than he protected himself. Clearly, his lesson wasn't harsh enough. Clearly, he didn't learn anything.

It's one thing to see the parts or faces of bodies that you never knew. Let's see how the pup does when he sees the bloody corpse of someone he loves.

The Hope

I'm frightened for them. How many more people are going to have to die so that virtue can triumph? Can one man really stop the evil one? One man who isn't even pure of spirit.

I pray that he can turn from the evil inside him, turn to the light.

I don't know how much longer she can remain in the dark. She must be made aware of the way she is being hunted. Perhaps they could work together to overcome what is coming.

I pray together they can be strong.

Heven

Kimber lived on a lake. Even though the house was large, it looked like a cozy log cabin from the road. Only after you came down the driveway to park next to the four car garage did you realize just how big it was. It was a beautiful, peaceful place that had views of the lake from every room in the house. Full-grown trees canopied the lawn making it feel as though you were in your own private space all the way down to the water.

I was surprised that Kimber wasn't having a huge party like she had last year on her birthday. Instead, all she wanted was to hang out here at her place with the people she was closest to. Frankly, I was relieved. The last big party I went to didn't turn out too well.

"You look good tonight," Sam said when he picked me up for the party, opening the truck door to help me in.

I felt my cheeks burn. "Thank you."

I was wearing one of the new outfits I'd bought when Kimber and I were at the mall. It was a nice outfit, but more understated than what I would have chosen *Before*. Even though it was early spring, it was still pretty cold, so I was wearing a fitted pair of jeans with a few strategically placed rips, a pair of brown suede boots that came to the knee and a white button up shirt with ruffles around the neck instead of a collar. Over top I added a deep red military-style jacket with pewter buttons that I found hiding in the very back of my closet (leftovers from *Before*). The only jewelry I wore was the whistle, which was tucked beneath my shirt and the bracelet Sam had given me.

Sam shut the truck door behind me and hurried to get it. He picked up a curl of blond hair from my shoulder. He rubbed the strand between his fingers before giving it a light tug and letting go. His arms wrapped around me and towed me up against his chest. All the breath whooshed out of me and my heart thudded. "Hey, beautiful," he rasped.

God, that voice of his. And he knew how to kiss. It's like he knew exactly how to get to the very depths inside me and lure me out and into the palm of his hand. I could never go back to anything less ever again.

He pulled back, and I was dizzy. When my head cleared a little I looked up – he was watching me with an amused yet smug smile on his face. Could he possibly know what he did to me?

I cleared my throat. "Thanks for coming with me tonight."

"Where else would I be?" he asked, lacing his fingers through mine. "Besides, I like Kimber."

I tried not to think about when he was 'dating' her. "I guess you got to know her pretty well when you two were together." I wanted to kick myself for those words. *Dumb ass.*

"I wouldn't really say we were together. Even then I knew she was totally hung up on Cole. Besides, I had my eye on someone else." He looked over at me and winked.

I laughed. "She must be pretty special."

"Eh, she's okay. Sometimes she can be a real pain."

I put my hand to my chest in mock distress. Then I shrugged. "You should dump her."

He laughed then laced his fingers through mine. "That's the thing. I kinda love her."

My belly flipped over and my heart skipped a beat.

"Yeah? I bet that she really …" As I talked I noticed a dark shape – an animal – dart out onto the road. I screamed. The truck swerved violently, and Sam jerked the wheel and let out a colorful swear.

"What was that?" I gasped, trying to slow my racing heart.

"Probably just a deer or something."

It didn't look like a deer, but I kept my mouth shut. His hands were gripping the steering wheel so hard that his knuckles were white. His chest was rising and falling as he took in short, deep breaths.

I unhooked my seatbelt and slid closer to him. "Hey, are you okay?"

"Put your seatbelt back on!" He demanded.

I drew back in shock but used the lap belt in the center. When I was done I stared out the windshield.

Sam's arm slid across my shoulders and his hand splayed over my arm. "I didn't mean to yell at you. We almost had an accident and then you took your seatbelt off. I was just scared you could get hurt."

I nodded and laid my cheek against his chest. Sam was very intense sometimes. One minute he was laughing and teasing but the next he was rigid and protective. I often wondered if he was so protective because I was all he seemed to have. I wondered about his parents and why he didn't live with them. I was just about to ask when he spoke. The words vibrated his chest and tickled my cheek.

"Please don't be upset. I know that sometimes…I can be kind of an ass."

"You're not an ass, Sam." Then I smiled. "But you are bossy."

He snorted. "If I am bossy then you are pig-headed."

I gasped and sat up. "I am not!"

He made the sound a pig makes and I laughed.

Just like that the mood from earlier returned. We laughed and teased each other until we pulled into Kimber's driveway.

Sam got out and came around to lift me out of the truck. It wasn't that high of a step but I let him help me because I enjoyed when he touched me. As he lifted, he brought me close and let my body slide down his. He made a deep sound in the back of his throat and his eyes darkened.

"Kiss me," I whispered.

He lifted me back off the ground and covered my mouth with his. When he finally set me down my skin was flushed and my vision was blurred. He chuckled at my state and put an arm around me, leading me toward the house.

It wasn't fair. I always seemed to be the one affected when we kissed.

"How big is this party anyway?" Sam asked as we walked along the deck toward the back of the house.

"She said just a few of her closest friends."

Sam looked over at me with a small smile.

We rounded the corner of the house, and I stopped cold. I absolutely should have known. There were at least fifty people in the back yard. How had I not seen this one coming? I felt relaxed all day thinking that this was some sort of small get-together, so now seeing the crowd, my nerves skyrocketed.

"You alright?" Sam asked, concerned, moving to stand in front of me. What a favor that was because he blocked everyone from my sight.

"I guess I didn't expect this many people."

"You didn't see the cars out front?"

I shook my head, dumbly. All I saw was him.

"Hey," he said softly. "Want to go?"

"No! It's Kimber's birthday, I cannot miss this party. She's my best friend."

He nodded and turned back to the party. I saw Kimber making her way through the crowd toward us. I took a deep breath.

"Would you mind sticking close to me tonight? I don't know many people." He shrugged. "New kid and all."

Everyone loved him, and he knew it. He'd said that for me, and I loved him for it. "Like glue," I said, grateful.

"Happy Birthday!" I sang out to Kimber and went to hug her.

"'Bout time you got here!"

"I thought this was a small party," I laughed, hoping my nerves didn't show.

"It is," she said, exasperated. "Gifts go on the table inside the door. There's a bonfire with marshmallows at the fireplace, and the food and stuff is on the upper deck. The spiked punch is on the lower deck." She leaned in to whisper, then laughed. Someone called her name, and she spun to wave. "I'll be back," she said, scampering away.

I turned toward Sam. He was watching me. "Guess I'll go put this gift inside."

He took my hand and deftly steered us through the crowd. By the time we made it to the gift table I was shaking inside. "Everyone is staring," I said, feeling silly and self-conscious.

"It's because you look so beautiful."

I snorted. It was very unladylike. I gasped and brought my hand up to cover my mouth.

Sam laughed. "You're so cute."

I put the gift on the table and then turned to look out the huge glass doors at the crowd.

"This is a nice place," Sam said into my ear from behind. He was standing super close, and I knew all I had to do was lean back, just slightly, to be surrounded by the warmth that emanated from him.

"It's beautiful." Past the multi-tiered deck and across the grass-covered lawn, the trees seemed to part just for the gorgeous view of the rippling lake. Evening was falling, and the sky was streaked with pink. Soon the sun would slide beneath the water, and we would be blanketed by night.

"So where are the marshmallows?" Sam asked.

I giggled and pointed through the glass toward the lower deck. "There's a huge stone fireplace down there."

"Come on," he said, grabbing my hand and leading me out into the music and crowd.

Not many people were gathered around the fireplace, which was a relief. Sam grabbed a bag of marshmallows off the coffee table and a long stick and sat close to the flames. He patted the bench beside him.

"I guess everyone's where the spiked punch is," I said almost to myself.

Sam shrugged and pulled a flaming marshmallow out of the fire. "I like them crispy."

"Ewww," I said, batting it away. "I like them lightly brown."

He shoved his into his mouth and grinned.

"Be careful! That had to be a hundred degrees!" I waited for him to scream. Surely he was burned.

"Taste's good," he said, licking his fingers. Talk about a distraction. How in the world could he stand his food so hot? It made me remember that day in home-ec when he shoved the fresh from the oven pizza right into his mouth. Just like tonight, he hadn't even blinked at the extreme temperature of the food.

Next thing I knew there was a perfect, lightly-brown marshmallow in front of me. I grinned. "For me?"

"I wouldn't eat that undercooked thing." He said, screwing up his face into a grimace.

I laughed and accepted the treat. I took a bite, and it was good. Crispy on the outside but warm and gooey inside. "Mmmm."

"You've got it all over your lips now." He grinned. "You're supposed to eat it all in one bite. Less messy."

I made a face and started wiping at my mouth with my fingers. He grabbed them and leaned in, his lips doing a far better job of getting the candy. "Much better," he said, pulling back.

I caught movement out the corner of my eye and looked over. Amber and a few other cheerleaders were standing there with their mouths hanging open. I blushed.

"Marshmallow anyone?" Sam smiled, holding out the bag.

I held my breath. They were going to run off. No one wanted to hang with the disfigured girl anymore.

"Only if it's extra crispy!" Amber said, sitting near me and grabbing a stick. All the other girls did the same.

"Ah, a woman who knows how to cook them. Hev likes hers *browned*."

Amber laughed. "I know." She turned toward me. "Remember that insane campout we had last spring?"

I laughed. "That was a crazy weekend."

"Totally," Amber agreed, looking at Sam. "We decided to go hiking, and we got lost."

Everyone laughed at the memory, and Sam smiled, the corners around his eyes crinkling. I grabbed his hand, lacing our fingers. "When we finally made it back to camp, it was dark."

"And there was a bear ransacking our campsite."

"It was eating everything it could find!" one of the girls laughed.

Sam didn't laugh, he stiffened. "Did it attack you?"

I squeezed his fingers. "No. It left when all the food was gone."

He relaxed and smiled.

"Yeah, and then we had to spend the rest of the night trying to set up the bent tent and cleaning up the mess," Amber exclaimed.

"Some weekend," Sam said, smiling. The firelight cast a beautiful glow across his face.

"That wasn't even the half of it." Amber grinned. "But I'll never tell…"

We all laughed. I could hardly believe that I was sitting at a huge party with a cute guy holding my hand and the friends I thought I'd lost all around me, laughing.

Maybe this night wouldn't be as bad as I thought.

Chapter Twelve

Heven

"I see you're having a good time," Kimber said, sliding beside me.

"Actually I am. You throw a good party, friend."

"It's a talent." She sighed, taking a sip of her drink. By the way she was swaying, I would say it was spiked.

"Where's Cole?"

"Getting some food. He thinks I need some." She took another sip and giggled.

"We were just thinking of getting some food, too."

Kimber looked past me to Sam. "Looking good."

Sam smiled. "How much punch have you had, Kimber?"

"Just a few."

Cole walked up behind us with a huge plate of food. "Here, Kimmie. Eat."

She laughed. He looked at me and rolled his eyes.

I grinned. "Hey, Cole."

"Birthday girl's had too much sauce."

Kimber laughed.

"We're going to get some food," I told them.

"Oooh, meet me on the dance floor!" Kimber said.

"Sure, Kimber." I agreed, hoping she'd forget.

Unfortunately, she didn't.

Couples were dancing on the grass beneath white lights that glittered in the trees. Kimber managed to drag Sam and me, along with several others, onto the dance floor with her. I tried to stay as close to the edge of trees as possible. Sam and I moved enough to make it look like we were trying to dance. I think Sam hated dancing more than me, which was a little surprising. He moved so gracefully all the time, and he always seemed so comfortable in his skin that I figured he'd be a natural. Instead, he was tense and almost nervous, his hazel eyes scanning the trees and the shore of the lake. If he wasn't sticking so close by I would think he was embarrassed to be dancing with me – the girl with no rhythm.

Finally, a slow song came on, and I thought we would make our escape, but Sam towed me out into the crowd and wrapped his arms around me. This kind of dancing was really good. I took a deep breath and closed my eyes, Sam relaxing right along with me. We moved with each other to the music, and I hoped the song would never end.

Then the power went out.

The music stopped playing and all the lights went out. I didn't realize how dark it would be without any lights. Sam stiffened and tightened his arms around me. People around us screeched and laughed. Some of the guys made ghostly sounds.

Then a wolf howled.

It sounded way too real for it to be a drunken guy. People around us started whispering nervously.

Sam tucked my head further into his chest, and I could feel his heart hammering away. He leaned in to whisper, "Let's make our way toward the house. Don't let go of me."

I nodded.

"Do you have your whistle?" he asked.

Panic bubbled up in my chest. Did he think that some wild animal was going to take advantage of the dark and start attacking people? What if it was the same animal from the other night? I reached under my shirt and palmed the whistle.

"Sam?"

His muscles were bunching and rippling beneath his skin in a way that I never knew was possible. I tried to take comfort in the fact that he was clearly ripped.

Before I could truly start freaking out the lights came back on. Kimber's dad was on the upper deck and yelled down at the crowd. "Sorry! The breaker blew!"

Everyone cheered, and the DJ started up another slow song. I wondered when my heart would return to normal. Sam titled my head back and stared into my face. "You okay?"

"Yeah. Are you?"

He nodded and pulled me close again. Seconds later he pulled back. "I'll be right back."

"Where are you going?" I asked, alarmed.

"The bathroom," he called and ran toward the edge of the dance floor. Instead of turning toward the house, he disappeared into the trees.

Where was he going? Last time I checked, the bathroom was not in the woods. I was about to follow when someone caught my hand. I turned, ready to yell, when I saw who it was. "Brice."

"I thought he'd never leave you alone." He smiled.

That smile used to make my palms sweat. *Before.* We were practically an item last summer. Then I was attacked, scarred, and emotionally wrecked. Brice had come to visit me in the hospital once. He'd taken one look at my face and hadn't talked to me since.

"Who? Sam?" I stuttered.

"Dance with me," he said, flashing a smile and blinding me with his dimples. I let him sweep me forward because I was so shocked.

"You want to dance with me?" I asked. He was holding me a little too close so I eased back, creating some distance.

"Haven't seen you around much this year," he said.

"I've been busy."

"I've missed you," he whispered, leaning in.

"You have?"

He nodded. "It's good to see you out, having fun. Like old times. Remember?"

Was he hitting on me?

"I heard you were going to take Jenna's place on the cheer squad next year as team captain."

Ahh, he thought I was going to be popular again. I stepped back, cutting off our dance. "I need to go find Sam."

"Let him go. We had something good last year."

"Maybe," I said, wetting my lips. "But that was before you came to the hospital and were disgusted by my face." Where had that come from?

His blue eyes widened, and he shoved a hand through his perfect blond hair. "I wasn't, I'm not…"

"It's okay, Brice. Really. I'm with Sam now."

"You're going to blow me off?" He seemed incredulous. "For the new guy?"

I noticed that people around us were staring. This was going to be all over school tomorrow.

I tried to think of something to say that wouldn't embarrass him. Or me. A deep hard voice answered for me. "You heard her. She's with me now."

Sam stepped around me to face Brice. They measured each other for long moments, and I held my breath. Then Brice smiled. "Hey, man. That's cool. Can't blame a guy for trying."

He walked away.

When he was gone everyone turned toward Sam and me. Kimber came through the crowd. "The DJ's giving away free stuff at his booth!" she announced.

That took all of the attention away from us. I let out a sigh of relief. "Thank you," I told her.

"You looked like you needed some help."

I turned questioning eyes to Sam. "I thought you were going to the bathroom."

"I did," he answered vaguely, his eyes darted through the crowd to land on Brice again. I wasn't worried about Brice. He was an idiot.

I grabbed his hand. "You went into the woods, Sam. You didn't go to the house."

Beside me Kimber burst out laughing. "Guys pee all over the place, Heven."

Sam laughed and looked down at me, his eyes twinkling with amusement.

"I guess they do." I laughed, feeling silly. What else would he go in the woods to do? All the excitement lately has been going to my head; I'm seeing danger in my boyfriend peeing in the woods, what next?

Some guy walked by carrying a tray full of drinks. The cups were so full they splashed over the sides as he danced. "Oooh! I need one of those." Kimber said and went off to grab one.

Sam touched my fingers. "Are you alright?"

"Yeah. I guess that blackout just made me a little nervous."

Sam wrapped an arm around my shoulders and pulled me close. "You're safe."

I shifted and rose up on tiptoes to brush a kiss over his lips. He always made me feel so much better. He made a low growl in his throat as he deepened the kiss. I laughed against his lips.

"Break it up you two." Kimber exclaimed. Sam pulled back but swiftly came back to press a quick kiss to my lips.

I giggled. Kimber reached out and wrapped her arm through mine. "Let's take a walk."

"Sam and I were dancing," I protested.

"Oh, please. You managed to find the only person on this planet as bad at dancing as you are." Kimber said. "Besides we haven't had any girl time." As she towed me away I looked back over my shoulder. Sam was standing in the crowd with a frown on his face. I smiled and blew him a kiss. His lips titled up.

Beside me Kimber slurped her drink. "Maybe you should take it easy on those," I said, eyeing the cup.

"It's my birthday."

For the first time I noticed that she was towing me toward the lake. At the water's edge she stepped onto the dock. "Kimber, this is far enough."

"Oh, come on, the stars are beautiful over the water."

Fear licked into my belly, and I turned back to look for Sam. He wasn't far behind us, someone had stopped him to talk, and he was smiling.

"Oh, come on, Heven. Don't be such a baby." Kimber said a hint of annoyance in her voice.

Maybe it shouldn't have, but her comment stung. I knew she was half-drunk, and I knew that she was probably kidding, but she hit a soft spot. I *was* scared a lot. I was always looking over my shoulder, and I was always seeking out reassurance from Sam. I *did* act like a baby. But, I didn't want to. Bravely, I stepped up on the dock, ignoring the shivers of fear that ran up my back. I looked up at the stars and realized that Kimber was right. They were beautiful. When we stopped I realized we were almost to the end and the lake stretched before us. My nerves, not long forgotten, returned. "Let's go back now."

She didn't respond, and I looked over at her. She was drinking her punch and looking out across the water. "What did Brice want?"

I rolled my eyes. "To get back together."

She turned and stared at me.

"He somehow got it in his head that I would be back on the squad next year and be team captain. He's only interested in popularity."

"Sam and Brice."

"What?"

"You have two hot guys after you."

"C'mon Kimber. You know how Brice is. *Sam* and I are together."

"Soon you'll be back on the squad, head cheerleader."

I shook my head. "I don't want that anymore."

She snorted and rolled her eyes. "Get real. I saw you earlier with the girls. Giggling, laughing – just like old times. Everyone just loves Heven, even my own boyfriend. "

I drew back in shock. She seemed angry that I was having a fun time tonight. "We were just reminiscing, telling Sam about that campout last year."

"They just ate up your words. This is my party. My night." She pointed to herself as she spoke.

"I wasn't trying to take anything from you." I said, still trying to understand what her problem was. How drunk was she?

"You never mean to take anything – but somehow you are always the one who has it all."

"Kimber–" I started but she ignored me and plowed on with her words.

"*Before* your accident everything was always all about you. No one ever saw me. I was always in your shadow. But then you started hiding and everyone started to see me." She looked over at me, her eyes spearing me through the dark. "Now you're trying to take what I finally have."

"Kimber, I had no idea that you felt this way – I …" My words trailed away when she pulled her shirt over her head and kicked off her shoes.

"What are you doing?" I asked nervously.

"Doing what you're too chicken to do." With that she dove off the deck and into the dark water.

" Kimber!" I yelled after her. Was she insane? That water had to be freezing! And she was half-naked.

I waited a few beats, but she never came back up.

"Kimber!" I yelled again. "This isn't funny."

My stomach began cramping. What if she'd hit her head? What if she was too drunk to swim? I looked across the water, praying she would pop up and laugh.

She didn't.

I itched to jump in after her, but I couldn't. She knew I couldn't. Terrified of the water from a young age, I'd never learned how to swim.

I wondered if my stupid fear would get my best friend killed.

Frantic now, I turned to yell for help. I knew Sam was close by. Just as I was about to yell, a group of guys ran by without their shirts.

"Skinny dipping!" one yelled and they all began jumping.

I tried to step back, to hurry out of their way. But the dock was narrow and there wasn't anywhere else to go.

Except down.

I slipped right off the dock and plunged down into the dark water.

I struggled, trying to find my way to the surface, but everywhere I turned there was water. I couldn't see anything, and it was so cold. Panic seized me, and I felt as if a giant hand reached out and squeezed my lungs. My chest burned as I struggled to figure out which way was up. I forced my eyes opened searching for light, but there wasn't any. Only darkness. I felt something brush against me, and I reached out, hoping that Kimber had seen me fall and was trying to help. My hand closed over something soft. Something furry. I let out a scream, bubbles filling my vision. The next thing I knew I was being tugged down, toward the empty bottom of the lake. My body spun into action, kicking out, trying to get away. I looked down trying to see what had me but strands of my hair covered my face and I pushed at them all the while kicking. When I realized that my kicks weren't strong enough I let go of my hair and started punching. I felt a surge of satisfaction when my fist connected with something solid.

Unfortunately, my satisfaction was short lived, and I blacked out.

When I opened my eyes the first thing I saw was the stars. Then I felt an enormous pressure on my chest, like someone was sitting on me. Then, Sam's face filled my sight, and I stared up at him, breathless. My face and limbs were numb from the cold. I opened my mouth to breathe or speak but nothing happened. Swiftly, Sam flipped me onto my side and water poured out of my mouth. I gagged and coughed, gasping for precious oxygen to fill my lungs.

"That's my girl," Sam murmured, his voice sounded strained. "That's it, breathe."

My throat and lungs burned, and I coughed some more. Sam hunched over me, rubbing my back and whispering words of encouragement. I collapsed back onto the deck, exhausted. I heard someone screaming and noticed a commotion just off to my side. Then Sam was shoved aside, and a dripping wet Kimber shoved her face close to mine.

"Oh my God, Heven! Are you okay? I was so worried!" Her hands pushed at my wet hair, and she checked me over for injury. "Should I call 9-1-1? I am so sorry! I don't know what I was thinking!"

"I'm okay," I whispered, grabbing at her flailing hands.

She collapsed on top of me, the strands of her hair felt like icicles against my already frozen skin. I wanted to push her away, but I couldn't seem to find the strength. But then Sam was lifting her away and crouching over me.

"Hey, beautiful." He tried to smile but it didn't reach his eyes. "What happened?" he asked, trailing a finger down my cheek. His skin was blissfully warm, and I turned my face toward his hand. He splayed his palm out, cupping my face and looked at me expectantly.

I tried to explain, but my teeth were chattering together.

"She can't swim." Kimber wailed from behind him.

"So you brought her out to the end of a dock?" Sam asked, standing to face her.

She had the grace to look embarrassed. "I'm sorry, Heven, I just wasn't thinking. I just wanted to…I don't know, I wasn't thinking, I'm so sorry!"

Sam made a rude noise and turned his back on her. I had managed to sit up but was still shaking from the cold. He pulled off his sweatshirt and yanked it down over my head. Delicious heat surrounded me. "Relax, honey. Just breathe and try and get warm." He sank down onto the deck and wrapped his arms around me, pulling me into his lap. My shivers eased immediately; his warmth was exactly what I needed. I noticed that there was a crowd gathered around where the dock met the yard, but I didn't care. I closed my eyes and leaned into Sam's chest.

I heard footsteps pounding across the deck, and I opened my eyes to see Cole running towards us. "I was up in the house – what happened?" He gaped at Kimber standing there all wet and in her bra.

"I just wanted to have a little girl time; I just thought we could talk," Kimber cried, throwing herself into Cole's arms.

"Why are you guys so wet?" he asked, shifting Kimber into one arm so he could bend and pick up her shirt. "And why are you half naked?"

"I f-f-fell in," I stammered and Kimber began to cry.

"Geez, Heven." Cole sighed.

"Are you feeling okay? Can you walk?" Sam asked me.

"I think so," I said, trying to climb out of his lap. He tightened his grip.

"We should go," Sam said, talking more to my friends than to me. Instead of allowing me to stand, he stood up, taking me with him, holding me against his chest.

"I can walk," I told him, half-heartedly.

"I know," he said simply and began walking toward the house.

"Wait!" Kimber exclaimed, running after us. "Let's go change into some dry clothes."

I stared at Kimber, trying to decide if I should be mad or not.

"It's the least I can do," she begged, wiping at the tears on her cheeks. "I feel awful."

I kind of thought she *should* feel awful. But still. She was my best friend, and it was her birthday. Even after she said those things to me I still didn't believe that she wanted me to drown. So I nodded, and we made our way to the back door of the house.

I looked like a drowned rat. My clothes were rumpled and soaked, my hair was plastered to my head, and my skin was an unnaturally pale shade. And to top it all off, I felt odd. Something wasn't right…but I couldn't figure out what it was. I figured that it was because I just almost drowned and tried to push the feeling away.

While Kimber pawed through her extensive closet, I shut myself in the bathroom and made use of the hair dryer. My perfectly tasseled waves were gone, and I wasn't even going to bother to get them back. I wished I could pull the blond mass up on my head and call it a night, but I couldn't. I dried it until it was only slightly damp and brushed it out, knowing that it would have to do. I used Kimber's face wash without asking, needing to get the lake water off me and not caring if she minded. When I was done I stepped out of the bathroom. Kimber was standing at the foot of her bed fully changed into dry clothes. Her hair was brushed out and pulled up high, like I wished to style mine.

"I got you some dry clothes." She motioned to a pile on the bed. "Just leave your outfit here. I'll wash it for you."

"That's not necessary." I walked to the bed and looked down at a pair of black yoga pants, a white tee and a pink GAP hoodie.

"I thought the pants would fit you better. I know my jeans are too big."

I nodded and began changing. When I pulled off Sam's sweatshirt and looked down I realized that something was missing. Something important. My bracelet was gone. What if it fell off in the lake? What if it was gone forever? I should have known better than to wear it tonight with the clasp so undependable. *This* is why I was feeling so off. *This* is what was wrong. I wouldn't feel right again until that bracelet was back where it belonged.

"Heven," Kimber began, drawing my attention away. She looked more sober now than she had all night.

"What were you thinking?" I cut her off, angry. "You scared me on purpose."

"No! I wouldn't do that. I never meant for you to get hurt."

"Well, I did." I snatched up the sweatshirt and shook it, hoping the bracelet was lost inside. It wasn't. I grabbed my wet clothes and went around the bed.

"Please," Kimber said softly, grabbing my arm. I turned back. "I had way too much to drink. I don't know what came over me. I didn't mean any of that stuff I said out there. You're my best friend. I'm sorry."

I laughed a humorless laugh. "You think saying sorry is going to wipe away everything you just said and did?" I glanced down at the floor, hoping to catch sight of my bracelet. It wasn't there and it made me even madder. "You might have been drunk when you said those things, but you know what? Alcohol doesn't lie, if anything it loosens your tongue. You might not have wanted to say those things to me but on some level you meant them."

"No – I –" Kimber began, but I sliced my hand through the air and cut her off.

"Just save it, okay? I almost drowned, and I'm too tired to hear your excuses." I tossed the pink hoodie aside, choosing to put Sam's sweatshirt back on. It smelled like him, and suddenly I wanted to see his face.

"I didn't mean for you to fall in. I guess I just got scared that you were becoming popular again, and I would be back in your shadow."

I actually appreciated her honest answer. "You'll never be in my shadow, Kimber. I am sorry that you ever felt that way. You should have said something before."

"You forgive me?"

I sighed heavily. "Of course I do." Even though I was still mad, I decided to let it go. Kimber was too good of a friend to let a drunken tirade ruin our friendship.

She sprang forward and hugged me. "Thank you! I love you."

"Love you too." I grinned.

"Let's go shopping next weekend for prom. I'll help you find a totally hot dress." That was Kimber's way of making things up to me.

"Deal," I agreed. But all I really wanted was my bracelet back. I decided not to tell Kimber just then that my bracelet was gone. What was the point? I already made her feel guilty enough, why make it worse?

"Good. Now let's get some cake!" Kimber swung open the bedroom door and made a sound of surprise. I peeked around her and saw Sam sitting in the hall with his back against the wall. When he saw me he stood and took a step forward.

"You've been waiting out here the entire time?" Kimber asked.

"I just wanted to make sure she was okay." Sam said, not taking his eyes off me when he spoke.

Kimber looked between the two of us and then took off downstairs calling, "I'm cutting the cake!"

"We better go," I told him. "If I don't see her cut the cake, she'll be pissed." I said the words lightly, but deep down it bothered me because, now, I knew that it was true.

"Hey?" He grabbed my hand, lacing our fingers and pulling me around to face him. "What's wrong?"

Without warning my eyes filled with tears. Sam let out a low curse and pulled me against his chest. "It's okay," he murmured.

"No, it isn't." I sniffled. "I'm a horrible person." I wiped my face against his shirt.

"Why would you be a horrible person?" I could hear the laughter in his voice, and I pulled back. His smile died on his lips.

"Hey," he whispered. "Tell me." He caught a stray tear with his thumb and brought it to his lips. I watched fascinated. "Heven?" he prompted after a few silent moments.

I took a deep breath. "I lost my bracelet. I think it fell off in the lake." I looked at the floor not wanting to see the disappointment in his face when I said the words. I was afraid that he would think that I was careless with it, or that it didn't mean anything to me.

"Damn clasp," he murmured then tilted my chin up so he could look into my eyes. The gold was a little deeper tonight, and it reminded me of the burnished gold color of the fall leaves that made Maine so famous. "Don't worry about it. I'll find it."

I shook my head. "It's probably at the bottom of the lake."

"Maybe not. Maybe it fell off before that." He took my hand and began leading me away, toward the party.

"I feel kind of empty without it." I whispered.

He squeezed my hand as we walked out onto the deck where a huge cake burning with candles sat, and everyone gathered around while Kimber blew them out. I made sure that she could see me before she started cutting the cake and handing out large slices.

After almost drowning, losing my bracelet and hearing the awful things Kimber said to me, I was ready to go home. Instead I was sitting here pushing cake around on my plate.

"Are you okay, Hev?" Cole leaned over to ask me.

"I'm fine." I said, pushing the uneaten cake away. "I lost my bracelet."

"Oh, no!" Kimber gasped. "I know how much it means to you. I am *so* sorry."

"It's okay." Underneath the table Sam squeezed my fingers.

"I'll go ask the DJ if anyone turned it in to him." Kimber said, jumping up.

"You don't have to do that," I said.

"It's the least I can do." She argued. I didn't say anything else because she was right.

Before she walked away, a guy in our class came up to the table. "Hey, guys. Have any of you seen Andi around?"

"Sorry, Sean, I haven't." I said. Everyone else shook their heads.

His shoulders sagged, "I can't find her and she isn't answering any of my calls or texts."

"When's the last time you saw her?" Sam asked.

"Right before the blackout. We were dancing, the lights went out and when they came back on she was gone."

"I was just on my way to the DJ booth. Come with me, and we will have the DJ page her. Maybe she went off with friends and lost track of time." Kimber told him.

He nodded, but his eyes were worried. I watched them disappear into the crowd and an uneasy feeling came over me.

Sam stood up from the table. "I'm going to go look for your bracelet."

"I'll come with you."

"No. Stay here. I'll be right back."

"I want to help."

"Please," he sounded weary. "Just stay up here."

"You act like I need to be watched or something. This is my best friend's house. I have been here a thousand times. I know the place better than you do."

"I don't think you need to be watched, Heven." He said patiently. "But you almost drowned, it's chilly, and now there's a girl missing."

"Missing? She isn't missing. She probably just wandered off, drunk."

He nodded, but his eyes said something else.

"As much as I hate to admit it, dude's got a point." Cole said.

We both looked over at him, forgetting that he had even been listening.

"Fine," I muttered and looked at Sam. "Go. I'll stay up here."

"Thank you. I'll be right back." He kissed my forehead then brushed a stray piece of hair out of my face.

Dammit, how was I supposed to be mad when he treated me with such tenderness?

"Hurry back." I whispered. He smiled then turned and walked away.

I sat down next to Cole, watching Sam gracefully forage through the grass. Suddenly, I felt as if I was being watched. I turned my head to see Cole staring at me with a funny look on his face. "What's the matter?" I asked.

"You really like that guy, huh?" he said, glancing in Sam's direction.

"Yea, I do."

"I just don't get it," he muttered.

I didn't have a response to that, so I turned back to watch Sam. He didn't have to get it. I did.

"Hey, Hev." he said, touching my arm. "I shouldn't have said that."

"It's ok."

"But I feel it is my duty as your friend to inform you that you will not be winning any Olympic swimming medals anytime soon. My two-year-old cousin swims better than you." He grinned, and I smacked him playfully on the arm.

"You know I can't swim," I said.

"Maybe I can call up my cousin and have him give you a few lessons, you can pay him in goldfish."

Sam

I tried to appear casual as I looked through the grass. This entire night had been a great lesson in control for me. Sometimes it scared me – how good I had become at lying. I didn't bother to wish for a normal life because that wasn't going to happen. But, I did wish that I could be honest with Heven about myself and for her to still want to be with me. Was it really fair of me to ask her to live a life that would be so chaotic?

I pushed the thoughts aside and concentrated on my task. I looked back over my shoulder to where I left Heven. She was still sitting on the deck and Cole was talking, making faces, and she was smiling. I hated that guy. He acted like he was so much better than everyone else, like he was *good*. There was something about that *goodness* that really ticked me off. But there was one other thing that really got to me about Cole. He was normal. He could give her normal. But he would never love her like I do.

Focus.

Checking once more that Heven – or anyone else – was no longer looking my way I ducked into the trees. The monster was out here. Waiting. That little stunt earlier with the truck was just the monster's way of saying that it was watching and that it was back. I had a very bad feeling that the girl who couldn't be found – Andi – was dead.

I didn't bother trying to be quiet as I went deeper into the trees. I wasn't trying to hide. The monster knew I was here and knew that I would come. I took a deep breath to pinpoint where it was hiding so we could get this confrontation done with. I needed to get back to Heven. There were the normal smells of the night and the woods of course, but there was something else too…something that seemed to latch onto the inside of my nose and wouldn't let go.

I began pushing further through the trees, hurrying, but half afraid of what I would find. Seconds later my eyes focused on something lying up ahead. I ran forward then stopped.

And looked down in shock.

Pale blond hair, streaked with blood, covered most of the girl's face. Her arms and legs were bent at odd, unnatural angles. There were deep, bleeding gouges all over what was once flawless skin.

But those sights weren't the worst part. No, the worst part was the blood crusted charm bracelet that hung around the girl's wrist.

My knees threatened to buckle, but I refused to let them.

I felt blood, hot and urgent, rushing through my veins, pumping up my insides and surging energy through my limbs. I blinked, trying to clear my eyes and when they cleared my stomach revolted. Deep anguish settled on my chest.

No.

I just saw her with Cole; I thought was safe. How could he let anything happen to her? The monster better have killed Cole too because if he is still breathing, I will make him wish he wasn't.

I turned to run, to escape the sight, but I couldn't. I couldn't leave her here alone. How was I going to live with this? I stared down, swallowing past the lump in my throat. Then, a sound reached my ears through the dark.

My head snapped up.

Again. Please, God, again.

The sound floated to my ears once more, and this time I did fall to my knees.

Heven's laughter filled my ears, and I bit back a strangled sob.

It isn't her. She's alive.

The pressure in my chest eased, and I forced myself to get it together. I didn't have time for this. I looked back again at the crumpled body lying in the grass. It was easy to see why I thought this girl was Heven. She looked just like her with long, very light-blond hair and slender limbs. Around one of her wrists sat Heven's silver bracelet. Heven's bracelet with the skeleton key charms. It was bloody. I reached down and grasped it. It came easily, as if it knew that this wasn't where it belonged.

I stuffed it into my pocket and continued to stare down at the horrible sight, and I felt terrible knowing she died in Heven's place. Her skin was tan…and from here I could see a lot of it. If I had been thinking straight before, I would have realized that Heven wouldn't wear something so revealing. Then I realized that her outfit hadn't been revealing, but that her clothing was shredded. Scraps of fabric littered the forest floor and left her body vulnerable and invaded.

I reached for my sweatshirt to try and allow this girl some sort of modesty – some kind of respect in death – but I wasn't wearing it. Heven was. Heven – who was alive and breathing.

But for how long?

I jumped up and turned, ready to race to her side. To reassure myself that she was still safe.

The monster stood yards away, staring at me...smiling.

"Take a good long look." The voice was taunting and smug. "The way her blond hair hangs limp, the cuts and scrapes that still leak with blood, the way her blue eyes stare out, vacant and flat. The next time you see this sight, it will be her. And there will be nothing that you can do to save her."

Disgust, hot and acrid, speared through me. Before I knew it I was launching myself straight at the person I hated most in this world. We rolled across the ground, and when we stopped I was on top. I didn't even think twice before I plowed my fist into flesh and bone.

The monster yelled, and I shoved a hand over a wide-open mouth. The last thing we needed was for someone to hear and come running. I stared down at the struggling form beneath me. Teeth cut into my hand but I didn't care. There was only one way I could think of that would allow us to have it out with no one able to see and hear.

I got up, dragging the monster with me, and ran quickly through the trees. Thankfully, the walk wasn't far, and when I got there I delivered another solid punch before tossing the body in the lake.

Then I jumped in too.

The water was cold and dark. In that moment I realized the fear that Heven must have felt when she was drowning. How overwhelming it would be if I didn't know how to swim.

But I did.

And I was very good.

I looked through the dark water, my eyesight already adjusting to the murkiness. The monster was there, a body in transition. My body quivered with need, but I held back. If I transformed now my clothes would be ruined. How would I explain that?

Fortunately for me, I wasn't that worked up. The minute I realized that it wasn't Heven lying there mauled and dead, I calmed down. I knew that I should feel guilty for not mourning that dead girl, and there was a part of me that was, but Heven was my only priority, and I couldn't think beyond her.

Strangely, I felt calm...almost resigned to this fight, to this battle. I knew what I had to do and I knew that there was only one acceptable outcome. I could do this.

I had to.

The monster came at me, and I was thankful we were underwater. It made it easier to flip myself around and throw both legs out in a hard kick. My feet caught the beast and sent it floating back. I cut through the water, grabbing out but coming up empty. I ducked just as a hit was about to connect with my face and I swam down, deeper into the water.

I was grabbed from behind and slammed into the rocky floor of the lake. I spun and kicked out again. I sat crouched and ready for the next charge but instead I watched as the monster swam away.

When I was certain that it wasn't coming back, I pushed up to the surface of the water and took a deep breath. I swam quickly to the shore, making sure I was still away from the house and walked up onto the shore.

I stuck my hand in my pocket to be sure the bracelet was still there. It was. Then I rushed to the edge of the trees and looked through the crowd and up to the deck. Heven was still sitting there, her eyes scanning the crowd below. No doubt, she was wondering what was taking me so long.

The DJ turned down the music and spoke into the microphone. "Will Andi Richards please come up to the booth? Sean is looking for you."

My heart sank at the thought of the body lying in the woods. She wouldn't be coming back to the party. She wouldn't be doing anything ever again.

I couldn't risk her being found. I couldn't risk calling the cops. I shuddered at the thought of answering their questions and seeing their suspicious faces.

There was only one thing to do.

I made my way, quietly this time, back through the woods. Her body was exactly as it had been before. I reached down and pulled her around; her body fell heavily onto her back. Her eyes stared up at me, vacant and shocked. The last moments of her life had been horrible and no one should have to die that way.

Her face was mauled and bloody. Her body was broken and almost naked. Her skin and lips were already blue, and I closed my eyes to the awful sight.

Trying to detach myself, I picked her up and ignored the way her eyes seemed to stare at me. I went quickly to the lake shore, thankful that there was still the cover of trees and walked right into the water. For the second time that night, I threw a body into the lake.

Except this time, this body wouldn't be coming back out. I watched the girl float and realized that I would have to weight her body to make it sink. With a sick feeling in my stomach I dove to the bottom and grabbed a heavy rock. Then from beneath the water I grabbed her leg and pulled her down....then further down still.

At the bottom of the lake, I held her body and placed several large rocks on top of her. There was some long vegetation growing, and I wound it around her hands and arms. I looked down at her face, her eyes still wide open. I reached out and closed them, hopefully bringing her some peace.

I'm so sorry. You didn't deserve this. But it was you or Heven. I won't let this happen to her. So it had to be you.

Then I swam away without looking back.

Heven

One second he wasn't there but the next he was, striding through the crowd, dripping wet and pushing the hair up off his forehead. He seemed to walk like he was weighed down, like something was wrong. I took that as a sign he didn't find my bracelet. I resolved to myself that it was gone, and I vowed to not show him how upset that made me.

From across the table Cole and Kimber were talking, but I wasn't paying any attention. I was focused on Sam. He stepped up onto the deck, and I couldn't help but notice the way his wet t-shirt was plastered to his broad chest. When he caught me staring, he smiled, and his face transformed from torment to peace.

He slid into the vacant seat next to me and icy droplets of water fell against my hand. "You are soaking wet!" I exclaimed.

"I found you something." He grinned.

"You did?" I asked.

He held out his palm and uncurled his fingers. My bracelet was there, nestled against his skin. I gasped and threw my arms around his neck. "You found it!"

He laughed, his arms clasping me tightly, his face buried in my neck.

"It was in the lake?" *How did he find it?*

"I guess I got lucky." He said, kissing me on the nose. I laughed and scooped it out of his hand.

"I am so glad that you found it, Hev." Kimber said.

"Thanks." I smiled. "Can you put it on me?" I asked Sam.

"I think I better fix the clasp first, before you wear it again."

I felt disappointed but he was right. I would rather not wear it than risk losing it again. "Okay," I agreed and handed it back to him.

"I'll give it back to you tomorrow."

I nodded. I knew it would be safe with Sam.

"We should be going." Sam said quietly to me.

I nodded, ready to leave.

He stood, his keys appearing in his hand, and Kimber came over to give me a hug. "I'll call you tomorrow."

"Sure. I can help you clean up all this if you want."

"You're the best friend ever, Heven," Kimber said, hugging me again. "And I am so, so sorry about what happened earlier."

"I know. Happy birthday." I returned her hug.

I gave a wave to Cole as Sam's hand found mine. When we were around the side of the house I said, "That was quite a night."

He made a sound in his throat. "How are you doing? You feeling okay?"

"Yes. Thanks to you." I smiled, but he didn't smile back. "Are you okay?"

His arms surrounded me and his chin rested on the top of my head. He was so solid and even though he was wet, he was still incredibly warm and I couldn't help feeling safe, even when he acted so mysterious. When he didn't answer I tried to pull back, but he wouldn't let me and finally he spoke, his voice a mere whisper, "When you fell into the lake…I had no idea that you couldn't swim. I never would have let you wonder off that far."

"I was hardly twenty feet away!"

"It was too far," he murmured, squeezing me tighter.

"But you pulled me out. And everything's okay."

"Let's try and take it easy for a while, huh? At least until prom."

"Prom?" I stepped back and looked up.

He grinned. "You are going with me aren't you? You didn't agree to go with that jock, did you?"

"Who?" I wondered.

His grin got bigger. "Good answer."

"Oh. Brice? Yeah, right." I rolled my eyes.

"So…me and you?" he asked, his tawny eyes turning serious.

"Of course," I said, transfixed. I would go anywhere with him, even the depths of Hell.

"That's my girl," he whispered, hooking his arm around me and settling me in the truck.

As he walked around to the driver's side, I came out of my happy fog just long enough to see his eyes scan the trees one last time before climbing in and locking the doors behind him.

The Hate

Rage boiled my blood, and I screamed at the sky. I could feel droplets of spittle gathering around the edges of my mouth as I screamed, but I didn't care. I pretended the moisture was blood…and it had come from Heven.

But I loved to see the complete devastation that he felt when he saw that corpse in the woods. He thought it was his precious little love. He's so pathetic, standing in the woods and mourning over a silly girl. Love is for the weak.

The only way to make him strong…to make him see who he truly is…is murder. The bitch must die. Though her death will mean his suffering, it isn't enough. I want him to feel as much pain as possible. I want his soul destroyed.

So before I murder her and spread her insides out for him to see, I have a plan. I will whisper all the lies he tells her, the secrets he keeps, in her ear.

How satisfying it will be when he sees her gaze of love turn to disgust. She will rip out his heart. I will rip out hers.

Then his soul will be mine.

The Hope

But the path of the righteous is like the light of dawn, which shines brighter and brighter until full day. The way of the wicked is like deep darkness; they do not know over what they stumble.
—Proverbs 4:18-19

Chapter Thirteen

Heven

A masquerade ball – the perfect disguise. My stomach fluttered and anticipation curled around me. I almost forgot what this feeling was like. This feeling of *excitement*. *When was the last time I was excited about anything?* (Besides Sam, of course!) I couldn't remember. I do know that it had been *Before*. Tonight was different, though. Tonight things felt almost normal.

I turned up the volume on my stereo, not caring a bit if Mom thought it was too loud. Tonight was my night. I was going to enjoy it, because come midnight, I turned back into a pumpkin. Pushing that bit of depression back into the corner of my mind, I stepped in front of my mirror, not an ounce of trepidation in the act. I knew what I was going to see and what I wasn't.

I smiled, my glossy pink lips glistening. I looked hot. Just like *Before*. I giggled a little, almost giddy. I took a moment to really look at myself because I hadn't in so very long. My long blond hair was parted down the center, with two loose French braids woven with peacock blue satin sweeping the hair away from my face and stopping just behind my ears. The rest of my hair was left loose to trail down my back, and its softness brushed against my bare shoulders. My dress was strapless, a deep, vibrant shade of blue, fitted at the top to lightly flare out just beneath my bust and float to the floor. At my knees the color of the fabric began to fade, and where it skimmed the floor, it turned silver. Around my neck hung a silver teardrop pendant, and on my feet were strappy silver flats. No heels for me. Secretly, I liked being short. Especially when I stood next to Sam. He towered over me, always, unknowingly, making me feel protected. My stomach did a little flip at the thought. I could almost die waiting to see what he would say when he saw me tonight.

Tonight things would change for us.

I was ready.

Ready to say the words he wanted to hear.

The doorbell rang, and my heart fell to my belly. He was here! I took a calming breath, not that it helped, and looked back in the mirror once more. I did my makeup tonight, lining my eyes in charcoal, giving them a smoky look, and adding a silvery shadow to my lids. The rest of my face was more natural, but it needed to be because of the mask. At first I was thrilled to wear a mask because it was a chance to cover up my scars, to be like everyone else for a night. It definitely hid my scars, but it also looked dramatic, stylish and a little bit mysterious.

"Heven, you're date is here," Mom called up the stairs.

"Coming!" I called, checking the mask one last time.

It was the same color blue as my dress. It molded perfectly around the side of my face with soft feathers tipped in silver, curling around my cheek and eye. It managed to cover every inch of my ugliness and highlighted the blue of my eyes and the creaminess of my skin.

Like I said, I was hot.

With a spin I grabbed my bracelet off my dresser and left my room, practically running down the stairs.

Sam was waiting.

When I descended the stairs a hush fell over the room. I realize that there was only mom and Sam, but I swear it felt like every single noise, every single movement stopped for a few precious seconds. How could I have ever doubted my beauty, my confidence…my self-worth?

"Heven, honey, you look beautiful." My mother gasped in a hushed tone. "You're just stunning."

"Thanks, Mom," I said, but I didn't look her way. I was too busy looking at Sam.

His whiskey colored eyes widened at the sight of me and I saw him draw a breath that he never let out. The hand to his side flexed, almost as if he ached to touch me. I liked to imagine that he did.

The silk of my dress brushed against my ankles as I stepped down off the last step and Sam closed the distance between us in two great strides. But then he stopped, not touching me the way I imagined. Instead he stared, those honey gold eyes never leaving me.

"You two are just gorgeous together. Let me get a photo." Mom ran from the room to get a camera, but I barely noticed.

"Hi," I murmured.

"Hi," he said, clearing his throat. "You look…" his words fell away and I saw his Adam's apple bob against the collar of his shirt. "I've never seen anyone so beautiful."

"You clean up good yourself." I blushed. "Is that for me?" I asked, looking down at the clear box that held a flower.

"Yes." He fumbled with the lid, having to try twice to get it open. I smiled. It was the first time I had ever seen him fumble at anything. Usually he was so sure of himself. Finally he lifted out a delicate flower. It was a white lily with blue and silver ribbons. I held out my arm and he slid it over my wrist. It was perfect.

Mom rushed back in the room with a camera and another clear box. "Oh! I forgot," I said, rushing over to take the box. "Thanks, Mom."

Mom snapped pictures as I leaned in close to pin the boutonniere on the jacket of his tux. It was also a white Lily with blue and silver ribbon. I couldn't help but breathe deeply of his deep, natural scent. I was so proud to call him mine.

We posed for several pictures and for once, I didn't mind being in front of the camera. With my head held high I smiled while Sam placed his arm around my waist. When we were finished, Mom reminded me of my curfew, and then Sam whisked me out the door.

It was the start of what I hoped would be a very memorable evening.

He couldn't keep his eyes off me. Or his hands. It was amazing the number of ways he could find to touch me in some small way: his palm at the small of my back, knuckles across my cheek, and his fingers playing with the ends of my hair. If this night was a dream, I prayed I'd never wake up. He pulled the truck into one of the last parking spaces and shut off the engine. His eyes were unreadable and delicious as he leaned toward me, brushing his arm across my lap to open my door.

"Stay put," he whispered, withdrawing his arm. "I'll be right there to help you."

And he was, placing his hands at my waist and lifting me from the truck's cab. "You're so beautiful I can barely breathe tonight."

I didn't respond because I couldn't breathe either. These last few weeks had been like a fairytale.

He stood me on my feet and leaned in close. "Your heart is racing."

I nodded. The way he smelled, the heat of his body…I was surrounded by him. I leaned back, mere inches, to rest against the side of the truck, settling in.

"Careful," he warned, slipping his hands between me and the truck. "Don't want to get that dress dirty."

At the moment I didn't care.

"Ready to go in?"

I shook my head.

He laughed softly and dipped his head. His lips were like they always were – warm, soft and giving. His breath was sweet like a candy only he knew about, and his tongue was just the right combination of rough and gentle. I moaned and wrapped my arms around his neck, kissing him back, hoping that maybe my kisses were just as sweet to him.

"Careful," he warned a second time. "Kiss me like that again and your dress may not make it."

I blushed, secretly pleased, and pulled back. "Can I get my bag?" I motioned at the door.

He opened the door, and I reached in to grab my handbag. Out of it I pulled my pink gloss and reapplied it. He watched as if fascinated by my movements. When I was done he asked, "Where is your whistle? You aren't wearing it."

I smiled. "It's in my bag. It didn't match my dress."

He smiled and offered his arm. "Ready?"

"One thing?" I held out the bracelet he gave me. "Clasp this on me?"

He took it and did as I asked, his fingers checking the clasp twice, even though it hadn't come loose once since he'd fixed it. I could have had my mother do this for me at home, but I wanted him to do it. I liked the intimacy I felt between us when he put it where it belonged. When he was satisfied that it was closed, he leaned to press a kiss on the inside of my wrist. Goosebumps broke out across my arms. He looked up. "Cold?"

"No."

He smiled, offered his arm and walked me toward the party. At the door he moved to open it for me, but I stopped him. Nerves were making their way to the surface, taking away my earlier elation.

"What's the matter?" he asked, leading me off to the side.

"I..." I didn't know how to explain to him that for the past ten months I hadn't walked into any building or room without pulling up a hood or trying to hide. I almost felt like I didn't know how to enter this ball with confidence. "Is my mask on straight?"

His eyes softened. "Your mask is fine. You're the best looking woman here."

"How do you know?" I teased, "We're not even inside yet."

"I don't have to be inside to know this. Besides did you see that girl that just went in? She had toilet paper stuck to the bottom of her shoe." He laughed.

I laughed too. "Why were you looking at her shoes?"

"Because there was a huge wad of toilet paper hanging from it." His eyes twinkled as he laughed.

And just like that my nerves vanished. I was merely a girl going to a dance with a guy who was incredible.

"I'm ready," I told him as I slipped my hand into his. As long as he was with me I would be okay. When we entered I couldn't help but brace myself for whispers and stares, tucking myself close to Sam's shoulder, trying to hide.

"Not tonight," he whispered, pulling me from his side and taking my hand instead. "You're far too beautiful to hide."

I blinked once at his words, shocked that he would take away my comfort. Then something horrifying happened.

People came running toward us.

Sam stiffened, just slightly.

All my old friends from cheerleading and their dates stood close, staring. I wanted to run and hide, but we were surrounded. Sam squeezed my hand in reassurance.

"Hey guys." I meekly said.

Chaos erupted.

"OMG, that dress is gorgeous!"

"Who did your hair?"

"Who did your makeup?"

They were all talking over each other, reaching out to finger the satin of my dress and the curled ends of my hair. I was shocked. No one had given me this much attention since…well *Before*.

I smiled a genuine smile and stepped forward, out of Sam's shadow. Just like that my old confidence came back to me. I gracefully accepted their compliments and dished out my own just like I used to. When everyone fell quiet, and I was about to turn back to Sam, Amber cleared her throat. "I think I speak for us all when I say it's really good to have you back."

"T-thanks."

"I mean, we were all really worried. We knew you wanted space, but it's nice to have our friend back."

I didn't know what to say. They'd stayed away from me all those months because they thought I wanted space? They weren't grossed out by my face? They hadn't thought I was a freak! Amber was still staring at me, waiting for a response, so I said, "I'm ready to have my life back." I couldn't keep a large smile from taking over my face. My friends had always been my friends! The reason they had stayed away was because I pushed them away. Those baggy hoodies, my curtain of hair – I used it as a wall. I made myself unapproachable; it had all been me. My friends were far more accepting than I gave them credit for.

Joy burst through me, and I felt like I might be glowing. I could have it all again. And I could have Sam. I felt so amazing…like I was soaring. I made everyone promise to stop by our table before I let anyone go, and when they did move away they were all smiling.

I turned back to Sam, still smiling. "Did you hear that?"

He stroked his hand across my neck and nodded. His eyes were a little sad.

"Heven?" Kimber gasped from the entrance way. "OMG!"

I turned to face her as she rushed over. "Holy crap! You look awesome!"

"Thanks!" I said, enjoying her compliment and accepting it. I deserved it.

"And so damn skinny. You bitch."

Beside me Sam stiffened, I squeezed his hand and laughed. "You look beautiful tonight, Kimber."

She was wearing a gorgeous designer gown in gold. Her red hair was up in a mass of curls, and she carried a glittery gold mask that had a handle on one side. She lifted it to her face and peered out of it. "I know."

Beside her, Cole rolled his eyes. He was wearing a mask that looked like the one the guy in *Phantom of the Opera* wore. That made me realize that Sam wasn't wearing a mask at all…

"Hey, Hev. Lookin' good," Cole grinned.

Kimber elbowed him. He grinned again. I laughed, and it felt good.

Kimber hooked her arm through my free one and began walking us all toward the ballroom. "Come on everyone," she called. "Heven needs a few pieces of cake. When I stand next to her I look fat."

The ballroom was spectacular. The setting actually made me think of *Phantom of the Opera* in a way. The hotel was old and carried an authentic charm. The lighting was low, and large candelabras, dripping white wax, were centered every table. It should have looked messy, but it didn't. The DJ was set up in the far corner with large swags of golden fabric draping from the ceiling to the floor, partially concealing his booth. Refreshment tables lined the left side of the room with a large punch fountain dominating the center of one round table. There was also a huge white cake adorned with iced roses in all shades of red. The center of the room was a giant wooden dance floor where many couples were already dancing. Round tables were scattered about the room, each one draped in a pale gold tablecloth.

"This place looks great," Kimber said as we approached our table. "This must have cost a fortune."

"It does look good," I agreed as Sam pulled out a chair for me.

"We're going to dance," Kimber said, pulling Cole toward the floor.

I turned toward Sam and smiled. He pulled his chair so close that my knees bumped his as I turned. He leaned in and kissed me softly.

"The feathers on that mask tickle."

"I noticed you aren't wearing a mask. How come?"

"I get tired of wearing a mask all the time," he murmured.

"What?" His words confused me.

He blinked and leaned in. "I didn't want you to confuse me with anyone else tonight, so I chose to keep my face revealed to you all times."

He was so romantic and charming. But still, what he'd said before…why do guys always have to be so cryptic?

He palmed my face in his hands and drew me near. "Kiss me, beautiful."

"You guys need to get a room," Kimber griped from behind. Sam drew away and looked into my eyes, smiling tenderly. What had we been talking about?

"Speaking of…" Cole drew a key card out of his pocket. "I got us one."

"You did?" Kimber gasped, grabbing at the card, but Cole was too fast, tucking it back into his pocket.

"It's for later," he told her.

She kissed him. Kimber and Cole had taken the 'next step' in their relationship last summer. I used to think that they were way too young, that she hadn't been ready. But now…

I looked into Sam's whiskey eyes and thought that maybe if it was with the right person, maybe, age was just a number. I knew for sure that no one could ever make me feel like Sam, even if I lived for a hundred years. The words I knew he waited for were heavy on my tongue; I wanted to let them out right then.

"Yes?" he asked, leaning in, as if he knew what was on my lips.

I opened my mouth. "Dance with me."

I thought I saw a quick flash of sorrow in his eyes, but then he was standing, holding out his hand and leading me toward the dance floor. On cue, a soft, slow song began to play. His body molded against mine in a way that made my skin burn. I looked around sure that one of the chaperones would come and tell us to separate. No one came, and I sank even deeper into his warmth. If I wasn't careful, I knew that I could completely lose myself in him. Something told me that was already happening. A stray thought whispered that perhaps that could be a bad thing, but I pushed the thought away. I'd think about that later, not tonight.

"Are you having a good time?" he whispered in my ear.

"The best."

"I want this night to be perfect."

"It is." Again, the words *I love you* were heavy on my tongue. I could just lean up and whisper them into his ear…

He stiffened and stood a little straighter, gazing around the ballroom.

"Sam?"

He stayed that way for several long moments, then finally, relaxed and looked down. He smiled ruefully. "Sorry, I thought I heard something."

I frowned. All I could hear was the music.

"Did you want to say something?" he asked. The alluring hazel of his eyes almost, but not quite, recaptured the previous moment.

Slowly I shook my head. "Never mind."

"You sure?" he pressed.

I nodded. "Later, okay?"

He gave in, and I laid my head against his chest. Our moment would come soon and nothing would spoil it.

The Hate

I'm sick of watching. Of waiting. I am always so close…but never close enough. She thinks she's something tonight. Everyone is just fawning all over her. It makes me sick. I can see the smugness in her eyes and in the way she walks. She thinks tonight is going to be perfect.

It's not.

He's thinks he's won, but it isn't over.

He's wrong.

It all ends tonight. It's time she knows who lover boy really is. Little girl's dreams are going to be shattered, and I am going to enjoy it.

The Hope

I sensed a change in the air. Tonight she would be put to the test. I feared she wasn't ready.

"There's no way she'll accept him."

I turned and took in his bleak, sad face. With a caress of my fingers, harmony and peace went to him, hopefully wrapping him in comfort. "Pray she does, or all could be lost."

"I wish she didn't have to be involved."

"Trust Him. He knows what He is doing. Trust in love."

He nodded and came to join me at the water.

"Let us watch," I murmured.

Gentle waves rippled the surface of the water. Images formed and solidified. A beauty and her beloved danced...

We waited.

Heven

The night passed by in a haze of dancing and laughter. I reconnected with friends I thought I'd lost, and slowly, I learned to accept myself a little more. I hoped that come morning, when the mask I wore was gone, that I would still feel the same. Sam never left my side, except once to get some punch and cake, which he was currently feeding me. It was decadent, and I couldn't remember the last time I'd enjoyed food more. He tried to fork another bite into my already-full mouth, and I shook my head and stole the fork from him.

As I chewed I pointed at him with my fork, scooped up another big bite and held it out. He opened obediently, watching me as I fed him. His eyes flickered pure gold like they sometimes did.

"You guys totally need to get a room," Kimber groaned.

I kept my eyes on Sam and smiled. His eyes flashed once more. I marveled in the fact that it no longer frightened me, I liked it. It made me feel...wanted.

"Are you ready to go?" he asked, his smoky voice sending shivers up my spine.

"Yes." I glanced at my cell. It was eleven. "I have an hour before I have to be home. Can we go somewhere and talk?"

He nodded, reached into his pocket and pulled out a key card. It looked identical to the one Cole had. My breath caught. Did he think...?

He leaned close and whispered in my ear, "Relax. I got it in case we wanted to be alone tonight."

I pulled back, slightly shaken. I was ready to tell him that I loved him, but I didn't think I was ready for a hotel room and all the things that went with it.

"Heven?"

I shook my head.

Understanding lit his eyes, and he grasped my hand. "I didn't get it for *that*."

I lifted a brow.

"I promise. I know you aren't ready." He cleared his throat. "Neither am I."

Instead of being relieved, I was hurt. Why wouldn't he want to? What *guy* didn't want to? Maybe I was getting too attached to him; maybe he wasn't as attached to me as he said.

He let out a low sound, almost like a growl, and pulled me forward. "It isn't what you think. I love you, and of course I want you."

"Then, why?" I whispered.

"I just want you to get to know me a little better. I want you to be ready."

I nodded, accepting this.

"So will you come with me? To talk? I promise I won't pressure you." He kept his sometimes-golden gaze steady on mine. His eyes were so gorgeous, almost hypnotizing.

"I will," I vowed.

He smiled.

"Let me go to the ladies room first, okay?"

"I'll walk you," he said, standing.

"I think I can find my way," I joked.

"I know. You're just so beautiful I'm afraid someone might try and steal you away." He smiled.

"Well in that case," I said, holding out my arm. He took it and tucked it beneath his and off we went. The trip to the bathroom was stalled by many people that we stopped to laugh and talk with. Then a slow song came on and Sam pulled me out for one last dance. I knew I would never forget how it felt to be in his arms. Finally, we made it near the restroom where Sam was distracted by a group of waving guys. He didn't want to go to them, but I shooed him away. "It's only the bathroom, Sam, I'll be fine." He nodded once and went to join the laughing group as I turned to slip inside.

The inside of the tiny room was cold. Clearly the staff had the AC cranked up in the ballroom, making this much smaller room freezing. I went to the sink to check my makeup and mask. I took out my compact to quickly dust away the light shine on my nose. When I was finished, I put away the case and washed my hands. I heard the stall door behind me open then bang shut, but I didn't bother to look up. When I did, there was a masked woman standing directly behind me. She was standing much closer than necessary, and I moved to try and put some distance between us.

She wouldn't let me.

When I stepped she stepped, where I went she went. My hands began to shake.

"Excuse me," I told her, trying to get by once more.

"He should have done his job, and then I wouldn't have to be here right now." Her dark red lips moved beneath a black mask that looked like lace. Her raven hair was bound up with a huge bunch of black feathers sticking out of the up-do.

"What?" I tried not to sound intimidated.

"How much do you know about your precious Sam?" the woman practically snarled. I watched in horror as she reached out and grabbed my arm. Hard. I looked down at her bronze hand grasping my thin, pale arm. Her nails looked like sharp, red talons, ready to draw blood.

"It's time, little girl. Time you knew the truth."

I had no idea what she was talking about and I didn't want to know. I opened my mouth to scream, and she pinned me with a hard stare. "Make a noise, and I will slaughter you. Then I'll slaughter him."

Sam! She was threatening Sam! My head spun with what this woman could possibly want.

Just then the door burst open, and Kimber came striding in. "Heven, why didn't you tell me you were coming in here?" She stopped short when she saw the woman grabbing me.

"What's going on?" Kimber demanded.

The woman dropped my arm like I'd burned her and leaned in to whisper "Get rid of her. Or I will."

I believed her, and I was terrified. Why would she threaten to kill me? To kill Sam? Was this some kind of sick joke? My skin broke out in a clammy sweat and glanced to the stall she'd come out of. *Had she been waiting in there for me? Who was this woman and why was she saying these things?*

"Kimmie," I said, using the name only Cole called her. I prayed it would be enough to let her know that something wasn't right. "Would you mind grabbing my clutch? I left it at the table."

Kimber smoothed out the gloss she was applying and hardly glanced at me. "Sure. Be right back." She walked out without even a nervous glance.

Not even two seconds later Sam burst through the bathroom door with a wild look on his face. When his eyes landed on the woman and her hand grabbing my arm, he let out a roar and lunged. In one smooth moment I was behind him, pressed up against the door. And he was leaping at the woman.

"When I tell you to – run!" he called over his shoulder.

What he did next shocked me.

He punched the woman right in the face.

She fell backwards, but caught herself against the wall and stood. "Ask him about his secrets!" She yelled at me. "Make him tell you what he really is!"

With that she practically climbed up the wall and disappeared out the tiny open window.

I stood there in shock, my mouth hanging open. Then I started to shake.

Sam ran over to me, his eyes sweeping my entire body. "What did she do to you? Are you hurt?"

"She didn't hurt me." I said, a strange feeling settling over me. I looked into his eyes, so guarded and wary.

She might not have hurt me, but he was about to.

I felt it down in my bones.

Kimber picked this moment to rush back in the bathroom. "Are you okay? What happened?"

I straightened and turned. I prayed the smile I plastered on my face looked real. "Sorry about that. She was just getting a little too pushy. I think she might have been drunk."

"Some people have no class." Kimber said, buying my story. "And who told her that outfit looked good? And where the heck did she go?"

"I have no idea." I said, fear pumping through me. "But thanks for that."

"Anytime." Kimber smiled. "Cole and I are leaving."

"Sam and I are too," I said, trying to sound normal.

"You okay?" Kimber asked, turning to look at me. "You look pale."

"I'm fine, just tired."

She nodded. "I'll call you tomorrow?"

"Sure." I said brightly.

She went out the door, leaving me alone with Sam. I dropped my act and looked at him, about to ask what was going on. "We have to go." He said, grabbing my arm and rushing from the room. We got a few stares when people saw him coming out of the girl's bathroom, but he didn't seem to notice.

"Sam?" I began.

He was busy towing me toward our table to get our stuff. His eyes traveled the room and never stopped. I planted my feet on the floor, and he swung around to face me.

"That woman said you had secrets. She said that you lie. Do you know what this is about?" I asked a tremor in my voice. I was half afraid of the answer.

He aged about ten years right before my eyes. He nodded miserably. "Yeah."

"What's going on?"

"My time has run out."

Sam

Heven was in her element. It was something to see. I had a feeling that the way she was acting tonight was a glimpse at the way she was before I came into her life. So vibrant and real. She had this sort of charm, this way of making people feel good about themselves, and people wanted to be around her.

In a way it made me sad. Not sad that she was coming back into herself, but sad that I had been involved in taking that away from her to begin with. My thoughts drifted to the body in the bottom of the lake: Andi. Tonight should have been her prom night as well. Instead, she was alone in a watery grave, and there were people out there mourning over her status as missing. The police had been searching to no avail. I had heard some talk that they were going to list her as a runaway.

Music flowed out of the ballroom, it was something upbeat and loud. I heard Heven laugh at something her friends were saying, and I thought how odd it was that I was standing in this place thinking about a dead body.

I pushed the dark thoughts aside as the evening went on, determined to have a good time. All the masks made it hard to relax. Every time someone drew near I would have to decide if they were friendly or not, if we knew them or not. Word of Heven's mood, and I suspect the way she glowed, drew people to us like a magnet. I hadn't realized how popular she had been *Before*. It was almost intimidating. How could I compete with all of these people? How long until she figures out that she can do better?

I squelched those thoughts as well, telling myself that Heven's feelings for me weren't the issue right now, keeping her alive was. Hopefully, someday when I removed the threat to her life she would be able to tell me that she loved me. Words I hadn't heard in so long. My eyes scanned the crowd once more, searching for anyone suspicious. Damn these masks and formal attire. Thankfully, I had a profound sense of smell, and I didn't catch any familiar scents from my roommates so, for now, we were safe.

Turns out Heven isn't much of a dancer, which comes as a bit of a relief to me. I didn't dance. It made me feel like an idiot out there trying to move to some impossible beat. But I did like the slow dancing…I smiled at the thought of allowing my hands to roam just a little bit lower on her back as we moved.

The slow dances were much less common than the fast dances so when the upbeat music was playing we mingled in the crowd (by Heven's request) and made a stop at the giant punch fountain. It seemed like a silly thing to me. If I wanted a drink why not just pour it out of a pitcher into a glass? Instead we stood in a long line (who knew a punch fountain could be such a draw?) and waited with clear plastic cups in hand. When it was your turn you were supposed to let the punch flow down into your cup until it was full. The liquid splashed and splattered, and I thought it was annoying, but then Heven laughed at the silly thing, clearly pleased.

Maybe punch fountains weren't that annoying after all.

The food was good. I was always hungry, and there was a lot to eat. Heven seemed amazed at the amount of food I could put down and watched as I shoveled in a couple of plates of mini sandwiches, cookies and fruit. She sampled a few things off my plate, but otherwise sipped her punch while socializing with the crowd that surrounded us.

When a slow song came on I pulled her out onto the darkened dance floor and slid my arms around her.

"Are you having a good time?" I whispered in her ear.

"The best."

"I want this night to be perfect."

"It is." She said, gazing at me like she wanted to say something more. My stomach dipped a little with what I hoped it might be. She rose up on tip toe…

The sound of a muffled bang caught my attention, and I stiffened, looking around for the source of the noise.

A large, swinging door opened to the room the caterers were using and I saw a whole box of trays had fallen to the ground.

"Sam?"

I swept my eyes around the ballroom one last time, making certain I didn't sense any threat before I looked down. "Sorry, I thought I heard something."

She frowned, and I thought she might ask what was wrong so I spoke before she could.

"Did you want to say something?"

"Never mind."

"You sure?" I was an idiot. I ruined the moment for nothing, and now it was gone.

"Later, okay?" she asked, her blue eyes wanting understanding.

I pulled her close and let the moment go. Hopefully, I would get another chance to hear the words that I thought she might be ready to say. I thought of the keycard in my pocket and wondered if I took the chance of getting her alone that maybe she would say them. Then everything would be different. If I knew she loved me, maybe I could tell her the truth, maybe she would be able to look past what I am.

The rest of the night passed in a blur. I couldn't quite relax after that ridiculous scare I had earlier. I found it hard to believe that the monster would leave us alone for one night. Maybe there was another lead on what we had been looking for. Maybe it would keep Heven safe for one more night.

An hour before her curfew, we were sitting at our table feeding each other cake. I decided to take the chance and show her the keycard to the room I got. At worst she would rebuff my attempt to be alone, but at least I would have somewhere to shower without wondering who would come home and if there would be a fight. I pretty much had been living out of my truck for months. I despised the people I lived with but felt locked in to my life. How could I leave the only people who knew what it was like to be a freak? Until I had found them I lived alone – I hadn't been frightened of myself, but I was scared that no one would ever accept me. My own parents wouldn't accept me. Isn't it better to be accepted by someone than no one at all?

But it had become harder and harder to stay with people who had no thought to the people they hurt. I was grateful that they had taught me the things I needed to know about myself, but I was a little older now. I was stronger. I had my own path that I wanted to follow, a path that was leading me away from them.

"Heven?" I asked – her response to the keycard hadn't been as positive as I would have liked.

She shook her head, a fine blush spreading over her cheeks.

I realized then that she thought I was asking her for something she wasn't prepared to give.

Sex.

I grasped her hand. "I didn't get it for *that*."

If she threw herself at me right now, I definitely wouldn't turn her down. I wanted to laugh but didn't think that it would be appropriate. I looked into her blue eyes and realized she didn't believe me. Crap, what girl would?

"I promise. I know you aren't ready." I cleared my throat, not really knowing what to say. "Neither am I." Just because I wanted to do it didn't mean we should do it.

My words seemed to have the opposite affect than what I was hoping. I thought she would be relieved to know that I didn't plan on pressuring her for sex. Instead she seemed disappointed. Could she possibly think I wouldn't want her? Man, girls were tough to figure out sometimes. "It isn't what you think. I love you, and of course I want you."

"Then, why?" she whispered.

"I just want you to get to know me a little better. I want you to be ready." I want her to know *all* of me, which is exactly why I got this room.

"So will you come with me? To talk? I promise I won't pressure you." I tried to keep the hope and nerves out of my eyes while I waited for her answer.

Her soft acceptance sent joy through me, and I smiled.

I insisted on escorting her to the ladies room, still uneasy and not wanting to let her out of my sight for long. I thought she might protest, and she did, so I ended up next to the bathroom pretending to socialize.

I really wanted to be right next to her – for her to stay in sight. There was something inside me, telling me something wasn't right. But I had no choice, so I stood as close to the ladies' room as I could, waiting for her to come out. A couple guys that I knew, mainly due to my relationship with Heven, called out to me, and I hesitated to walk over and say 'Hi'. It was only a few steps, but I wasn't sure I should even go that far. Then Kimber walked by smiling and went into the bathroom. I figured that at least Heven wouldn't be alone so I went to see what the guys were laughing about.

Seconds later Kimber came out of the bathroom with a worried look in her face. The door was just closing behind her, and I caught a glimpse of black. She began to motion to me, but I was already moving, bursting into the ladies room.

She was there. How had I missed her? I looked up and saw the open window and realized that she must have been hiding in here all night. I didn't smell her because the heavy door blocked her scent, and we hadn't been over here at all except for now.

Damn, I was stupid. And I may have just cost Heven her life.

Heven was frightened, her eyes were wide with fear and her skin had gone white. I lunged at the pair, snatching Heven away and putting myself in between her and this bitch. I was beyond angry. Angry at myself for missing her hiding in here and angry at her for being such a devious creature.

"When I tell you to – run!" I yelled at Heven, unsure how ugly things were about to get. I didn't want her in here; I didn't want her to see what I was capable of.

I couldn't hold in my anger, though, and I threw out my fist punching the bitch right in the face. I didn't care that she was a womanI'd kill her right then if I could.

She fell backwards but caught herself against the wall and stood. "Ask him about his secrets!" She yelled to Heven. I caught the evil glint in her eyes "Make him tell you what he really is!"

Then she escaped out the tiny open window. I realized then that she hadn't come here to kill Heven. She had come here to tell her my secrets to drive a wedge between Heven and her protector. Now I was going to have to tell her. I couldn't lie anymore. I wondered if this would be my last memory of actually being with Heven.

I rushed to her side, worried that she might be hurt. "What did she do to you? Are you hurt?"

"She didn't hurt me." A wary look crossed her eyes, and she looked at me like I was a stranger.

You know me. Deep down, you know who I really am. Please accept me, don't push me away.

Kimber picked this moment to rush back in the bathroom. "Are you okay? What happened?"

To my surprise Heven pulled it together. She knew that there was something going on here, she knew that I had been lying. Yet, she lied for me. Maybe there was hope after all.

"Sorry about that. She was just getting a little too pushy. I think she might have been drunk."

"Some people have no class." Kimber said, oblivious to the undercurrents circling the room. "And who told her that outfit looked good?"

I tuned out the rest of their conversation; my head was spinning. What was I going to say? How much would I tell her? What would her reaction be to who I really was? I've never once told anyone what I am – I've never had to. I was alone until I met the others. I didn't have to tell them anything, because they already knew. How did you tell someone that you were a monster? That you weighed bodies down in the lake and had roommates who hid severed body parts out of the prying eyes of normal people? How did you tell someone that you've been stalking them, that you lurk in the shadows, and that if it wasn't for you, their face would be whole, and no one would be trying to kill you?

My chest felt tight because I couldn't do it…but I had to. I was going to mess this up, and she was going to hate me.

I looked up just as Kimber was leaving the bathroom; Heven and I were left alone. "We have to go." I told her, grabbing her arm and leading her from the bathroom. I was almost positive that she wouldn't be coming back tonight. She got what she came for. She blew my whole world apart, and now I had to pick up the pieces. But still, I wasn't about to hang around and be caught by surprise again. We got a few stares when people saw us coming out of the girl's bathroom, but I didn't care. These people were the least of my worries.

"Sam?" Heven's voice was quiet and laced with uncertainty and fear. She was already pulling away.

I turned away, not wanting to see the look in her eyes, to see what it would like when she turned me away.

"That woman said you had secrets. She said that you lie. Do you know what this is about?"

I thought about making something up, to spin an elaborate tale. But I was exhausted, I was tired of lying, of wearing a mask. I decided then that even though I had no clue how to say it, the truth was going to come out tonight. Maybe she would give me a chance to explain. Unfortunately, I didn't think that she would be proclaiming her love for me tonight. The loss of that potential moment cut me like a sword.

With a heavy heart I answered her question. "Yeah."

"What's going on?"
"My time has run out."

Chapter Fourteen

Heven

"You're scaring me," I said for the twentieth time.

"I'm sorry," he answered for the twentieth time.

The elevator dinged open, and I moved to step out, but he caught me and pushed himself out into the hall ahead of me. Did he think that woman was going to come back and find us? A violent shudder ran up my back at the thought. She was scary. There had been something in her eyes that wasn't right – unbalanced.

Sam towed me along beside him, stopping a few feet down the hall and swiping his key, all the while keeping his attention on our surroundings. The door buzzed, and he shoved me into the room, snapping the locks behind us.

Unease began churning in my belly, and I felt panic rising up in my chest. I fought it back –going over by the window, hoping the view outside would calm me. It didn't. I was going to have a panic attack if I couldn't get some air…

Sam's strong arms circled me from behind and he pulled me into his chest. "Easy," he murmured, stroking my hair. "You're safe. I won't let anyone hurt you."

I trembled in his arms and fought for control. He kept murmuring, gently rocking me back and forth. To my relief I began to calm. I could think again.

What was going on? Who was that woman, and how did Sam know her? All the previous warnings that I sometimes felt with Sam came back to me, and I felt foolish for ignoring them. I stiffened in his embrace, and with a sigh, he let me go. I turned to face him. I took a moment to study him, to memorize the angles and plains of his face, to remember the way his shaggy blond hair fell over his ears and the exact color of his eyes. I needed to remember these things. Because something deep down told me that I might never see him again.

Pain. I thought I understood pain when I was in the hospital after the attack. I thought I knew it the first time I went out in public wearing my scar. While those things hurt, this was a far deeper kind of pain. If I lost him, I know I would never forget, never escape this pain. Compared to the scars on my face the ones this pain would leave inside would be, by far, more horrifying and more traumatizing.

"Sam?"

"It's pretty bad."

"What is?"

"I had hoped…"

"Hoped?"

Despair showed in his eyes. "That if you loved me it might make a difference."

I do love you! I wanted to shout, but I couldn't. Something had changed.

"What I'm going to tell you is unbelievable."

I swallowed.

"Will you give me the chance to explain it all to you?"

I nodded.

"Promise me, Heven."

"I promise."

He shot forward and seized me up and before I could protest his lips were on mine, and I was instantly reminded of all the things I loved about him, of the safety and security I felt when he was near. But there was also something about this kiss that was different – it was desperate and a little sad.

He tore himself away and put some distance between us.

I put a hand to my tender lips.

"I know what happened to you."

My hand fell away. "What do you mean?"

"Your attack. I know who did it."

"You know who attacked me? You know why my face is like this?" Denial – sharp and strong bit through me. He didn't know. How could he? If he did he would have known something, he would have told me. He knew how much that night haunted me. He knew that I looked over my shoulder everywhere I went. He knew that I was frightened of every shadow that appeared when the sun went down.

He nodded. "There are people out there who aren't completely human."

"Why are you saying these things?" My head was swimming; he was saying things that made no sense. First, he says that he knew what happened to me, and then he says something completely ridiculous. Was he trying to be cruel? If he knew how my face got destroyed why wouldn't he just say it? This is not funny. This is not a game.

The hazel of his eyes smoldered, and I couldn't look away, even though I was completely terrified. "Some people can't help how they are born."

I hated the tortured look on his face, the overwhelming sense of loss that was permeating the room. I wanted to go to him. To touch him. To feel him. But I was too afraid to get that close. He was scaring me.

"I made choices that hurt you. Choices I regret…" his voice broke. "I never asked for any of this."

"If you know what happened to me – then spit it out! Tell me!" The only way he would know about my attack was if he was there…if he had been involved. I wanted to gag. He couldn't have done this to me. I trusted him.

"It was my family." His eyes begged for forgiveness.

"Your family?" I squeaked. My mind was racing and I couldn't form a thought. He never talked about his family; he'd said he didn't have one.

He'd lied.

"Yes." He pushed his hands through his hair.

I shook my head trying to clear it, he wasn't making sense. "I don't understand." He couldn't have done this to me. The marks on my skin were made by an animal. I was almost positive. In my dream something heavy and warm had pressed me down. I felt sharpness of claws and heard the inhuman sounds it made. No, I hadn't been attacked by Sam. I had been attacked by an animal.

"I'm not like you," he bit out.

"You're not?" An echo of his earlier words floated through my head. *There are people out there who aren't completely human.* I swallowed past the bile rising in my throat. I wanted to sit down, but sitting made me feel vulnerable. I couldn't let myself feel any more vulnerable right now that I already did.

"No. I'm different."

"Are you telling me that you aren't human, Sam?" The words felt wrong coming out of my mouth. How could he not be? I'd felt his heartbeat. I'd touched his warm, rough skin and felt his chest expand with air when he cradled me against him.

He flew across the room and grabbed the mask on my face and tore it away. I flinched and stumbled away, his sudden anger and violence scared me. I stared at the pieces of the broken mask as they fell to the floor. I had a feeling that my heart was going to look like my mask very soon. "They did that to you!" Sam yelled. "That woman in the bathroom, she did that! She isn't human. Neither am I!"

Any other time I would have cowered. I put a finger up to my puckered scars. The source of all my pain. "You did this to me? How?"

He unbuttoned his tux jacket and tossed it on the bed. Then he undid his tie, shirt, white T-shirt and belt, tossing everything on the bed.

"What are you doing?" I couldn't help but look at the door; he was standing in my way.

His pants joined his other clothes, and I began to panic once more. I backed up as far away from him as I could get. Why was he taking off his clothes? What was he going to do to me? Too soon, my back hit the wall. I reached around behind me and grabbed fistfuls of the heavy curtains that framed the large sliding door. I was searching for anything that would anchor me – that would keep me from collapsing in fear. Then it dawned on me that I should be looking for a weapon.

The very fact that I needed a weapon to protect myself from Sam was enough to make me hysterical. I released the curtains and grabbed up a heavy brass lamp from the desk. I held it up high, over my head. "Don't come near me. I'll use this."

The thought of hitting him with anything made hot tears spill over onto my cheeks. But I would do it. I was tired of being scared all the time, and in that instant, I decided I would never be helpless ever again.

"Just watch for a second," he pleaded with me, making no move to come closer. He pretended that he didn't even see me wielding a lamp. Was I that unthreatening then? Another violent shudder wracked my body, and I nearly dropped the lamp.

I glanced to the side at the sliding door. It led out onto a small balcony. I wondered how far down it was and if I would survive the jump.

"Don't run." He said, his voice going deeper than it ever had before.

I shook my head. Given the first chance I would run like hell.

"I mean it, Heven. Please, stay and give me a chance to explain."

I nodded. I couldn't help but stare at the strong angles of his body. The rippling bronze muscles of his chest and arms. He was so utterly beautiful. How could anyone so gorgeous not be human – not be made by God? I forced my thoughts away from his beauty. Beautiful or not, if he came at me, I was going to have to hurt him. I couldn't let my feelings get in the way of my safety.

Some strange sounds drew my attention, and I looked over to Sam. Or…what I thought was Sam. He was hunched over, his face pulled taunt in pain, and it seemed as though his body was tearing itself apart.

There were horrible sounds. A sharp, popping sound that echoed through my ears, and every time something popped, his limbs seemed to sag lower from their sockets. There was a terrible ripping sound, and Sam arched his back, the muscles in his jaw flexing. My hand flew to my mouth as I stared in horror as his body ripped itself apart. I whimpered; the sound was terribly weak compared to the sounds of Sam's destroyed body.

He dropped onto hands and knees, his arms looking like Jell-O. This weakness made me wonder if maybe I would be able to escape. Then, he looked at me. His eyes were hard and glowing. The gold that sometimes streaked through his eyes seemed to catch on fire and light up. It burned through his stare and his eyes changed…turned. They weren't Sam's eyes anymore, they were the eyes of an animal – a predator.

I screamed and threw the lamp. It hit the bed and bounced away. I ran toward the glass doors and began tugging on the handle, trying to open them. They were locked. I was trapped. *Think!* I began searching for the lock, trying to see where to unlatch the door.

"You promised!" Sam yelled. His voice was not his own. It was deep and the words vibrated my bones. "Wait!"

The last word he yelled came out as an inhuman growl and I froze. I recognized that sound. I'd heard it in my dreams. Slowly, on shaking knees, I turned.

Sam stared at me, and the rest of his form seemed to fall away. His face transformed, elongating, widening. He made a sound like he was in pain and his back arched up like a cat. He stretched out his arm – only it wasn't an arm any longer.

It was a paw.

And it was covered in black fur.

Razor sharp claws shot out of the ends and flexed, ready to attack.

Black fur seemed to spout over his entire body, and I watched – terrified – yet morbidly fascinated as his ears disappeared and sprouted up higher on the top of his head. They stood up in angry triangles, reminding me of my old neighbor's Doberman pinscher.

Then his ears flattened against a giant head and a horrible sound ripped from between its teeth. Teeth that were so long that they stuck out from beneath its black gums and hung forth in promise of harm.

"Shit!" I screamed and renewed my search of the lock with force. I finally found it and yanked, the door giving way and the cool night air rushed in around me. I tripped running out the door, my dress catching beneath me. I tugged at it and got up, reaching for the balcony rails. My hands closed around them, and I sobbed in relief. I didn't even bother to look down because I didn't care how long the drop was. I would take my chances.

I would rather die down there than be eaten alive up here.

I hurried to climb on the railing as I heard a commotion behind me. I held my arms out and stepped off, closing my eyes and waiting to fall.

Instead, strong jaws caught hold of the length of my gown and yanked me backwards. I fell, but arms caught me. Black furry arms. I screamed when I saw the claws so close to my skin. I fought. I kicked and struggled. I punched and clawed. It didn't matter. This thing was so much bigger than me. I was going to die.

I found myself on my feet as the animal walked, on two legs, back to the other side of the room. He was so much scarier on two legs than four. He towered over me this way, and I knew that even trying to kick him would be stupid. My foot wouldn't even reach its waist. At least when he was on all four I had a chance at kicking and hitting it in the face.

I made a move back toward the door and he – it – Sam – growled. I froze and turned back. It dropped to all fours and sat down. I took a minute to fully stare at it. In a way it was beautiful – scary as hell – but beautiful. The black fur that covered its body was sleek and shiny. It had the grace of a giant cat and a long whip-like tail. Its eyes were hauntingly gold, and they blinked as if waiting to see what I would do.

It kind of looked like a panther. A giant, 'kick your ass; eat your mom', kind of panther. Except its teeth were bigger, its eyes were meaner, and it was huge. "Sam?" I whispered.

It made a sound and lay down.

A sob tore from my throat, and I let it out, it hurt. This hurt.

He was a beast.

As tears leaked from my eyes, thoughts of despair and disbelief ripped through me. This thing…this beast…was the boy I thought I loved. How could I have spent so much time with him, *loved* him and never sensed this?

"Are you a werewolf?" I asked, not even believing that I was standing here asking such a ridiculous question. This stuff didn't exist. This wasn't some bad horror movie where the girl ran screaming up the stairs instead of out into the night. Well, I had tried to run into the night, and I was dragged back into this room. By teeth. How could I deny what was right in front of me? "Are you?" I asked again, watching the beast warily.

He shook his head.

Then what the hell was he?

Suddenly, he shot into the bathroom. I heard the same popping and tearing as before. I imagine the pain on his face that I has witnessed earlier and felt a pang of sadness. That little pang pissed me off. I shouldn't feel bad for him. I should be feeling bad for me! *He* was the reason that I was disfigured. *He* was the reason my life was torn apart, and I was haunted by nightmares and pain. Screw him! I was leaving.

I went to the hotel room door and threw the lock and opened the door.

"Heven, please wait." Sam begged mere inches behind me.

I turned. He was there, and he was the Sam I knew. At least, he was the Sam with the *body* I knew. He wasn't wearing anything but a towel around his waist. I looked away from his rippling, corded muscles. I would *not* be distracted by his golden good looks.

"I'm leaving. I never want to see you again."

"You can't leave," he said softly. Gently he reached around me and shut the door.

I allowed it, transfixed by his rich, deep voice. And because part of me wanted to hear what he was going to say. I mean a girl didn't find out her boyfriend – her ex-boyfriend – wasn't human every day.

"If you touch me I will scream my head off." I told him.

"I won't touch you." He said, watching me walk across the room. He grabbed up his clothes and went back into the bathroom.

I watched him go feeling like everything I ever believed had been a lie.

I was sitting on the bed when he came back out of the bathroom. He was fully dressed, wearing black tuxedo pants and the white button up shirt. The sleeves were rolled to the elbows and the buttons at the throat were undone showing a patch of smooth tan skin. He was wearing socks and shoes, and it gave me the feeling that he was ready to run me down if I tried to escape again.

I rubbed my temples. I was *so* going to be late for curfew. I looked up when I saw movement. Sam knelt down in front of me, his hands reached out, but he dropped them when I stiffened. He fell backward to sit on the floor.

"You have some major explaining to do." I said, weary.

"Where do you want me to start?" The words rumbled from his chest, and he looked up in my eyes, his face was open and truthful.

"Why don't you start by telling me exactly what you are."

Sam

She wants to know what I am. I guess I should be grateful that she's still here and listening instead of still fighting and clawing to get away. The sight of her face as she watched me change was heart wrenching. It was more painful than the transition itself. She was horrified. She was literarily shaking with fear so much that she tried to jump off a balcony seven stories high.

I'd driven the girl I love to suicide. Talk about a punch in the gut.

She'll never love me now.

I sank back onto my butt and leaned against the wall. I wanted to reach out and touch her. I wanted her to stop looking at me like I was a complete stranger.

I wasn't going to get what I wanted.

So, I would settle for giving her what she wants. Answers.

"I'm a hellhound."

She stared at me for long moments. It almost looked like she was deciding whether or not to believe me. "A hellhound?" she finally asked.

I nodded. "There's so few of us left, saying we're almost extinct is an understatement." In fact, I hadn't even known they existed until I changed into one a few years ago.

"You never told me. You lied to me." She accused, her blue eyes flashing up to mine. I knew she would be angry, but her anger was still like a slap in the face.

"I didn't have a choice, Hev."

"No?" she snapped. "You always had a choice. You could have told me the truth." She jumped off the bed and began to pace. Her shoulders were tense, and I couldn't help but stare at the hemline of her dress. It was torn.

"What was I supposed to say?" I asked, staying sitting on the ground. I wanted to pace the room like she was to walk off some of my anxiety, but I was afraid if I got up I would frighten her. "Was I just supposed to walk up to you and say 'you don't know me, but I'm a hellhound, and someone is trying to kill you?'"

"Someone wants to kill me?" She stopped cold and turned, her eyes wide. I could actually see some of the anger drain out of her.

"Yes. It's what I'm trying to say. You're in danger."

"That woman tonight…she's involved?"

"Yes, that's China. She's the one…she's the one that attacked you that night. The night you can't remember."

"How do you know this?" she asked, tension building up around her.

I swallowed. "Because I was there."

Her entire body stilled. She was calculating my words, deciding what they meant. There was only one conclusion. I did this to her, or that I was an accomplice.

All of a sudden it's like a fire started within her. Her hands balled to fists at her sides, and she speared me with a look. "You're telling me this now? Is this some kind of twisted joke? It took me a long time to make some semblance of a life for myself after my attack. My entire life was destroyed. *I* was destroyed. Just when I had my life figured out you came along and changed everything again. You made me care about you, you made me feel like I could have a real life again. And now you drag me up to some hotel room and change into a beast in front of me and then you tell me that everything between us had been a lie, that you, *you* of all people, Sam, were the one that destroyed my life in the first place!"

She was practically hyperventilating, her breaths were coming in short gasps, and her face was turning red. Alarmed I jumped to my feet. I promised her I wouldn't touch her, and I wanted to honor that promise, but I couldn't stand to see her this way.

"I'm leaving!" She yelled and ran for the door.

I lunged after her, she couldn't leave. People out there wanted her dead, and I had to protect her. I wrapped my arms around her waist and towed her away from the door, back into the room. She turned and shoved me, both hands slamming into my shoulders. "Get away from me."

"Stop it, I need to talk to you, there are things you need to hear." I reached for her again and she slapped my hands away.

"I hate you!" She yelled as she rushed forward and began hitting my chest with the sides of her clenched fists. "I hate you for this!"

I let her pound me, I deserved it, and she needed to get out her anger. Because I still had to talk, and she still had to listen. And because I hated myself too.

After a few minutes of her hitting me she collapsed against my chest and sobbed. I was afraid to put my arms around her so I just stood there, my hands at my sides and shaking with the need to touch her while she cried hot tears all over me.

When her sobs became hiccups, she whispered, "I thought you loved me."

I groaned and wrapped my arms around her. "I do. More than anything."

My voice or my touch seemed to break through her emotion, and she stiffened and yanked herself away. "Don't touch me."

I held up my hands in surrender and took a few steps back.

She wiped at her eyes with the back of her hand and her make-up smeared, leaving black streaks against her pale skin. "I don't want to see you again."

"That's too bad, you don't have a choice."

She turned away and stood, staring at the door probably wondering if she could beat me there. I was tired. My body felt drained and exhausted. My mouth was dry and the muscles in my back were sore from tension. I wondered how I could get through to her, how I could make her understand. As she stood there with her back to me I realized that talking to her this way might be easier. I wouldn't be able to see the hate in her eyes, and she wouldn't be able to see the devastation in mine. Maybe if I just started talking, explaining, she would stay and listen.

So I began talking.

"I live with three roommates; I sometimes call them my family because they are hellhounds like me. When I met them I was alone, and I knew nothing about what I was or how to control myself. I thought I was a freak, an outcast, and that there wasn't anyone else out there that could do what I could. But then China – the woman you saw tonight – found me one night and offered me a place to go where people understood."

Heven made no comment or even moved from the spot she was standing in, but I knew she was listening. So I continued, "At first I liked being with them. I learned a lot about what I am, and it was a relief not having to be alone. But China, started to change, she became harder, meaner somehow."

Heven's head tilted just slightly and a little ray of hope bloomed in my chest. *I have to make her understand.* I went to the mini fridge and pulled out a bottle of water and downed it all. I was so thirsty. Then I reached for another and uncapped it. When I lifted it to my lips I realized that she was no longer turned away. She was looking at me. "Would you like some?" I asked.

She shook her head. "How did she change?"

"China's been looking for something, an object that she heard about, something that no one has ever seen. We'd been helping her look, even though we really didn't know what we were looking for. All I know is that it is a map of some sort."

"Like a map to gold?"

I nodded, pleased that she finally seemed interested. "Exactly. We used to go out every night searching. Our apartment was here, but we went all over the state looking. We could never find it, and as time went by she became angry and frustrated."

"Then what happened?"

"She started killing people, Hev." I heard her soft indrawn breath, but I continued to talk – anxious to get it all out before she began yelling again. "We began fighting because I tried to stop her a few times. She would get so angry at me. It was almost like she had to kill them, and if she didn't…" I shook my head not bothering to finish the sentence.

"She didn't what?" Heven asked, I noticed she had come forward to sit on the edge of the bed.

"If she didn't she would get punished or something. I never understood it because I didn't think China was scared of anything." *So why would she feel like she had to kill?*

"Then what happened?" Heven asked. Her voice was deeper than normal because of all the crying she had done.

"Then I saw you." My voice softened at the memory. "I was running through the woods, and you were out riding Jasper. I thought you were the most beautiful thing I'd ever seen. You were so pure and carefree. I envied that in you."

I stole a glance at her; she was staring at the wall, her face drawn.

"So I started watching you. Sometimes running in the woods where I knew you rode, and hanging near the library… I liked being near you, even if you never knew I was there."

"Why didn't you talk to me?" she asked, curious.

I barked a laugh; it was an empty sound. "Why would you ever want anything to do with someone like me?"

She didn't answer.

"Anyway, I started skipping the nights that we went searching. I started pulling away from the pack. I hated that she was killing people, but I didn't know how to make her stop. The others didn't seem to care what she was doing...I think they even might have helped her. I couldn't go up against all three of them. I just wanted to be normal. I wanted a real life."

"One day China followed me, and she saw me watching you. She became angry. She became fixated on you. She got it into her head that I was pulling away from the pack and not helping them search because I was infatuated with you."

"Were you?" she asked softly. Her eyes were riveted on my face and most of her fear had drained away. She was becoming fascinated by my tale.

"I loved you from the minute I laid eyes on you. I've lied about a lot of things, Hev, but I have never lied about that."

Her eyes seemed to melt a little but then she caught me watching so she sat up straighter and all the emotion left her face.

"China threatened to kill you. I told her that if she left you alone that I would go back to searching. For a while that worked, and I thought she had forgotten about you, but she hadn't. One night she killed someone, completely ripped them to shreds, and it made me sick. I told her how disgusting I thought she was, and I refused to help her hide the body. That's the night she attacked you. The night you can't remember."

"Why didn't she just kill me?"

She said the words almost as if she were talking to herself. So I didn't bother to answer. I didn't want to rouse her memory of the attack because I didn't want to give China any other reason to come after her.

A lonely tear slid down her cheek, and she glanced at where my hands gripped her. I let go and put some distance between us once more.

"I'm sorry," I whispered. An apology was not enough, nothing would ever be enough but I was out of words. How did you make up for practically robbing someone of their life?

"For a few months after your attack she left you alone," I explained. "I did everything she asked, and I only watched you when I was sure she was out of town. She came home early from one of her trips and caught me following you again," I said, pushing my hands through my hair and shoved away from the wall. I had to move. I was edgy and tired of trying to find ways to make her understand. "She's crazy! She became convinced that I was going to tell you about us, about what we are. She said that you would tell – that we would get locked up. I enrolled at school to keep a closer eye on you; I didn't like leaving you unprotected for so many hours in the day."

"Just during the day?" she asked.

I felt a fine blush spread over my cheeks as I nodded. "I watch your house at night. To keep you safe."

"All this time I thought I was crazy," she murmured to herself.

"Why?"

"Because I always felt like I was being watched. I always sensed that something was there, in the shadows watching me."

"I didn't know you felt that way. I never meant to scare you." I said.

"Just like you never meant to lie?"

"I lied to protect you. I thought I would be able to kill China before now."

"Why haven't you?"

"She's strong and whenever I manage to get the upper hand, something always manages to get in the way."

"So that's it then? She's going to keep coming at me until I'm dead?"

"No! I won't let that happen." I rushed to her side and sank down on the bed next to her. "That's the reason I can't let you leave, and why I can't stay away."

"Please," I whispered. "I want to go home."

"Okay. I'll take you." The truth was out now, and I couldn't keep her here. She wouldn't want me around but that was okay; I could protect her from afar, and I would.

She didn't refuse the ride, and I took that as a good sign. With a ballroom full of people downstairs she could have asked anyone for a ride. But she didn't. Maybe there was a chance for us after all.

The drive to her house was quiet and sad. I had hoped this night would be so different. I thought it would be the beginning for me and Heven – not the end. I thought that finally, tonight, she would confess her love. I was naive to think that she would love me at all.

When I pulled into the driveway, I shut off the engine and turned to face her. "Want me to explain to your mother why you're late? I can make something up."

"No. I'll do it," she said, reaching for the handle.

"If you want to talk you can call me anytime."

She wasn't going to call. I knew that. She got out of the truck and I scrambled out after her, not needing to walk her the short distance to the door but wanting to prolong my time with her. At the door she refused to face me.

"I love you, Heven." I told her, needing to say the words.

She put a hand up to her scars, whispering, "Your love comes with a heavy price tag."

She walked into the house and shut the door in my face. I didn't know if she would ever talk to me again. I didn't know how to make things right. The only thing I had left to offer her was my absence. And her life. Standing there in the dark, my heart in a million pieces, I made a vow. I would give Heven back the life she lost. I would kill China. And then, if she wanted me too I would walk away and never look back.

Chapter Fifteen

Heven

    I spent the weekend avoiding Kimber's phone calls, claiming I had a stomach bug. I used the same excuse to stay in my room all weekend, away from my mother. When Monday morning came, I pleaded I was still sick, even going as far as running into the bathroom to make retching sounds while I poured water in the toilet. Mom was convinced and let me stay home from school. At eight-thirty I felt my first breath of relief when she left for work. Finally, I was blissfully alone. I lay in bed a while longer wallowing in misery. The guy I loved wasn't even human, and it felt like my heart would never mend.

    I padded down to the kitchen and made some hot tea and brought it up to my room, crawling back under the covers. I thought about everything he told me, about the danger I was in and how a crazy hellhound wanted me dead. I knew I should be terrified, but my emptiness at the loss of Sam muted those feelings. And to make it worse the nightmares kept coming, but instead of the animal-like claws attacking me, there were long, red fingernails biting into my skin, drawing blood while Sam stood watching in the background. When I would wake up, I would lay there and cry wondering how my life got so messed up. I was so incredibly miserable. What made everything that much worse was the one person who could make it all go away was the reason for the pain. How could I miss Sam after all he'd done? I burrowed further under the covers, trying to go back to sleep, except I wasn't tired. I'd slept too much this weekend. I was wide-awake with my misery.

I threw the covers back and sat up, reaching for my tea. I jumped and screamed, tea spilling everywhere, when I saw Sam sitting on the floor by my dresser. "Owww!" I wailed, scrubbing at the hot liquid.

Sam jumped up. "I'm sorry." He rushed to the side of the bed.

"I've got it," I told him, pulling the shirt out away from my skin. It burned and stung. Tea dripped down my arms and legs making me feel sticky and wet. Like I wasn't already miserable enough, now I had to have burns?

I gathered up the soaked bedding and tossed it on the floor. Then I grabbed a clean shirt and went into the bathroom to change. When I came out Sam was stuffing the bedding into the washing machine. He looked up apologetically, "I don't know how to use this."

I sighed and gave him a quick lesson, putting in the detergent and showing him how to use the settings. When the task was complete I went back to my room. Sam followed.

"What are you doing here?"

"You didn't go to school. Your mom finally left and I wanted to make sure that you're okay and see if you needed anything."

"I'm fine. You can go."

"You can't be here all day alone, Heven."

"This is about China." I was sorely disappointed. Was I hoping he would say he missed me, that he wanted to see me?

"It's about your safety."

That didn't make me feel any better. "I'm fine."

"I'll just stay and make sure."

"You can't stay."

"Why?"

Because it hurts too much. Because I want to throw myself into your arms and never let go. Because I want to forgive you, but I can't. "Just go."

"I'll be outside if you need me." He walked to the door.

"Outside?" I couldn't stop myself from asking.

"I've been here all weekend."

"*What?*"

"I told you I would protect you."

He stayed outside all weekend to protect me? To watch over me?

He nodded, looking exhausted. When he was halfway down the stairs I went after him. I couldn't let him go again; he made me feel better even though I didn't want him to.

"Have you eaten?"

"I'll get something later."

"I'll fix you a sandwich."

He looked up, his eyes flashing gold.

My heart leapt.

He followed me into the kitchen, seeming tired and worried, which for the life of me I could not understand. After admitting to sitting outside the entire weekend to keep watch over me like a stalker, coming into my house without being invited, and scaring me almost to death…and only now that I was to make him a sandwich he was worried?

"Like any sandwich I made could be that bad…" I muttered, grabbing the bread.

"What?"

I jumped a mile high because I had no clue that he was inches behind me. "Geez, stop sneaking up on me!"

"Sorry." He moved to the other side of the kitchen, giving me some space. This was a good thing, right?

I sighed and focused on the turkey sandwich I was slapping together. Extra mayo, extra turkey, cheese…I held up a tomato and he shook his head, making a face. I put the tomato down and topped the sandwich with another slice of white and carried it over to him. He reached for the sandwich, and his fingers brushed mine. I felt the jolt as if I were electrocuted. He froze and looked up at me. I ignored him and went back across the kitchen to grab a soda. When I turned back, half the sandwich was gone. I began making another; clearly, he was starved.

"When's the last time you ate?"

He shrugged and shoved the rest into his mouth. Geez, did he even chew? After I handed him the second sandwich I turned to walk away, but he grabbed the hem of my T-shirt and pulled me back. "Hey."

My stomach did that flippy thing, and I prayed that he couldn't hear my heart accelerate. Who knew what a hellhound was capable of? "What are you?" I whispered.

His hand slid away from me. "I'm the same guy I've always been."

"I never really knew you at all." I had no idea that he was a hellhound and lived on his own with a bunch of other hellhounds who liked to kill.

"I only hid *what* I am, not *who* I am." He sat the sandwich on the table like he'd lost his appetite.

"Isn't that the same thing?"

Slowly he shook his head.

I wasn't sure how to respond, so I busied myself by cleaning up. "You don't need to stay."

"I'll go outside, but I am not leaving." he said being stubborn.

"Fine! Do what you want anyway!" I said, exasperated. I wanted to run from the room, but he was near the door, so I settled for turning my back on him.

I shouldn't have been surprised that he appeared behind me instantly, soundlessly, but I was. I felt his hands hover above my shoulders before they settled, warm and heavy. With gentle hands and strong arms he turned me around and cupped my face, forcing me to look into his hypnotic eyes. "I don't want to hurt you. I would die to protect you from pain."

My skin tingled under his touch, and it was his words, not his eyes, that hypnotized me. "Sam..."

His lips brushed over mine, and while I willed myself to push him away, I pulled him closer. I opened my mouth wider and his tongue slipped in, making me groan. There was a sharp thump and a gasp from the door of the kitchen. Before I could register anything, Sam flipped around, tucking me behind him. I stared at the tense, rippling muscles of his back.

"What is going on here?"

Oh, crap. It was my mother.

I tapped Sam on the shoulder and he turned, his eyes full of regret. "I wasn't paying attention," he whispered. "I didn't hear drive up, I was so focused on you..." his eyes dropped back to my lips. I understood because everything else fell away when I was with him too.

I stepped around him to look at my mother. "Mom, this isn't what it looks like."

"You mean you didn't pretend to be sick so you could skip school and…and…act like a harlot?"

A harlot? What the heck was that? Sam must have heard it before because he actually growled. Like that helped anything.

"Mom…"

"I do not want to hear it, young lady," she said, bending to pick up her dropped keys and purse. "You and I are going to have a talk. And you," she said pointing at Sam, her face flushing, "you are going to leave. You are not welcome here."

"Mom!"

Sam turned to face me, his hazel eyes darkening. "I'll see you later," he whispered.

"Go!" Mom told him.

When he was gone, Mom stared at me, hard. "Are you proud of yourself?"

"He came by to see if I was okay, that's all."

"Are you even sick?"

"Yes." At the moment I felt like hurling.

"I didn't want to believe…" she murmured, sitting down at the kitchen table. I don't even think she heard me.

"Believe what?"

"I thought you understood; I raised you with the Lord."

"Mom, it was one kiss." It wasn't as if we were naked on the floor.

"You did so well after the accident. I understood that you were sullen and self-conscious about your scar."

She wasn't making any sense.

"But these past few weeks, I began to see the change in you: the cheering, the parties, the boys."

I felt like she'd slapped me. "I was helping the cheer team out at a competition so they wouldn't get disqualified. It was two parties, this whole year, and the only boy is Sam."

"It's a slippery slope to sin."

"What are you saying, Mother?"

"After you missed so much Bible study lately the pastor tried to tell me, but I wouldn't listen. But after what I just saw…I can't ignore it."

My stomach cramped. This wasn't going to be good. "I'll be better," I promised, not even understanding what I was promising.

"It's too late. You were marked, the damage is done."

"Marked?"

"By evil. That scar on your face proves it."

"You…you… think I'm evil?" I swallowed the bile rising in my throat.

Mom stood from the table and smoothed her skirt and top. "Don't worry, we can fix this."

How do you fix someone you thought was evil?

"There is this camp, beginning right after school lets out. It will save you."

"I…" My own mother thought I was evil, and that my scars proved it. I'd thought a lot about these scars, how they made me look and feel. But never once, not in a million years, had I ever thought that they were because I was marked by evil. But my mother had. My own mother didn't think I was good, she was ashamed of me. I felt myself worth shrivel.

"I know you have questions about camp. I need to use the restroom, and then we can have a long talk."

Numbly I nodded as she went. At the door she paused and looked back. "This is for the best, Heven. Someday you'll thank me."

When the bathroom door closed behind her, I went to the back door and opened it soundlessly. There, beneath a large oak tree was Sam. His face was drawn and pale. He'd heard everything. We stared at each other from across the yard; the distance between us seemed tremendous. From inside the house I heard the toilet flush. I jumped, and Sam stiffened. Moving quickly I stepped out onto the porch, shutting the door behind me. I couldn't stay here. When I reached him he held out his hand, and I took it.

Then we ran.

Chapter Sixteen

Heven

Where did you go when your life was spiraling out of control? To a place that felt safe. A place you knew you could be yourself.

Even if being yourself meant being evil. Deep down I knew I wasn't evil but a small part of me whispered, "What if?"

"Take me to my grandma's. Please," I whispered. It hurt to talk. It hurt to breathe. How could she think that I was evil? Was I?

Sam nodded and fired up the engine of his truck. At first I thought him watching over me was like being stalked. Now, I was thankful. Things between me and him were not even close to being good, but if I was honest with myself (and right now I had to be), I trusted him. I peeked over at him to see him staring through the windshield, jaw set, face hard. My mother hadn't been nice to him, banning him from the house and looking at him like he was trash.

"I'm sorry."

The wheel jerked beneath his hands and he looked over at me. "You're sorry?"

"My mother was very rude to you."

"Rude to me?" he choked. "I don't care about me. I'm so sorry that she said those things to you. It's all my fault. If I hadn't brought China into your life then your mother wouldn't think that you are evil. Shit, because of me, your own mother thinks you were marked by Satan."

I stared out my window. I didn't want to think about the things she'd said.

"It's not true," he said roughly.

"Maybe it is." Ahh, and there was the thought that bothered me most. What if there *was* something bad inside of me?

He laughed a hollow sound. "I know all about evil, and you are not it."

"Do you?"

"I'm a hellhound, Heven."

I still had no clue what that really meant. We turned onto the dirt lane that led to Grandma's house, and I began to panic. What if Mom called her? What if Grandma turned me away and said she agreed with my mother? What would I do, where would I go? I couldn't breathe, and I clawed at my throat, wheezing. My whole body began to shake and I broke out in a clammy sweat.

I felt a strong hand on the back of my head, forcing it down between my knees. "Deep breaths, honey. In, out, in, out."

I tried to match my breathing to his voice, and after several tries, some of the tightness in my chest receded. I kept my head down because I didn't want him to see my tears. This was by far the worst day of my life.

"It's okay. Everything's going to be fine."

I noticed that the truck wasn't moving anymore. I looked up. We were parked near the house, beneath a tree. Sam swiped the pad of his thumb across my cheek. I sighed, sitting all the way up. He already saw that I was crying. "Thanks for giving me a ride." I placed my hand on the handle to get out.

"What? I don't even get a thank you for giving you a ride?" he asked in mock horror.

I smiled and turned back toward him. "Thank you, Sam. For the ride."

"There's that beautiful smile. I missed it." He said, his fingers inching across the seat toward me.

I turned away, pulled the handle and opened my door.

"You can walk away from me just like that?" he asked low, all trace of joking aside.

No.

I was in his arms, crushed against him so fast that I wasn't aware he'd moved. A broken sob escaped me, and I pushed closer against him. I knew that I should think about everything he'd done and all the things I had yet to know, but in that moment I didn't care. He made me feel better, and that counted for something, didn't it? I felt his lips brush the top of my head, and I let him hold me a little longer. Too soon, I sat up, putting distance between us. Out of the corner of my eye I saw movement and looked toward the house. Grandma was on the porch, watching us with the phone clutched in her hand.

"I have to go."

"I'm coming with you."

"You can't."

"I will not leave you here unless I know she…"

"Doesn't think I'm evil too?"

He gave a tight nod. I looked past him to Grandma. She waved. Swallowing my fear I got out and went around the truck toward the porch. I couldn't stop the tears that filled my eyes.

"You're mother called," Gran said, frowning.

I nodded.

"I told her you would be staying with me for a while."

Relief poured through me so great that I staggered. I heard a truck door slam behind me, and I held up my hand to tell him I was fine. "Thank you, Grandma."

Her eyes softened. "You couldn't possibly think I'd turn you away? My favorite granddaughter?" She shook her head. "Come inside, you look like you need some coffee. And bring your friend; it's clear he's not leaving until he knows you're safe." The door shut softly behind her.

I turned and motioned for Sam. He was out of the truck instantly. A hysteric laugh bubbled out of me. Sam reached my side. "What is it?"

"She invited you in."

"Well of course I did, I know a good man when I see one," Grandma called from behind the screen.

I laughed again. Sam took my elbow and guided me into the house.

If Grandma only knew.

"Tell me," Grandma said, sitting down across from Sam and me.

I looked down at the coffee she'd just handed me. Sam paused in his inhalation of a plate of muffins that sat between us. My stomach revolted just looking at them. "I thought Mom called you."

"She did. I'd like to hear your side of things."

"She doesn't approve of me," I said, skirting around the 'E' word.

"How so?"

I sighed. "She thinks I'm evil. She thinks my scar proves it."

"She said that to you?"

I nodded, wrapping my hands around the mug. It was nice and warm. Beside me, Sam was quiet.

"What else?"

I repeated everything that happened from the time Mom found me in the kitchen making sandwiches with Sam. I left out the part about us kissing, because that was private. I ended with, "She wants to send me away to some church camp so that they can 'fix' the evil inside of me. I couldn't be there, so Sam brought me here."

Throughout the explanation, Grandma sat quietly listening, sipping her coffee. When I was finished she sat silent a few more minutes before speaking. "It's utter nonsense. I'm glad you came here."

"You mean you don't agree with her?"

"No. I knew your mother was very dedicated to the church, but I had no idea that she believed such…nonsense."

"I can stay?"

"Of course you can. Now don't you worry." She reached across the table and patted my hand. "I'll take care of your mother."

It was only early afternoon, and yet the day felt as if it dragged on forever. I was so exhausted, and not just from today, but since prom. After Gran promised me everything would be all right, she made lunch and insisted that Sam stay. It wasn't uncomfortable because Grandma didn't let it be. She seemed genuinely interested in getting to know Sam, and he didn't seem to mind the questions. Probably because the questions were light, and the food was good.

"Will you be in school tomorrow?" he asked now, standing beside his truck, keys in hand.

"Yeah. Will you?"

"I'm not sure."

"I have a few things to take care of."

"Well, thanks for today. For the ride." I started to turn away.

"Heven." His voice was rough and so was his hand when he pulled me back. I looked down at where he held my arm, and his touch lightened, his thumb stroking the inside of my wrist. "I'll be by in the morning to pick you up for school."

His light touch and gentle words made my eyes sting with tears. I willed myself to be strong, not to cry, but the idea of not seeing him really hurt. I didn't want to send him away. Even so, I said, "I loved being here with you today, like this, I loved pretending that everything was okay, but it isn't and I need time. Time to decide what I am going to do."

"Why?"

"Because you lied to me. I don't know if we can be together anymore."

Hurt flashed across his face, but he covered it. His grip tightened on my arm before he let go. I couldn't help but feel like he was giving up, by not arguing, by not fighting to be with me. I wanted to be angry, but then I remembered what I'd just said. I couldn't fault him for doing what I asked him to do.

"If you don't want to see me anymore then I accept that, but I will be around, watching."

"Is she really going to come after me?" Without thinking I reached up and touched my scars.

"I won't let her hurt you," he vowed.

But she already had, and really, hadn't he been the one that had brought her attention to me? "I have to go."

He sighed and jammed his hands in his pockets. "If you need me, just call out my name. I'll hear you and come."

"Go home, Sam. I don't need you." I tried to convince myself of that as much as I was trying to convince him. I knew I would need him if China came back to finish her task, but it was just as hard thinking about him being so close, when I didn't know if I could trust him with my heart, but knowing he was the only one who would ever have it.

It took all my courage to walk away. And when I did, I blinked back my tears because I had to be strong. I needed time – time to really convince myself that I didn't need him, because deep in my heart I was afraid that I did.

That night I had a nightmare.

And the night after that.

And the night after that.

In fact, since I told Sam to go away, I had a nightmare every night for two weeks.

They were always the same: dark, scary and lonely.

They all started out the same. I was alone, walking home in the dark. I'd stayed too late at the library and the clicking of my high heels on the pavement was like an exclamation point that danger was lurking. Then there was the rustling of the bushes and the running...

I woke up screaming.

Every time.

The first few nights Grandma came running into my room to see what was wrong. She'd rub my back and hum a lullaby, and I would pretend that it soothed me. When she was gone I would get up out of bed on shaking knees and run to my dresser for the bracelet Sam gave me. The metal always felt warm in my hand and the weight of it around my wrist was comforting.

Only then could I sleep. I should just wear it to bed, but I was terrified that it would catch on the sheet or my PJs, and the clasp would break again. If it broke again who would fix it? I sent Sam away, and the bracelet was all I had left – except for the whistle. I still wore it every day; I wore it now, but it didn't give me the same comfort.

Grandma stopped coming in after a while, because I learned to quiet my sobs of fear. Sometimes I think she suspected I still had bad dreams, because every morning we would have breakfast together, and she would ask me how I'd slept. I didn't bother lying like I would have to my mother. Grandma knew better, and I didn't like the fib. She assumed my dreams were because my mother thought I was evil, and other than dropping off camp registration papers to Gran one day while I was at school, she hadn't been by to see how I was at all.

But I wasn't having nightmares because of my mother.

I was having them because of Sam.

I missed him. Like a ghost, pain haunted me day and night, no matter where I went. He did come back to school, but he didn't bother me; he didn't even look at me. It was like he completely forgot I existed. Kimber was sure that it was just a fight (I didn't tell her otherwise) and that we would make up, like her and Cole. I spent most of my lunch hours avoiding one of her schemes to get Sam back.

I was so grateful when Friday came. I was exhausted and depressed. The weekend stretched before me, and I looked forward to being able to nurse my broken heart. It was a stroke of luck that Gran had her monthly bridge meeting at a friend's house, and I was going to be spending the evening alone. Grandma made some noise about not going to stay with me, but I protested, saying I wanted to read a new book I found at the library.

Once she was gone I changed into a pair of cotton pajama pants and a tank top and crawled into bed. I tossed and turned for a while, but my exhaustion won out, and I slipped into sleep…

The dream began as it always did. I tried to wake up, but I was caught between the dream and reality. I got to the part where I was running and running, knowing that something was after me, and then I fell, scraping my knee on the hard pavement.

This was where I always woke up.

But the dream continued…

The sting on my knee was burning, but it was the least of my worries. Whatever was chasing me had caught up and flipped me onto my back. I screamed and fought, flailing my arms and kicking my legs. I was no match for what had me, but I didn't stop fighting.

Until I heard the growl.

I went still, peering up at my attacker. I thought my heart would pound out of my chest because the person who had me wasn't a person at all. It was an animal: a large black animal that was snarling and showing its very lethal-looking teeth. Danger was screaming in my head, and I just wanted to get away. I tried to roll myself out from under it. Razor sharp claws bit into my arms, pinning me down. I felt the first warm trickle of blood on my skin, and I knew then that it would kill me.

So I played dead.

I lay utterly still, holding my breath, praying the thing would lose interest in its game if it thought it had already won. Miraculously, the creature began to back off. It took everything in me not to whimper from fear and pain. I lay there still as I could, barely breathing for long minutes after it left.

When I was sure it was gone I opened my eyes and sat up. But the creature hadn't left at all. It tricked me, and now it crouched before me ready to finish off its prey. Right before it launched I saw two others just like it approach. Their golden eyes glistened in the dark, almost hypnotizing me.

Agony searing through my body made me scream. I felt blood oozing all over me, but I had no idea where it was coming from. All I heard was snarling and high pitched screams as my flesh was torn again and again.

Then it was over.

The screaming stopped.

Something warm surrounded me, making me feel safe.

"You're going to be fine," he said.

I liked his voice. It was raspy and deep. I tried to open my eyes to tell him to run away. It took several tries and when I did my vision was blurred.

Even so, I would know him anywhere.

Sam.

"Help," I choked.

"Shhh. You're safe."

"A…animal."

"I scared it away. I'm going to get you some help."

"Th-thank…you."

"I'm so sorry."

I didn't understand why he sounded so sad. I couldn't hold onto the thought because the pain was so bad that I began vomiting. Minutes or hours could have passed, but the next thing I knew I was at the hospital.

"Please take care of her." The warm safety of my savior's arms was being taken away, and I wanted it back. *Don't leave me here!*

"Strap her down, she's hysterical!" someone yelled.

I began to scream and fight.

"Heven, it's me!"

His voice was a lifeline, and I fought even harder to get to it. I heard a grunt and a swear before I managed to open my eyes. "Sam?"

"You're safe, sweetheart. It was only a nightmare. A dream."

I sagged against him and sobbed, griping fistfuls of his shirt. He held me for a long time while I cried. I couldn't even be embarrassed because the dream was still so fresh in my mind. After a while my sobs quieted and I just lay against him, boneless. "I had a nightmare."

"I know." His voice was hoarse. "This was the worst one yet."

I pulled back and looked up. "You know about my dreams?"

"I hear you every night, crying. It's horrible. Every night I pace the grass beneath your window, willing myself to stay outside. The fact that your grandma was here held me back, but tonight, she isn't here. And..."

"And?"

"I just couldn't bear to hear you scream like that."

"It was horrible," I whispered. "I remember all of it now."

He stilled. "The attack?"

I nodded against him. "Usually I get halfway through the dream and wake up. Tonight I dreamt it all..."

He held me tighter.

It felt so good to be in his arms again. He was warm and strong and safe. It made me remember... "You saved me."

"I didn't get there soon enough," he whispered.

I fought his embrace and as he let go, I sat up. "It's true?"

"What did you dream?" His face was drawn and pinched.

"Something was following me, but every time I turned around, it wasn't there. I was scared, so scared, and I started running. But I wasn't fast enough, and the beast caught up. And it was so heavy, its claws felt like broken glass against my skin."

"Then what happened?"

"Then the animal was gone, and there was warmth. I felt safe. When I opened my eyes it was hard to see, my vision was blurred."

"There was blood all over you," he murmured, rocking me gently.

I nodded. That must have been the wetness I'd felt. "But then I saw you. You were holding me. You took me to the hospital."

"I hated leaving you like that. I couldn't stay; they would have asked too many questions." I felt his arms shaking. He sounded sick.

"I didn't want you to leave me."

He groaned. "That's why you fought with the nurses? That's why you started screaming?"

I nodded.

His eyes were far away. "I thought you were scared of me. I thought you were in pain." His eyes cleared and he looked down. "You weren't afraid?"

"Not of you." Never of him.

He kissed me hard, grabbing my face and pressing his lips against mine with a fierce desperation that stole my breath. When he pulled back I said, "Why didn't you tell me?"

"Tell you what?"

"That you were the one who saved me."

"I was the one that lead China to you in the first place. I didn't save you."

It was the very same thought I'd had too. Then I had this dream and it changed things forme – for us. "You never wanted to hurt me."

"No."

"What are you doing here tonight, Sam?" I sat back. I wanted to see his face.

"I'm always here. I told you I would watch over you."

"You've been here every night for two weeks?"

He nodded. "Except when I am out looking for China."

"Where?"

"In the loft in the barn."

"You ignore me at school. You don't even look at me."

"You told me to leave you alone."

"But you still watch over me."

"I've never stopped loving you, Heven."

A thrill went through me. It wasn't too late! "I've missed you so much."

"I've missed you more."

I laughed.

"Can you forgive me?"

I didn't have to think it over. "Yes."

He hugged me, and I fell over backward, laughing. When I looked up, his eyes flashed gold. Slowly, he reached out and brushed a hand through my hair and traced his fingers along the raised, ugly scars on my face. "You're the only one who's ever touched them," I confided, my lashes dropping.

"I never wanted you to get hurt. If I had known…"

I put my hand over his lips, "Shhh. It doesn't matter anymore. If I didn't have these scars I never would have met you."

With both hands pressed against the mattress on either side of my head, he leaned down to kiss me. I opened my mouth wider to accept more and wrapped my arms around his waist. His body pressed fully against mine; the feeling was so delicious I shivered. Sam took this as a sign that I was cold and reached down to pull the blankets over us. Then there was nothing but him. Soon, I was breathing hard and straining against him for more…

"Sam."

His response was to rake his teeth over my earlobe and growl low.

Was I ready to give him everything I had? I wanted to – oh God, I wanted to. I loved him so much I could barely breathe.

"We should slow down," he said, putting a few inches between us.

We absolutely should. "I don't want to."

He kissed me again, his hand sliding up beneath my tank to cup my breast. I wasn't wearing a bra, and I gasped at the contact. His hand stilled, and he looked into my eyes. I pushed my chest against him harder and he groaned, his eyes sliding closed.

"You're so soft," he whispered, before sitting up to straddle me.

I opened my eyes. "Sam?"

"Are you sure you want to do this?"

"Yes. Aren't you?" Insecurities came flooding into my head.

"I don't want to rush you; I can wait. I love you so much."

Is this why he was hesitating? The night of the ball I was ready to hand him my heart with the three words I knew he wanted to hear. But that night turned out much differently than I'd planned. Nothing was going to stop me from giving him those words right now. "Sam, I…"

He stiffened and looked toward the window.

"What?"

"Your Grandma's home."

Already? I looked over at the alarm clock and winced. It was much later than I thought. He jumped off me, landing silently on the floor. I sat up in protest; I didn't want him to go. Grandma's footsteps on the stairs had me looking toward my bedroom door.

"Go to sleep," he whispered, then jumped out the window.

I flopped back on the pillows and closed my eyes as she opened the bedroom door. Light from the hall filtered in, and I concentrated on keeping my breathing even and slow. She stood there a moment, then the door closed, and she moved down the hall. I breathed a sigh of relief and rolled over toward the window to watch the curtains floating in the breeze. I wondered if he would come back. I wondered what we would be doing if Gran hadn't come home. Would this have been the night I lost my virginity? Would I have gone through with it? *Yes.* I would have said those three words that Sam wanted to hear so badly, and he would have made love to me.

His blond head poked in the window, "Is she gone?"

I giggled. "Yes."

"I thought she'd never go to bed." As he walked toward the bed, I admired the way he moved with such grace, and I thought of how hard his body had felt pressed against mine. I was disappointed when he crouched down beside the bed instead of climbing in.

"You okay?" he reached out and threaded his fingers through mine.

I nodded. "I'm glad you came back."

"Yeah?" His smile was quick and my heart sped up at the sight. "Want me to hang out awhile?"

I tugged his hand and pulled the covers back in invitation. He slid between the sheets, and I threw an arm and leg over him then rested my cheek against his chest. "Can you stay?"

He pressed a kiss to my forehead. "Yeah."

I yawned as my eyes slid closed. He was comfortable, and I felt safer than ever before. When I opened my eyes again Sam was slipping out from beneath me. I made a sound of protest and clutched at him. He leaned in close and whispered, "The sun is coming up. I have to go."

It was morning? I looked toward the window and saw that the sky was lightening. I couldn't remember the last time I'd slept so peacefully. I started to pull myself up but Sam pressed me back against the pillows. "Go back to sleep."

"Miss you."

"I'll be in the barn, up in the loft. Come see me later." I grabbed his hand, and he kissed me. I heard a sound in the hallway – Grandma was up. "I have to go," he whispered, tucking the blanket around me.

I nodded. "I'll meet you in the barn."

"I love you."

Before I could tell him the same he disappeared out the window.

Chapter Seventeen

Heven

"You're up early," Grandma said, not bothering to hide her surprise. She was measuring coffee into the pot and then turned it on to brew.

"I fell asleep early last night."

"Sleep well?"

"Yes."

"How about I make a big breakfast to celebrate?"

My stomach grumbled loudly, and I nodded. "I'm starved."

"Wonderful!"

"I think I'll go see Jasper and give the horses some hay."

"They'll like that." She was already pulling out pans from the cupboard.

"Would you like some help?"

She waved me off. "Shoo!"

I shoved my feet into my sneakers and palmed the doorknob. Nervously, I turned back. "Uh, Grandma, would it be okay if I called Sam and invited him for breakfast?"

"Now that's a name I haven't heard in a while."

"I – uh asked him for some space. You know after Mom…"

"I understand." She nodded, not turning away from her cooking. "Sure, honey, call him. The more the merrier!"

I swallowed past the lump in my throat. Her love and acceptance meant more to me than she could ever know. "Thanks, Gran. I love you."

"I love you, too. Now go on and feed the horses."

My pace quickened the closer I got to the barn. Anticipation curled around me as I swung open the barn door and shut it behind me. I ran to the ladder that led up to the loft, calling his name as I went. He appeared at the top with a smile on his face. I climbed up the ladder as fast as I could. Once at the top I launched myself at him, eager to feel his arms close around me.

"I didn't expect you until later," he laughed.

I snuggled in closer, enjoying his scent. "I couldn't wait."

He chuckled again.

"You're invited to breakfast!"

"I am?"

"Uh-huh. Grandma was so happy I got up early and wasn't depressed that she is cooking a huge breakfast. She said I could call and invite you."

"Sure beats the power bars I've been eating."

I remembered that he was spending his nights here, and I pulled away, feeling guilty. A pile of clothes lay off to the side, and a single blanket was tossed across a loose bed of hay, near it was a small flashlight and a book. His book bag and sneakers were tossed in another corner. "Have you been spending all your time here?"

He shrugged.

"But why?"

"I told you why."

"So she's still around?" The thought gave me the willies.

He shook his head. "Not since right after prom. She took off, and I haven't seen her since."

"She left?"

"Yeah, I think she's still out searching."

"Then why are you practically living in the barn?"

"She'll come back."

"Because she wants to kill me."

"She won't." His voice was harder than I'd ever heard it before. "I'll kill her first."

The absolute resolve in his voice scared me. Was he really capable of killing her? Of killing anyone? I backed up toward the ladder. "I need to feed the horses."

"I'll watch from up here." He smiled a tilted smile, and just like that, he transformed back into the boy I loved.

"You have something against horses?"

"More like they have something against me." Again he smiled – a quick flash of white teeth.

I paused climbing down the ladder and looked up at him. He stood over me all bronze and gold. His skin always looked kissed by the sun, and his hair always glistened with beautiful gold highlights. It was so incredibly easy to forget what he was, but even as I remembered, I noticed his full peach lips and round hazel eyes. That's when it hit me. I didn't care what he was or wasn't, because to me, he was everything, and nothing was going to change that.

"Heven?"

I shook my head, trying to clear it. "It's nothing." I smiled and finished going down the ladder. "Grandma mentioned that the horses seemed restless to her lately. I guess I know why."

"I stay up here away from them. I don't want to make them uneasy."

"I know." I headed into the tack room to get a bag of grain. When I came back out I looked up, and he was peering over the edge watching me. "So tell me…"

"Tell you what?"

"What exactly is a hellhound?"

He was quiet awhile, and I wondered if he would tell me at all. Before going back into the tack house to put away the grain, I glanced up. He was still in the same spot, but he looked a little pained, like he might be ashamed to tell me about himself. It made my heart hurt to see him that way. I didn't ever want him to feel ashamed to be who or what he was with me. I walked to the bottom of the ladder and dropped the bag of feed as his gaze flickered to me. "Never mind," I told him, gently. "I've already decided that it doesn't change things between us – me knowing. I still want to be with you."

He was shocked by my words, judging by the way that his body jerked and his eyes widened. His lips parted, and a small sound came out but otherwise he said nothing. I smiled to show him that I understood and then walked back into the tack room. When I turned from the cubby after putting the bag away, I was met with intense hazel eyes. "You could be with me, not knowing anything about what I am?"

"I already am with you."

"It's about time." He smiled quickly. "You made me work hard enough for you."

His smile fell away and he grabbed me and began kissing me aggressively, almost like he was angry that I dared to make him feel that way. I answered his kiss with my own. I was frustrated. Frustrated that my love didn't come through enough for him to be able to tell me about himself. But this wasn't the way to show him. I grabbed his wrists and tugged, pulling his hands away from my face and placing them at my hips. Then I reached up and gently ran my fingers through his hair and gentled my lips upon his own. Just as I'd hoped, the kiss transformed into something softer, and it became more about giving rather than taking. Every beat of my heart screamed out my love. I wanted to tell him, so I pulled back and took a deep breath, but he spoke first.

"You deserve to know."

"You don't have to."

"Yes," he said, pushing a hand through his hair, "I do. We can't really be together with this between us."

"So tell me."

"I didn't know what a hellhound was either until I turned into one when I was thirteen."

I wanted to gasp at the young age, at the innocence that must have been stolen away in that moment, but I didn't. Telling me was clearly hard enough for him and I didn't want to make it worse.

"I was sitting in the kitchen doing my homework one minute, and the next I was off running into the yard...I didn't understand what was happening to me. My skin, it burned. It felt like it was on fire – like it was just going to melt right off my bones. Every bone in my body started shaking and making these sounds...this groaning and crunching." He shook his head as if to clear the vivid memory and looked up at me. I nodded and reached out to lace my fingers in his.

"I thought the pain would never stop. I fell onto the ground, onto my hands and knees. I remember thinking that I was dying, and then everything just sort of snapped. And the next time I looked down I was standing on four paws covered in midnight black fur. My torn clothes were lying on the ground at my feet. I could still think – I was still me on the inside, but on the outside I was something completely different.

I thought that maybe I was just dreaming, that I fell asleep at the table doing my homework. But then I heard my mom crying. She was crying and calling my name. I looked behind me where she stood; the phone was clutched, forgotten, in her hand. I wanted to tell her that I was okay, and when I opened my mouth, this growl ripped from my throat. My mother jumped, and the phone fell out of her hand onto the ground. I moved to pick it up, and I stumbled. Walking on four legs instead of two was much harder than you might think. Before I could fall, though, my reflexes took over, and I sprang up and forward. My mother screamed and ran. She ran into the house and locked the door." His voice had grown quiet and hollow. I couldn't even begin to imagine how frightened he must have been, and then his mother ran away, she turned her back when he needed her most.

"Sam," I said, gently. "You don't have to tell me anymore."

"I want to." He said quietly as he moved across the room to stare at the row of saddles hanging from the wall. "She wouldn't let me in at first. I didn't stay as a hound for very long but changed back about ten minutes later. I stood there shaking, trying to conceal my naked body. I couldn't cry because I was so shocked. Shocked from what was happening to me, but also shocked because she wouldn't let me in the door. She just stood there and stared at me like I was a monster, like she was afraid. I heard her talking on her cell phone to my dad. He was at work, and she was hysterical. He came home early. I'll never forget the look on his face when he came into the kitchen and looked at me. I was sitting at the table, my whole body hurt, and I was so confused. He was mad, I could tell by the way the vein in his forehead stood out and by the way he clenched his jaw. I apologized for what I'd done, and I swore I wouldn't do it again. My mother was crying, but he just stood there, staring at me, like there was no hope. Then he turned to my mother and told her to get rid of me."

I gasped, my hand flying up to cover my mouth.

He smiled a sad kind of smile and shook his head. "It's okay, don't be upset. It was a long time ago."

It hadn't been that long ago…but it was brand new to me. The things that Sam had lived through were things that he wouldn't ever forget – neither would I.

"Mom sent me to my room, and they got into a huge fight. I could hear it all, even after they started whispering. Apparently, Dad had a few skeletons hiding in the family tree. He carried the gene mutation for hellhounds, something that was passed down through the members in his family. He said he never told her because they thought the gene had died out because a hound hadn't been produced in three generations. Usually it's every other one. Guess I got lucky." He laughed, but it was a bitter sound.

"What happened?"

"My mom was scared of me. She was furious that my Dad wouldn't tell her something like that, but to her, I was still her son. My dad didn't want me around, I heard him say it, loud and clear. He thought I was a disgrace. He thought I was weak. How come all the other generation could manage to overcome the gene when I couldn't? I think that deep down he was scared of me. He was afraid that I would hurt him, my mother and my little brother. But I wouldn't do that. I would never do that." He said the last like he was trying to convince me, like he was trying to make me believe.

"I know that, Sam. Of course you wouldn't hurt them. They are your family." I said the words because I believed them, but more importantly because he needed to hear them.

The tension in his body seemed to ease, and he turned back, able to look at me once more.

"My mom convinced my dad to let me stay. He didn't have a choice really. He lied to her for years and allowing me to stay was the only thing that would even come close to making up for it. For a while we lived like nothing happened. They ignored when I impulsively went out into the night, because no matter how hard I tried, I couldn't stop from changing. They pretended that my quick growth spurts were because I was a boy, and that it wasn't unnatural. I wasn't allowed to talk about it or ask any questions about what was happening to me. But even though they pretended that nothing was wrong, there was. My mother was terrified of me. She didn't understand how my body could transform, to twist myself into something else. She used to pray constantly asking for me to be spared. She couldn't accept that I was a freak. My dad just kind of ignored me, tried to pretend I wasn't there. He would take my brother out into the yard and play football, but I was never allowed to play. My mother was terrified that I would hurt him – the only normal son they had left. Right before I turned sixteen, Dad brought some paperwork home and handed it to me. Emancipation papers. They wanted me to file for emancipation and move out, so I did. They bought me my truck and paid the rent for six months in advance for a crappy studio apartment on the other side of town. When they dropped me off there, Dad handed me an envelope with some cash in it and told me that from there on out I was on my own. I haven't seen them since."

"They let you go? Just like that?" My words were an echo of the time I tried to walk away and he'd asked me the same.

"Yeah."

"How dare he!" I raged, pacing away, fists clenched at my sides.

"He?"

"Your father," I spat. "He did this to you, and then he had the nerve to disown you! If I ever see him I'll…"

Sam seemed amused by this, and I had no idea why. "You'll what?"

"Punch him in the nose!"

He laughed.

"It's not funny." I glared at him.

He sobered. "Of course it isn't," he rasped and walked to me, grasping my balled fist. "You're cute when you're mad."

A frustrated sound escaped me, and I leaned into his chest. "I'm so sorry."

"Don't be."

"Not for you."

"No?" He pulled back and lifted an eyebrow.

I shook my head. "For them. They made a huge mistake by not keeping you in their lives. I can't imagine not having you in my life."

His eyes softened, but then he stepped away. "You turned me away too."

I winced and stepped forward. "Not because you're a hellhound. Because you lied to me and it hurt. But even before my dream last night…I was on my way back to you."

"You were?"

I nodded. "I couldn't stand being apart."

He swept me into his arms and held me. He was solid and strong; he'd always been those things. Except now he was even more so because of what he'd managed to live through. He rested a cheek against my hair and his raspy, deep voice filled the room. "Original hellhounds were used a long time ago to take souls through obstacles into Hell. To enter Hell one must pass through a wall of fire and a body of water. They were used as guardians to the gates of Hell, and sometimes souls would escape, and they were sent to hunt them down and drag them back."

"How did the hellhound gene end up on Earth?"

"Hellhounds were cast out of hell and sent to Earth, where they took human form and lived among humans."

"Why were they cast out?"

"Hellhounds were extremely uncontrollable. Not even Satan himself could make them do what he wanted. So he banished them, he cast them out of Hell and gave them human traits. He sent them to live on earth where he had hoped they would spread evil throughout the human race. The hellhounds began to reproduce, and the gene was passed down from family to family, skipping a generation. Best I can figure is that eventually the gene pool became diluted and the children became more human and less hound. It was Satan's ultimate revenge against God. He was using his evil to contaminate some of God's children and twist them into sin."

"I don't believe you are evil, Sam." I told him wholeheartedly.

"I don't believe you're evil either." He said, giving me a knowing look. It dawned on me that we had more in common than I thought. "It's why I got so upset that day at your house. *I'm* the one who came inside and kissed you. *I'm* the one who was so caught up in you that I didn't hear your mom. And *you* are the one who got blamed for it. She said the exact words to you that my father said to me. He said I was marked by evil"

"We have each other," I said, "and what happened with my mother isn't your fault. It had been brewing for a long time, and I just never noticed." I had been too caught up in my own pity.

In two short strides he was in front of me, pulling me close for a long, hard hug. I tightened my arms around him and sighed then stepped away and pushed the hair from my eyes.

"How do you know all of this?"

"China. It was one of the reasons I went with her when she found me – and one of the reasons I stayed. I dropped out of school because she convinced me I would never fit in. She's older than me.

Older than my roommates. She's lived longer inside her body, and she knows how to use her abilities. She taught us, showed us how to live and how to keep our secret."

"Does it hurt very much?" I asked. "When your body changes like that?"

"Not anymore."

"That's good." I didn't want to think of him in pain.

I needed a minute to digest everything he was saying, so I went to the fridge to get a bag of carrots. They were a little wilted because I hadn't been in here for a while. Sam watched me from the door as I went to each stall and fed the horses. They all eyed him warily, but the lure of the carrot was too strong, and soon they just ignored him. "They're getting used to you."

I looked over my shoulder at him. He was looking at me from beneath lowered lids, almost like he was shy. "I understand now why you love comic books so much."

He grinned. "Oh, yeah? Why's that?" He settled his shoulder against the doorjamb and made himself comfortable.

"Because you can identify with the guys who are different, with the guys who can do things that no one else can." It made me think of something else... "Do you have any cool superpowers?"

He laughed. But I saw some sort of smug satisfaction in his eyes. The kind that guys always got when they scored a touchdown or pulled up in front of a crowd in a muscle car.

"Maybe," he teased.

"It's okay if you don't," I said, feeling mischievous. "I guess turning into a big dog is cool enough."

For a second his mouth dropped open, but then he laughed. It was a rich sound, and it drifted to the rafters. It was a sound I wanted to hear over and over again. *This* was the real Sam. My Sam.

"I hear really good. And I have inhuman strength."

"I figured that out." I said, trying to sound unimpressed, when really I was totally impressed.

"I'm fireproof."

"You are?" Now this was pretty cool.

"I can stand in the middle of a fire and my body won't be affected; my core temperature would rise, but that's it."

"Interesting," I said, patting Jasper. That would explain why the night I almost fell into the fire, his jacket and shirt got burned through but not his skin.

"I can survive being frozen, too. I would only lose consciousness until my body temperature returned to normal."

"You've tried freezing yourself to death?"

His teeth flashed as he laughed. "No. China told me. I also read that we are really great swimmers. I've tried that one out." He grinned again. "It's definitely true."

"Well aren't you just a show off?" I smiled. I liked being like this with him. With everything out in the open, no secrets between us. It felt lighter, easier.

But then a stray thought pierced through my happy mood. I returned the bag of carrots to the fridge and cleared my throat. "I should be getting inside before Gran comes looking for me."

He frowned and hooked me around the waist, towing me near him. "Hey, did I frighten you?"

"No. I…" I tried to step out of his hold.

He wouldn't let me. "You what?"

The words rushed out of me, toppling over one another. "Can you live forever?"

He paused, weighing my words and searching for something in my eyes. "The idea upsets you?"

I was embarrassed, and I shrugged.

"Why?"

Because the thought of me aging and dying while he stayed behind was depressing. I wanted him all to myself; I was selfish. When I got wrinkled and old and died, he would find someone new, young and beautiful. I turned and buried my face against him, inhaling deeply of his scent.

"Heven?"

"Because I have to get old and die. I want to stay with you."

He chuckled. "I have to get old and die too."

"Really?" I pulled back searching for the truth in his eyes.

"Yes. You seem thrilled at my impending doom."

"*Our* impending doom," I said, burrowing against him once more. "And it won't be for a long time."

His chest vibrated with laughter, and it tickled me.

"You'll come for breakfast?"

"Sure. I'm going to go home and shower first, then I'll be back."

At the barn door I stopped but didn't look back. "Sam? I never really walked away. I thought of you every minute, and I couldn't sleep without your bracelet. It was a terrible mistake that I never, ever plan to make again."

I heard his breath hitch as I let myself out the door.

The scent of breakfast wafted all the way upstairs and made my stomach growl viciously. Throughout my routine of showering and dressing, I couldn't stop thinking about the things Sam confided in me. I didn't understand how his parents could turn him away. It made my stomach ache.

I stepped in front of the mirror to brush my hair, and my gaze landed on my scars. After everything Sam had been through, they seemed small and insignificant. Staring at myself, I pulled all my hair back, away from my face, into a high ponytail. If these scars were the worst that ever happened to me then I was lucky. My mother's words floated through my head, *marked by evil.* I guess I could understand how Sam's parents treated him. Wasn't my mother treating me the same?

How could she raise me for sixteen years and then blame me for how I turned out? It hardly seemed fair that something I didn't ask for or want could make others judge me. But, to be fair, the only one who truly judged me was my mother. My friends, they never judged me, I allowed myself to believe that is what they were doing, but they weren't. Hadn't they just explained that to me at prom? So, yeah, I guess I did know how Sam felt, only it was worse for him because his rejection is real. The realization was humbling. Suddenly, I ached for Sam, ached for his crooked smile and golden gaze. I wanted to touch him and feel his strength. A strength that not only came from his true identity, but from everything he had already overcome.

Downstairs Gran was heaping steaming blueberry pancakes onto a huge platter. "I hope you're hungry," she said, adding the platter to an astonishing array of other loaded-down platters. Eggs, bacon, sausage, toast, fruit...

"Holy cow! You made enough for an army."

She laughed. "I noticed how that young man of yours likes to eat."

Her words caused a stirring inside of me. Sam was mine just as I was his. "I'm not even sure *he* can put a dent in all this food." I went over to the coffee and poured a mug, adding sugar and cream. "I'm starving."

"Grab a plate!"

I sipped my coffee instead, wanting to wait for Sam. There was a knock at the back door, and I ran to it, my face breaking into a wide smile at the thought of him standing there.

Except it wasn't Sam.

It was my mother.

My smile vanished.

"Mother," I said, stepping away from the door as she stepped inside.

"Hello, Heven. Good morning, Silvia."

Grandma turned from the sink. "Good morning, Madeline. I didn't hear you pull up."

"Yes, I'm sorry for stopping by without calling, but I was just coming from church."

"You're welcome anytime. Would you like some breakfast?"

My stomach suddenly lurched at the idea of food. Surprisingly, it made me angry. Seconds ago I was happy and felt really good for the first time in a long time, and she ruined it.

"No, thank you," she replied, looking me over. "You pulled your hair up."

She disapproved. I realized I didn't care. "Yes. I decided that my scars are not something that I need to be ashamed of. Worse things could happen to me than this," I motioned to my face.

"You accept your scars?"

"Yes." I guess I did.

This seemed to worry her. "Have you filled out the registration forms for the camp this summer?"

I looked to the top of the fridge where I'd put them, hoping to forget about them. "No."

"Fill them out now. I'll mail them tomorrow."

"No."

"No?"

"I'm not going to that camp."

"Yes, you are."

"No, Mom, I'm not. I won't let you punish me for something that wasn't my fault. I am not evil. I am the same girl I've always been." I hadn't really believed that myself until I said the words just now.

"That's the evil inside you, influencing you. You must turn away from the bad, Heven."

"That's quite enough," Grandma said, coming to stand beside me.

"You agree with her?" Mom seemed surprised.

"Do you think my son would approve of the way you are treating his daughter?"

Mom paled. "Jason isn't here for me to ask, so I must do what I think is best for our daughter."

I wished my father *was* here. Things would be very different. Mom would be different. Grandma stepped toward my mother and placed a hand on her shoulder. "I know. You have done a wonderful job with Heven these last years. Jason would be proud. But this, this…"

"Is my decision to make. Fill out the papers, Heven. I will be by tomorrow after work to get them, and you."

"What do you mean?" My heart began hammering in my chest. I couldn't go back home. I wouldn't be able to see Sam.

"She's welcome to stay here," Grandma said, alarmed.

"I won't have my daughter staying with someone who doesn't have her best interest at heart."

"She's been such a great help here. The barn and land can be a lot to take care of…" Grandma said, wringing her hands. I knew she was searching for a way to keep me there, and I loved her for it.

"She can come out on the weekends after church to help you out."

I saw the defeat on Grandma's face. I couldn't stay here unless Mom allowed it.

"I'll fill out the papers." I said, low.

Both women looked at me, surprised. "What did you say?" Mom asked.

"If you let me stay here, with Grandma, I'll fill out the papers for camp right now. You can take them with you."

"You like it here that much better?" She seemed hurt by this.

"I'll start going back to church too," I added, hoping to sway her.

"How are your grades?"

"Really good."

"Oh yes, she studies every night," Grandma agreed. Minutes ticked by, minutes of Mom studying me, judging me. Suddenly I wished I had left my hair down.

"Fine," Mom relented. "Get the papers."

I hurried to fill out the papers and shove them into the envelope, not wanting her to have enough time to change her mind. When they were finished I handed them to her and turned away.

"I'll see you tomorrow night at Bible study?"

Inside I cringed. "Yes."

"All right then." I heard her hesitation, and I stared at the wall just praying that she would go. "Bye, Heven."

I didn't trust my voice, so I nodded. I barely heard her saying goodbye to my grandma and the sound of her car pulling away from the house. I felt as if I'd just signed my life away, and all I could hear was the ticking of the clock. It was ruthlessly counting down the minutes until I had to show up at church tomorrow.

Grandma hugged me from behind. "It's going to be fine."

Her hug reminded me that what I did was necessary. If I hadn't signed those papers and agreed to church, then I wouldn't be here. I would be a prisoner with Mom acting as my jailer, and there was absolutely no way I would get to see Sam. Yes, my sacrifices were nothing compared to living without Sam. There was just one thought that made my insides shake: if I was the evil one, why did it suddenly feel like I'd just made a deal with the devil?

Chapter Eighteen

Heven

"I need to tell you something."

I knew by the tone of his voice and the look on his face that it wasn't good. After my mother left, I'd come outside to sit on the porch steps to wait for Sam. I knew I made the right decision by signing those papers and promising to go back to church, but I still doubted myself. I knew that once I saw Sam my insecurities would go away.

When his truck came up the long dirt drive my heart fluttered in anticipation. But hearing his words now did not erase any of the tension coiled inside me. "Okay." I clasped my hands in my lap and waited for more bad news.

The screen door squeaked open and Gran poked her head out. "Breakfast is getting cold."

"Thank you for having me," Sam said politely.

"My pleasure, Sam. Come on in."

I stood to follow Grandma, but felt Sam grasp me from behind. "Hey."

I looked over my shoulder.

"Don't look so sad, honey." He pulled me close. "It's not terrible. We'll talk after we eat."

I nodded.

"Where's the smile I saw this morning?" He tickled my ribs.

I squirmed, a giggle escaping. He pressed a kiss to my cheek. "Everything is going to be fine."

The way he said it, I wondered who he was trying to convince.

"You think this isn't terrible?" I asked, my stomach turning.

"I know it isn't."

"You just told me that China is back." From wherever it was that she went.

He nodded.

"The woman who attacked me–" I reached up to my unsightly scars and continued, "–has been stalking me, has threatened you, and wants me dead?"

He sighed.

"This is terrible."

He grabbed my shoulders and leaned down to look directly into my eyes. "Listen to me, do not freak out. I just wanted you to know so that you would be more careful."

Oh, that made me feel better. Now I could add worrying about him getting killed to my list.

"Breathe, honey," he reminded me. "In. Out. In. Out."

My lungs obeyed.

"That's my girl."

We sat there a long time, in the middle of my grandma's orchard, beneath the newly budding fruit trees. I felt grateful that Sam had suggested we walk after breakfast, because this news, coupled with my morning adventures with Mom, did not put me in the frame of mind to hide my anxiety from Grandma.

"What else happened this morning?"

"What?"

"Heven, I know something happened. When I left you this morning everything was good. The next time I saw you there was pain in your eyes. What happened?"

I felt so safe with him that the words tumbled from my lips without thought. "My mother."

He stilled. Even his heartbeat slowed. "She came to see you?"

"Yeah. She threatened to make me move back home."

He sucked in a breath.

"But I filled out the papers for that camp and promised to go back to church."

"Why would you do that?"

"Because if I had to move back home, she wouldn't let me see you. She wouldn't let me do anything."

"I'm sorry you had to go through that."

"I think I hurt her feelings." I regretted that much more than I'd realized.

"Your mother's?"

"Yeah. She was shocked that I wanted to stay here so much."

He grunted.

"For a long time now it's been just me and her. I thought that wouldn't change, you know? But now it's like we are two completely different people, and she doesn't understand me at all."

"I understand." I heard the emotion behind his words. He did know. More than anyone ever could.

"I'm sorry," I murmured, wrapping my arms around his back and pressing in closer.

"Aren't we a pair?" he wondered, pressing a kiss to the top of my head. Then, "You always smell so good."

I wondered how I would live if he ever got taken away from me.

Too soon we had to leave the orchard. Sam had to work. I was sitting at the table with my second steaming cup of coffee at my elbow. I had a feeling I was going to need the caffeine today. Sam entered wearing a pair of clean khakis and a polo shirt embroidered with the *Planet Fitness* logo. The shirt was tucked in neatly, and he was wearing a brown leather belt. I smiled at his cuteness.

"Well, Sam, don't you look ready for a day at work," Grandma said, looking up from her crossword.

"Thank you for letting me change here," he mumbled, looking a little embarrassed. I wanted to jump up and kiss him. I settled for a grin instead.

"What time does your shift end?" Grandma enquired without looking up.

"Uh, six, ma'am."

"Just in time! I just put a roast in the oven. It should be ready right around that time. Why don't you come back and join us for supper?"

My heart soared. Now I wouldn't have to make an excuse to hang out in my room or the barn all evening so I could be with him. I tried to control my smiling. It was no use.

"Thank you," He accepted graciously.

On his way toward the door he paused and turned back. "Ma'am? Would it be all right if I took the want ads from the paper with me? I could take yesterdays or last week's if you still have them," he rushed to add.

Grandma shuffled this morning's paper around and pulled out a thin section. "Searching for another job?" she asked, handing them over.

"He already has two," I blurted out. He couldn't possibly have time for a third job, school, and me.

He grinned, his eyes sliding over to me. "I live with a few roommates right now that I don't really get along with too well. I was hoping to find a smaller apartment or an efficiency that I could rent on my own."

Excitement whirled through me. If he moved, there would be somewhere we could go to be alone! I would know where he lived and might actually be allowed to visit him!

"Good luck with your search," Grandma told him, returning to her crossword. "We'll see you at dinner."

"Yes, ma'am. Thank you." I followed him out to the back porch, closing the door behind us. I whirled around to see him smiling at me. I launched myself at him, laughing.

"Really? You're moving?"

"Yes." He kissed the tip of my nose.

"Will I be allowed to visit?" I batted my eye lashes at him.

"I'll give you a key."

I bounced around in his arms. The words *I love you* sprang onto my tongue. Instead I said, "Can I help you look?"

"I don't know, it's going to be pretty boring," he teased, faking a yawn.

I smacked him in the stomach. He made an "oomph" sound and then grinned. "Okay, you can help."

"I can't wait!"

He was still grinning, which took all the warning out of his tone, "It's going to be a few weeks until I can move."

I nodded sagely.

"It probably won't be that nice of a place."

"Any place with you will be heaven." I ducked my head shyly.

He lifted my chin with his finger; his eyes were soft. "I feel exactly the same about you."

"Have a good day." I said, sorry he had to leave.

"I'll see you later?" His voice was deep and low.

I shivered, liking the way he made me feel. I walked him to his truck, and just before climbing in, he looked at me with somber eyes. "Would you please stay inside today? I'll worry less if you do."

I nodded. "Be careful."

"I will." He kissed me softly, briefly. "Go on in the house."

I went, wondering the whole way how long until China came for me.

"What's going on with you?" Kimber demanded.

"What? Nothing."

Her eyes narrowed. "I know you better than that. We've been friends forever."

"Why would you think there was something wrong?" Like say, my boyfriend is a hellhound, and it turns out that his hellhound roommate is stalking me and trying to kill me? Or maybe my Bible-beating mother thinks that the disfigurement on my face (that said stalker put there) is because I have been marked by evil and that she thinks I'm about to go completely postal at first chance?

She studied me. I felt like she was trying to pick out which lie she should call me on. Then she shrugged. "You just seem kind of jumpy and a little more quiet."

"Me? Jumpy? Queen of the panic attack and not wanting to go out in public?" I pressed my hand to my chest like I was shocked she would say such things.

"Shut up." She laughed. "I guess you are like that all the time." But then she looked around her bedroom as if to make a point. *I* had been the one that wanted to hang out there instead of going to our fave coffee shop. "I just thought that stuff was getting better. You know with the wardrobe changes and prom and Sam. But lately, since prom actually, you seem to be worse."

I never really thought Kimber was that observant of anything that didn't revolve around her. I scolded myself immediately for that mean thought. Hadn't she been the only one (besides Cole) who came to the hospital and treated me semi-normal after my attack? Hadn't she stuck by me through all my moodiness, my crying, and my panic attacks after I came home all scarred and disfigured? She deserved more credit than I was giving her.

Tears sprang to my eyes. Kimber was my best friend, and she was right. Things had been super hard lately. But I still couldn't tell her why. "I'm sorry."

"I'm here if you need to talk," she prompted, dutifully ignoring my tears.

"My mom thinks I'm evil," I blurted. Then I slapped my lips together.

"What?" Kimber cried, dropping her hair brush and rushing over to the side of the bed.

I nodded, wiping at my eyes. What was the harm in her knowing this? Other than it being embarrassing, it wasn't some big secret. "That's really why I am staying at my grandma's."

"You said she needed help at the farm."

I nodded. "I was embarrassed, and she really does need the help, but that's not why I am there."

"Tell me."

So I did. I told her about Mom finding me in the kitchen with Sam, and how he was only there to check on me because I was sick (she still didn't know the real reason I'd missed school). I told her the things Mom said and about the camp she was forcing me to go to this summer.

When I was finished talking, she looked at me with wide eyes. "Whoa. Makes me kind of glad my parents ignore me all the time."

"I don't know what to do," I whispered.

"It's going to be okay." Kimber leaned in and side-hugged me. "Your mom will realize she's being crazy and back off."

"You think so?" I'd never considered that before. I was always too busy wondering if she was right.

"Absolutely. Your mom is strict, but she loves you. Maybe you should talk to her; try to work it out."

"Maybe," I murmured. The idea had some merit. Maybe I wasn't giving Mom enough credit. Maybe if I went to her to talk, like an adult, then she would see I was still the same girl I'd always been. I looked up at Kimber. "Thanks."

She smiled. "Anytime. Next time, don't be so slow in telling me what's wrong."

If she only knew.

At least she was satisfied that she knew everything. I changed the subject. "How are you and Cole getting along?"

"Great! I would totally suggest a double, but what the heck is up with Cole and Sam?"

I rolled my eyes. "I have no idea."

"Why can't they just get along?"

"They would if they could get over the 'who's more macho' thingy." I said.

"For real, girlfriend."

Downstairs the doorbell rang. I stiffened, a moment of panic freezing me. Would China find me here? Was Kimber in danger by being with me?

"Pizza's here!" Kimber sang out and left the room.

I took a moment before following her, taking a deep breath as my fingers found my bracelet. The metal was warm, and I thought of Sam. The safety I felt with him was so strong that when we weren't together it was like a hole in my chest. My hand found my cell and my fingers itched to call or text him, but I resisted. I shouldn't rely on him for everything – how exhausting that must be for him. I was his girlfriend, not his child. I needed to act like it before I pushed him away.

Chapter Nineteen

Heven

"I was hoping we could talk," I said, using the most respectful tone I knew.

"Sure honey, come on in."

We both sat on the sofa. It was the same sofa we'd been sitting on for years. "I wanted to apologize for just leaving that day. We didn't really have a chance to talk things over."

"You mean the fact that you are marked by evil?"

She said it so casually, like she just accepted it.

"I don't really feel like I am marked by evil, Mom. I feel like the same girl I've always been."

"That's the evil inside you, influencing you, making you think that you are on the right path."

"I am not on an evil path," I said, trying to hold on to my patience.

"You need to come back to church."

"I will. That's a great idea."

"Break up with that sinner boyfriend of yours."

"I won't do that, Mom." How could she ask that of me?

"I know what he is, Heven. He's part of the evil in your life."

"No, Mom. Sam is a good person."

"Don't worry, Heven. I found someone to help get the evil out of you."

"You have?" A knot formed in the pit of my stomach.

Mom got up and went to the front door. She opened it and in walked China. She had long, flowing black hair, and her red nails looked like claws. She smiled a feral smile. "I'm here to help you." She laughed.

I jumped up from the couch and screamed. "She's the evil one! Don't trust her!"

"Turn away from the evil, Heven."

China advanced on me, her movements like that of a big cat.

"Sam," I whimpered.

China laughed. She laughed so hard that I could see the back of her throat. In a low, flat voice she said, "He's dead. I killed him. You'll never see him again."

"No!" I screamed, panic filling my chest. "Sam!"

China leaped on me and I fought. I fought so hard…

"Heven! Wake up, sweetheart. Wake up!" Sam shook me, whispering fiercely.

"Sam?" I blinked. Fear made me tremble.

"I'm here, honey."

A broken sob escaped me, and I fell into him. "You're safe," I murmured. "You're safe."

He tensed and swiftly pulled away. "No!" I cried. He disappeared out the window. Tears streaked my face. He was gone.

The bedroom door swung open and Grandma was backlit by the hall light. "Heven? Are you all right?"

I cleared my throat. "I'm fine, Gran. I'm sorry I woke you. I was having a bad dream."

"Want me to sit with you awhile?"

"No. Thanks. I hardly remember what it was about."

"Well if you're sure…" she came farther into the room to peck a kiss on my forehead. "Sleep well."

"I love you," I told her.

"As I love you." She closed the door softly behind her.

I looked at the window. I waited and waited. More tears gathered in my eyes only to spill over. Where was he? I buried my face in the sheets and cried softly, trying not to disturb my grandmother again.

Gentle hands pried the sheets from my fingers and smoothed them on the bed. "I'm so sorry I had to leave like that," Sam said, his voice pained.

I nodded.

"She went downstairs for a drink before she went back to bed. I had to wait. I'm so sorry."

"It's okay." My voice was husky, like I hadn't used it in years.

"You had a nightmare." He slid beneath the sheets and gathered me against him, pulling the blankets around us. "You're shaking."

"China said she killed you." My voice wobbled. "She said I would never see you again."

"I'm here," he murmured, brushing his strong hands through my tangled hair.

"I tried to be strong."

"You are strong."

"I need you," I admitted. I couldn't help it.

"You've got me."

"For how long?" I whimpered.

"As long as breath fills my lungs, I will never leave you."

I pressed myself so close to him I thought he might complain.

"She's coming for me." I felt it in my bones.

"Not tonight, baby. Sleep. I'll watch over you."

I slept.

I woke groggy and tired. I rolled over, reaching for Sam. He wasn't there. I sat up, forcing my eyes open. "Sam?"

The room was empty. I flopped back down on the pillows as last night's dream filled my head. China was back, and I was in danger, but I wasn't worried about me, I was worried about Sam. What if he'd gone out this morning to find her? What if he was hurt? I groaned and swung my legs over the mattress. A piece of paper was propped up against the clock.

Don't worry – I'll be back soon.

I love you.

It made me feel a little better. I tried my best to push away the cobwebs and went to take a hot shower. The water felt good, and I stayed until the water turned cold. I took my time in the bathroom, blowing my hair until it was smooth and shiny. It had grown long this past year, falling to just beyond the middle of my back. Knowing I couldn't stall the day any longer, I dressed in a pair of jeans and a pink and white striped T-shirt. I gave Sam's note one last glance before heading downstairs for breakfast.

I was crunching on some cereal when Grandma came in from outside. "Aren't you going to be late for school?"

"Nope, teacher workday."

"That's nice." She went to the sink to wash her hands. "Now that spring has arrived, there's going to be a lot more to do around here."

"I'll help out. Just make me a list of what needs to be done."

She turned from the sink, smiling. "You already do too much."

"Taking care of the horses and the barn isn't that much," I argued. "I was wondering if maybe you could teach me about the orchard? Maybe I could take care of it?"

"You're interested in the orchard?" She seemed surprised.

"I walked up there the other day. It's really peaceful and beautiful." Not to mention that Sam and I spent precious 'alone time' there.

She got a wistful look in her eyes. "Your father always enjoyed working in the orchard."

I smiled. "I remember. We always had so much fun picking fruit." I wondered why I'd never thought of this before.

"The orchard hasn't been a priority of mine for a few years. I am sure it needs some work," she said, thoughtful.

"I can do it!"

"It's hard work," she cautioned.

I nodded emphatically. "I'd like to try."

Grandma grinned. "Wonderful! If we get a lot of good fruit then we can set up a farming stand and people can come and buy bushels of apples or pick their own. I haven't done that in years," she mused.

"Can I plant some pumpkins, too?" An image of Sam carving out a pumpkin popped into my head. It made me smile.

"I grew those when you were little."

"I remember."

"It's a plan, then." She nodded, smiling. "Are you sure you're up for it?"

"Sure." I pulled out the newspaper. "I was thinking I might get a job too, just for the summer."

"A job?"

"Mmmhmm. So I can start saving for a car and to have some spending money."

"I think that Sam is a good influence on you."

I nodded. "He works really hard. He has two jobs just to support himself. He pays rent and buys his own food..." my voice trailed off. And he does all of that while taking very good care of me. How is he not utterly exhausted?

"He's emancipated?" Grandma asked. I'd told her that he was when I first came to stay.

I nodded. "He didn't get along with his dad at all. It caused his parents to fight a lot, so Sam figured that it would be best for his mom if he moved out." It was as close to the truth that I could get.

"Well, I like him. He has good manners, and he always cleans his plate."

I giggled. "You really approve of him?"

"I really do," she said, sitting at the table across from me with her coffee. "But don't tell your mother," she whispered.

I laughed, but inside I felt really nervous. I decided to take Kimber's advice and try to talk to my mother. I mean really, how could things get any worse?

Grandma and I were making plans for the orchard and looking over the want ads when Sam knocked on the door. I was so relieved to see him that I bounded through the open door and flew right into his arms.

He chuckled. "Good morning."

"Morning," I said, stepping back and returning to my chair.

Sam closed the door behind him and came into the kitchen.

"Help yourself to some coffee, Sam," Grandma said. "I didn't make breakfast this morning; I was out in the barn doing chores."

I froze, remembering that Sam was staying there and had a bunch of stuff in the loft. I caught his eyes, and he shook his head slightly. I relaxed, guessing he cleaned it out.

"I already ate," Sam said while he poured some coffee. I got up and got out the cream and sugar for him and handed him a spoon. Then I got down a bowl and poured some cereal, adding milk. I sat it in front of him at the table, giving him a stern look. Power bars were not breakfast. Especially for someone with his metabolism.

He dug in with gusto.

I sat down, satisfied.

"Here's one, Heven," Grandma said, pointing. I leaned over to see. The local ice cream shop was hiring part-time help for the summer. It was a possibility. Then, I wondered if I could take strangers coming in every day staring at my face. *Get used to it,* I told myself.

"I'll check it out later," I said.

"Check what out?" Sam said, draining the bowl of all its milk.

"I'm getting a job this summer."

His bowl hit the table with a clink. "A job?"

I nodded.

I could see he didn't really like this idea, but he couldn't say so in front of Gran.

"The ice cream shop is hiring. I'll give you free ice cream," I sang.

He smiled, but it didn't quite reach his eyes. "Sounds delicious."

"Grandma is going to show me how to take care of the orchard this year, too. We want to open a farm stand when the fruit is ripe."

His eyes displayed real interest. "The orchard we walked to the other day?" Was it a special place for him too?

I nodded with a small smile.

"Cool."

"That reminds me, Sam. I have an offer for you," Gran said, cutting into our private moment.

Sam turned his eyes to her. I felt a little hollow for the loss.

"I know you have two jobs and may not want another, but I could use a farmhand around here for the summer."

"Yes, ma'am." Sam nodded.

"You could come out early in the morning, or in the evening – whatever works for you. I'll pay you, and you'd be welcome to stay for supper or breakfast, whichever you're here for."

I could barely contain myself. I was so excited.

"I could come first thing in the mornings," Sam told her, "before I go to my other jobs."

My excitement dimmed. Would this be too much for him? How much could one person take? Maybe he shouldn't take the job.

"Wonderful. I'll show you how to work the tractor tomorrow. You can do all the mowing, and I'll show you where everything else is. I'm sure Heven will need help with the orchard, it's probably really overgrown.

"Thank you for the opportunity, ma'am." Sam smiled. "You know, I would do this work for you for free."

My heart melted. He was so, so sweet.

Gran smiled. "I know. But it's honest, hard work and you deserve to be compensated for your time."

"Yes ma'am."

She chuckled. "And please call me Silvia."

He nodded and stood, taking his empty bowl to the sink. My breath caught when he looked at me. He was so completely gorgeous that I wanted to pinch myself.

"So, I need to go somewhere, and I was hoping you…"

"I'll go anywhere with you," I rushed out, cutting him off.

He grinned and Grandma laughed. I blushed so much my face felt hot.

"Don't you want to know where we're going?" he asked, his honey eyes twinkling.

"Yeah," I said sheepishly.

"I found a place to rent, I am supposed to go look at it this morning."

I jumped up. "Let's go!"

He smiled and went to the door. I turned to Gran. "May I?"

She made a shooing motion with her hand. "I'll see you later."

I raced out the door after Sam.

The place was a dump. Okay, it wasn't that bad, but it wasn't great either. It was an efficiency apartment, which meant that it was one room with a bathroom. It had everything he needed: a fridge, microwave and a sink in the small kitchen, which was off to the right of the front door. The landlord seemed to think that the stove and oven was a big deal. I guess that not many tiny apartments had them. The rest of the room was a big open space. The floors were nice, which were a light-colored hardwood. They were scratched up, but a rug would fix that. There was enough room for a TV, a bed and a small table. The bathroom was off to the left of the space. It had old tiles that I guess you could call retro, that were shaped like small hexagons and were in alternating colors of blue and white. There was shower stall that needed a curtain, and there was a pedestal sink and a toilet. It all needed a good cleaning.

"Well, what do you think?" the landlord asked Sam. We were standing in the center of the room, hands clasped and taking in the little space.

"I like it." He shrugged.

At the same time I said, "It needs painting."

The landlord must have really wanted to rent the place because he said, "I'll pay for the paint if you keep it neutral and do the painting yourself."

Sam was about to agree when I squeezed his hand. "He needs a rug. For the floor," I added when the guy looked a little blank. He still didn't say anything so I said, "The floors are a little scratched." Actually, a lot.

The man sighed. "Okay, you can pick one out that I have downstairs in the shop."

I nodded. The apartment was above a secondhand store.

"The place rents for three hundred a month and includes all utilities but cable."

"Two eighty," I tried.

The landlord narrowed his eyes. "Who's going to be living here?"

Oops. Maybe I went too far. Sam cleared his throat. "Just me, sir."

"Aren't you kind of young to be renting on your own?"

"I'm emancipated," Sam said and held out the document proving it. The landlord looked it over and handed it back.

"This your girlfriend or your agent, son?"

Sam grinned. His hand returned for mine. "Girlfriend. She can be a little bossy."

"Hey!" I argued.

"What woman isn't?" the guy muttered.

I sputtered. But Sam said, "I'll take it."

"Good." Then he looked at Sam. "You into partying?"

"No, sir."

He pointed a finger at Sam and said, "There will be no wild parties here."

This made me angry. Sam worked hard, he didn't need this. I stepped forward. "Listen here, he works three jobs. Three. And he goes to school. He doesn't have time for parties."

Sam pulled me back to his side, but I still glared at the landlord.

"Three jobs, huh?"

Sam nodded.

He sighed. "All right, then. Come on downstairs and sign the papers."

I cleared my throat. "Two eighty?" I asked.

The guy laughed. "Geez, you should be a lawyer. Two eighty it is."

I grinned. Sam shook his head. When the landlord left the room Sam leaned over and kissed me. "You're amazing."

"I wish I could have got you more." He deserved everything. More than he had.

"I already have everything, sweetheart." He pulled me close. "So what do you think of the place?" he asked, leading me from the room.

"Ask me again after we paint, and I scrub the place with bleach."

"You're going to help me?"

"Of course. When I'm done with this place it will be perfect."

"I don't know about that." He smiled.

"I do. You'll see."

The morning I spent with Sam was close to perfect. We had time to be alone, and we found him an apartment (which, yes, needed some work – okay a lot of work), that promised even more time to be alone. I couldn't quite explain it, but there was something inside that was urging me to find places for us to be ourselves. Almost like we needed a place that could be a sanctuary. I didn't tell this to Sam because it sounded a little weird, and he was already worried enough. Everywhere we went he was constantly searching, his eyes were never still, and his shoulders were never relaxed. He stayed as close to me as possible, as if he was prepared to jump in front of me at any given moment. It made me nervous, and I was constantly reminded that we were not safe and that someone sick was after me.

He seemed angry when he dropped me off at Gran's before he went to work. When I asked him about it, he scooped my face up in his huge palms and said fiercely, "I love you." He made it sound like a sacred vow that no one would dare challenge. I was left staring at his retreating truck through the house window with a ball of ice in my belly and goose bumps on my arms.

I spent some time staring out the windows and jumping at every strange sound I heard until my own paranoia began to annoy me.

I couldn't live my life like this.

Sam couldn't live his life like this.

For months and months I'd lived under a hood, beneath my hair and in the shadows. How much longer was I going to hide? My life was here now, and it was waiting. I looked out the window once more, not to be certain that no one was there, but to see the blue sky and the bright, shining sun. I looked out to the orchard where the trees were budding with new life. For too long I'd lived, mostly without knowing, in fear of China.

It ended today.

For me.

For Sam.

School would be out very soon, and I wanted us to have the best summer we could. If we were going to do that, it meant no more looking over our shoulders, no more hiding, and definitely no Bible camp to exorcise my demons. I wasn't exactly sure how to accomplish my first two goals, so I decided to begin with the easiest: my mother.

She was surprised to see me on the other side of the door, waiting to be allowed in. "You don't have to ring the bell," she told me.

"I knew you weren't expecting me."

"Come in," she said, opening the door wide.

I ignored how nervous I felt and walked in. It was exactly the same as always. I don't know why, but I was surprised. Maybe because *I* felt so different.

"What brings you by?"

"Uh, I was hoping I could get some of my spring and summer clothes to take to Gran's."

Was that disappointment in her eyes? She nodded, "Of course."

I sighed. "I was hoping we could talk, too."

She smiled and some of the tension fell from her face. "Would you like to stay for dinner?"

Oh, God. Chicken. I couldn't say no, I was here to make our relationship better. "Sure. I hadn't realized it was so close to dinner already." I guess I would just eat again later with Sam and Gran.

I followed her into the kitchen, where she began going through the cupboards. "Have you had a busy day?"

Before I could think better of it I said, "Yes. I helped Sam find a new apartment."

I saw her shoulders stiffen, but all she said was, "That's nice."

"Mom," I began, but she cut me off to say, "I don't have any chicken. Would it be okay if I just make us some soup and sandwiches?"

"That'd be great!" Anything was better than chicken!

I started putting together some grilled cheese sandwiches while she heated the soup. It was a little awkward at first, but then I found myself telling her all about my classes and how I applied for the job at the local ice cream shop. I also told her about Gran's and my plan for the orchard and pumpkin patch. I even invited her to come help one weekend.

I had devoured half of my sandwich when I noticed how quiet it was and looked up. She was staring at me with the spoon in her hand and an unreadable expression on her face.

I swallowed. "Is there something on my face?" I asked, picking up my napkin.

"You're happy," she said, somewhat stunned.

Slowly, I nodded. "I am."

"Living with Silvia has been good for you."

I nodded again, looking down at my soup. Living with her was easier. I didn't feel like I had to hide myself, but I didn't want to say that out loud. "Things have just seemed a little easier lately, you know?"

She nodded slowly, setting down her spoon. "I don't know what to say."

She was hurt. I'd hurt her feelings. I felt bad. "I miss you, though! That's why I'm here. I hate the way things are between us. I was hoping we could be close like we used to be." I reached across the table and touched her hand.

"I would like that too." She smiled.

Feeling better, I took another bite of grilled cheese. Mom got up and went over to the counter and picked up a large white envelope and brought it back to the table. "This came for you the other day. It's your itinerary and packing list for Camp Hope."

"Camp Hope?" I asked, clueless. Then I remembered. "I was hoping we could talk about that."

"What is there to say?"

That I'm not evil? That I don't need to go to some cult camp? "I'm doing good; I'm happy. I don't think I need to go there."

"We've discussed this, Heven," Mom said, weary. "You're going."

I jumped up from the table, sending my chair clattering to the floor. "That's just it! We *haven't* talked about it. You came home one day and declared that you think I'm evil, and that I need to be sent away!"

"You haven't been making the right choices."

"Why? Because I went to prom? Because I helped out the cheerleading squad when they needed it? Because I have a boyfriend?"

"You're not allowed to date that boy. He's a bad influence."

"This is because I have a boyfriend?"

"Part of the reason. You'd been late several times for curfew, you pretended to be sick to skip school, and I caught you making out with that boy."

"He has a name."

"You're moody and sullen, you hardly eat."

"I've gained five pounds!" I yelled. "And I was attacked and left disfigured! You can't expect me to walk around singing and happy after that!"

"It was a sign." How could she just sit there calmly like that? I was so upset my hands were shaking. I could feel the muscles in my neck bunch with tension, and I was seriously sorry I ate that sandwich.

"A sign?" I said flatly, taking a deep breath through my nose.

"That you would be tested. The devil has glimpsed the bad in you, he seeks to try and turn you from God. It's a test, Heven. You have to turn your back on sin and choose holiness."

Was she serious? "You don't really believe that?" I let the words slip.

Her cool exterior finally slipped. She stood up from her chair and planted both palms on the table, leaning forward. "I do, young lady, and you'd better, too. This is your very soul that's in trouble. I will not take that lightly."

A hysterical laugh bubbled out of me. What would she think if she knew I was dating a hellhound?

"You think this is funny?" She was incredulous.

"No! Not at all," I said, suddenly very, very tired. "I can't believe you think I'm evil." I picked up my chair and sank into it.

"I don't think *you're* evil, honey; just that for some unknown reason evil has chosen you. I want to help you fight that."

"By sending me to summer camp."

She sighed. "It's a retreat. The people there are very educated; they can help you."

"You don't know me at all," I sadly said.

"Someday you'll thank me for this."

"No. I won't." I looked straight into her eyes when I said the words with absolute conviction. The tiniest bit of fear shone in her eyes. She not only thought I was evil, but she was scared of me. I stood. "I'm leaving."

"What about dinner? Your clothes?"

"I've lost my appetite."

"Heven," Mom called when I was at the door. For the first time I heard regret in her voice.

It was too late.

I left without looking back.

The Hate

She forgives him for deceiving her. She knows what he is, and she still wants him. She knows I watch her, stalk her. She pretends she isn't scared. I hear her mockery clear as a bell.

My claws sink into the ground, ripping open the earth. This wasn't what I was supposed to come home and find. I expected to find Sam shredded and bleeding from her rejection. His world was supposed to be falling apart.

But it wasn't.

No matter. I have found what I have been searching for. Finally it is mine. It's my ticket to power. With this I can finally do what Satan sent us here to do: tip the balance between the divine and the vile.

When word gets out that I have what those below have been searching for…it will be my chance. My chance to rule and be followed. Feared and hated.

Everything I ever wanted. Mine.

I don't need Sam anymore. I don't need the others. I had never really needed them at all. Because in the end it had been me who had found what I sought. Proof that it belongs to me.

I'm afraid my find doesn't bode well for others. What do you do when you no longer need something? What do you do when it loses its value?

Get rid of it.

Throw it out like yesterday's trash.

Finally I can do what I have longed to do.

Watch out, pup. I'm coming.

Game over.

The HOPE

The situation was not going well. The enemy proves to be persistent, and I wonder how much longer she will wait. She's been very busy wreaking havoc and stealing. I felt sorry for her lost soul, and I took a moment to say a short prayer that her soul might someday find rest.

"It may be time," I spoke aloud because I knew I was not alone.

"Time?"

I looked over my shoulder. "For me to pay them a visit."

"We don't know yet if he can be trusted."

"All the more reason to go."

"What's happening?" He came forward to gaze down into the water. The images rippled away. "I need to see."

"Things have changed. You are not to get involved."

"Keep her safe," he implored.

I intended to.

Chapter Twenty

Heven

I drove for a while without caring where I was going. I felt numb. Thinking I could fix things with my mother so easily had been naïve. I guess I didn't realize just how far apart we actually were. I felt like I had to mourn our relationship because a part of me knew that it was over. How could I be close to anyone who honestly believed that I was marked by the devil and meant for evil?

When the headlights of Gran's car automatically turned on, I was shocked to realize that it was almost dark. I glanced at the clock; Sam should be getting off work now. I missed him so much there was a sharp ache in my chest. I wanted desperately to hear his husky voice and see his liquid-gold eyes. I needed to tell him that I loved him. I felt deep regret that I'd waited this long. Knowing his love was there was carrying me through tonight. How did he get through his tough days?

For the first time since I'd started driving, I paid attention to where I was. I was farther from town than I wanted to be. There was no one else on the road with me so I did a U-turn right there and started heading toward Gran's. I searched through my bag for my cell, but I couldn't find it. The bag was too deep, and there was too much clutter, so I pulled the car to the side of the road to find it.

I dialed Sam's number and anxiously waited to hear his voice. It went to voicemail. With a sigh I left a message, "Hey, it's me. Went to visit my mom. It didn't go well. I've been driving around; I'm on Seven Hills Road, heading back to Gran's now. There's something I need to tell you so will you meet me there when you get off? Bye."

I frowned at the phone and dropped it on the seat next to me. I thought he would be off by now. A bolt of lightning shot through the sky and landed in the field to my left and was followed by a deafening boom of thunder. I shivered and reached over to turn the heat on. Anxious to get home and see Sam, I put the car in drive and pulled out onto the road, only to immediately slam on the brakes.

Standing in the center of the road was a large black animal. Its flaming red eyes stared at me through the night.

It was a hellhound.

It wasn't Sam.

Which meant it must be China.

I watched in horror as the animal stood on hind legs and pulled its lips back to reveal razor- sharp teeth. A threatening growl, a promise of harm, carried through the rising wind to reach my ears. A dim thought from earlier speared through my mind: the hiding and fear would indeed end tonight.

Another flash of lightning streaked the sky as the hound sprang forward.

I hit the gas and with a squeal the car gunned forward. I hoped to run the beast down. Instead, China jumped high into the air, landing on the roof on the car. I screamed, and the wheel jerked beneath my hands. *Stay calm.*

Yeah, right.

I reached for my phone to dial Sam, but it was just out of reach. I turned the wheel sharply, and the phone slid into my hand. I punched in Sam's number and was about to hit SEND when China ran, head-on into the side of the car. I felt the impact like she was made of steel. The door bowed and screamed in protest, and the car careened into the wrong lane. My cell went flying out of my hand to disappear beneath the seats.

I looked up in time to see a large truck driving straight at me. I screamed and swerved back into my lane. The loud, angry honking of the truck filled my ears. I wanted to pull over. I wanted to catch my breath. I couldn't. From out of nowhere, China landed on the hood of the car. I was paralyzed by the pure hatred in her blazing red eyes. *This* was evil.

The speeding of the car didn't seem to affect China's balance. She stalked forward, her claws digging into the metal of the hood as if it were butter. On impulse I slammed on the brakes, and she went sailing through the air. I didn't look to see where she landed, but I hit the gas and sped forward, praying she was hurt. I prayed her legs were broken, and she couldn't catch me. I prayed to be back in my room, safe in Sam's arms.

It was too late when I saw her. She was low in the grass and charged, throwing her surprisingly lithe and strong body under the car and flipping it into the air. As the car careened off the road and rolled again and again, I had only one thought: I never got to tell Sam I loved him.

Pain is a funny thing. You know that you hurt. You know that your body isn't working the way it should, but you can't really feel it, you know? The pain is sometimes so intense that you're numb. Maybe it's your body and mind's way of protecting itself. Maybe it's your body's way of dying.

"Hev, I'm here," a faraway voice reached me. "I'm going to get you out of there." I knew it was Sam. It was always Sam. My fierce protector. I tried to call out, to warn him about China, but no sound left my lips. I felt warmth and silk brush by me, and I longed to move closer to the sensation. But I was pinned, held prisoner, by what I didn't know. Then, I was falling forward against the heat I so badly needed.

"I'm so sorry," Sam whispered.

I reveled in the sound and smell of him. I was safe…there was something I needed to tell him. Something he needed to be warned about…"Sam." *We have to get away! She's going to come back!* Why wouldn't the words come out?

"I'm here. You were in an accident. I'm going to get help."

An accident? Panic stole through me. I concentrated hard for the feeling of metal along my wrist. "B-bracelet" I wanted it. I needed it to feel better.

"I'll get you another."

"N-no." Pain filled me, and a cough burned my throat.

"Shhh. I'll get it. Then we're getting you to a hospital."

I was so cold. Wasn't it spring? Where was the sunshine – the warmth? I was so tired. Maybe I could just go to sleep. I tried to open my eyes, but they were just so heavy.

Then I heard his voice. He wanted me to look at him; his voice was filled with panic and pain. I wanted to take away his pain. It took me a few tries, but I finally opened my eyes. I wanted to see his beautiful whiskey-colored stare one last time.

"Heven, thank God."

"Sam." My mouth and throat felt weird.

"Hang on, baby. We're going to the hospital right now."

"Too late."

"No," he cried, but his voice was hoarse.

"I love you, Sam." Peace filled me. I could let go with no regrets now.

"I love you," he groaned.

A last moment of clarity jerked me. Fight! Stay with Sam! But it was no use. I was too weak, and I felt the last bit of my energy drain away.

I died the only way I would ever want to die: in the arms of my beloved.

Chapter Twenty-One

Sam

I glanced at the clock for the tenth time in the past ten minutes. My shift tonight felt endless. The gym was practically empty with only two people still here, finishing their workouts. All the cardio classes were over, and there were only a few people left in the pool. Usually, I liked this place. Usually, the sound of weights hitting together and the constant hum of the treadmills was a sound I didn't mind. Not tonight. Tonight the sounds and people seemed to overwhelm me. My senses, already acute, hummed with every single sound in the place. It was maddening. My skin tingled and itched, and there was a fire in my veins.

I couldn't shake the feeling that something wasn't right.

Heven promised to stay in the house tonight. She promised to be careful. I shouldn't be worrying about her. But I did. It wasn't something that I could ever shut off. There was a constant voice in the back of my mind whispering, reminding me to stay alert. I already messed up once when I dropped my guard with Heven when her mother caught us kissing. Heven paid the price for that. Her mother said things to her that cut deep, things that would probably haunt her forever. I didn't want that for her. I wanted better for her, so I would be better, which meant that I couldn't drop my guard. I refused to let her pay for my mistakes.

I wished I didn't have to work. Sometimes I felt like I was trapped here, and that I was going to miss the moment that Heven needed me most. A nagging thought accosted me like it always does when I get like this.

You don't have to work. You can get the money you need to live without a job.

I shook the thoughts away, just like I always do. Sure, I had the strength, speed and even the perfect disguise to steal. I could probably be in and out of a place with a bag full of cash in mere minutes. But it was wrong. I walked a thin line everyday between sin and faith. The things I've done aren't all good. But they were things that I had to do. And they were things that I felt sorry for. But stealing wasn't something that I could justify to myself. What was the point of being with Heven if I couldn't be the man she deserved?

I was behind the front desk when the door off to my right opened, and someone came in. I turned, annoyed because it was so close to closing. I did not expect to see whom I did.

"Riley. What are you doing here?" I said, not being able to keep the shock out of my voice. It was my roommate. The one who held me down while China beat me then stayed behind from a day of searching to make sure I would live.

He looked around the place for a moment before speaking. When he looked back at me he smirked at the Planet Fitness shirt I was wearing.

"I don't have the patience for you tonight," I snapped, keeping my voice low. "What the hell are you doing here?"

Riley sauntered over, his dark eyes narrowing on my face. "Watch it pup, I might change my mind and walk out before I say what I came to say."

"Just tell me." Even though I kept my face as controlled as I could, my insides were going crazy. Something had to be very wrong for Riley to be in here. Riley didn't even like me. I don't think he liked anyone.

"China is going after your girl tonight."

My hands flexed on top the counter, gripping the edges until my knuckles turned white. "How do you know?"

"She was ranting and raving earlier. She said she doesn't have any reason to keep you around anymore. She said she was going to start with the girl then come for you."

I launched across the counter and grabbed him up by the front of his shirt. "If you're lying to me right now I will kill you."

Riley's eyes narrowed on my face, and I felt the muscles beneath his skin shift – I didn't care. One on one, I would tear him to shreds.

I was so sick to death of everyone underestimating me, treating me like a kid because I was the youngest.

He reached between us, shoved my hand away and then reached up to smooth his shirt. "Believe what you want. I came to tell you and I did. Whatever you do with the information is up to you."

With that he walked out the door.

Steve, one of the personal trainers came around the corner. "Hey, man."

The door was swinging shut as I turned. "I have to go." I said, trying to sound normal.

"Is everything okay?" he asked, concerned. His eyes drifted to the door that Riley just went through.

"That was a friend of mine. My girlfriend has been in an accident." My heart was pumping, and my hands were beginning to shake. I had to get out of here.

"Oh, shit, man. I'm sorry. Go, I'll cover for you..."

I didn't even wait to hear the rest of what he said. I shot out of the door and was in my truck and speeding away towards the farm before I even took a breath. I grabbed my cell and noticed a missed call. I pulled up the voice mail and listened to her soft voice fill my ears.

"Shit!" I yelled and slammed on the brakes. She wasn't at the farm. She was out driving...alone!

I made a sharp turn in the middle of the road and pressed the gas, thankful that she told me what road she was on. I broke every law possible on my way to find her. I pushed the truck way past its comfort zone, and I swerved around and passed people who were in my way.

I glanced down at the clock and wiped the sweat off my forehead with the back of my hand. *Seven minutes.* It had been seven minutes since I left work. I prayed that in those seven minutes Heven was not being killed. I prayed that China couldn't find her. Maybe it would work in Heven's favor that she wasn't in her usual place.

When I barreled onto the road that Heven said she was on, I pulled to the side of the road. If China was here, it would be faster to catch her on foot. I would be able to use my senses and hopefully catch her scent to know where she was

I got out of the truck and ran across the street. There were trees along this side of the road, and I went into them, hoping the darkness and the trees would be enough concealment for me. I started running and my body shifted, changing into my other half. Tonight, I was grateful for this form. The speed and agility might come in handy.

I took in a deep breath and caught the scent that was distinctly China. I willed myself to move faster. I could hear the sounds of a speeding car, and I prayed that it was Heven. That she was getting herself to safety.

But then another sound filled my ears.

The hideous sound of grinding metal and crushing glass.

My steps faltered. NO! With a burst of speed I rounded a small turn in the road and looked through the trees. The sight ahead was my worst nightmare. I was too late.

Heven's car was overturned and the sharp smell of gasoline filled the air. Glass littered the ground and the guard rail was ruined. China saw me racing their way, and she leaped at me, baring her teeth. I didn't think – only reacted by leaping on her back and sinking my teeth into the soft, vulnerable flesh at the back of her neck.

Then I ripped it right out.

She made a blood-curdling howl and tried to buck me off, but I dug my claws in and held on. I managed to rip out two more chunks of her flesh before she managed to shake me off. I landed on my back and rolled, my jaws snapping out to grab her front leg. I chomped down hard and twisted, sick satisfaction flowing through me when I heard the bones snap and the tendons tear. China fell down, and I used that moment to rip at her ear. It came off, and I spit it right beside her where her head now lolled.

How do you feel now, seeing severed body parts that belong to you.

I was about to lunge again when the heavy smell of gasoline made it past my rage. Heven was inside that car, probably injured, and it could blow up at any moment.

I looked down at China, who was almost unconscious and then turned my back. I would finish her off once Heven was out of the car. When I knew she was safe.

I transformed back into my human form and ran up to the car, lying on my stomach to peer in the window. The car was lying upside down, but she was still inside, unmoving in the driver's seat.

From what I could see, the only reason she was still inside was because the seatbelt did its job and clasped her tightly against the seat. Blood covered the side of her face and her breathing was shallow. The scent of fear filled my nostrils. Anxiety filled my chest. I was scared. More scared than I had ever been before. But I had to keep it together. She needed me.

"Hev, I'm here," I told her, praying she could hear me. "I'm going to get you out of there."

The seatbelt made it impossible for me to just pull her out the smashed window, and I couldn't reach the clasp. It was all too easy to rip the fabric free, and Heven's body fell forward. I caught her, pulling her awkwardly through the window. I sat amidst the broken glass and gasoline cradling her limp body in my arms.

"I'm so sorry," I whispered.

She made no response. The injury to her head looked pretty bad. Aware the car was a ticking bomb, I moved farther away from the wreckage. She stirred in my embrace.

"Sssamm." Her voice was slurred.

"I'm here. You were in an accident. I'm going to get help."

"B-bracelet," she whimpered. I could feel her body tense as if she wanted to get up.

I looked down at her wrist, hoping to see what she wanted. It wasn't there. It must have fallen off during the crash. Damn that stupid clasp.

"I'll get you another."

"N-no." Her body spasmed and she coughed.

"Shhh. I'll get it, and then we're getting you to a hospital."

Cautiously I laid her down on the ground and went to the car. The bracelet was there, caught between some wreckage on the ground. I palmed it and ran back to her side.

Her eyes weren't open, and she was so pale and lifeless looking. I felt tears gather in my eyes.

"No!" I cried, hoarse. Gently, so gently, I grabbed her. "Heven. Can you hear me? Open your eyes."

She gave no response as I slid the bracelet in the pocket of her shorts. "I found your bracelet, honey. It's in your pocket." I thought the news of her treasure would make her open her eyes. It didn't. "Please, baby. Wake up."

Just when I was about to break down, her eyes fluttered and she stared, without really seeing.

"Heven, thank God." I sucked in a deep breath, trying to ease the pain in my chest. *Please don't die.*

"Sam," she whispered then began coughed, and blood leaked from between her lips.

I hugged her a little bit tighter, and I stared at the trail of blood slowly running down her face. I couldn't face this. I couldn't sit here and watch the only thing I loved die.

"Hang on, baby. We're going to the hospital right now."

"Too late," she rasped.

"No." I grabbed at her hand. She was ice cold. "You're going to be okay, we'll get through this."

"I love you, Sam."

Words I'd longed to hear. They pierced me to my very soul. I had been desperate to hear those words. But not like this. Never like this. She coughed some more, then gurgled. Blood filled her mouth, choking her. I turned her head to the side so that the blood could come out and she could breathe. It didn't help.

"I love you," I groaned, clutching her tight. A sob built up in my throat and ripped from my throat.

Her body jerked and she stared up at me. I cut off my emotion and focused on her, brushing her hair away from her face. "Easy, honey. It's okay."

Then she was still.

It took me a moment to understand, to realize that her eyes would never open again.

Heven was dead. She died in my arms.

Had she even heard me tell her I loved her?

A tear slid from my eye and trailed down my face. Heven was dead, and it was my fault. I would never see her smile again, never hear her laugh.

"No!" I yelled and shook her. Her head lolled around unnaturally. A sob escaped me, and I clutched her harder against my chest. The scent of death filled my nostrils. It made me sick. I turned my head to the side and retched.

Just then the car went up in flames. A deafening explosion at my back. I hunched around her broken body, trying to protect her from the heat and flying debris.

A loud clap sounded above and the sky opened up, rain pounding down around us. I let it slap against my back, each icy drop feeling like a knife.

"Heven, please," I moaned, rocking her back and forth. "Please don't leave me here."

I sat there for long moments, rocking her, buffering the rain and watching the car burn, the rain doing nothing to extinguish the flames. I looked back down at her – the sight of her in my arms caused grief so deep that I knew I would never be the same again. I wanted to die right along with her.

The blood on her face was rinsing away with the heavy rain. Even in death, she was so beautiful, even her scars glistened beautifully in the downpour.

I did this to her.

If I had just stayed away from her, if only I hadn't let myself fall in love with her that day, China would never have become obsessed. Maybe she was right after all…maybe hellhounds weren't capable of love…maybe my kind of love was twisted and unclean just like my soul. How could I live the rest of my days knowing that because of me this beautiful, innocent girl was dead? How could I wake up in the mornings and not feel her body against mine, not hear the lazy, peaceful beating of her heart?

Before I kill China, I will make her suffer. Even a slow painful death is too good for her.

The thought snapped my head up, and I peered through the night to where I left her laying. I would just go finish her right now. The things I would do to her…

China was gone.

I should have known that she would drag her beaten, broken body away when she had the chance. I looked back down at Heven. Her lips were blue. Filled with so much grief and sorrow I did the one thing that I hadn't done since I became a hellhound. The one thing I thought I might never do again. I prayed. I begged God to listen, not for me but for her. I prayed that she was at peace.

I prayed that loving me didn't give her a one-way ticket to Hell.

Something hot and heavy hit my back, something from the fiery wreckage, but I paid it no attention, my concern wasn't for me but for her. I wondered what I was going to do. Should I take her to the hospital? To her mother? I snorted at the thought. Her mother would say she got what she deserved because she was evil. I looked down. Heven wasn't evil. She was the opposite. I brushed the blond hair away from her face. She was an angel, my angel.

"How will I live without you?" I whispered. Another tear escaped me; it dripped off my chin and onto her cheek. I brushed it away with my thumb. I paused. Something wasn't right...

There was an intense heat at my back, almost uncomfortable. I figured that it was from the blazing fire, but now I realized that I no longer heard the angry flames. It was quiet, too quiet.

And I sensed that I was no longer alone.

I clutched Heven tightly against me and sprung up and around. I wasn't prepared for what I saw.

There was a woman, a beautiful woman, standing in front of the wreckage, which was no longer on fire. She was dressed in an elaborate white robe, and I swear the very air around her shimmered. She looked so out of place, here, in this place of destruction and death.

"Who are you?" I asked, instinctively curling around Heven's body.

The woman smiled. Peace wrapped around me. "My name is Airis. I am here for the girl."

"You can't have her!" I all but snarled, half-turning away.

"I am here for you, too."

"What do you mean?" I asked suspicious, turning back.

"Will you come with me?" Her voice was as kind as her face. She made no move to come at us, nor did she try and lure me closer.

"Who are you?"

"Someone you can trust."

"Not likely."

"I can help her, but you must come with me."

"You can't help her. She's dead."

"Is she?"

"Yes," I said, hoarse. I smelled the death on her skin; I'd felt the life leave her body.

"It is not her path."

"Why are you doing this?" My head was swimming. I didn't understand what she was saying, and she talked like there was hope. Hope that Heven might live. Why would she be torturing me this way?

"Will you come?"

"She stays with me?" Why was I considering this? Because if there was even the slightest chance for Heven to live, I would do whatever it took.

"Of course." Airis came forward and my heart picked up its pace.

"Stay back."

"I won't hurt you."

It wasn't me that I cared about. Airis reached out a hand and placed it on my shoulder, causing warmth to spread throughout my body. The air around the three of us began to shimmer.

"What…?"

Before I could say anything else everything went white.

Airis brought us to a place – a void – where there was nothing. No color, no life, not even any noise except for the sound of two people's breathing. I wasn't scared of this place, but I wasn't at complete peace here either. It was a totally neutral world – a place where you waited. Waited for something else to come along. My eyes watered as they tried to adjust from the darkness I had just left to this never ending sea of bright white.

"Would you give up your life for hers?" Airis asked, breaking into my thoughts.

"Yes."

"Just like that?" She seemed surprised that I didn't need to think about it. I would do anything for Heven, including dying so she could live.

"Yes."

"All right then." She inclined her head and raised her palms above her. Light seemed to gather in her palms, but I couldn't be sure because everything here was so bright. I watched as the light grew brighter and brighter, then Airis made a motion like she would fling the light right at me.

"Wait!"

Airis paused, lowering her hands. "Have you changed your mind?"

I recoiled from the idea. "No." I waited a moment for some of my disgust to dissolve then said, "Can I have a moment with her?"

Airis inclined her head, "Of course."

For the first time since Airis brought us to this place, I looked down. Even in death she was the most beautiful thing I'd ever seen.

Holding her tightly I looked around for somewhere to lay her. Almost as if I conjured it, a bed swathed in very pale gold appeared before me. I went to it, gently laid her on the satin and kneeled before her. I always knew that I would leave her eventually; what was between us couldn't last. The knowledge didn't make saying goodbye any easier.

I cupped her cheek, turning her face to the side to see her clearly. "I love you," I whispered, brushing the pad of my thumb across her bottom lip. It was like blue ice. "I did this to you...but I'm going to make it right." I leaned in and kissed her, the last time I would ever do so.

"Who's going to protect her when I am dead?"

"There is a plan in place for her safety," Airis responded.

"Goodbye," I whispered before I took one last look before making myself straighten and walk away from her. It was the hardest thing I'd ever done. I looked up at Airis who stood in the same place as before with the same ball of light in her palms. "I'm ready."

I didn't lower my head or shield my eyes from death. I stood tall and watched the ball of light spiral toward me. Dying is easy when you do it for someone you love more than yourself. The light got closer, and I felt its heat. It burned fiercely when it slammed into my skin, but I didn't feel the pain long. That was the one good thing about death: no pain.

Chapter Twenty-Two

Heven

My eyes jerked open, and I gasped for air so forcefully I sat up. Where was I? What was happening? I focused on my surroundings, but couldn't really settle on anything to tell me where I was. Everything was very bright and quiet. "Sam?"

"You are safe here."

I spun around to see who spoke. It was a beautiful woman dressed all in white.

"Where's Sam?"

She didn't answer but her eyes drifted to something lying on the floor.

"Sam!" I surged across the room to where he lay, and I noticed right away that his bare chest did not rise and fall with breath. My stomach clenched. He wasn't moving, and he didn't respond to my cries. I shook him, slapped him, even pulled his hair but he wouldn't wake up.

"Help me!" I cried to the woman who stood and watched me flail about to help him.

"You cannot help him, he has died."

He wasn't dead. He couldn't be. He wouldn't leave me. I screamed his name once more, the shrill sound sure to wake him. It didn't. "No," I sobbed and lowered my head to his chest. I waited and waited for the sound of his heartbeat. It never came.

Sam was dead.

"What did you do to him!" I screamed, standing up to face the woman.

"He exchanged his life for yours."

"No!" I shook my head. It was impossible! I wasn't dead. I hadn't died! I looked around for some sort of reality. There was nothing. There was no color except for the three of us and a bed draped in pale gold satin. How did we get here?

"I brought you here," the woman spoke. "You were in a car accident."

Realization dawned. I remembered China chasing me, the car running off the road. I was hurt and wanted Sam…I gasped. Had I died?

The woman nodded gently. "He loved you."

Loved. Past tense. "He died for me?" I whispered.

"He wanted you to live."

"I don't want to live without him."

"Why is that?"

I dropped to my knees before him. A lock of hair had fallen onto his forehead, and I brushed it aside. Tears slid down my cheeks and dropped onto his. "Because I love him." My words were broken.

If the woman made a response I didn't hear it. I curled up next to him and put my head on his chest. I felt the loss of him so deeply that I was sure I would die from it. I wished I could – then we could be together again. Suddenly I felt very warm so I looked up. An intensely bright light surrounded us. I reached up, put a hand over his face to shield him and ducked my face into his neck. It was so hot…

Then there was nothing.

A cool breeze brushed over my skin, cooling and soothing me. My entire body ached, and I moaned.

"Heven?"

His voice was so sweet. I'd thought I would never hear it again. I must be dreaming. Not wanting to wake I burrowed further into sleep and willed him to come to me.

"Heven?"

Sam.

"Why isn't she waking up?" His voice was anxious, not as it should be in a dream. "What's wrong with her?"

"She's dreaming," the woman answered.

Sam let out a frustrated sound. I felt hands in my hair and on my face. "Wake up, Heven. Please."

I opened my eyes. Sam's face was so close I actually flinched. He didn't move but his eyes flared gold and stared into mine.

"You're alive?" I asked, hope welling up inside me. I prayed that my mind wasn't playing a cruel trick on me.

"Either that or we're both dead."

A small smile splayed across his lips, and I squealed coming up off the ground so fast he fell backward with me landing on top of him. "You're alive!" The relief was so great that I laughed.

He laughed too and wrapped his arms around me and squeezed me until I couldn't breathe. "You have no idea what I went through…you died in my arms. Oh God, Heven. You're alive. Oh God, you're alive."

His hold on me was iron clad but there was a fine tremor in his muscles. I could imagine what he went through because seeing him lying motionless and cold on the floor was a sight I never wanted to see again. Those few moments had been the worst of my life. "I couldn't stand to see you that way…so cold…so still. I wanted to die alongside of you." Tears leaked out of my eyes to stream down my cheeks.

He buried his face in my neck and inhaled, his hold iron clad. I left him that way until my lungs began to burn, and I truly had to have oxygen. I wiggled, and he eased his hold while I gulped for air. "Sorry," he murmured, pulling back and taking my face between his palms. "Don't ever die again."

"You either," I whispered, more tears falling. He wiped them away with his thumbs and paused.

"Are you okay?" he asked, tilting my face and studying me. Something passed behind his eyes, and it looked like shocked disbelief. It was the same way I was feeling.

"I'm okay," I whispered.

"Where are you hurt?" He ran his hands along my arms and shoulders, coming back to brush the hair away from my face and stare at me again. "Your head…so much blood…" his voice caught and his eyes glazed over in panic.

"Sam." I caught his hands and pressed a kiss to the inside of his palm. "I'm not hurt. Not anymore."

He groaned and pulled me into him again. I fit against him so perfectly and he felt so right that I knew I never would have been able to live without him. I loved him so much that I could feel the connection between us, pulling me closer. *God, I love you.* The words pounded through my head over and over almost like a mantra. I couldn't stop thinking and feeling them.

Sam held me tighter still, his face buried in my hair. *I love you...*

My head snapped up at the same time his did and we looked at each other, both our eyes widening in surprise. "Did you say that out loud?" I whispered.

"No. Did you?"

I shook my head.

"I heard you."

"I heard you, too."

His eyes held mine and he stared at me hard. *I love you, Heven.* His lips did not move yet I heard the words as if he'd spoken them. He was watching me for a reaction, something to let him know what he suspected.

I love you, Sam.

He jerked like I hit him, his eyes closing for a second only to reopen and stare at me, shocked. *I thought this was just a legend.*

A legend?

His eyes flared again because I heard his thought and answered. "*Mindbond,*" he said, mostly to himself.

I had no clue what that was or what it meant, but whatever it was seemed to be a big deal. But right now we had bigger problems. "Where are we?"

"I don't know." He frowned, and in one fluid motion stood, pulling me with him. "What's going on, Airis?"

I completely forgot about the woman in white. "You know her?"

"Allow me to explain," she graciously answered.

Sam settled an arm across my shoulders.

"You are safe here," Airis said.

I believed her. I did feel safe here. Besides, if she wanted to harm us she would have just left us dead.

"Where exactly is here?" I asked. *And how the heck did I die and then come back to life?*

"The InBetween."

"The what?" I asked, and Sam stiffened. *He had heard of this place?*

Yes.

I jerked when he answered my thought with his own.

"It's a place where people who have died come before passing over completely to Heaven."

"Or Hell," Sam finished Airis' explanation.

"Why are we here?" I asked.

"Because you died."

"We're still dead then?"

"You were. But you passed the test."

"What test?"

"Sam gave up his life for yours. He made the ultimate sacrifice for you, proving his loyalty – his love. Your clear distress and utter certainty that you would not go on without him proved your love for him

You wouldn't live without me? Sam's thought speared into my brain, and this time I didn't react.

Never!

My response seemed to anger him and he glared at Airis. "You killed her to see if I would give up my life for her? You killed her for a stupid test!"

"I had nothing to do with her accident. She died because of China's decisions."

I shuddered at the memory of China's soulless, red eyes.

Sam made a sound in his throat. "How do we get out of here?"

"I can send you back."

"Do it," he said, not unkindly.

I wondered how much time had elapsed since we got here.

"Not just yet," Airis began. "When I spared both of your lives you acquired a debt. I need to explain this."

"You want me to pay back a debt because you spared my life when I didn't ask for it?" Sam vibrated with confusion.

I began to worry. I was thankful that we were both alive, and I was beyond grateful to this woman…but I didn't like the idea that we were now indebted to her. What would she want from us? I pulled away, but he anchored his arm around me harder. I felt trapped…

Calm down, Hev.

I can't breathe.

Yes, you can. He removed his arm from around me to rub slow circles over my back.

In. Out. In. Out.

Air found its way into my lungs to the tune of his voice, and the panic ebbed.

That's my girl.

I kind of like hearing you when no one else can.

He smiled.

"You did ask me to spare her life, did you not?"

He gave a tight nod, "I thought the debt was my life."

"Your life is too valuable."

"*My* life?" He seemed surprised, but I wasn't. His life was more valuable to me than my own.

"If she lives, then you must live as well."

"Can you please say something that makes sense?" I asked.

She inclined her head and spoke to Sam. "How much do you know about being a hellhound?"

He sighed. "Hellhounds are not as common as they used to be. Rare, in fact. They were once used to guard the gates of Hell and help souls pass into the World of Sin. They were also responsible for dragging escaped souls back to Hell."

"Do you know why they have fallen out of favor to use?"

His feet shuffled a bit then he cleared his throat, "They were too hard to control. Even Satan couldn't handle them when they wanted to disobey."

"Did you know that hellhounds have been asked to undertake other duties in the recent past as well?" Airis asked.

"No." He seemed genuinely confused by this.

Airis nodded. "Yes. And I have come to offer you a job."

Something told me that this job wasn't something he could turn down. He squeezed my hand again. "What's the job?" he asked, grim.

"We would like you to guard a Supernatural Treasure."

"We?" Sam asked.

Airis lifted her eyes to the heavens. I felt Sam recoil. "You can't possibly be saying that…"

"Yes, you have been chosen, Sam, by the highest power there is."

"That's impossible."

"Why?"

"I'm a *hell*hound. We usually operate on the other side, for the sinners. We are sinners."

"You were created by God, but twisted by the wrath of Satan. Satan twisted two beasts, coerced them into his evil and the hellhound was born. You were always children of God, but you were led to believe otherwise. But then hellhounds were cast out of hell, and your lineage changed. Hellhounds realized that they, too, had free will. A choice of who you would become. Tell me, Sam, do you think that you are a sinner by birth?"

"Yes."

"You have a dark soul?"

"No!" I yelled. I'd stayed quiet until now, but I couldn't stand here and allow this woman to call Sam evil, to imply that he wasn't good. "If he was a dark soul he wouldn't be capable of love. He wouldn't have given up his life for mine."

"The test," Sam murmured.

"Yes, the test. Now you have proof that you have always wanted – you have proven you are pure of heart." Airis smiled brilliantly.

"Are you telling us that God now wants to employ hellhounds to do good?" I asked skeptically.

Sam laughed. "If Satan couldn't control us, then how will He?"

"He does not seek to control you. He seeks the abilities that were sired to you, that are yours by birth; He prays that you choose to use them for Glory and not for evil."

"By guarding a Supernatural Treasure?" Sam asked.

Airis nodded patiently, kindly and Sam fell silent. It was a lot to take in, and I don't think Sam ever thought of himself as a child of God before. If he could accept that, then everything could be different for him, better.

"Are all hellhounds being offered these jobs?" I asked.

"Not all," Airis replied. "Some are indeed what they were originally twisted to be; they have turned their back on God and have chosen darkness. They will not be welcome."

Sam was quiet for so long that I began to worry. I could feel that he was intrigued by the idea of being something better than what he thought he was. I already thought he was wonderful. This could be good for him, giving him something to be proud of. It didn't take long, though, for doubt to creep into my head. Selfish doubt. If he was off guarding some Supernatural Treasure, then when would I see him? We couldn't be together. The thought made panic begin to build in my chest. I couldn't live without him.

"I can't do it."

Did my ears deceive me? Did he just refuse this?

"Sam." I tugged on his hand.

"Can I ask why you would refuse?" Airis asked calmly.

He looked down at me. Love swelled in my heart for him. He was doing this for me. I turned my back on Airis and faced only him. "You can't refuse."

"I already did." His chin jutted out and he had a stubborn glint in his eyes.

"You cannot refuse God to be with me!" I hissed, even though I wished he could.

"I was meant for Hell anyway. I'm staying with you. Besides, who else is going to stop China?"

"You are not meant for Hell. You have a good heart, Sam. You need to do this; your eternity depends on it." As much as it hurt, I knew I was right. I would give him up if it meant saving his soul so that when he — *gulp* — died, he would spend his eternity in peace.

"I want you. To hell with my soul."

I gasped.

From behind me Airis spoke. "Perhaps you would like to know about this Supernatural Treasure that you would be guarding?"

Sam shook his head, but I turned around to say, "Please. Is it something that he can take with him and keep where he lives?" Then he could still be with me.

"It must stay with him, and he must go wherever it goes."

"Oh."

"What is it, anyway?" Sam asked.

"It's actually a 'who,'" Airis replied.

"A 'who?'" I didn't like the sound of that. What if it was a girl? A beautiful girl without scars and a crazy mother…

Cut it out. Sam's words cut through my thoughts. *No one could compare to you, and I am not doing this.*

"It's why you were given your life back, Heven." Sam and I both looked over at her. "The Supernatural Treasure is *you*."

"I'll do it."

"You've changed your mind then?" Airis asked.

"I wouldn't have said 'no' at all if I'd known it involved Heven."

"I was hoping you would agree before you knew."

"Guess I'm not as pure of heart as you think."

I heard the exchange, but I was scarcely paying attention. Did no one seem concerned that Airis just announced that I was some kind of treasure? It was ridiculous. I was hardly a treasure; my own mother thinks I'm evil, and I'm dating a hellhound. Admittedly, he is a hellhound who has a moral soul, but still, he was a hellhound.

"Heven?" I looked up at Sam. "You okay?"

I shook my head.

"Could you explain to us exactly what a Supernatural Treasure is and what that means for Heven?" Sam asked Airis.

"A Supernatural Treasure is a person who has been gifted supernatural powers. The ones that discover their powers are generally guided by us to accomplish good things in the world. We use them as tools. The noble, extraordinary deeds you witness are usually the work of Supernatural Treasures."

"I don't have any powers." I said, confused. There was no reason that I should be considered a Supernatural Treasure. "And I haven't done any noble deeds unless you count not kicking the crap outta Jenna a noble deed."

Airis smiled at me like I was a two-year-old, then she turned to Sam. "So you agree to be the guardian, the protector of Heven, a Supernatural Treasure? You choose to denounce sin and accept virtue?"

"Yes."

"Why me? What makes me a Supernatural Treasure?" I asked, suddenly.

Airis regarded me with patience. "Because of who you are, for reasons you have yet to understand."

"Explain them to me."

"You will learn in your own time. For now, I would like to awaken the gifts that slumber within you."

"Slumber within me?" I murmured.

"Many Supernatural Treasures live their entire lives without realizing what and who they are. Many of them never know of their abilities. That knowledge isn't always necessary, but sometimes it is. You, Heven, have a path to walk. I pray that you will be strong enough to take what I awaken within you and use it for Glory."

"I don't under–" I began but Airis turned to Sam.

"Step aside please, Sam." As we watched a giant ball of light swelled in her palm. It grew until I thought the weight of it must be unbearable, but she never seemed to struggle. It shimmered and glittered turning so bright that I had to squint, yet I couldn't look away.

"What are doing?" Sam asked, his muscles tensing.

"Step aside," she repeated.

"I can't. You have asked me to protect Heven, and I agreed. While you have given me no reason to think you mean us harm I cannot just let you do whatever it is you are about to do to her, I have to know that she will not be hurt." Even as he said the words he angled his body in front of mine.

Airis, still holding the swirling ball of light, inclined her head. "Your loyalty is commendable. I give you my word that I will not harm her. I am only doing what I said, awakening her abilities."

Sam turned to me, his body completely blocking Airis from my view. He cupped the side of my face in his palm, his eyes lingering on me. "Your face," he murmured.

I knew I probably looked horrible from the accident and I laid my hand over his. "I know, I…"

"It's beautiful." He said, smiling. "She will not hurt you." He told me, he said the words like he knew them to be true. "Trust me?"

I nodded. "Always."

He backed away from me, never once looking away. I got lost in those honey-colored eyes, and I barely noticed when Airis sent the ball of light at me. Only when Sam looked away did I look up. I braced myself for the impact, for the searing heat, but there was none. The ball of light hit me and spread out, enclosing me in a bubble. The bubble floated up off the ground and hovered high above Sam and Airis. Sam stood below watching. I didn't want him to worry, because I didn't feel afraid at all.

"I'm okay," I called down to him. I wasn't in pain and for several moments I floated in the bubble of light, and it was almost peaceful. But then something changed. The air around me became electric and charged. I could feel it vibrating, making my skin tingle. "Sam," I croaked, but my voice caught in my throat. The pain was sharp and quick, and if I hadn't been floating, I would have fallen to my knees. My whole body jolted as if I was being electrocuted, and I couldn't breathe. Over and over again I felt the jolts until I was so exhausted I yearned for sleep. A loud 'pop' sounded, and it jerked me back to reality. The electric jolts stopped, and my body was left shaking. I crumpled forward only realize there was no floor to catch me; my heart seized, panic assailing me once more as I barreled from the sky toward the ground.

The feeling that I was free falling lasted only a second before my body was lowered to the ground with ease with deliberate care, and Sam reached out to catch me, holding me close to his chest.

I let my head rest against his shoulder, my body feeling drained.

Sam stiffened and looked at Airis. "That didn't look pain-free."

"She is just fine. She only needs rest."

Sam relaxed as he shifted my weight higher into his arms.

"I will transport you home now."

"You haven't told us anything about her abilities, or what she needs protection from."

"She will soon learn of her gift, and she needs protecting from anything that may cause her harm."

"But," Sam began, only to have Airis cut him off. "You have been through enough today. Everything else you will figure out. I will be there if you truly need me."

Just like that she dismissed us. Seconds later, we were standing in the rain on the side of the road where my wrecked car lay smoking. I was still in Sam's arms, and I looked up at him through the falling rain. "What in the world do we do now?"

The Hate

The bitch was alive. I stalked her all day for nothing. Finding her alone was more than I could have hoped for – the perfect opportunity. I was sure that my final attack would have finished her off. But then he showed up and ruined it. How did he know where to find her? I had escaped, fleeing the scene, but I couldn't help but come back to watch Sam grieve. The draw of that kind of hell was just too great. But when I got close I saw that they weren't there. Where had he taken her?

My body was damaged, and I was in immense pain; I sat down to rest. As I lay there, licking my considerable wounds they reappeared. Now she stands in the rain looking whole and healthy. By the stark relief written all over lover boy's face and the way he is hunched over her in the rain, protecting her still, I would say that she was nowhere near dying.

How did she manage to defy death? He couldn't possibly have saved her from what I did to her? But seeing her now, it looks like I never even touched her. I felt satisfaction knowing that her scars from this encounter might be invisible, but the ones I inflicted before were permanent.

I watched in smug satisfaction as she came to stand over the wreckage that used to be her car, her face twisted in pain. He called out to her and she lifted her face and turned. Pain screamed through me with my sharp intake of breath. It couldn't be!

There was only one way that she could have survived my attack and have this 'miracle' occur. The rumors I'd heard down below were true. The scrambling for power, the plan to upset the balance of Glory and evil, was not going unnoticed by those who wanted things to remain as they were.

But what did she have to do with it? What did *he* have to do with it?

Pain, sharp and pungent, ripped through me. I had to get out of there before I passed out; he would smell me and come to finish me off. I was lucky he was so busy mooning over her and calling the police to catch my scent now. This wasn't over, not by a long shot. It didn't matter how they were involved because I would take them out of the game before they even got a chance to play.

Chapter Twenty-Three

Heven

Hospitals suck. I swore after my accident that I would never go back to one, yet here I was. Sam sat over by the wall, his hair wet and mussed from the rain with an unreadable expression on his face as he watched the nurses poke and prod me. He was lucky they weren't torturing him this way, too. Sure, he hadn't been in the accident, but the clothes he was wearing (the shorts Airis seemed to conjure right on his body and the shirt he got from his truck) were ill fitting, ripped and covered in blood. He looked like he needed medical attention, even if I knew he didn't.

Just as I thought it, a new nurse came into the room with what I thought of as a blood bucket (a kit to draw blood) in her hands and an intent look on her face as she headed for Sam. "We would like to check you out as a precaution."

His face stayed the same, but I felt his panic like a slap to my face. Having his blood down in the lab would raise all sorts of questions. As a hellhound, Sam has an extremely high white blood cell count, which he believes is the reason that he heals quickly and rarely gets sick. If his blood went down to the lab and they saw how unusually high his count was, they would want to study his blood further which would lead to the discovery that he has an extra chromosome (which is what I learned enables him to change into a hellhound). These kinds of discoveries would only lead to more questions…questions that Sam (and I) didn't want to answer.

Thinking fast I moaned and caught the nurse as she brushed past me. "I don't feel well."

She stopped and turned to me, her face softening. No doubt I looked horrible, so my lie appeared true. "Did you get some pain meds yet?"

"Yes, they made my stomach upset," I gagged and lurched forward at her.

She jumped back, stumbling a bit. "I'll get the trash can." She hurried over and grabbed the bucket and thrust it at me.

"Thank you," I responded weakly. "Could I have some ginger ale and some crackers? It might settle my stomach."

The nurse patted my hand and ran from the room. I tossed the trash can down and looked over at Sam. He lifted an eyebrow. "Pretty convincing."

I shrugged. It wasn't all an act. The thought of anyone finding out he was different made me nauseous. He appeared before me and I blinked.

You have to go. The idea really made me feel like barfing.

No, I don't.

The nurses are going to want to check you out.

I'll handle it.

Just then Grandma ran into the room. "Oh, Heven, honey, what happened?"

Sam went back to where he'd been sitting before. "I'm sorry, Grandma, I wrecked your car." Seeing her made my eyes fill with tears. Up until this point I think shock kept me from feeling overly emotional about everything that had happened tonight.

"Don't worry about the car. How are you?"

"Okay, a little shaken up. I'm not hurt too bad." I sniffled. Lucky for me most of my injuries were healed when Airis brought me back to life. I was still bruised up and my body really hurt, but at least I was alive. Thankfully a good amount of the blood that I lost had been washed away with the rain. Having that much blood all over me would have looked suspicious considering my lack of injuries.

She grabbed my face and kissed me, brushing the hair away from my face. I looked up to smile and reassure her, but her eyes went wide and she gasped.

"What?"

Your scars are gone. They disappeared when Airis brought you back to life. Sam hurried to say.

"What happened to your scars?" Grandma whispered.

My hand flew to my face. It was smooth and flat. I felt around again and again. I looked up at Grandma. "They're gone?"

She nodded.

"I want to see." I jumped down off the gurney. My legs felt like Jell-O and wouldn't hold me up, but Sam appeared, slipping his arm under me for support.

"You have good reflexes," Gran murmured.

You didn't tell me! I told Sam as I headed for the bathroom and the mirror.

I forgot.

How could you forget this?

I never see your scars when I look at you.

When I was in front of the mirror, I took a breath and looked up. They were gone.

I wasn't disfigured anymore.

I burst into tears.

"Bring her out here," Grandma told Sam from the bathroom door.

"Wait!" I cried. Lifting my head from his chest, I stared back at my reflection. He kept a hand at the small of my back as I stepped closer to the mirror. My skin was splotchy from all the crying I'd done in the past few hours…but the scars were gone. I stared at myself, at the face I'd wished for since the accident, the face I'd always had – except it wasn't me anymore.

What's the matter?

I looked in the mirror at Sam who stood behind me. *I don't recognize myself.*

I do. You're beautiful.

I burst into tears again.

"Come lie down," Grandma ordered.

Sam led me out of the tiny room and all but lifted me onto the gurney. Instead of going back to his chair, he sat beside me. His body heat and scent calmed me. I loved him so much that I would go through everything we'd just gone through again just to be here with him.

"What happened?" Grandma asked from the foot of the bed.

"It was raining really hard, and the car just hydroplaned. It was dark, and I ran off the road." After Airis had sent us back to the scene of the accident, we called the police, and the ambulance brought us here to the hospital. While it hadn't been raining when I wrecked the car, it did start right after, so I didn't have to stretch the truth too far. "I called Sam while I was waiting for the ambulance, right after I called you."

"Well, thank you for coming, Sam."

"Anything for Heven."

The nurse bustled back in carrying some crackers and a ginger ale. Her eyes bounced back and forth between me and Sam.

"Hello," Grandma said, drawing her attention away from us. "Is that for Heven?"

"Yes, ma'am."

I turned to Sam, "Would you mind getting me some ice for my soda?"

He frowned. *I stay with you.*

It will get you away from nurszilla over there for a minute.

He looked like he might protest.

I'll be fine.

He nodded and rose from the bed. "Could I get you some coffee?" he asked Grandma.

"Well, yes. Thank you, Sam. Decaf, please."

His eyes returned to me before he ducked out, and they flashed gold. *I'll be right back.*

I smiled and waved. When he was gone I turned to my grandma and the nurse. "How much longer do we have to be here?"

The sooner we got out of there the better.

"If you could have any super power, which one would it be?"

"Uh…"

I giggled, "I guess you already kind of have a super power."

"I wish I was normal."

"I love you the way you are."

He shifted beneath the covers in my bed to face me. It was late and I didn't think we'd ever get here. It took me awhile to convince everyone I was fine, and then I'd had to ride home with Gran and Sam was left to find his own way (Grandma thought he had his truck at the hospital, and we let her believe it). I know it made him crazy to let me go off with her alone, but there was no other choice. Once we got home I took a quick shower and then stood in front of the mirror staring at my new face. The face I had to die and then be brought back to life by an angel to get. It was all so unreal, and every time I caught a glimpse of myself, I did a double take. I didn't recognize myself. How could I not? I looked like this all my life and only spent ten months disfigured, so how did that girl become more familiar to me than this one? It wasn't like I was unhappy to have this face back because I was happy. It just felt strange, to get back something that I lost, something I had learned to accept.

Sam shifted beneath the blankets, bringing my attention back to him. "I didn't think I would ever hear those words from you."

"I love you," I whispered. Just saying those words spread joy throughout my body.

"I love you, too."

I scooted forward, and he wrapped me in his arms. It's like my body knew exactly where to go and where each part of me fit perfectly against him. My eyes drifted closed at the familiar safety I felt only with him. For the first time all day I relaxed. "Sam? I'm not sure I want super powers or to be a Supernatural Treasure."

"According to Airis you have always been a Supernatural Treasure, so it shouldn't be anything new." I heard a smile in his voice and looked up.

"Do you think this is funny?" I couldn't help but smile.

"No," he said, running his fingers through my hair. "But I can't bring myself to be upset that you are a Supernatural Treasure, if you weren't you might not be alive."

"When you put it that way…" I said, tucking my face into his neck. He smelled good.

"What kind of power do you think I will have?" I said after a minute of us just lying there quietly.

"I don't know." Then he laughed. "Maybe you'll get x-ray vision."

"You might want x-ray vision, but *I* don't." I said, grinning.

He lifted his head and looked down at me, wagging his eyebrows. "You never know what you might see."

I laughed. He pulled a pillow over our heads. "Shhhh."

I giggled. "Sorry."

It felt so good to laugh and just be together, especially after dying then coming back to life. We lay there for a while in our own little bliss, and I prayed nothing would break the moment. Of course, it did. I had almost forgotten about the after effects of Airis 'awakening my abilities' until another tremor licked through my body. It started in my legs and worked all the way up through my head, and then it was gone. It made me a little queasy and a little dizzy. I pressed closer to Sam.

"What was that?" he asked, pulling back to look at me.

I clutched at him, bringing him close once more. "I've been feeling them all night. It's like an after effect of whatever she did to me."

"Why didn't you say something?" His was voice concerned.

"I didn't want to worry you."

"I'm supposed to protect you."

"It's like your official job now." I giggled.

"I wasn't so good at it tonight."

"But Airis didn't hurt me," I protested.

"I'm not talking about Airis."

"You mean China." A little bit of fear burned in my belly, and the image of Gran's smoking car flashed in my head.

"Did you kill her?"

He made a sound in his throat. "No. She ran off, and I let her go because I was worried about you."

"She's still out there?"

"Don't be afraid," he whispered, "she's not coming back tonight. She's injured pretty bad."

"But she will come back."

"Yeah."

"What are you going to do?" I anticipated his answer and it made me nervous.

"Kill her."

While I didn't mind so much about her dying, I did mind that Sam would be doing the killing. I didn't want him to have to do something like that for me.

I will do anything for you.

I can't believe that God wants you to kill someone to protect me.

Maybe that's why I was chosen. Hellhounds don't have a problem with sin.

I gasped out loud and my hands gripped his shirt. "Don't say that. They chose you."

Because I love you and would do anything for you.

Yes. But you're a good person, Sam. I yawned loudly.

Sleep, you're exhausted.

But I haven't asked you about what we're doing now.
Talking through our thoughts?
Yes. Do you know how?
China told me about it once. She thought it was a myth associated with being a hellhound. It's called a 'Mindbond.' Hellhounds can only do it with one person during their lives. It is very strong and even distance cannot break this communication.
You mean we'll be able to do this forever, no matter what?
Yes.
Pleasure bloomed in the center of my chest. *You can't do this with anyone else?*
I felt him smile. *No.*
I can sleep now. I was smiling too.
Sweet Dreams.
I love you
We slept

Chapter Twenty-Four

Heven

The sheets felt rough against my skin. Even though they were made of fine cotton, every movement I made against them felt like sandpaper. I moved again, looking for something to ease the feeling, and brushed up against something not as soft as the sheets; its rough texture surprisingly something I wanted more of. I moaned, but the sound was instantly swallowed by a pair of soft, moist lips capturing my own. Again and again they moved against mine, eliciting a delicious ache in the center of me. Curious and hungry at the same time, I reached out to touch more of this sensation, to pull it closer. I encountered more cotton – sandpaper to my skin. In protest I tried to rip it away and soon it was gone and a delicious warm weight settled over me. My lips moved deeper, my tongue traveling out, finding something to dance with. I pressed my body closer, moving with rhythm against the only thing that could make this ache inside me go away.

We have to stop.

Lips left mine, and I was bereft. The delicious weight started to pull back. *Don't leave.*

I pulled him back down and my lips found his shoulder; the taunt muscle was straining against his skin, and I scraped my teeth over the firmness. I heard him groan, and then he was gone.

"Sam?" I sat up, opening my eyes. He was across the room beside the window, pacing. It took a minute for a full thought to form in my head because it was fuzzy, and the tantalizing dream I'd just had wanted to hold on. As he paced I watched him; he was beautiful, and he was shirtless. Abruptly he paused in his pacing to turn and look at me. There was a red mark on his shoulder...*oh boy, it wasn't a dream.* Sam and I just got majorly hot and heavy, and if I he hadn't pulled away...

You thought that was a dream? He seemed exasperated and let down at the same time.

I just know that it felt really good, and I didn't want it to stop.

He groaned again and resumed his pacing. I felt a little rejected.

Did I do something wrong?

He swung toward me. *God, no. But your grandmother is right down the hall!*

I guess it wasn't the best time to get busy.

I want to take my time with you. Things right now aren't really...

I know. I scrubbed my hand over my face, my eyes felt like they had sand in them. *We should wait. I'm sorry.*

The bed dipped with his weight when he sat next to me. "Don't ever be sorry, not for that."

I nodded. "What time is it?"

"Late."

I looked at the clock and gaped. Half the day was gone! *So much for going to school.* I went to the window, pulled back the curtains and lifted up the blinds, releasing the cord, and looked out at the sunny day. I gasped and stumbled backward, my hands coming up to shield my eyes.

"What's the matter?" Sam asked, coming to stand at my side.

Close the blinds, the blinds!

He ran to the window and pulled them down, yanking the curtains closed as well. "They're closed."

Tentatively, I opened my eyes and blinked. They were watering and stinging, but I could see fine. Even worried, Sam's face was beautiful to me, which was good because it was super close to mine.

"What's up?" he asked.

I shook my head. "It's so bright out. My eyes hurt."

"The sunshine hurts your eyes?"

"Yeah." I blew out a breath. "Tell me, do they look bad?"

He came even closer and took my head in his hands and tilted it this way and that. I waited through his scrutiny, preparing myself for news of some new disfigurement. "They look fine," he declared.

"I want to see." I looked in the mirror above my dresser. He was right, everything looked normal. I turned back to Sam and shrugged. "I guess I just wasn't fully awake yet."

"Are you awake now?"

I nodded.

He went over to the window and lifted the shade. My eyes burned and watered when the light bounced around the room, but it wasn't as bad as before. "It still burns."

He closed the blinds again, frowning. "Are you feeling okay?"

I took a moment to take inventory of my body; everything seemed fine. "My muscles are sore, but the accident and then whatever happened with Airis…"

He nodded.

"But otherwise I feel okay." Then I remembered something. "Except for those tremors I was getting last night."

"Had one yet this morning?"

"No."

"You should take it easy today."

"Yeah. I'm starving though, want to eat?" I went over to the bedroom door.

He appeared beside me and placed his hand over mine as I reached for the doorknob. "I can't just waltz downstairs with you."

"Oh. Right."

He smiled. It was crooked and playful and my heart turned over.

His smile faded and he skimmed his knuckles down my cheek.

"Maybe you could come visit me? You know – to see how I am feeling after the accident."

He nodded. "I'm going to run home and shower first, change my clothes."

I didn't like the idea of him going to the home he shared with China and the other hellhounds. *Will she be there?*

Nah, she's probably hiding.

He said this just to make me feel better. I could feel that he hoped she was there so that he would get a chance at her. Anticipation coiled inside me and my body was ready to jump into a fight. I frowned. I was scared of China; I did not want to see her.

It's the Mindbond. It's called bleeding. The mental state of one can 'bleed' to the other and affect their mood.

All emotion, all the time? I asked and frowned. While I loved having this Mindbond with Sam, I didn't exactly like the idea of him hearing and feeling every thought I had. Some things were just meant to be private.

No, honey. The bleeding would only occur when we are standing this close to each other. Unless it is very intense emotion, like if you were hurt or something bad was happening to you, then I would feel it. It's the same for you and feeling my emotions.

I nodded, warming to the idea of bleeding.

The Mindbond means we can talk like this, through our thoughts, no matter the distance between us. We can only hear the thoughts we project out to the other, and again, unless of course you were thinking very loudly or forcefully, then I might be able to pick up on them.

I understand. But then I had a thought. *Sam? If China thought this was all a myth, then she must have never experienced this or known anyone who has either...who's to say the stuff she told you is true?*

Sam took my hand and brought it to his lips, pressing a soft kiss to the tips of my fingers. *I guess I can't be sure. But so far everything else she told me has been true. I guess this Mindbond/bleeding thing will be something that we figure out together.*

I liked that.

He smiled then turned away, but I pulled him back.

You feel that much anticipation at seeing China?

Anticipation to remove the threat she poses to you.

Stay.

I'll be back.

I'll miss you.

He tapped my forehead with his finger and smiled. *We can still talk.*

I'm the only one that you can do this with?

His grin was quick and devastating. *The one and only.*

I could get use to this Mindbond stuff.

If you need me...

You'll know.

"Yeah," he whispered and pulled me close for a quick kiss. Then he disappeared out my window.

You forgot your shirt! I told him, wanting to see if it really worked when he wasn't in the same room.

Keep it.

I picked it up from where it lay on the floor and raised it to my nose. It smelled just like him, spicy and masculine. After hugging the cotton to my chest I tucked it beneath my pillow. With any luck the scent of him would still be there later when I wore his shirt to bed.

Sunlight filtered in from every window downstairs. As I walked through the living room my eyes stung more and more until they watered. I hurried over to my book bag and found my sunglasses. Thankfully the dark lenses gave me a semblance of relief. Grandma was in the kitchen, moving around. I could smell fresh coffee and muffins. The big windows next to the table were uncovered with sun streaming through them, and I had to squint when I entered the kitchen. I bolted for the coffee pot, turning my back on the sun to pour the brew into a giant white mug.

"Good morning!" Grandma called. "Did you sleep well?"

Taking a breath I turned around, leaning against the counter.

"What's the matter?" she gasped, looking at my glasses.

"I have a headache," I murmured, taking a sip of coffee. Which really wasn't a lie, the sun was so bright it was starting to hurt my head.

She hurried over to a cabinet and pulled out a bottle to shake two pills out into her hand. "Here, this will help."

I took the pills and swallowed them with my coffee. "Thank you." On my way to the table, I snagged a banana muffin and then sat with my back to the window. I blinked a couple of times trying to clear my vision, which was slightly blurry.

You doing okay? Sam's raspy voice floated through my head.

I'm fine. The light still hurts, though.

I'll be there soon.

Okay. I really wanted to tell him to hurry and that I missed him terribly but he already felt an extreme obligation to protect me, why make it worse? Besides shouldn't I deal with my own problems myself?

"I spoke to the insurance company; the car was destroyed completely from the fire but is completely covered. I should receive a check very soon to buy a new one."

"That's great. I'm so sorry about the accident."

"Hush, I know it was an accident. I'm glad you weren't hurt."

If only she knew.

I concentrated on my muffin. It was good, and I found myself wishing that it was somehow magical and healed whatever was wrong with my eyes. Grandma 'tsked' at my silence and walked over to the window above the sink. "I'll lower the blinds, maybe it will help your headache."

"Thank you." The room darkened just slightly when the shade was down because the windows at my back were the biggest. Still the little change in light seemed to make my eyes worse. It seemed like my eyes were trying awfully hard to adjust to their surroundings, and the slightest bit of variation in light made them work even harder. I stared hard at Grandma as she refilled her coffee mug; she was so blurry I could hardly make her out. I squeezed my eyes shut hard and took a deep breath. When I looked up she was watching me, frowning.

"Here let me get the other shades." She jolted forward, and her burst of movement caused something in my brain to snap.

Intense, bright color exploded around me.

I have to get out.

I have to get out.

The mantra pounded through me. Something was so wrong with me. My head pounded and even though my eyes were closed, blindingly bright color swam in front of me. I worked really hard not to show my alarm. After several long seconds during which I only tried to breathe, I managed to thank her for lowering the shades. She didn't seem to notice that I was suddenly overwhelmed, and for that I was thankful.

"You should take it easy today. Yesterday took a lot out of you."

"I plan on it," I answered. Should I open my eyes? Would everything be normal, or worse? My stomach twisted in panic as I fretted about what to do. What if I opened my eyes and I couldn't see anything? What if I could see, but everything was so blurry I couldn't make my way out of the kitchen without bumping into everything?

There was a knock on the door, and I heard Grandma open it. "Sam," she said.

"I thought I would come and see how Heven was feeling after the accident."

I fought not to slump with relief. *Something's wrong.*
I know. Breathe.

"Well come on in. Let me get you a muffin and some coffee."
"Thank you."

I felt him drawing closer. His scent reached me, and I wanted to cry. From right before me he spoke, "Hey, Hev. How are you feeling today?"

"Except for this headache, I'm good." *Bright colors are everywhere.*

Close your eyes.
They are closed!

"I like those glasses." I knew he was smiling for the benefit of Gran. Except I felt robbed of his smile. I wanted to see it too. Oh God, what if I couldn't see his beautiful face?

Open your eyes; focus on me.

I opened my eyes. For a few seconds bright blotches of color obscured my vision, and I panicked, reaching out to grasp Sam's hand. But then, slowly the blotches faded away and my vision became clear. Sam was squatting before me, staring hard, worry on his face.

You're so beautiful. I couldn't help but think.

He smiled but not enough for the worry in his eyes to disappear. *Does the light hurt your eyes?*

Not too bad. It was actually better than before.

"Here you go." Gran set a plate and mug next to him on the table. I looked up at her and gasped, jumping in my chair.

"What!?" she exclaimed.

I shook my head, "Sorry, you startled me." It was a pathetic lie.

"My goodness, you about gave me a heart attack." I stared at her even when she moved away.

What's going on?
There's a huge ring of color around her. It keeps changing.
Are there colors around me?
No.
Anything else?
No.

Sam glanced at Grandma and moved to sit at the table next to me. "I brought some movies with me. I thought maybe you might like to watch them today, if you don't have plans, that is."

"No plans," I said and then turned to Grandma, who sat down across from us. "Would it be okay if Sam hung out for a while?"

"That's fine dear. A movie day is just what you need. And I won't feel guilty for leaving you alone to go to the store."

Sam palmed a few movies that I hadn't even noticed and stood, pushing in his chair. "Thank you for the muffin and coffee, Mrs. Montgomery."

"You're welcome, Sam."

I stared at Grandma as the colors around her shifted some more.

Come on, Heven.

I stood, grabbing my coffee. I felt sluggish and tired. Sam took the mug from me and led me into the family room where the TV and DVD player were. He went about sliding a movie into the player, and I settled on the couch, pulling a blanket over me. When he turned around I slid the sunglasses up over my head. *What's happening?*

Looks like we just discovered the supernatural ability that Airis gave you.

We did?

You can see people's auras.

Did that even count as some sort of supernatural ability? It wasn't particularly exciting. And it wasn't that useful. Sam settled down on the sofa next to me, and my first thought was to curl up in his lap and lay my head on his chest. But then Grandma banged a pan in the kitchen and put an end to those tempting thoughts. With a sigh I settled for scooting a little closer and laying my head on his shoulder. With one hand he pressed some buttons on the remote, and the movie flashed on the screen. I didn't notice what he put in because his other hand was busy slipping beneath the blanket to slide his fingers through mine. I closed my eyes and sighed, thinking that maybe if I went to sleep, when I woke up my headache would be gone and there wouldn't be a ring of colors surrounding my grandma. Except I couldn't sleep. As exhausted as I felt, my mind wouldn't shut off and leave me alone. It was annoying.

Questions plagued me. If I really could see auras then why didn't Sam have a ring of color around him? Would I be able to see colors around everyone that I looked at? That was going to be extremely distracting. How was I supposed to walk around school and not let on that everyone was glowing? I felt like such a freak; first the hideous scar and now this. At least this was something that no one else had to know about. And how was I going to explain at school tomorrow where my scar went? I couldn't possibly tell the truth.

And what about my eye sensitivity? When would that go away? Wearing sunglasses 24/7 just wasn't an option. I guess I could–

Stop.

Sam's demand brought me out of my swirling mind. *What?*

Stop worrying. We'll figure it out.

I can't, I have too many questions.

Then let's get some answers.

How?

He hit the pause button on the remote, and I looked over at the TV, noticing the movie for the first time. *How to Lose a Guy in Ten Days?*

He shrugged, "You've seen it?"

"Sure. Have you?"

He shook his head. "It looked like a girly movie, and I thought it would make you happy."

I smiled. "You'd sit through a girly movie just for me?"

"Yes, although, I actually think it's kind of funny."

"Let's finish watching it."

He shook his head. "Later. We have something to do."

"We do?"

"Go offer to go to the store for your grandma. I'll drive you."

"I don't know if I want to go out…"

"Wouldn't you rather learn about what you're seeing today at the grocery store with me instead of at school tomorrow?"

"Totally." I tossed the blanket to the side and tugged his hand as I stood.

We went into the kitchen where my grandma was reading the newspaper. I stood there a minute trying to get a handle on the colors that circled around her. The brightest, most dominant color was blue. I watched in fascination as other clouds of color in green and purple floated around her. Sam squeezed my hand, and I cleared my throat. "Grandma, if you give me your list I would be happy to go to the store for you."

She looked up from her paper. "I thought you had a headache."

"The pain reliever you gave me really helped."

"Well, good. But I still think you should rest."

"I really feel fine, and you do so much for me. I really don't mind. Getting out for a while might be nice."

"You'll drive her, Sam?"

"Yes, ma'am."

"All right then." When she walked across the room the colors went with her. She pulled out a list and some cash. "Here you are. Make sure that you pick up something for dinner tonight. Sam, you are welcome to join us."

I leaned forward and kissed her cheek. "Thanks, Grandma. I love you."

She smiled and the colors around her flared a shade of pink. Somewhere inside me a voice told me that the color of pink stood for love. "Love you too. Don't stay out too long."

Sam waited downstairs as I went to change out of my PJs. As I dressed I couldn't help but feel the irony. Just last week I would have been thrilled to go out in public without my gross scars, and now that I could, I was too nervous to enjoy it. I was afraid that Sam was right and that I really would see everyone's aura. It made me feel like I was still a freak, just in a different way.

Chapter Twenty-Five

Heven

The parking lot at the grocery store wasn't crowded. I was incredibly relieved because I was already shaking. From the minute we'd turned onto the busy street I was assaulted with too many bright colors. Everywhere I looked there were people exploding with different hues, so much so that my head began to pound all over again. It was sensory overload to the tenth degree.

Sam parked the truck and turned off the ignition, but made no move to get out, instead turning to look at me.

"How am I supposed to process all of this at once?"

"You don't have to."

I snorted. "Are you kidding? I don't have a choice."

"Yes, you do." The raspy quality of his voice soothed me. "It's like going to the mall. There are dozens of stores all with different colors, lights, music. There are different scents from all the different food places, there's a lot going on. But you don't really notice it, you know? Sure you know it's there, but you aren't really thinking about it all at once."

The idea made sense. "Just because I can see the colors doesn't mean I have to pay attention to them?"

"Exactly. Unless you want to."

I nodded. "I guess I could try it."

I took Sam's hand and let him lead me through the parking lot, keeping my head down and my sunglasses on. The light was still a little too bright for my eyes. Once inside I took a breath and looked up. I couldn't help but notice every person that was near. Each one of them had colorful rings of color around them. All of the colors varied in shade and intensity. It overwhelmed me, and my chest began to feel tight.

Don't pay any attention to them. Look at me.

It wasn't hard to lose focus of everyone else and concentrate only on Sam. I did it all the time. He was gorgeous and if that wasn't enough, now I had another reason why he took my breath away. He was the only person I looked at that wasn't surrounded by color. He made me feel like things were normal.

He laughed out loud, drawing a few stares. *I make you feel normal?*

Stop listening to every thought I have.

He had the grace to look chagrinned. *Sorry.*

I pulled Gran's list from my pocket. "Come on."

Thankfully, I didn't see anyone that I knew. At first it was hard to concentrate on the list because seeing a rainbow of color at every turn wasn't as easy as I'd hoped. Sam was super gracious leading me from aisle to aisle, only stopping in front of the things I needed to get. When we finally made it over to the dairy aisle (the last aisle that we needed to go), I was relieved and a little more relaxed. I somehow managed to get through the store and no one seemed to notice that I stared at everyone and everything. I reached into the large cooler for a gallon of milk and stepped back when a man brushed by me. I gasped, dropping the gallon at my feet where milk exploded everywhere. I pressed my back against the cooler door and stared at the man who glared at me before stalking away.

Sam stepped in between me and the view of the man. "What's the matter?"

That man is so ugly.

He glanced over his shoulder. *He isn't that scary looking.*

I shook my head. *Ugly on the inside. Angry too. The colors around him are icky and brown.* I shuddered.

Block it out, Hev.

"Guess I'll get someone to clean up this mess I made."

"I'll go." He turned just as someone was coming out of the stockroom. The man looked at the mess and told Sam he'd come back with a mop. When he returned I smiled. "I'm really sorry about the mess."

"Don't worry about it."

"Can I help?"

"Nah, it's okay." The colors around him were mostly blue, and it felt like he wasn't angry at all, and it made me feel better. After the milk was mopped he reached into the cooler and grabbed me another gallon. "Here you go."

"Thank you," I accepted the milk and added it to the cart.

After we paid for the groceries, we loaded them in the truck and were walking back from the cart return when Sam pointed to the ice cream shop next to the grocery store.

"Can we get it to go?" I asked.

"Sure."

The place was packed, and I panicked. Quickly I slid the sunglasses over my eyes to help keep out some light and hide my expressions. Sam put a palm to my lower back, and I concentrated on the feeling it gave me. I managed to make it through the line to order (strawberry in a cone for me, a to-go cup of butter pecan for Grandma and a double scoop of chocolate for Sam) and navigate through the crowd. Outside on the sidewalk I took a deep breath of the spring air and enjoyed a taste of ice cream. It was silly to feel proud of myself, but I did. I managed to get through the menagerie of colors without losing it in front of everyone.

Then I looked up.

Kimber and Cole were coming through the parking lot toward us with Kimber waving at me fanatically. I checked my watch. Yep, school let out just twenty minutes ago. I looked back up at my friends. Colors of bright shades in yellow, orange, red and most dominantly – turquoise – shot out around her, almost like flames. Her aura was so bold that it practically fought for space with Cole's. His was bright too, but the colors were not as frantic; they didn't burst around him like they might attack me. They were much more soothing to my eyes in green and blues. There was also a dominant magenta shade, a mix of purple and pink that surrounded his head. It was the first time I had seen a color like this. Sure, I have seen pinks and purples, but they were always temporary bursts, they never stayed like this color, and the purple and pink never mixed together to create a new shade. It was different, but it seemed to fit him perfectly somehow.

I'm not sure I'm ready for this.
I'll be here at your side.

It gave me the strength to wave and smile at them. If I wasn't so nervous I would have laughed at Kimber's aura. It fit her perfectly and explained her exactly. It was disconcerting to know that everyone's aura I saw probably fit them the exact same way too. I would never have to get to know someone before I knew if they were a good person or not. A giggle escaped me. *This sure cuts back on time.*

Sam grinned and then attacked his cone.

"I have been calling you all day! Why haven't you answered? And why weren't you at school today?" Kimber said, stopping before us. She put her hands on her hips and glared at me.

"Hey, guys." I said, getting ready to spew a lie. But I didn't even get a word out because Kimber gasped loudly.

"Oh My God! Your face!"

I swallowed hard as people turned to look. Sam shifted closer beside me, and I resisted the urge to shrink into his side.

"Kimber," Cole warned, quietly. He looked at me though, with wonder.

Surprising myself I lifted my chin and let them look, I even lifted my sunglasses. "I know, pretty awesome, huh?"

Kimber was actually speechless for once, her jaw falling open as she gaped. Her aura flared red, and I frowned. "How?" she croaked.

"It's the reason I wasn't in school today. I have been talking with this plastic surgeon for a few months now…I never thought I would be able to get in, but he had a cancellation late Friday afternoon, and he called me. I got laser surgery and had the scars removed."

"Why didn't you tell me?" Kimber exclaimed, smiling. "We are supposed to be best friends, how could you keep this from me?"

"I never thought I would get it done, and I certainly had no clue that it would work. It's usually supposed to take a few treatments, but he said that once the laser touched my skin the scars just seemed to come right off."

"That is awesome!" Kimber said, clapping her hands. "I am so happy for you!" Colors exploded all around her, and I was reminded of the fireworks that Sam took me to see.

I was beyond happy that Kimber and Cole believed me and that they were happy but their emotions were slapping me in the face. It was almost too much to handle.

"Yea, Hev. That's awesome. You deserved something good like that to happen to you." Cole reached out and hugged me with one arm. Surprisingly, some of the emotion that was berating me fled. I was suddenly wrapped in the soothing blues and greens of his aura and even some of the rare magenta shade.

"Thanks, guys. I was still feeling kind of funny this morning from the pain medicine the doctor gave me during the procedure, so I stayed home and slept in. I didn't call you back because this isn't something I wanted to tell you over the phone." I hoped I wasn't blushing but judging from the heat I felt in my cheeks I figured I probably was.

Sam cleared his throat and stared pointedly at Cole and the arm that was still around me. Cole looked up at Sam and a smug look flickered behind his eyes before he released me.

Before I could do anything else, Kimber lunged forward and hugged me. It was a tight, quick hug that left me speechless. "Are you kidding? I forgive you! Wait here while we get our ice cream, and we can sit together and talk."

Just the idea was exhausting, but I saw no way out.

Sam ran a hand down the back of my head and spoke to Kimber. "We have groceries in the car for her grandma, and she's still pretty worn out from the procedure."

"Of course." Kimber nodded. "Will you be in school tomorrow?"

"Sure."

"Cool. I'll see you at school in the morning?"

"I'll see you then." This time my smile wasn't forced because I knew I was getting out of there very soon.

I waved to Cole as Sam led me toward his pickup. *You saved me.*

You're worn out.

Yeah. Thanks for the ice cream.

You let him touch you. Sam said, steering the topic toward something I thought I had avoided.

He's my friend, Sam. He was happy for me.

Sam walked along beside me, not saying anything and I prayed that he wouldn't ask me to stop being friends with Cole. I felt like everything was spinning out of control, and I wanted my normal routine, my friends. I wanted things to feel normal. I didn't know if they ever would again. Sam lifted me up into the cab of the truck and hurried around to get in. As he turned the ignition he said quietly, "I won't ask you to give up your friends. I would never ask something like that of you, but I don't like when he touches you."

"I understand." I did understand. But I couldn't help but feel like I was somehow disappointing him in not offering to end my friendship with Cole. As he drove I closed my eyes, wondering if a quick trip to the grocery store was this hard, how an entire day of school would be tomorrow.

It was pure hell. I arrived the next morning feeling like I could handle it. I'd handled the grocery store yesterday, so I already knew what to expect. At least I thought so. Now I understood that I didn't know anything at all.

It might have been okay, but I forgot one major thing: my scar. Or rather, the lack thereof. I thought since people didn't much pay attention to me they might not notice right away that it was gone. Wrong. From the minute I walked through the doors, an onslaught of my classmates were coming up to me, marveling at my face.

Before people only stared and looked away, whispering behind my back. Since the masquerade ball though, things had changed. My old friends weren't as concerned with giving me space. I'd encouraged them: talking, smiling, and trying to get some of what I'd lost back.

Now I wondered if that had been such a good idea.

I couldn't get *Before* back. There was no going back to that girl. She was gone.

Forever.

"What happened?" a voice asked from beside me.

Amber came running up, "Oh My God! You look so great!"

"Heven, did you have your scar removed?"

I barely heard their words. All I saw was color. It exploded right on top of me, around me and it was all I could see. The more that gathered, the harder it was to focus on anything.

Sam was right there with me, thank God. He tucked me into his side and smiled at our audience. *Say something, honey.*

What?

Tell them about your surgery.

Knowing I had a lie ready to go and that Kimber and Cole already bought it made me feel more in control, and I looked up, trying to focus on faces, not colors, and I plastered a smile on my face and managed a fake laugh. "Yeah, I got totally lucky, and this plastic surgeon had a cancellation at the last minute. It was this new laser surgery." It sounded convincing, and I held my breath while waiting to see if everyone else thought so too.

"It looks so great!" Amber said enthusiastically.

"Totally," another classmate agreed. To my absolute horror, she reached toward my face.

Sam moved smoothly, swiftly, turning so that the girl brushed his shoulder. "Heven needs to get to her locker," he announced. He shouldered us through the crowd but it didn't go away, it moved with us.

I can't do this.

Yes, you can. Focus on me.

We made it to my locker, Sam opened it, and I practically thrust my head inside.

"Geez, people! She isn't a circus show!" Kimber's loud voice came from behind me. I grinned into the locker. "Let me through! Go on, shoo!"

People began moving off, and I sighed. "Thank you," I groaned to her, keeping my face in the locker.

"No problem." She sniffed. I turned to look at her and stumbled backward, Sam steadying me.

Colors flamed around her; she had to have the strongest personality of anyone I knew. It was unsettling. I glanced at the floor trying to get control. When I looked back up she was still flaming colors, but I tried to look past them.

"You look great," I said, lame.

"Thanks." She grinned.

Cole walked up behind her, smiling. "Hey, guys." He tipped Kimber backward, kissed her, then he glanced at me and grinned. "Looking good, Hev."

I smiled, but it faltered. Red exploded around Kimber, and I knew instantly what it meant. I guess I came hardwired not only with the colors, but their meanings as well.

"Hey? You okay?" Cole stepped forward and laid a hand on my arm. The same vibrant magenta shade from yesterday surrounded him, and he was still the only person I have seen that carried that color. More red burst around Kimber, masking Cole's aura completely and making me jerk back.

"Yeah, great!" I reached into my locker and grabbed a handful of books, not even looking to see if they were right. "Better get to class," I said, moving backward, Sam moving with me.

Cole frowned, but Kimber smiled and waved, her aura returning to its less-intense colors. I heaved a sigh of relief.

What was that all about?

Kimber's aura is totally intense.

That's not all. Sam insisted. *I can feel it.*

It's just...never mind, I might be wrong.

You aren't wrong, Heven.

How could it be? I wondered.

Say it.

Kimber's jealous of me.

You didn't know this? To Sam it was obvious.

No. I...we're friends.

Sam shrugged. *Sometimes friends get jealous.*

He was right. It happened to me sometimes, but seeing it in her aura made it seem worse somehow. The way the red burst around her seemed violent.

It made me wonder if having my old face back was going to put a strain on my friendship with Kimber. She already admitted to being jealous once and that was before I got my old looks back. I never imagined that not being disfigured might actually cost me a friend. I shook the worrisome thought away. Kimber was my best friend; she would see that nothing between us had to change. Then, hopefully, everything would go back to normal...

If only I could remember what exactly normal was like.

Chapter Twenty-Six

Heven

As soon as Sam's truck got close to Gran's I saw it. As if my day hadn't been bad enough – the entire weekend really. First, I realized that my mother was going to believe I was evil no matter what I said. Then, psycho China tried to kill me – well, actually, she did. Then Sam sacrificed himself and died. After we were both brought back to life, I was hit with a ball of light, got a massive headache, and now I saw auras. Did I mention that my BFF's aura isn't looking like a BFF's aura should?

Sam stiffened and the wheel jerked in his hand. "We're leaving," he growled.

I sighed. "No. Let me just get it over with."

"You're sure?"

Round two with Mom. "Yep."

"I can't stay," he worried.

"It would make things worse anyway," I mumbled. Then I gasped. "I didn't mean…"

"I know, honey." He took my hand in his and pulled the truck to a stop next to my mother's car. "It's all right."

"I love you." I wanted him to know.

"I know. I love you too."

Despite my mother standing on the porch watching, the bold colors exploding around her, I leaned over and kissed Sam. Surprise flickered in his eyes as I leaned close, but he didn't push me away. He did what he always does: welcomed me with open arms and took my breath away.

I hope you don't pay for that, he said when I pulled back.

I would pay any price for that.

His fist clenched in his lap, and he looked up with fierceness in his eyes. *Sometimes I love you so much I can hardly...*

I touched his cheek, "I know. See you later."

"Hev." He caught my hand. "If you need me..."

"I know you'll come."

I got out slowly and walked to the porch to stand next to my mother. I waved as he drove away. My mother just stood there in shock. Then she went into the house. I followed.

Sam reached out. *Let me know how it goes.*

You'll be the first. I prayed that this wasn't going to be a scene. I prayed that maybe she was just here to make sure I was okay after the car accident.

Gran was at the kitchen sink rinsing some baking potatoes. She turned when Mom and I walked through the door. "Hello, Madeline. Heven, how was school?" The dominant parts of blue and green in her aura were muffled by a burst of brown. Clearly, she knew this meeting would not go well.

"Fine, thanks," I answered, as Mom turned to face me.

"You are still seeing that boy!" Colors in purple, turquoise and orange floated around her – but mixed with those vibrant colors was an ugly one – a mustard shade with tinges of brown. The colors of worry and anger.

"Yes." I crossed my arms over my chest.

"You kissed him," she practically hissed.

"I love him."

She stared at me for long moments. "Your scar is gone."

"I thought Gran told you."

She nodded. "But to see..."

"Guess I'm not as evil as you thought."

Her eyes flashed with pain but then it was gone. "I wanted to come see you as soon as Gran called me about your accident, but..." her aura flashed with a mustard color and a strong pink shade. Worry and love.

But you felt too guilty maybe? I left your house upset and got into an accident. The words were on my lips, but I didn't say them. It wasn't her fault, it was China's. "I don't blame you, Mom."

"You don't?"

"It was an accident."

"I would never want you to get hurt."

"I know." It was written all over her aura. I knew she loved me. It was something.

"About that boy…"

"Sam is in my life, Mom. For good. I will not stop seeing him."

"Don't you take that tone with me, young lady. You'll move back home."

A potato hit the sink with a thud. I felt exhausted. I just wanted to be alone. To not have to see colors swimming around everyone I looked at. Mom wasn't going to change her mind about me. She could force me to go to church, to camp, or back home, but she couldn't take away Sam.

"You can make me move home," I said, going for the door leading to the living room, "but it won't change anything. This is me, Mom." I turned to Gran, "Would you please call me when dinner is ready? I'm going to my room. I want to take a nap."

Gran turned to look directly at me. Respect shone in her eyes. "I'll call you."

I didn't bother looking back at my mother. I'd said all I had to say.

The barn was quiet, and to my great relief I couldn't see the auras of the horses. Actually I'd learned that I couldn't see the aura of any animal. I puzzled over why I wasn't able to see Sam's, because he isn't what I would classify as an animal. Sam is human, he was born to two parents, and he is a child of God. Yet I couldn't see his aura…the best I could come up with was that it had something to do with the extra chromosome that he had and that it somehow threw off his energy.

I took my time currying Jasper, relishing the fact that it was Friday. Finally. The whole weekend stretched before me, and I didn't have to go out and deal with anyone.

How is work? I asked Sam, smiling.

Boring. No one wants to work out on a Friday night.

See you soon. Love you.

I can't wait. Love you too.

I led Jasper out of the barn and hoisted myself up onto his saddle. I looked forward to a long, relaxing ride beneath the trees and amongst the spring air. The trail was exactly as I thought it would be. I rode for a long time, feeling the week's tension seep out of me. School would be out next week, and I couldn't be happier. My eyes finally adjusted to my aura ability, and I had no more eye sensitivity and no more headaches. There was still no sign of any other abilities, but I was okay with that. I liked the idea of getting used to this one first before another was sprung on me. Hopefully, I would be able to enjoy a fun, stalker-free summer with Sam and my friends.

I was heading back toward the barn when Jasper stiffened, his ears going flat. A moment of panic rolled through me, but I breathed through it, looking around for anything that might have spooked him.

Out of the corner of my eye there was movement. I turned toward it, and a streak of black dove behind the trees. I laughed.

"Did they let you leave early?"

Sam peaked out from behind a tree. Jasper danced. "Easy, boy." I felt a moment of hesitation at Jasper's uneasiness. He was usually much more comfortable around Sam these days.

Want to race to the barn? I asked him, gathering the reigns and readying myself to urge Jasper forward.

What?

I see you, silly. Want to race?

Where are you? There was a feeling of stillness that washed over me with his words.

Right in front of you, silly.

Are you alone?

Panic assailed me, and I realized that I was getting an example of how Sam's feelings could bleed to me in intense circumstances from afar.

I'm at work, Heven.

I looked up to where the hound had been. It was gone. Crap. Panic pounded through me. It was China. She was back from wherever she kept disappearing to. There was a loud thump behind me; Jasper reared up and fled away from where China stood. I had to grope for his neck just to stay on.

I dared a glance over my shoulder to see the hound running after me, bouncing off trees and leaping into the air. "Run," I urged Jasper. "Faster!"

Heven!

China's back.

Get to the barn, lock yourself in! I'm coming.

There was only one problem. China was between me and the barn, and Jasper was running as fast as he could in the wrong direction.

Chapter Twenty-Seven

Heven

She was toying with me.

I knew this because I knew that she could run faster than Jasper. She could have taken us down the minute she came upon us, but she didn't. She simply ran behind, chasing us, scaring Jasper and scaring me. My heart raced at a speed I never thought possible, and I struggled to get air into my lungs. Why was she delaying? Was she so vile that it wasn't enough to kill me but she had to torture me before I died? Visions of the car crash filled my mind and so did flashes of the newly discovered memories of the attack that left me disfigured. I wanted this torture to stop; yet, at the same time, I knew I should be grateful, because the more she played, the longer Sam had to get here.

Heven? Are you all right?

She's still chasing us. I don't know how much longer Jasper can run like this.

I'm almost there.

Hurry.

I was deep into the woods and knew that we should be nearing water. Grandma owned a lot of property that backed up to a small lake. I wasn't familiar with this part of the property because she didn't own the lake, and I'd never ventured this far in. I dared a glance behind me and earned a smack from a low-lying branch for my effort. I put my hands up trying to protect myself, but nearly lost my balance. I buried my hands in Jasper's mane and bent over him, trying to stay on. If I fell off...

She's getting closer.

Use your whistle!

Of course! I'd forgotten! I fumbled beneath my shirt and pulled out the small, silver whistle. With shaking hands I put it in my mouth and blew as hard as I could.

I heard nothing.

But the horse sure did. He reared up and I fell off, hitting the ground and rolling. Pain rocked my body, but I kept rolling and pushed to my feet. I looked back in time to see him stomp down right where I fell. I shuddered, thinking how close I came to having a broken bone and giving China even more of an advantage.

Heven!

Jasper heard it, too. I fell off.

Are you hurt?

No.

My legs were shaking as I tried to quickly calm Jasper. It was no use. I looked around for China, frightened that, because I was no longer running, she would decide just to end things now. My anxiety grew the longer I went without a glimpse of her jet black form – maybe I should be thankful for the lack of her presence, but I knew how cunning she was. I couldn't let my guard down. Just because I couldn't see her didn't mean that she wasn't there and ready to pounce. I made a feeble attempt to get back on Jasper, but he wasn't having it; he was too upset. After a few tries I gave up trying to mount him, and instead I got him to turn toward the house. I hit him on the rump, hard. He took off without looking back.

Then I was alone.

China slithered from behind a large tree.

We stared at each other.

She sank down low and prepared to jump.

I blew the whistle again and she dropped down, cringing. Taking advantage of the moment I looked around for something to use as a weapon. There was nothing I could use against a large, angry hellhound.

She stood, shaking her head. I placed the whistle against my lips and she lunged. I blew it and she fell out of the sky onto the ground. The noise didn't appear to hurt her, it just seemed to stun her enough that she couldn't think.

Climb a tree! Sam told me urgently.

Just my luck, there was a tree nearby that I thought I might be able to hoist up into. I blew the whistle as I ran toward it, keeping China back. I scrambled up about halfway. Perched on a teetering branch, I looked down. China was growling and pacing at the bottom.

I put the whistle back to my lips.

I'm here.

I let the whistle fall, not wanting to hurt Sam with it.

I'm up in a tree.

I can smell you. Stay put.

China put her big paws up on the tree and tried to shake it. When that didn't work she tested her claws for climbing. My breath caught in my throat as I looked down in panic. Could she climb this tree?

A streak of black shot out from behind the tree and came around the side, barreling into her and knocking her to the ground. The two animals went rolling, and I bit my lip to keep from screaming. I watched as the two went at each other again and again. They were so tightly wound together that I could barely distinguish where one began and the other ended. It was beyond maddening. The angry howls and snarls that they were making would echo through my nightmares forever. I watched as razor sharp teeth gnashed together and white, angry foam filled their mouths and pooled around their lips. They were fighting to the death.

I bit back yet another cry when China sunk her teeth into Sam, and he let out an enraged yowl. Tears pooled in my eyes and blurred my vision. I swiped them away and looked for something, anything that I could use to help. I shouldn't hide up here like this, I should help – or at least attempt to help myself and Sam.

My eyes landed on a branch not far above my head; it was bare, and the leaves hadn't grown on it. The branch looked angry and stark against the greenery of the other branches. The end of it was pointed and sharp, emphasizing its lack of fitting in amongst the others. I reached for it, my arm not long enough, and the branch remained out of reach. I let out a frustrated sound that mixed with the snarling below, and I glanced down. China was charging Sam, leaping off a tree into mid-air, but Sam met her half way and sent her body spiraling back and into a large, mature tree. It shuddered with the force of her hit but it stood tall and strong. Seeing the way the tree held its ground inspired me. *Don't give up.*

On trembling knees I raised myself up to balance of the shaky branch, pausing only long enough to reach out to steady myself against the tumultuous ledge I perched on. Then, pushing past my fear, I leaned up and grasped the dead branch in my hands and pulled. It wouldn't give. Sure, it bowed to me. It bent. But it refused to break. I felt it mocking my weakness.

I heard another scream below, and I saw China take Sam by surprise and tackle him to the ground. She lifted her claws and made a motion to slash open his belly. I screamed and grabbed up my whistle and blew long and hard. I blew so hard that my lungs seized for air and I felt lightheaded. China collapsed on the ground next to Sam and neither of them moved. I took my chance and quickly stood, ignoring the way the branch bowed and sagged beneath my weight. Then I grabbed that dead branch – my only available weapon – and I yanked as hard as I could.

It gave way with a sharp, ear piercing crack.

My triumph was short lived because the branch I was standing on also gave way. I fell, down through the hard, unforgiving branches and leaves, gripping the weapon I fought so hard to get, refusing to release it.

I didn't hit the ground. It seems my weapon, the angry branch, saved me. It got caught between two other branches and I hung there, my feet dangling a few feet above the ground. China's red, vile eyes laughed with glee as she raced toward me. I went to grab for my whistle and realized I couldn't – if I let go of the branch I would fall into her waiting claws.

I prepared to kick out but Sam launched off the ground and snatched her backwards by the neck and ripped out a clump of black fur. China screamed in agony and turned. She swiped at him with her claws, catching him at the shoulder. He stumbled only to get right back up and snap his ferocious teeth at her. His black lips folded back over blacker gums and his teeth dripped with excess saliva. His pointy ears laid flat against his head, and he keened a sound that made my ears ring.

China jumped at him, but Sam slammed her sleek and bloody figure into the hard earth without any trouble, pinning her down with his considerable weight. When she struggled he used his teeth on one of her legs, a loud, snapping noise announced the bone breaking. When he let go it fell at an odd, painful angle.

My shoulders were burning and shaking from holding myself up here for so long. The weight of my body seemed to drag me down, and I could feel the skin on my palms ripping from the rough bark on the branch. I looked down, wondering how much it would hurt when I fell.

I heard another yelp and I looked down – expecting to see another leg broken for China. I screamed, realizing that the yelp hadn't been hers but Sam's. China had managed to get on top of him and was biting into the vulnerable flesh of his neck.

The scene frightened me so much that, without thinking, I let go of the branch and fell to the ground with a thud. Stunned, I went to my hands and knees and looked up, through the hair that fell around me. China was still biting down on Sam's neck, but she was looking at me.

I stared her down, I looked into her red unblinking eyes with a glare that I hoped challenged her. "Come on, you sick bitch," I taunted. "Come and get me."

I saw her eyes flash, and she released Sam to come after me. I reached for my necklace only to realize that I must have lost it when I fell through the tree. *Shit!* China was on me in mere seconds. I tried to kick out – to fend her off. She snapped at my shoe, ripping it off my foot and tossing it away. I tried to see past her, to see if Sam was alright, but her huge black mass filled my vision.

She smelled…like rotting meat and bleeding flesh. When I sucked in gulps of oxygen I could taste the metallic hint of blood on my tongue. She was definitely injured with what looked like two broken legs. How she supported herself at all was astounding. Hate was an incredible motivator.

I fell back when she pounced on me. Blood from her cuts dripped onto my face, and I wanted to flinch away, but I wouldn't allow myself. I wouldn't show her my fear any longer. She bent low, blowing her putrid breath into my face and then snapped her teeth at me. I did not flinch.

She raised her paw – an unbroken one – and I knew that she meant to maim my face once more. I lifted my chin and turned my cheek giving her full access. "Even if you tear half my face off, I'll still be more than you could ever be," I taunted her.

With an enraged roar, she brought her claw slashing down, but it never met my skin. Sam ripped her away, and they went crashing into a tree. I watched as he grabbed hold of her tail and ripped, the terrible sound of ripping flesh was hideous. Then another crack filled my ears as yet another of her bones broke. She tried to dash away but fell. Three broken legs and a missing tail rendered her too injured to run.

Sam didn't seem to notice that she was nearing defeat. He kept attacking, launching himself at her. The sounds he made were inhuman as he ripped her apart. I turned my face away, waiting for the horror to end.

I thought of slapping my hands over my ears, but I figured there was no use. The sounds that they were making – there was no escape. From the sound of things, China had found yet another burst of life and the two went at it again...

Until all fell silent.

I sat up from my position against the tree, pushing at my hair and looking around. *Sam?* I pushed out hesitantly, using the Mindbond. For some reason disturbing this silence seemed wrong.

He didn't respond. What if China had somehow gotten the upper hand and Sam was killed? What if I had laid here and did nothing while he died?

My eyes took in the patches of black fur and the lumps of body parts littering the forest floor. *Sam!* I stood, ignoring the way my legs threatened to buckle and turned in a circle, searching...

My eyes landed on a large black heap.

He was alive! He was there, lying on his belly. I jumped up and ran toward him. He lifted his head as I rushed forward and dropped to my knees beside him.

She's dead. He told me, raising his bulk up into a sitting position. His usually gleaming black fur was matted and dull from dirt and blood and other things I didn't even want to think about. Then he peeled back his lips in what looked like a snarl, but I recognized it as his houndish smile.

China was dead.

For good.

Excitement and relief coursed through me that this nightmare was over. I turned and looked once more at the body parts that lay scattered. The enormity of what just happened hit me, and it was all too much; my stomach lurched. I ran to the trees and vomited.

When I turned back, Sam was standing near a tree watching me with unreadable eyes. "I'm sorry you had to see that."

"Are you all right?" I asked, wiping my mouth with the back of my hand.

He nodded.

He was completely naked, and I kept my gaze up over his shoulder. "You're bleeding."

"Just a scratch," he sounded exhausted. And something else…"You were out here alone."

He was angry. At me.

"I…I didn't think."

"You didn't think at all! You almost got yourself killed!"

I recoiled from being yelled at. I didn't like it. Mostly because I realized he was right.

He sighed. "Do you have any idea how close that was? How afraid I was I wouldn't make it in time?"

"I'm sorry." I said, feebly. My legs were shaking and I leaned back against the tree. I closed my eyes. "I'm sorry you had to do that."

I heard his movement, but didn't open my eyes. I couldn't stand to see him so angry at me. "She can't hurt you ever again." His voice was soft and came from directly in front of me.

I opened my eyes. His were burning with golden flames.

Is it wrong to be so relieved that someone is dead?

He shook his head and a smile took hold of his face and lighted his features. The he grabbed me up and spun me around, his laugh echoing in the trees. It was so wonderful that it pushed away the memory of the horrific sounds from before. "Finally! She's dead!"

He sat me down and pressed a quick kiss to my lips and grinned again. *We can actually go out without looking over our shoulders.*

I reached a hand out to his chest and splayed my fingers along his heart. It was pounding. With happiness and relief. Then I noticed all the blood smeared all over his chest and the long jagged cut near his collar bone. "Sam!"

I tugged off my hoodie and pressed it to the wound. Breath hissed between his teeth. He took the sweatshirt and wrapped it around his waist.

"I need to clean that."

He nodded. "Let's go."

I hesitated and he turned back, a question in his eyes.

"What about her?" I whispered, daring a glance at what was left of China.

He made a rude noise. "Leave her. The birds and animals will eat what's left."

"But won't she smell? What if someone finds her?"

"No one will know what she was, she's too unrecognizable for that…besides the animals will make short work of her remains."

I nodded and turned away, hoping that the sight of her and the images of birds pecking at her decaying flesh wouldn't haunt me.

Sam squeezed my fingers. "She's gone now. Let's put her wrath behind us."

I nodded and together we started in the direction of the house.

A few feet later he stopped and hauled me against him, twirling us around once more. I giggled. He bent low and his breath ticked my ear as he whispered, "Just me and you now…no more stalkers in the shadows, and no more worry over leaving you alone."

"I like the sound of that." I sighed.

He smiled and that mischievous glint came into his eyes. Just as he was about to say something, he stiffened, his head snapping up. Quick as lightening he shoved me behind him and a low menacing growl escaped his throat.

I peeked around him to see what was wrong. Two sleek hellhounds stood just feet away.

In a hard, cold voice that he never spoke to me in he said, "China's dead. She attacked me and Heven; I killed her. Anyone have a problem with that?"

I held my breath wondering about the wisdom of his words. He made it sound like a challenge. He was already hurt and exhausted – could he take on two more? I rested my cheek against his back, feeling the way his muscles rippled. *Maybe he could.*

There was some rustling around and then I heard a deep human voice say, "Yeah, we saw. You really let her have it."

They had been watching? I was beyond appalled. Did that mean they stood around and watched Sam battle for his life – for my life? What kind of people were they? I looked around Sam again to see that the hellhounds had transformed into two guys who stood there, both naked. I averted my eyes. A girl with any sense of modesty is going to have a hard time with dealing with all of these shiftings.

They were the same two guys we saw on the street weeks ago in Portland: his roommates. The guys he got into a fight with and then disappeared for three days to hide his injuries from me.

"She got what was coming to her," Sam said, his voice strong but quiet.

"That was brutal," one of them said. "The way you just went at her..." His voice trailed away, and he cleared his throat. "I didn't know you had that in you..."

"Are you claiming leader?"

Sam's muscles bunched and shifted. In him I felt an overwhelming sense of power and need. He was quiet for long moments. "Yeah, I am," he said, the challenging tone back in his voice.

What did they mean 'leader'? Did that mean that he was going to control what they do? Did that mean they were going to be around a lot? I didn't like that idea. I didn't really know these guys, but I knew enough to know that I didn't like them.

"What if we don't want you to be leader?" one of his roommates asked, his voice laced with menace.

"Bring it on," Sam snarled and motioned behind us to China's scattered carcass. "Here's a preview of what will happen to anyone who challenges me."

One of them snorted.

I stood and stared in shock as the rapid movements of Sam caught me off guard.

He grabbed one of his roommates by the neck and slammed him into the ground. He made a move like he would bend low into the struggling man's face, but then he swiftly pulled back and delivered a hard punch to his face.

He spoke so quietly that I had to strain to hear his words. "I am not in the mood for your shit. I've put up with a lot from you two and I'm done. You have a choice: accept me as leader or die." The last word came out as a growl and the way his body arched over the stilled and listening roommate made me think he was fighting the urge to change. Then he shoved himself away and stood. "What's it going to be?"

"You're crazy," the guy on the ground said, his eyes narrowing.

Sam didn't respond. He just stood there waiting to see what they would do.

"What do you want us to do?" The guy on the ground gave in while the other nodded.

"As leader I'm telling you to leave town. Don't come back."

"What if we don't want to leave?"

"You don't have a choice." His hands flexed at his sides as he waited for them to argue.

I sucked in a breath. My legs were shaking, and I reached around my neck for the cord that held the whistle, thankful I found it at the base of the tree after the fight was over.

"Mind if we get our stuff before we go?"

He shook his head.

"Thanks for taking her down. She was a real bitch." The dark-headed roommate said.

"Stay out of trouble," Sam said, and I thought I heard the slightest hint of fondness in his voice. It made me wonder if he regretted sending away the only people he knew who understood what it was like to be a hellhound.

"Not everyone's a hero like you." With that the two of them turned and walked away.

Sam didn't respond, but stood and watched until they were out of sight. A million questions raced through my head, and I opened my mouth to start asking. But then he turned toward me, and my words died on my lips. His eyes were hard, but the weariness was undeniable.

He approached and held out his hand, and I took it. We walked through the woods in silence.

The scent of peroxide filled my nostrils as I doused a cotton ball in the bubbly liquid. Sam watched me quietly as I leaned forward to begin cleaning the deep cut on his skin. "You might need stitches." I told him, as I gently wiped away blood and dirt.

"I'll heal," he murmured as I went for another cotton ball to repeat the same process as before. "I have to go back to work."

"Did you get in trouble for leaving?"

"No, but I need to go back."

"Would you have killed them too? Your roommates, I mean?" I asked, picking up a tube of antibiotic ointment.

"I would have done what I had to do. If they had challenged me...I wouldn't have had a choice."

I nodded and focused on taking care of his injury. "I understand," I said quietly even though I didn't really know what it meant for him to be 'leader'. I didn't want to get into it now after everything that just happened. I wanted to relish in the fact that my stalker was dead, and we could finally relax, let our guard down, and just be us – even if it was for only a little while.

Thank you for coming after me. I pushed at him, looking up into his eyes to smile.

He grasped my hands and kissed the tips of my fingers. *Always.*

Once the bandage was applied and I cleaned up the first aid kit, I handed him his shirt. He accepted it but made no move to put it on. He looked down at the kit in my hands and grinned. "I carried this thing around for months, thinking that I might need it for you – praying that I wouldn't – but wanting to be prepared if I did. I'm glad it's only me who's needed it."

"You carried this around for me?"

He laughed. "Do I look like the kind of guy who would need to carry around some Band-Aids?" He arched an eyebrow and looked down at me.

"No?" I asked laughing, injecting a bit of doubt into my voice.

He growled and came forward, tackling me to the ground. "You would dare insult me after everything I just went through for you?" He pinned me to the ground, his eyes sparkling gold again, and I enjoyed the sensation of his bare chest against me.

"What are you going to do about it?" I asked, breathless.

He lowered his head, his full lips parting slightly, and my eyes fluttered closed. I waited for that first moment when his lips would brush mine, that first little brush of excitement before the fire he always lighted in me took hold.

"I sure could go for one of those Bubble Teas about right now," he said mere inches from my lips.

I paused and my eyes flashed open. "What?"

He laughed. "They're pretty good, and I'm hungry."

I attempted his growling noise, and he laughed. I pushed at him, but it was half-hearted. Then he finally pressed his lips to mine. Laughter spilled through his mouth and into mine. The kiss was full of swirling emotions: happiness, fear, relief.

When he pulled back he sighed. "I wish I could stay, and we could celebrate."

"You'll be back later…" I smiled. "We can go get one of those teas then."

He grinned, a wolfish grin, and stood, pulling me up along with him and reached for his shirt. I watched, a little disappointed, as he covered up his spectacular body.

"I think when I get back I want to be alone with you." His deep voice dropped and goose bumps raced along my arms. I hoped that the excitement I felt wasn't tinting my cheeks pink.

He smiled and caught my chin to look into my eyes, "I'll be back later."

"I'll be waiting."

Sam

I could still taste her on my tongue. The metallic tang of blood seemed to fill my mouth and stick between my teeth. I swallowed, forcefully. It made me sick. Ripping China apart had been good, exactly the kind of vengeance I wanted…but now that it was over – it made me sick. How she could destroy people like that and enjoy it was beyond me. A flashback of flinging around her remains made my stomach turn and the truck veered toward the side of the road. I righted the truck and fought back the memory. Sounds of ripping flesh and ragged breathing filled my head.

China had fought for her life…until there was literally nothing left to fight with. I could still see the look in her evil eyes when she realized that she was dead. I shuddered and tried to blink the memory away. But it wasn't leaving. Her eyes…they had looked almost smug in a sick sort of way. Who acted smug when they knew they were going to die? It was almost as if she knew that she would haunt us even in death. But that was impossible. Wasn't it?

Even still, that hadn't been the worst thing about killing China. The worst thing was that Heven had seen it – seen what I was capable of.

How she still looked at me with love in her eyes I didn't always understand. But I was grateful for it. I wasn't going to let anyone take her from me. China had to die; she should have died a lot sooner than today. Refusing to give her a single second more of thought, I turned my attention back to the road and glanced in the rear view mirror.

Every mile I drove further away from Heven felt like a knife in my chest. I had wanted nothing more than to stay with her, just to reassure myself that she was fine and that the threat to her was gone.

Even though I knew that there was no longer a threat to Heven I still wasn't able to relax. I guess I spent too long protecting her for those feelings just to vanish. I glanced at the clock and sighed. I still had two hours left on my shift at the gym. Thankfully, we weren't busy, so when I told my supervisor I had to go home because a pipe had burst beneath the sink, he let me go. But only after he told me to come back once I shut off the water.

I pulled into the parking lot of Planet Fitness and parked the truck. *Two hours* I told myself. You can do this. Act normal for two hours. Forget that you just ripped apart your roommate and claimed leader over the group. Forget that they may not have listened to the order you gave them and you would have to take action.

The two hours I dreaded so much turned out to not be as bad as I thought. I thanked the Mindbond that I shared with Heven for that. The sound of her voice purring through my head throughout the remainder of my shift kept me from staring at the clock. When I finally walked through the parking lot toward the truck it was dark. The air wasn't cold, but without the sun it wasn't hot either. I knew that Heven was fine and safe at home, so I decided to stop by the apartment to see if my roommates had indeed decided to accept me as the leader…the *Alpha*.

I would know as soon as I arrived because if they were still in town I would know where we stood. I had enough energy in me tonight for another fight, but I didn't relish the idea. I didn't want to make good on my earlier promise and rip them to shreds. But I would if I had to, so I prayed they left. I didn't enjoy killing, and while I might not like them…they were kind of like family. They were the only ones that I knew like me. Still, I couldn't have them stay. They were loose cannons, threats to Heven's safety and really to the entire town.

As I turned onto the main road I thought over the word that I really struggled to even say – Alpha. Being an alpha wasn't really even something that seemed relevant to me. To me an alpha controlled a pack; he was the strongest, most cunning of the group. He could take on any challenge thrown at him and win. An alpha was the term for a werewolf leader. I was not a werewolf, nor did I think that any of the other characteristics of an alpha applied to me.

Sure, I was strong and had abilities. I was young, which up until this point, I think the others saw as a weakness…they didn't realize that maybe it was a strength. But most of all, I think I was underestimated. They all thought my attraction to Heven was a phase, was just something that I played with. They hadn't realized how deep my feelings for her go…perhaps because they themselves are not capable of that kind of affection. I think what gave me the advantage was that I was incredibly *driven*. Driven to keep what was mine safe.

Did those things make me an alpha? No. But if my roommates wanted to think that it did then I wasn't going to argue. I could use it to my advantage and run them out of town. I could probably control Casey if they stayed. He was violent and he liked to stir up trouble, but I could probably convince him to lie low. But…Riley…he was a wildcard. I felt like he underplayed his abilities and his strengths. At first I hadn't noticed, but the more time I spent with the group, the more apparent it became that he allowed China to be leader. Really, if we wanted to get into naming and calling alpha – I would have said Riley had that in the bag. In fact, I found it curious that he let me strong-arm them earlier today, agreeing to leave. That only meant one thing: Riley had an agenda of his own.

I pulled up to the apartment and sat in the dark staring out the window. I was tired. Not so much in body but in mind. The events of the past year had been draining. Worry over Heven's safety and sanity had been all consuming. Now that the immediacy of the threats against her was removed, I felt as though I might be able to breathe easier.

I looked up at the apartment. A light was on. The tension that I had been allowing to drain away just moments before returned. There would be no relaxing while Casey and Riley were still in town. Maybe I hadn't been as convincing earlier today as I had originally thought.

When I got to the apartment door I paused. Then without another thought, I put a shoulder to the door and sent it crashing in. It banged against the wall and bounced back to slam behind me. I let out a growl and launched even further into the room, catching Casey off guard. I slammed him up against the wall and held him firm, ignoring whatever he dropped at my feet.

"I told you to leave town."

"Chill," Riley said coming out of the bedroom carrying a large black duffel bag. "We were just leaving."

I looked at Casey. He nodded, so I shoved away from him and looked down. There was a duffel bag at his feet as well.

"I thought you would be long gone by now."

"We were just getting our stuff together," Casey said, bending to pick up the bag and swing it behind his shoulder.

I glanced at the bedroom the two guys shared. It was bare of all their belongings with just the old wooden dresser and bed, which was switched down to the mattress. I watched as Casey grabbed up a few other bags and went to the door, then he turned back to Riley. "I'll be in the car."

Riley nodded. Casey's gaze shifted to me.

I wasn't really sure what to say to someone that I ordered to leave town. "Stay out of trouble," I said again to him, not sure he would take the advice this time either.

Casey's mouth tilted up. "As long as I ain't around here, what do you care?"

I shrugged, because, really, I didn't.

Casey's small smile stretched to a grin and then he walked through the door. I wondered if this was the last time I would see him.

I turned to look at Riley. He looked back with a level expression in his dark eyes.

"Why did you stay here? Why did you put up with China?" I asked.

He lifted a dark brow. "For the same reasons as you."

"You and I both know that you already knew all about being a hellhound before China found you."

If he was shocked I knew, he didn't show it. Calmly he shrugged. "I have my reasons."

"What are they?"

He said nothing just stared straight at me. I figured now would be the moment to see if he really accepted me as leader. Finally something shifted behind his eyes and then he said, "She never found it, after all this time."

"You mean China and that dumb map?"

Riley bent to pick up a few duffel bags and swung them over his shoulders.

"Is that why you were here? You wanted it too?" What was the big deal over some stupid map?

"I'll see you around." Riley said and headed for the door.

I hadn't really expected for him to answer my questions and really, I guess I didn't care. I just wanted him gone.

"I don't want you coming back here," I told him, the hint of threat in my voice.

"Relax," he said, "I'll stay away from her. I know who she belongs too."

"Don't forget," I growled.

He grinned. "You don't have to worry about that."

And then he was gone.

My conversation with him left me oddly unsettled. *Hev? You okay?*

Yup. Waiting for you. How to Lose a Guy in Ten Days *is being played on TV in half an hour.*

It's a date.

I looked around the room once more and my gaze landed on the open bedroom door. I moved quickly, pushing the door all the way open to survey the room. It was as I noted on first glance: empty. But there was something I hadn't noticed before. I went toward the bed and picked up the piece of paper lying in the center of the bare mattress. I recognized Riley's handwriting instantly. I stared down at the words and committed them to memory, not really sure why I bothered. Then I tossed the paper back down and left the apartment all the while wondering why Riley left me the location of where he was going.

Heven welcomed me as she always did, with warm eyes and smiling lips. I wanted to grab her and kiss her until nothing else existed but us…but I wasn't sure it was the right time. For some reason my brief encounter with Riley left me feeling restless. I felt like something was coming, like there was something out there that I didn't know about. I told myself that I was just too used to being on high alert, always on constant watch.

But those thoughts didn't go very far in fighting my instincts. Instincts, I had learned, were usually right. It wasn't until I was settled in the warmth of Heven's bed, beneath a blanket, with her at my side that I began to feel any bit of relief.

And if I held her a little bit tighter and a little bit closer…she didn't seem to notice, and I never once let on.

If something was comingI would be ready.

Chapter Twenty-Eight

Heven

"Can I ask you something?"

"Anything," Sam said, looking up from the bagged lunch I'd brought him.

I looked out across the lake. It was calm and peaceful, the waves moving in the breeze. It didn't appear at all the way I knew it could be: black, choking and life threatening. I shook myself and looked back at Sam.

"I'm going to teach you how to swim," he declared.

"What? No."

"Then you won't be afraid of the water."

"I'm never going to swim as well as you."

He laughed. "No, but at least you won't drown."

I looked back at the lake. Maybe learning to swim wouldn't be so bad…if Sam taught me.

He grinned and took a huge bite of the ham sandwich I'd brought for him. "Thanks for bringing me lunch."

"You weren't going to eat," I accused.

"I can't leave the shack. I'm the only one here renting boats today."

I know. So I brought lunch to you. I liked switching into the Mindbond sometimes, it reminded me just how close I was to Sam, and I liked having conversations that no one else could hear.

I like to eat. He grinned, taking another huge bite.

"I noticed," I said dryly, then laughed.

A car pulled up and a couple got out and walked up to the rental shack. "I'll be right back," Sam said, hurrying off to help them.

I watched him work. He was friendly and helpful, getting the couple into a paddle boat and seeing them off. He came back only after he was sure they could work the boat and were headed off toward the center of the lake.

"So you wanted to ask me something?" he said, picking up his sandwich.

I nodded. "They said that you're Alpha now."

He paused from chewing and looked up. *Not really.*

But they said...

He sighed. *Hellhounds were never made to be pack-oriented. We're too independent. That's part of the reason we were tossed out of hell. Too hard to control even by an Alpha. We don't really have Alphas.*

I don't understand. They said you were leader now. You told them to leave and they listened.

The four of us lived together for a while; China kind of took over and the rest of us let her because we were younger and weaker. It just kind of became our group dynamic.

Then you killed her.

He finished the sandwich and opened the bottle of water and took a long drink. *Then I killed her. I guess the guys thought I would try to take over where she left off.*

They wanted you too.

Maybe. But only because that's what we are used too.

You wanted to be Alpha.

He shrugged. *I guess part of me would enjoy the power, the control. But I have other responsibilities.*

"You mean me."

"I mean protecting a treasure who, luckily, is you."

"Why did you send them away?"

He sighed. "They aren't nice guys, Hev. They might have been willing to accept me as leader for a while, but then the fights and the power struggle would have begun. I don't want that. I don't want them around you. They are dangerous, and I don't want to deal with them."

I feel like you've given up so much for me.

He made a scoffing sound. *Those guys were nothing to give up. Besides, I wouldn't have anything if I didn't have you.*

His fingers stretched across the table to lace with mine, and we sat there quietly watching the people in the boat. They were definitely in love, I watched as the pinks and purples of love bloomed around their heads like little clouds and reached out to one another. As the man rowed the boat rocked and one of the oars slipped out of his hands. Mustard bloomed around the woman in worry when the man leaned overboard to grab the oar. Then he rocked the boat – on purpose – judging by the way his aura flared and the woman screeched. When she realized his trick, she playfully pushed him then slid over in front of him, as close as she could get, and he settled back into a harmless rhythm of rowing.

I smiled to myself. The guy sure knew how to get her closer.

"I know Airis said that there was a reason that I am considered a supernatural treasure, but I just can't imagine what that is."

He shoved a whole oatmeal cookie into his mouth as he thought about my words. The way his jaw flexed as he chewed turned me on. And shot of heat streaked through my body. He glanced at me, gold streaking his eyes. I was suddenly glad Sam wasn't able to see auras too. It was bad enough that he could practically hear every thought I had.

I blushed and looked down. Sometimes having a Mindbond was embarrassing.

"I don't really know what is going to happen." His voice was huskier than usual. "But to me, you are a treasure with or without a supernatural power."

He had a way of making me forget exactly what we'd been talking about. He came around the table and crouched in front of me, taking my hands. "Thanks for lunch."

"You're welcome." I stood, Sam moving with me. "I'll see you later."

He groaned and pulled me in for a long hug. *I wish I didn't have to work so much.*

When are you moving into your new place? It was a lot less rent and maybe he wouldn't need to work as much.

They called me today. I can move in tomorrow.

"Great! Want me to help you finish packing tonight?"

"Sure. I get off here at four. I'll come pick you up."

Sam's two roommates actually kept to their word and moved out. As far as he could tell they'd left town too. It was nice not to have to look over our shoulders everywhere we went. It was nice to see Sam actually relax a little.

I finally got to see the apartment they'd been renting. It was a lot bigger than the tiny efficiency he was moving to, with its two bedrooms, separate kitchen, and living area. But the place was more depressing than I could have imagined. It made me more determined than ever to make sure his new apartment was a real home for him.

Even though the place had two bedrooms, Sam didn't have one. China had claimed a room of her own, and the other two boys had shared a room. Sam had slept on the couch. It was an old sofa in blue plaid that sagged slightly in the middle. A threadbare, ugly, green blanket hung off the back that I pictured as being Sam's only source of warmth. Sure, he might be a hellhound, and he might not need a lot of blankets...but shouldn't he have a nice one just in case? Shouldn't everyone be entitled to at least one comfort? It made my heart hurt.

There was a TV on a little table across from the couch and a brown, wingback chair with holes in it adjacent to the TV. The walls had all probably once been white, but were yellowed with age, and the carpet was rust-colored shag that seriously needed cleaning. The kitchen was very outdated, and I wasn't sure if any of the appliances worked other than the fridge, which was pitifully empty.

I understood Sam's hesitation to bring me here, even after he knew it was safe. I knew, because of the Mindbond, that he hated for me to see the way he'd lived. He was embarrassed that he didn't have more.

I didn't acknowledge that I knew these feelings because I didn't want to hurt his pride. And honestly, it didn't matter. I loved him. He did the best he could to take care of himself, and I was proud of him for that. But I was equally thrilled that he was moving, and when I was done with his little apartment, it would be suitable for someone as special as he is.

I was taping up the last of the boxes from the kitchen when he caught me behind the waist and kissed the back of my neck. His tongue snaked out to trace a line up to my ear where he stayed to nibble. My heart thundered and my knees felt weak. Oh, what he did to me.

"Sam," I groaned.

"Sorry," he released me, keeping his hands out to steady me.

Passion and teenage hormones were pumping through my veins. I bit my tongue to keep from blurting out that I wanted him. Although I was certain he already knew.

"Soon," he murmured, taking my face in his hands.

"When?" I asked, breathless.

His lips brushed mine. Once. Twice. The third time they lingered. "Not here," he whispered against me.

I closed my eyes and willed myself to calm. I took in the feel and touch of him. Finally, I stepped back and cleared my throat. "This box, uh." My voice sounded like I'd eaten gravel. *This is stuff that is going to your new place. I put all the other stuff to be donated by the door.*

He stared at me for long moments before he nodded and took the box to add it to the 'keep' pile. "That should be everything then. There's just one room we haven't cleaned out…"

All the sexual tension disappeared. "China's room."

"Why don't you wait out here? I'll take care of this, and then we can leave."

"No." I shook my head. "I'll help. It will go faster and then we can leave."

"You don't have to," Sam said gently.

"I know." I grabbed his hand and we walked together back to Evil's den.

Her room was a little nicer than the rest of the place. That made me angry. She didn't deserve nice. Although, I guess it wasn't really nice, just more livable. If this room had an aura it would be icky brown. She had a double bed with sheets, a pale blue comforter and two pillows. A small ratty dresser with a mirror sat off to the right and a small closet filled with clothes. Two pair of shoes – one running, one heels – were tucked to the side of the bed.

"I'll get a trash bag," I murmured and went from the room to find a large bag. Half of her stuff was going out to the garbage. I would like to throw it all out, but some of it was usable and someone might need it, so those items would be donated. None of the stuff in here would be making the move with Sam. I shuddered at the thought.

"You really don't need to do this," Sam said, taking the bag from me.

I grabbed the shoes and tossed them into the bag. He chuckled and began taking the bedding off the bed. We made short work of the room. I filled a few boxes for Goodwill and two big trash bags.

I was giving the room a final 'once over' before shutting the door, when something struck me as odd.

"What is it, sweetheart?" Sam asked, coming up behind me to run his hands down my arms.

"There's something there. It looks like there's something sticking out beneath the…"

Sam moved swiftly, lifting the mattress up. Between the mattress and mattress pad was a cylinder-shaped tube. It looked like it was made of metal – bronze, in fact. Sam frowned and picked it up, letting the mattress fall back in place.

"What is it?" I asked, peeking around him to see.

He shrugged, "Probably junk."

It wasn't junk. "Why would she hide junk under her mattress?"

The object was pulling me forward. My hands tingled with the urge to touch it. "Can I see it?" I whispered.

Sam looked up, his eyes narrowing. "What's the matter?"

"Nothing," I said impatiently. "Can I see?" I held out my hand while studying the tube. It was maybe six inches in length and was about as wide as a drinking glass.

He handed me the object. My hand closed around it, and I swear the metal vibrated in my palm. It was lighter than I would have expected. I turned it around, feeling a little lightheaded. "Look." I pointed to the top of one end. "You need a key to open it."

He looked down. "Weird."

"Yeah, it…" my voice trailed off as the room began to spin. "I – I'm not feeling…" I reached out to grab for Sam.

"Heven?" He grasped me with both hands. "What's wrong?"

Everything went white.

Chapter Twenty-Nine

Heven

"Heven?" Sam called. He sounded so far away.

I turned my head toward his voice. Where was he?

"Not again," he murmured.

I could feel his panic and worry. I didn't want him to be worried. I forced my eyes open, blinking against the light.

My eyes adjusted to the light and I looked around. The place was familiar. We'd been here before.

The last time we both died.

"Hello, Airis."

"We meet again."

"Why is that?" Sam asked.

I realized that I was still clutching the bronze tube in my hands. I held it out.

Airis inclined her head. "You found it. Well done."

"I didn't know we were supposed to be looking for it," Sam said.

"It was time," Airis replied.

"I guess you want it…is that why we're here?" I asked, not quite knowing how I felt about that.

"It is yours, for now. We need you to keep it safe."

Curiosity flowed through me.

"Can you tell us what it is?" Sam asked.

Airis inclined her head. "You hold in your hands a true treasure."

Beside me Sam jerked. He looked down at the bronze tube in my hands with renewed interest. When he caught me staring at him he said, "This is what China has been searching for. She found it."

"So it's a map? Like – to find treasure?" I asked, knowing it felt wrong.

Sam shrugged. "I don't know. She never told us anything about it. Just that it was a map and she wanted it. I didn't really know what to expect."

We both looked at Airis, hoping for some sort of explanation.

"This parchment doesn't lead you to treasure. It contains very specific words of God's knowledge that reveals certain appointments for people who will do extraordinary things in their lives."

"It's a list of names?" Sam asked a little disbelieving. Then he muttered, "I've been searching all this time for a list of names?"

"It's not just any list," Airis said. "This list is very important. It contains the names of the people who will do extraordinary things…the people who cure cancer and initiate peace. This list contains the names of every single person, in the present and future, who are going to be responsible for stopping the evil influences that Satan has spread on earth. These people are going to return Glory to the world."

The bronze tubing that I held suddenly seemed heavier.

"And China wanted it so she could destroy it and spread evil." Sam stated, flat.

"It's possible." Airis said, bowing her head. "Those down below have been searching for that scroll for centuries. It could mean the difference between world salvation and world destruction. China was most likely looking for it at the request of a higher power. Someone was probably using her as a means to an end."

"That doesn't sound like something she would agree too." Sam said, shaking his head.

"Would she if she was promised power or something powerful that she wanted?" Airis asked, patiently.

"She was obsessed with power…" Sam said thoughtfully. "And that might explain why it seemed like she was killing people like she had something to prove."

Airis nodded encouragingly.

"But where did she find it, and what was she going to do with it?" I asked.

"I would think she meant to take it to Hell." Airis replied.

"Hell!" I exclaimed. "How in the world would she be able to do that?"

"There are portals to Hell all over Earth. Ordinary humans do not notice them; they never realize what could be right in front of them. Even if they did find one, they wouldn't be able to open it. But China was a hellhound. Hellhounds can sense them, sometimes they are drawn to certain places where the portals are. A hellhound has the ability to open a portal. The portal itself recognizes what once resided within, and the portal opens for them."

I glanced at Sam. "Did you know any of this?"

"No."

"I am thankful that you found the scroll before she was able to carry out her plan." Airis said.

I looked down at the bronze tubing that held the scroll. "She didn't get it open," I said with certainty.

"No. You cannot open this without a key."

"Where is the key?" I asked.

Airis stared at us without responding. I realized something I hadn't noticed; she didn't have an aura. I was wondering why when Sam seemed to become upset about something.

"Sam?" I turned to him, placing a hand on his arm. He caught my wrist and lifted it, staring. I followed his gaze to the bracelet he gave to me. My most prized possession.

Keys dangled from the chain.

"I have the key," I whispered. Sam released my arm, and I slipped the bracelet off and lined the largest key on the chain up with the keyhole at the top of the canister. It matched perfectly.

I slid the key into the lock.

"No!" Airis called.

Sam and I both looked up.

"It is not necessary at this time to look at it."

"Why?" I asked.

"It will only make what you need to do more difficult."

"What we need to do?"

"This treasure map is very sacred. It was stolen from its rightful keeper, and it has taken a long time to relocate it."

"What does that have to do with us?" Sam wanted to know.

"As a supernatural treasure, Heven, you are the rightful person to return this treasure to its rightful place."

"I don't understand," I said, frustrated. "I see auras. Who cares?"

"Do not make light of your gifts," Airis began, but I cut her off to say, "Wait. You said gifts with an 's.' I can only see auras."

"For now," Airis replied and pressed on. "Possessing this scroll puts you in great danger. Many will come from far and wide to take this from you. You cannot allow this. Use your gift to know with certainty that these people mean you harm."

So that was the reason I could see auras? To know who wanted to hurt me and who didn't?

"Where does the map need to go?" I asked Airis.

"To Rome."

I gasped. "I'm a high school student. A financially challenged one at that. How do you expect me to get to Rome?"

"You will find a way."

I laughed.

"More specifically, the scroll must be delivered to one of the catacombs in Rome. The Catacomb of San Sebastiano. It is located beneath the thirteenth century church, which sits atop the catacomb. You will find its entrance along the famous ancient road *Via Appia Antica.*"

"I can't," I told her.

"You do have a choice, you do not have to do this. I think that deep down you will find within yourself the desire and the fortitude to accomplish this task. Think about what will happen should you refuse. This treasure could once again fall into the wrong hands. If someone manages to get the cylinder open and read the contents, then every living person named on the list will be killed. Those not yet born will be born into a world of anarchy and their destinies will be ruined. The world will be doomed."

Is that all then? World damnation and death?

I began to shake as I thought about my decision. There really wasn't one. I knew what I had to do. The shaking in my limbs began to ease, and I glanced up at Sam. *We have to do this. We have to at least try.*

World damnation is a pretty strong motivator, huh? He smiled down at me.

I looked back up at Airis who stood, patiently waiting my decision. "We'll do it."

"I knew that you had it in you. Thank you." Airis said and waved her hand in our direction.

Everything went white. Again.

Just like that we were back in China's empty room.

"What have we gotten ourselves into?" Sam said, staring down at the scroll, still clutched in my hands.

"We were meant for this Sam. I don't really understand how or why but I can feel it, deep down. I – we – were chosen to do this for a reason; it's the right thing to do. Besides it's not really about us, it's about something bigger than either of us."

He shook his head slowly, digesting my words. His mouth drew into a straight line. "I can't say that I am happy that you're going to be in danger because of this, but I understand." I smiled and wrapped my arms around his waist and hugged him close. He said nothing for a while, just rocked me gently back and forth. When he pulled back he glanced down at the bronze cylinder that held the scroll. "I guess we can't let everything go to hell."

My lips twitched. "I guess not."

"I guess I'm back on the clock as your bodyguard."

I laughed. "You got, like, a whole ten minute break."

He hooked his arm around my shoulder. "Come on, sweetheart, let's get out of here."

"I'm hungry," I complained.

"Pizza it is."

Sam was loading the last box into the bed of his truck when I realized I left one last box up in the kitchen. I ran toward the stairs calling out what I forgot.

"I'll get it," Sam called after me.

"It'll take two seconds," I yelled back. I ran into the kitchen and grabbed the box. When I spun around I was met with a pair of curious dark eyes. I screamed and the box fell to the floor.

"Who are you?" I stammered, stepping back.

The boy (he was most definitely younger than me) seemed amused by my fear. He took a step toward me. Sam thundered through the front door. "I heard you scream."

The boy turned around, and Sam's mouth fell open.

"Long time no see," the boy said.

"Logan." Sam murmured.

"In the flesh."

Sam grinned and rushed forward, scooping the boy up in a bear hug. He came to my side, grinning, when he put the boy down. "Heven, this is Logan."

"Logan," I said, giving him a little wave. I felt a little recognition at his face but wasn't fast enough to put two and two together. I leaned in close to Sam to whisper, "Who is Logan?"

Sam laughed. "My brother."

Chapter Thirty

Heven

"Your brother!" I rushed forward to greet him, but something stopped me from throwing my arms around him in a big hug. Instead I threw out my hand. "Hi! I'm Heven."

Logan returned my handshake with a shy smile.

"So you are Sam's younger brother. I have heard a lot about you."

"Man! You have gotten so big! You're going to be as tall as me soon!" Sam said, smiling. "What are you, like, thirteen now?"

"Fourteen and a half," Logan corrected.

I saw pain flash through Sam's eyes, but he recovered and smiled. "Yeah, fourteen and a half."

"I went to that place Mom and Dad rented for you…" Logan said. Then, more quietly he said, "I've been looking for you for a while."

"Yeah?" Sam asked, concern masking his features. "Something wrong? Mom?"

I noticed he didn't ask about his dad.

"Mom's good. She really misses you."

Sam didn't react to that. Then I realized something. Something I couldn't believe; I hadn't noticed right away…

"So why are you looking for me?" Sam asked.

"Uh…" Logan slid a glance at me then turned back to his brother.

He doesn't have an aura, Sam.

Sam jerked like he'd been shot. "You – you're not…"

Logan nodded. "I'm like you now."

"No," Sam gasped.

"Can't you tell?" Logan asked.

Sam's muscles bunched beneath his shirt. I wanted to go to him, but I knew he wouldn't want that right now. He gave a curt nod to his brother then said, "It wasn't supposed to be both of us."

"It is."

"That's not possible," Sam said.

"Guess we have more screwed up genes than we thought."

"I'm sorry," Sam said, truly meaning his words.

I took a chance and went to Sam's side, reaching my hand toward his. He took it, grasping hard.

"Who's she?" Logan asked, looking at me.

"Heven is my girlfriend."

Logan was surprised by this. His eyes widened and his lips parted. "Does she…?"

"She knows," Sam nodded.

Logan looked at me. His eyes were darker than Sam's, so was his hair. He was also shorter and thinner, but I had a feeling he would be filling out soon.

"How long have you been looking for me?" Sam asked him.

"About six months."

Sam sucked in a breath. "I should've called you…"

Logan hurried to say, "Dad wouldn't have allowed that."

Sam stood there, in shock and regret.

"We were just about to go get some pizza. Want to come? You guys can catch up."

"I'm starving," Logan said.

Sam chuckled. It was a good sound and eased some of the tension that was inside me. "Let's go."

I bent to pick up the box, trying to settle what was left of my nerves. I didn't want Sam to pick up on them. At all. Sam made a sound and hauled the box out of my hands. I smiled.

He kissed my nose.

"Gross," Logan complained.

Sam laughed.

For some reason I didn't really feel like laughing.

Sam

My baby brother was like me. The thought made me sick. I accept what I am, I accept the hellhound in me…I even kind of like the stuff I can do. But would I choose this? I don't think so. And I certainly would never want this life for Logan.

They cast him out. My parents did to him what they did to me. I would expect that of my rigid, cold father…but not my mother. I told myself that the only reason she agreed to my leaving was because she was afraid for her youngest son. I told myself that if I had been an only child, she would have gone against my father and fought for me to stay.

Now I knew I was wrong.

She hadn't loved me at all.

She cast Logan out just like me, both her sons. How could anyone be so cruel?

I glanced over at him, sitting on a bunch of hay with his one bag of possessions. He had grown bigger in the past two years. He was taller, leaner and looked more like a man than a boy. How much I had missed.

A vivid memory, swift and strong, flashed into my head. We were outside in the yard having a sword fight with big sticks and laughing. He seemed so much smaller then, much more innocent. It made me feel sick to know that most of his innocence was now gone.

"So, what happened, Logan?" I asked, sitting down in the barn loft across from him. Below, the horses shifted restlessly.

He shrugged and sat down the flashlight he had been flicking on and off. "Pretty much what happened with you."

He flicked his dark brown eyes up to me but then returned them to the floor, shuffling his feet in the hay. "I just changed one day, Mom freaked out and Dad got all pissed. He said it made him mad that both his sons would have such weak genes."

"There's no way that the court would have emancipated you at the age of fourteen."

"They didn't." He said, his voice low. "I ran away."

"You did what?" I could help the way my voice raised in shock. "Why would you do that, Logan? If they were going to let you stay…"

Logan didn't look up at me when he spoke. "Mom probably would have let me stay; I heard her and dad fighting all the time. She was never the same after you left…she cried all the time."

His words left a hollow feeling in the pit of my stomach. Maybe I had been wrong, maybe Mom did love me…

"Anyway, I couldn't stand the way they fought all the time, the way dad tried to ignore me. So I left. I figured they wouldn't miss me anyway."

"Logan, you have to call them. They are probably worried – they've probably been looking for you."

"They aren't looking for me. Do you really think dad would call the cops and admit that a son of his ran away? Sure, Mom's upset, but she won't go against Dad."

"You don't know that."

"Yeah, I do." Finally he looked up. His face showed the misery he had been trying to hide. "I followed her one day. She went to the school and told them that I was visiting grandma and grandpa for the rest of the year. They don't care, Sam. I thought you would understand."

I sighed. "I do understand."

"I'm not going back there, you can't make me." He said, his chin jutting out.

"I'm not going to make you. You can stay here with me." I wondered how I was going to protect Heven from whatever she needed protected from and take care of my little brother. But he was my family, family that I thought I would never see again. He needed me. He probably was confused and knew next to nothing about being a hellhound. This was my chance to help him and get some of the family back I thought I lost.

"You're living in a barn?" Logan asked.

I laughed. "No, we can move into my new apartment tomorrow. I…uh…I stay here with Heven every night…in her room."

Logan made a face. "How long have you had a girlfriend?"

"For a while now. She's really great, Logan. You're going to like her too."

"I guess she is pretty hot." Logan said with a smile.

I widened my eyes in mock horror. "Thinking of making a play for my girl?" I said, then grabbed up a handful of hay and tossed it at him. "Better watch out, little bro."

"Whatever." He laughed, dodging the flying hay.

"Have you been alone the last six months?" I asked, dreading the answer wondering how he survived this long.

"Yeah. I went to the apartment that dad rented you when you first left…but you weren't there. I've been looking for you ever since."

I ran a hand through my hair thinking how stupid I had been for not trying to keep in touch with him. I could have found a way to see him, to at least get word to him about where I was. I never imagined, not in a million years that he would end up like me. "I'm sorry; I should have kept in touch."

"I don't blame you. I'm just glad I found you." He rubbed at his eyes with his palms, and I prayed he didn't start crying.

I had let him down.

From here on out I told myself I would be here for him.

"It was pretty tough, huh? To be alone?"

He shrugged and dropped his hands away from his face. I was relieved to see that he wasn't crying. "It wasn't that bad. I had some money…I took it from dad before I left." He glanced at me, looking a little embarrassed.

I nodded. "You needed it more than he did."

Logan seemed to relax at my understanding and then continued talking. "I moved around a lot, trying to find you. Then this one night in Portland…I ran into this woman who said she knew you."

Horror filled me. "What was her name?"

"China. She said she was like us and that she knew where you lived."

"Did she hurt you?" I asked, leaning toward him, grabbing his arm.

"What? No. Why would she? She seemed nice. She gave me your address, told me where I could find you."

I relaxed and released his arm. "She wasn't nice Logan."

"So you do know her?"

"I did. She's not around anymore." I hesitated to elaborate on the fact that I was the one who killed her. I was supposed to be making him feel safe, not scared.

"Where'd she go?"

"I'm not sure," I lied, feeling horrible for doing it. "Out of town."

"Oh." He seemed a little let down.

I moved over to sit next to him. "We don't need her around anyway, bud. I'll teach you everything you wanted to know and you'll be fine."

"I don't want to know anything!" he cried, catching me off guard. Down below Jasper whinnied his discomfort.

"What do you mean?"

"I don't want to be like this! I don't care about it. I just want to forget that part of me."

"You can't just forget it, Logan. You have to learn to accept it, you don't have to like it, but you do have to accept it and learn how to control it if you don't want it to take you over."

"I can control it just fine." He said, stubborn.

"Okay, cool. We don't have to talk about that right now." I was scared of running him off. Clearly my brother wasn't as accepting of himself as I was. I guess I could understand that. He'd run away from home because our parents wouldn't accept him, and he has been alone on the streets for six months, searching for me. I thought that right now my time would be better spent trying to rebuild our relationship before I tried to make him accept that he was a hellhound.

Logan stared at the floor, mutinous and silent. I sighed. I had no idea what to do or say. I wondered what Heven was doing. I imagined her in room brushing out her long, silky hair and suddenly I wanted to be there. I wanted to run my fingers through the softness of that hair and listen to the sound of her heart beating. I glanced at the screen of my cell. It was late. She was probably asleep by now.

I reached into the hay and fished around, coming out with a bag. My stash from when I was sleeping up here to be closer to Heven. "Here, look what I got."

Logan took the bag I was holding out. It was filled with power bars and some candy and a couple of comic books. "Have you read this one yet?" I reached in the bag to grab the book and held out the latest X-Men comic.

"No! Awesome!" A grin split his face as he ripped from my fingers. "This is so cool." He put the comic in his lap and reached in to grab a couple of candy bars and a bag of M&M's.

I smiled. Just like that he had transformed from a sullen kid to a happy one. Maybe this wouldn't be so hard after all. I sat there with him for a while and we joked and laughed about the comic. It felt good to have a brother again.

After a while he fell asleep in a candy induced coma with the comic clutched in his hands. I pulled out a blanket and covered him. I went to the ladder, planning to go see Heven.

When I turned to go down Logan's sleepy voice stopped me. "Hey, Sam."

I looked over my shoulder. "I was just going to go see Heven. Want me to stay?" It would be the first night I spent away from her in months, but for my brother, it would be worth it. "No, go ahead. But…thanks."

I smiled. "You sure?"

"Go away, I'm sleeping." Logan mumbled and rolled taking the blanket with him.

I laughed, he always was grumpy when he was tired. "I'll be back in a while, 'kay?"

He murmured something as I went down the ladder and he was snoring before I left the barn.

Heven

It was very late by the time Sam crawled through my open bedroom window. That all too familiar feeling of safety enveloped me.

You're awake. He was surprised when he slid beneath the sheets and rolled to face me.

I've gotten used to you being here. It's hard to sleep without you.

He smiled and caressed the side of my cheek with the tips of his fingers. I closed my eyes. Every time he touched me I felt a long sigh throughout my entire body. I snuggled closer and rested my cheek against his shoulder, pressing a kiss to the inside of his neck.

I missed you.

Is Logan okay?

Yeah. Thanks for letting him stay here. I don't know what I would have done with him tonight.

Sam was sort of in limbo tonight because he'd already given back the keys to his old place and wouldn't get the key to his new place until tomorrow. It wasn't a problem when it was just him, because he stayed here every night anyway.

Maybe you should have kept the old place.

Nah. We'll make it work with the new one. There just won't be as much space.

Or privacy. I couldn't help but feel a little upset about that. It made me feel selfish. I should be thrilled that Sam's brother was here; thrilled that he was getting a chance to have some of his family in his life. I couldn't quite get there. I wished Logan had an aura. I don't know why, but I didn't completely trust him. I couldn't tell that to Sam, and I needed to keep my feelings about it under control. Our Mindbond made things tricky. It wasn't always easy to keep our strong feelings from bleeding to the other. Logan was a kid and most likely was confused and hurt by what was happening with his body. Sam was his only link to anything stable. For Sam I would put my own fears aside and try to be there for Logan. Maybe he and I could be close.

Is everything okay? Sam asked, rubbing slow circles across my back. I worried for a moment that maybe I wasn't doing the best job

I could at hiding my feelings. Then he said, *Today has been a lot to deal with.*

He meant Airis and the treasure.

It's hard to comprehend that we have possession of something so majorly important.

Yeah, I know. Where is it?

Under my pillow.

Maybe you should let me hold on to it.

I knew that it would be perfectly safe with Sam, but I wanted it close to me. I felt like it belonged to me. *I kind of want to hold onto it.*

I think that you having it puts you in danger.

You worry too much, I grumped. If having it put me in danger, then it would put him in danger as well. Either way, we were both in danger, so I decided I was keeping it. *Sam? Something Airis said is bothering me.*

Just one thing? He snorted softly.

I smiled. *I guess that makes me crazy.*

I felt his hands in my hair and his lips on my forehead. *It makes you naïve.*

She said that seeing auras was not my only gift.

Swiftly he pulled out from beneath me and looked down through the darkness. *Are you feeling okay? Are you getting those tremors again?*

I'm fine. It makes me nervous though. What else is going to happen?

He stared at me for several minutes without saying anything. Then, with a deep sigh he returned to the mattress, lifting me gently and pressing my head back into his shoulder. *Whatever happens...I'll be here.*

My defender. I loved him for wanting to keep me safe, but it worried me. If Sam was busy protecting me, then who would protect him?

"I know what I am doing this summer," Kimber declared, waving a flyer over our lunch table.

It was finally the last day of school. The halls and lunchroom were buzzing with nothing but plans for the summer.

"Well, doesn't anyone want to know?" Kimber asked, dropping into a chair next to Cole.

"Let me see," Cole said, around a mouthful of burger. He grabbed the flyer and looked it over. "I heard about this trip," he said, turning the flyer around so Sam and I could see.

Sam pulled the flyer closer and kicked me beneath the table. I abandoned my Doritos and looked down. I sucked in a breath and got a hunk of chip caught in my throat. It was sharp and I felt it cut into the sensitive skin. I coughed and grabbed up Sam's water to take a drink. The chip went down, but it scraped the whole way.

Sam's big, warm hand landed on the back of my neck to rub.

"Where'd you get this?" I asked Kimber when I could speak.

"Mrs. Britt."

"You don't take French."

Kimber rolled her eyes. "You don't have to take French to go. It's a school-sponsored trip, Mrs. Britt is just in charge of it."

Sam and I glanced at each other then back down at the flyer. The words seemed to jump right off the page:

Trip to Italy
Explore Rome and its surrounding areas
Learn about other cultures — see stunning architecture and works of art by the most famous artists in history.

"This is a school trip?" I asked Kimber.

"Yep. Isn't it cool?"

"Yeah, it is." *This could be our way to get to the scroll to Rome. I'd say it's our only chance,* Sam said.

We'd been trying to brainstorm ways to get the scroll to Rome ever since our meeting with Airis. This was perfect.

"I've already filled out the consent forms, and my dad has already signed the check. All I have to do is pack."

"When is the trip?" I asked. Kimber named off the dates. It was the exact same dates of that camp my mother was trying to send me off to. "How much?" I asked. Kimber gave me an odd sort of look. Her aura flared all different hues. I tried to ignore it.

"Are you interested in going?"

I shrugged. "Maybe." Then, "It might be nice to get away for a while."

Kimber's eyes softened, and she nodded. Likely, she was thinking of the issues with my mother. "It's fifteen hundred dollars."

I sputtered. "Fifteen hundred!"

Cole whistled between his teeth.

"I doubt my job at the ice cream shop will pay that much," I muttered, knowing for sure that I would never be able to come up with that much money…Sam either.

"Maybe your Gran would help you out," Kimber suggested.

"Maybe." But even if she would I couldn't leave Sam behind.

"Go talk to Mrs. Britt. Get the permission forms. It would be so cool if you could come," Kimber said.

"Maybe I should come too," Cole said, grabbing up the flyer to look at it again.

"Really?" Kimber asked, a smile taking over her face. "We should all go!"

I faked my enthusiasm. I did want to go. Not for shopping and fun like Kimber, but for reasons that she would never understand.

"Just turn the forms in," I pleaded with Sam. He was being very stubborn.

"I don't want to turn them in until we know if you can go or not."

Right after lunch Sam and I went to see Mrs. Britt. There were still spots open for the trip and when I voiced my concern over the price she told us that there were scholarships for three students. The school would pay for them to go. There was one left. I immediately offered up Sam's name. Being that he was emancipated and worked so many jobs, Mrs. Britt helped to fill out the scholarship form and told us he would definitely be accepted.

Sam was not happy with me. In fact, I thought he might explode. So I took the permission forms from her and promised to turn them in as soon as possible. As soon as we were down the hall, Sam yanked me into a supply closet.

"What were you thinking?" he whisper-yelled at me.

"That there was one scholarship left, and you needed it!" I matched his whisper-yell with my own.

"We have no idea if you're going to be able to go."

I sighed. "Even if I can't, you have to. It's our only way to get the scroll to Rome."

"I will not go without you," he said through gritted teeth.

"We made a promise, Sam."

"*You* made a promise," he growled.

He was right. I was the one who told Airis I would do this. This was my responsibility. I should be the one to go. Sam grabbed me by the shoulders and leaned down close to my ear. His breath was warm and tickled my ear.

"I don't like when you're that quiet. I didn't mean to yell at you, honey. It makes my skin crawl to think of leaving you here while I go to another country."

I shivered. The scent of him was surrounding me and his shaggy hair brushed against my cheek. "Uh-huh."

He pulled back, just slightly, his lips pulling into a knowing smile. "Are you listening?"

I nodded.

He kissed me. I buried my hands in his hair and pulled him even closer. His tongue was the perfect combination of rough and sweet. My stomach fluttered.

After he pulled back I rested my forehead on his chest to catch my breath. Soon, reality came rushing back. *It's not definite that I can't go. I'll convince my mother to sign the papers. Yours are already filled out. You don't need a parent's signature, you have the scholarship. Just turn in the forms. I'll turn mine in soon.*

You're going to convince your mother to let you go? Especially during those two weeks? Sam was doubtful. So was I, but I didn't have a choice. There was no other option. Our lives and the lives of everyone on that Treasure Map depended on it. I would trick her if I had to.

Chapter Thirty-One

Heven

Of course it was rainy and chilly on the day Sam and I were supposed to fix up his new place. But I refused to wait another day. He had already moved most his stuff in yesterday, but we hadn't fixed it up yet because school sucked up most of the day and then he had to work.

I was sitting on the front porch of Gran's, under cover from the falling rain. My hands were tucked in the front pocket of my blue hoodie and wrapped around the bronze tube that held the scroll. I heard the deep rumble of the truck's engine before I saw it and my heart picked up.

Moments later Sam was jumping down from the truck and running through the rain to meet me. He was laughing and his eyes were warm and the color of honey. He shook his head and drops of rainwater sprinkled around us. His blond hair was wet, making it a darker color than usual and framing his eyes and beautiful face in a wild, playful manner.

"Hey, beautiful." He grabbed me up and smacked a big, wet kiss on me.

I laughed and went for another.

"You're supposed to be all girly and grossed out that I got you wet."

"I will never push you away. Even when you stink like wet dog." I laughed.

He made a few barking sounds and lunged, pulling me closer. He leaned in to kiss me but at the last second his tongue shot out and he licked me across the lips. I squealed and stumbled backward, knocking over a box that was behind me.

"What's that?" Sam asked, his eyes still twinkling with mischief.

I began putting the spilled items back into the box. "Just some stuff for your new place."

"Heven," he said exasperated. "That's a huge box."

"I didn't buy all of it. Gran let me go through the stuff in the attic and take a few things."

He seemed skeptical.

"Look." I pointed to an item not in a box. "This microwave is way better and newer than the one in your place now. I don't think that thing even works."

He laughed. "It doesn't even have buttons." He wound his fingers through mine. "You're so good to me."

"I'm glad you think so. Now, haul this stuff to the truck." I smiled sweetly at him and batted my eyes.

He crammed everything into the cab so it wouldn't get wet and only stopped once when he saw the cans of paint. I batted my eyes again and patted his butt. He grinned and shook his head. When the truck was loaded, he came back with a crooked grin and the next thing I knew, I was thrown over his shoulder and deposited in the truck right next to him. To my intense delight I had to sit extra close to him on the way to his place because of all the stuff.

When we arrived at his place, Logan opened the door and stuck his head out. I waved up to him and he waved back. The rain had stopped, but the dark clouds still hung low, threatening to open back up at any moment. Sam got out and loaded his arms full of boxes and trudged up the stairs and into the apartment. Filled with excitement, I got out on his side and went around the hood to the passenger side and reached in to grab the two cans of paint. When I pulled back out I gasped noticing a big black crow that had perched itself on the side of the truck. It was creepy with flat, beady eyes and it opened its large pointy beak to let out a loud squawking sound. I jumped back and dropped the thingy that opened up the cans. With a muttered curse and a glare in the direction of the bird I bent to retrieve it. When I straightened the bird was gone. In its place sat a man.

He was naked.

He had longer hair than I have and it was full of knots and leaves.

His toes, which were propped against the side of the truck, were unnaturally curved and looked like claws.

What was most disturbing was his aura. It was white. I knew for certain that it was not pure. White was the worst color an aura could be.

I shrieked again this time letting go of the paint cans, and they rolled out onto the street. That bird just changed into a man? *CRAP.* Was that even possible? Sam could change, so why couldn't others? *Double Crap.* And why was he looking at me with contempt and anticipation? I watched him warily, unsure what to say and do.

"Give me the map," the man hissed.

"I – I don't know what you're talking about." I lied, trying not to glance in the direction of the front seat where the scroll lay unprotected.

He cocked his head and stared at me. His eyes flashed red. "Liar." His voice was scratchy and high pitched, just like I would imagine a bird's might be if it could talk.

"No, really." I looked up toward the apartment wondering what this thing would do if I screamed. I pushed my hand through my hair and looked back at the man. "I don't have whatever it is you want."

I backed up a step, and he hopped down from his seat. Without a word he opened his mouth and this weird sort of yellowish-brown mist rolled out. It swirled around me making it hard to breathe. I coughed and tried to run but my movements were slow and sloppy. "Sam," I called, but it echoed around me, the weird mist was trapping in my sounds, not letting them out. *Sam.*

The mist grew thicker and thicker, making it hard to see. My vision started clouding, and I knew I had only seconds before I passed out. But then there was a hand reaching through the mist and wrapping around my arm and pulling me free. I gagged and coughed as fresh air filled my lungs. Through watering eyes I looked for the bird-man, wondering what he would do next.

Sam appeared through the mist, grabbed my face and forced me to look up at him. "What happened?"

"There's someone there," I said, pointing in the direction where the naked bird-man had sat, my voice hoarse from the weird mist.

Sam shoved me behind him and turned. The bird-man stepped through the mist he had just released – seemingly unaffected by its power – and grinned. "Give it to me," he hissed. As he spoke more mist floated out of his lips and reached for us. Sam was about to jump forward, but Logan shot out from the side and slammed his fist into the man's chest and the bird-man disintegrated before our eyes.

"What the hell was that thing?" Sam asked as we all stared at the spot he had been standing in.

I shook my head and looked at Logan. He was watching me. "How did you know how to kill that thing?"

"Yeah, bro. That was awesome." Sam said proudly and Logan beamed.

"There's this game that I play on the internet… there's a guy on there like him. It's how you destroy him. Figured it was worth a shot."

"A video game?" I echoed.

Sam laughed. "The World Wide Web saves the day."

Logan shrugged again and went to pick up the paint cans lying in the street. He took them without another word up to the apartment.

Sam waited until he had disappeared inside the apartment then looked down at me. "What the hell was that thing?"

Whatever that thing was…it's only the beginning.

Sam gave me a little shake. "What did it want, Heven?"

I went to the truck and pulled out the bronze cylinder. Sam's jaw tightened and with a curse he hauled me into his side. *So are those the kinds of things that are going to be coming after you now? I got rid of one stalker for her to be replaced with God knows what.*

My eyes fastened to the spot where that bird-man had been. How many more were out there like him? How many more were worse? I shuddered and forced my gaze away, looking up toward the apartment. Logan was watching us through the window.

I couldn't help but wonder if Sam and I understood exactly what we had promised to do.

The Hope

"She wasn't supposed to be involved," he said wearily.

"She has a greater destiny than what you wanted for her."

"Airis," he warned.

"She has shown great strength and courage."

"She's a child. You gave her something that both worlds are fighting for. How do you expect her to survive?"

"She has protection."

He let out a hard laugh. "Are you kidding? He's a child too. And he was created by the enemy."

"He might be twisted by sin, but he was created by God, and he loves her. Even you can see that. We both know that a love that powerful can slay evil."

He sighed, knowing that he'd lost his fight. "I hope you're right, because more evil is coming."

"Negativity does not belong here; all will be well. You'll see."

He didn't look convinced.

I smiled. "After all, she has the best protector she could have, someone with a heart from God, but abilities the enemies from Hell have. Who better to get the job done?"

Heven

The night had long since turned dark. Outside my window, night life sang a mellow song and helped to soothe some of my nerves. I stared a long time at the reflection in the mirror. Who was this girl? Long ago I thought I knew. How naïve I had been. My attack changed the way I looked and the way I felt. I realized that everything I thought I understood about myself wasn't really who I was. I made peace with that with the girl in the mirror.

But I wasn't her anymore.

I wasn't either of those girls anymore. I guess you could say that I was a hybrid of them, certain parts all smooshed together. And there were new parts, too.

I gathered my heavy mass of hair up and secured it high on my head. "Who am I?" I wondered out loud. The next few months would test me; there would be others who would try to break me – to kill me. My hand went to my wrist to check the clasp on my bracelet, even though I knew that it was fine. I didn't know why I was chosen, but it felt right.

Silently, Sam appeared behind me. We stared at each other through the mirror without speaking. I was reminded of the last time we did this when I'd kept half my face from the reflection. I remembered thinking how utterly gorgeous he was and how we just didn't fit. It seemed like a lifetime ago.

He was still beyond gorgeous, far more beautiful than I thought myself to be. But this time as we stared in the mirror…we fit. I was becoming the girl that deserved him. That knowledge gave me strength and courage to face the danger I knew was coming.

"You need to stop leaving your window open at night. It isn't safe." Sam's voice was deep and low. His eyes were the color of dark honey.

"I didn't think you'd come tonight."

His eyes darkened. "All the more reason to lock the window."

"But you did come." I turned away from our reflections and lifted my face.

"I may have a new apartment, but my home is with you." He didn't touch me. He didn't have to. His words were the softest caress he could give.

"Come to bed," I beckoned, walking toward it.

I felt his strong hands on my shoulders as he turned me. "Everything's going to be fine," he murmured, his face drawing close to mine.

I nodded, eyes drifting closed. I wasn't worried about what was to come because it didn't matter. Deep down inside me I felt that I could handle it. I could handle anything. I no longer had to hide behind Sam but I could stand beside him. He had unique abilities that made him who he was…but so did I. I was just beginning to realize just how much of myself I had overlooked, how much of myself I hid from. Well, no more. From now on I was going to be the girl that everyone else seemed to see. I was going to be strong and capable. I would be courageous.

This was the new me.

Cambria Hebert grew up in a small town in rural Maryland. She is married to a United States Marine and has lived in South Carolina, Pennsylvania and her current state of North Carolina. She is the mother of two young children with big personalities, is in love with Starbucks (give the girl a latte!) and she is obsessed with werewolves. Cambria also has an irrational fear of chickens (Ewww! Gross) and she loves to read and review books. Her favorite book genre is YA paranormal, and she can be found stalking that section at her local Barnes and Nobles (which happens to be her favorite place ever!).

Masquerade is her first published novel, but she has many more books waiting to be published and devoured by her fans, including the sequel to *Masquerade*.

Cambria also co-hosts a live, internet blog radio talk show, *JournalJabber*, (www.blogtalkradio.com/journaljabber) where she dishes about books, publishing and everything in between: hair in a can, toilet snakes, chicken phobias, etc..

You can find Cambria on Facebook, Goodreads (she is a moderator of the Creative Reviews group).

You can also drop by her website www.cambriahebert.com.